After coming down from Girton College, Cambridge, Victoria Petrie Hay worked at the BBC for a short time before entering publishing. She became an editorial director at Victor Gollancz Ltd and then at Weidenfeld and Nicolson Ltd, resigning in 1987 to concentrate on her writing career. Her previous books are *Forsaking All Others* and *Every Purpose Under Heaven*. She lives in East Sussex.

VICTORIA PETRIE HAY

The Bequest

WARNER BOOKS

A *Warner* Book

First published in Great Britain in 1993 by Michael Joseph Ltd
This edition published in 1994 by Warner Books
Reprinted 1994
This edition first published by Warner Books 1996

Copyright © Victoria Petrie Hay 1993

The moral right of the author has been asserted.

A CIP catalogue record for this book is
available from the British Library.

ISBN 0 7515 0837 3

Printed in England by Clays Ltd, St Ives plc

Warner Books
A Division of
Little, Brown and Company (UK)
Brettenham House
Lancaster Place
London WC2E 7EN

To the memory of my grandfather

Part I

I

The will was handwritten and photocopied, and the faded lines fell as though exhausted at the ends so that, by the bottom of the first page, there was a clear two inches of space at the left side and none at the right. As Emma read the closely written lines her eyes were dragged downwards and sideways and she found she had a sore neck as her head tipped to compensate. She flipped to the third page, the papers held together by a rusty bulldog clip, the writing now more weary than ever.

'. . . I give all my property not by this will or any codicil to it otherwise disposed of (my residual estate) to Les Embrassades Cats' Home, Guernsey, Channel Islands.' There followed a scrawled signature and two illegible witnesses' signatures. Documents attached to the will revealed that the amount given to the cats' home was nearly four hundred thousand pounds. A fair fortune now, let alone then. Cats in clover.

Emma massaged her neck and gazed around the attic. A cats' home! Was she, then, not the first member of her family to be claimed by the funny farm? No. You had to be of sound mind to make a will, and anyway the woman who had made this one might not be a relative. She didn't recognize the name, but her grandfather had been an executor, her grandmother had been left 'my family silver' and a clock, and her mother and aunt two thousand pounds apiece. The woman must have been very fond of cats.

Emma fished in the chest and was rewarded with a package of letters with Canadian stamps on them under which were two fat photograph albums. She took them out. The sunbeam allowed by the attic's single dormer window had moved a dust-ridden few feet away and she clambered over the other junk stored there, seated herself precariously in the light and opened the first album.

Her commercial brain was still functioning, she thought immediately (and, note: tell that to the psychiatrist), for hadn't she come across the unknown, unheard-of photograph albums of the young Ronald Colman? Hollywood memorabilia had gone mad, too, along with Emma Langton. Marilyn Monroe's shoes had changed hands (feet?) for thousands of dollars, paid by the Japanese, wasn't it? Emma had seen something about it, in the before time when she had read newspapers from the City pages outwards. It would have been in the outer bit, of course.

This was not Ronald Colman's album, though. He looked like him and was amazingly handsome, but even if Colman had gone on safari in Africa between shooting films in Hollywood it could not have been for the unbroken period of time the captions, written in white ink on thick black paper, suggested. The man identified himself only as 'self' and, once, in a page from the *Illustrated London News*, he was called 'My White Hunter' by a royal princess. In another picture she posed proudly before the massive hulk of a dead elephant, its tusks, her trophies, held for her by two black men. Emma had a 1990s' revulsion for such scenes, but somehow she could not extend it to the white hunter – who, presumably, had brought about the death of the elephant, whoever had fired the bullet – even given his own propensity for being photographed in the company of a variety of dead

4

animals. His smile was confident, casual, impudent; his charm oozed out of the photographs and across the years.

And then . . . good God! Emma peered closer. 'Idina, Joss, Alice, Self. Clouds, 1926.' And: 'Nell, Patricia, Alice. Race Week', 'Jack, Self at the Muthaiga'. Emma was sure she knew those names. Hadn't they made up the Happy Valley set in Kenya in the twenties and thirties? Joss Erroll had been scandalously murdered. There had been a film about it, *White Mischief*. It had been on television not long ago. She and Brian had watched it . . . No, she would not think of that. She turned to the front of the album and found a signature in white ink: H. G. A. Wittering.

Something tickled inside her head, but before she could give it a good scratch she heard her mother calling from below.

'Here,' she called back.

An interrogative shout in reply.

'In the attic.' The words were hopelessly lost in the confined space. She crawled towards the trap door and repeated them. Her mother was climbing the stairs to the first-floor landing.

'Emma, what are you doing?'

'Exploring. Who was H. G. A. Wittering?'

'Your great-grandfather,' Laura Langton said. 'Harold George Albert. Emma –'

'I've found his photograph albums. He was a dish.'

'Do you know, even as a child I could see that? I think he was the first man I had a crush on.'

'Tell me about him.'

'He had two tortoises called Laura and Julie, after your aunt and me. As children we were unbelievably flattered, though the tortoises seemed unimpressed.'

'Mum! Something juicy. What did he get up to in Happy Valley?'

'I've no idea. He was a district commissioner in Kenya. I don't think it was very glamorous.'

'He was, though. Who was it who loved cats so much she left them four hundred K and only two K to you and Julie?'

'His wife. But she hated cats. She bred and showed dogs.'

The conversation so far had been conducted between Laura at the foot of the stepladder leading to the trap door and Emma's disembodied voice in the attic, from where there also came monumental thumps as Emma moved around. Mice in an attic sound like a flock of sheep, Laura reminded herself, and refused to nag her daughter. The psychiatrist said she was getting better (which was obvious to everyone but it was nice to have it confirmed by the professional in the case) and it was time Laura gave her more rein. She had left Emma alone, driven into Chichester, shopped like a maniac and returned within an hour to find Emma in the attic. She was, she considered, being wondrously calm about it.

Now there was silence above her head. 'Emma –?' she said.

Emma's face with a cobwebbed grin appeared in the dark opening. 'She *hated* cats?'

'Well, she certainly preferred dogs.'

'An ossuary in the cupboard! And I thought my breakdown was the only scandal in our family history.'

'Hardly an ossuary.'

'A skeleton, then. Can you manage this?' A wooden chest replaced Emma's face and Laura stood on the second step of the ladder to receive it. Soon the three of them were on the terra firma of the landing.

'Attics are fascinating,' Emma remarked. 'I must play with them more often.'

'But what possessed you to go up there?' Laura regretted the querulous tone, but it was too late to retrieve it.

'Gran rang. She wants Granddad's sword for Al. They cost an arm and a leg, apparently, and she'd like it to join the Navy again.' The sword, in its scabbard, was leaning against the wall. Laura had not noticed it.

'Did Gran have any ideas about how we transport the thing to Al?' she said. 'We can hardly send it through the post.'

'No.'

'I wish she'd dumped her stuff on Julie instead of us when she moved. She's for ever wanting bits of it, usually for Julie's children, and Julie's much nearer.'

'Perhaps it's because you're older. The older one should inherit the secrets.'

'Secrets!' Laura said, laughing, at ease now there was a good reason for Emma's excursion into the attic and because there was none of the blankness in her eyes that had haunted the rest of them for the past month.

'Was Harold George Albert Gran's father?'

'Yes.'

Emma handed her the will she had found. 'Why did her mother only leave her the silver? And why so little to you and Julie and so much to the cats?'

Laura had not read the will before. The two thousand pounds had come when money was tight and had seemed like a windfall. They had put a new shower unit in the bathroom and taken the children for a holiday in France. Her mother had not said much about it, but Laura recalled she had gone to an auction in Guernsey to buy some china. 'My family silver' indeed! It bore the crest that was on the signet ring Laura wore. The will was a nasty document; it seemed to be exacting revenge from beyond the grave – but for what?

'Emma, she wasn't –' Laura began.

'Skeletons!' Emma announced, interrupting her. 'Explain this.'

It was a birthday card, still in its envelope, the stamp

Canadian. All the available space inside had been written on.

'Dear Olivia,' it said.

I don't expect you remember me for it's a fair thirty years since we saw each other last and you were a young girl then, but I had to write. I've felt so bad this long time about what happened, and me leaving without saying goodbye or even speaking to you. I couldn't help it. I had to go and didn't realize I was saying goodbye to service that day.

I married, Olivia, and came to Canada. I always meant to take my children (two boys and a girl) to see old Anglesey except there was never enough money, and when there was they were Canadians through and through and not interested in their mother's native land.

Will you write and tell me how you are? You've been on my conscience. I wish I'd been able to say goodbye.

With love,

Morfydd Johnstone (Jones).

Emma turned the envelope over and examined the postmark.

'She timed it to arrive on her birthday,' she said. 'After thirty years she remembered when it was. And she found out her married name and her address. How, from Canada?'

'From someone on Anglesey, I should think,' Laura said. 'Gran didn't live there for long, but her aunt did.'

They sorted through the rest of the bundle. It contained Christmas and birthday cards and photographs of tanned, handsome men and women, children of increasing size and in the centre of the group a white-haired woman and a tall bald man. In the last envelope was a black-edged card announcing the death of Morfydd Anne Johnstone, née Jones.

What happened? What could it have been to stay on someone's conscience for thirty years, finally prompting her to discover the name and address of the child she had known and begin a correspondence on that child's birthday?

'Skeletons and secrets,' Emma said, and took the chest downstairs.

She felt her mind turning a corner and heading into the light. It wasn't going back the way it had come, though; it was making a V shape, and she could see that the side she was on now was aiming for sunlight instead of the neon the first side had descended from. She'd had blips of optimism during the past weeks and was inclined to distrust this leap, but she examined it from every angle and decided that even if she slipped a few inches the turn was genuine.

She had thought she had been happy in the before time, and realizing that she had not – that she did not want to regain the neon – was a major step towards recovery. Earning the money she had been at the age of twenty-four had seemed an end in itself, the Porsche, the flat in Docklands predictable ways to spend it for there was not much time to dispose of it otherwise. She had regarded the weekends with Brian as periods of relaxation but, like so many of their colleagues, they had forgotten how to relax.

Brian was a shit, but that was his problem and not hers. She could recall his, 'You didn't think, did you, that you were the only one?' with dispassionate anger instead of the humiliation and hurt that had set her off on the slippery slope. She viewed the scene she had made with the most intense embarrassment. However justified, she should not have done it, not in the office anyway, even though Brian did another kind of 'it' there – frequently, so it seemed. The dishevelled secretary, the open-plan area beyond the office door where even the computers appeared to be listening . . .

The scene had cost her her dignity and her job. You do not make an idiot of the boss and get away with it. The pay-off had been – what was the word? Substantial? Generous? The financial director, delegated by Brian to do the deed, had called it both before inviting her to clear her desk and be gone. She rather thought she had refused the money, may even have stormed into Brian's office and shouted about how proud she was. She was around a thousand pounds a fuck. She had been sliding fast by then, going at Mach Three towards the bottom of the pit after a night when the stock markets of the world had been doing something similar.

She still could not remember, though.

'Did I get the money?' she asked her mother, looking up from H.G.A.'s albums which she had spread on the kitchen table. They were her past. Her past and her future. She was formulating a plan.

'What money, darling?'

'Brian Shitface's of Woodward and Shitface.'

'Language, Emma!'

'Sorry. Did I?'

Laura was grilling plaice for lunch. She had a notion that fish calmed the blood and was good for damaged brains. It had probably been put there by her mother, who had a facility for making obscure old wives' tales into incontrovertible fact.

'Yes, you did. You gave a cheque to your father when we came to fetch you.' While you were gabbling nonsense. 'He put it on deposit at your bank.'

'Oh.' She was silent until: 'It would probably do better in a building society. I don't reckon I'll be playing the market for a while.'

'Not for a while. Will you clear the table? We're ready to eat.'

Emma closed the albums and put them into the chest. 'I wonder if it really was a nervous breakdown,' she said.

'*Was?*'

'It's over. Finished.'

'Isn't this rather sudden?'

Emma explained about the V turn, about neon and sunlight. 'Isn't it more likely,' she concluded, 'to have been the result of exhaustion, pressure of work and ... heartbreak?'

As good a set of ingredients for a nervous breakdown as anyone could have wished for, but Laura said, 'Yes, darling. I'm sure you're right.'

'I'll go to the session tomorrow to thank Dave and say goodbye.'

'Will he let you discharge yourself so unceremoniously?'

'Why not? I haven't done anything criminal. My treatment is voluntary, isn't it?'

'At least listen if he thinks it's a bad idea,' Laura begged.

'Don't fuss, Mum. I'm better.'

Don't fuss, she says! Laura fumed. How am I to switch it off like a tap after a month of nothing but fuss?

Yet Emma was better. Her father confirmed it that evening when he got home.

'It's happened too quickly,' Laura insisted.

'It hasn't happened quickly,' Hamish said. 'Consider my hostas.' (They were in the garden.) '*Fortunei* Albopicta,' he added fondly. 'Their leaves are unfurled today. They weren't yesterday and a month or so back there was bare earth here. In one sense you could say it happened quickly – a grown-up hosta today and not yesterday – but in fact it has been slow, continuous growth.'

'Emma –'

'Has been getting better slowly. I've been telling you that. It's hard for you to see because you're with her all the time. She's unfurled a leaf or two and it's surprised you.'

'What if a late frost thumps them – her?'

'It'll be a setback, no more. The hostas will survive and so will Emma. Darling,' he went on, 'it's been dreadful for everyone, but think about it: she didn't slit her v⟶⟶⟶ or take an overdose. She got into terrible trouble and rang her parents, the most sensible thing possible. What's in the chest she's found?'

'Skeletons, she says. They aren't really – well, I suppose you could call it a bone or two.'

'They can't harm her,' Hamish said.

The psychiatrist discharged her and phoned Laura with reassurances.

'She says she's picked up most of the pieces of her head and knows where the rest are. I believe her. I wish the rest of my patients were so easy to treat.'

'She wants to start driving again.'

'That's all right. She's not on any medication. Go with her the first few times to make sure of her confidence, then short trips on her own. There's nothing the matter with her, Mrs Langton. Honestly.'

Yes, and who lets poisoners and rapists out of prison? Psychiatrists, that's who. Laura was suspicious of the whole breed, despite the miracle wrought by this example of it.

Emma was fine driving her car, except she went too fast in her mother's opinion.

'You can't help going fast in that thing,' Hamish said. He had driven it down from London and had been casting longing glances at it ever since. Emma was selling it, but not yet, she said.

She dispersed what she referred to as her golden kick in the bum – 'okay, *backside*, Mum' – in such a way that would provide income and some growth, phoning people up and issuing orders with what to Laura's ignorant ear sounded confidence and competence, using her financial knowledge with a utilitarian disinterest. She let her flat on a six-month lease to a Swiss bank.

She would take the summer off, she said, and then decide what to do. She was beginning to believe, she said, that finding Brian *in flagrante* whatever it was had been a blessing in wolf's clothing. She'd had a drink with some former colleagues. Had she really been like that? Working too hard, playing too hard, all nerves and talk of money?

She was going to take her grandmother the sword for her cousin Alistair. She was going to find out about Anglesey and Africa.

2

Her grandmother had moved to the kind of cottage grandmothers are supposed to live in: a privet hedge, roses and clematis growing around the porch, honeysuckle up the house beginning to show a coy leaf or two. It was detached, just, and on Chard St Sebastian's high street, if such a village could claim to own one. There was no answer to Emma's knock so she opened the side gate and went through to the back garden. Olivia Wheeler was at the bottom of it, feeding her hens.

'Darling!' she called. 'Lovely to see you. Do you want to collect the eggs?'

Emma was nine or ten years old again. She went into the hen run, kissed her grandmother, took from her a little basket and, crouching, entered the hen house. It was familiar, too. Gran had had it transported westward; and also familiar was the thrill of finding eggs, some still warm.

'How many?' Olivia said as Emma emerged.

'Eight.'

'Seven. You've taken a dummy one.'

'Whoops. I'll put it back.'

'Don't bother. Let me look at you.' She swept Emma's hair away from her brow. 'You seem all right. Better than you did at Christmas.'

'That was before this started.'

'I know. Have you had enough?' she said to the chick-ens and, when they did not reply, ushered Emma out of the run and closed the gate. 'Would you like a boiled egg for your tea?' she asked.

'Gran, I'm –'

'Twenty-four years old. I know that as well. I'm not entirely senile. Would you like a boiled egg for tea?'

'Yes,' Emma said.

They went in through the back door of the cottage. The television in the sitting room was on, the volume loud. Emma had heard it as she had knocked on the front door.

'It deters burglars,' Gran said. 'It's a fact.' She paused in front of it. 'Oh, well *done*, Nick. He's got a birdie. Isn't that good? You've still got that car, I see –' peering out of the window. 'You should have a nice little Metro like me. Did you bring the sword?'

It was like attempting to field a juggler's balls, five of them in the air at the same time. 'Yes,' Emma said again, hoping it covered everything.

'Good. I'll put water on for your egg while you bring your luggage in.'

The television in the sitting room was turned off, but there was another, a miniature one, in the kitchen. Olivia kept an alert eye on the golf while she prepared a casserole for their supper and Emma ate her egg. It was nice being nine or ten years old again. Emma half expected to be ordered to a bath and bed at seven o'clock, but instead was invited to the pub across the road. She had passed one at the other end of the village more suited to her grandmother, Emma considered, which advertised food and had a terrace outside for summer days. The White Horse was spit and sawdust with a dart board and a skittle alley. Olivia Wheeler was on the skittles team and there was a match tonight; Olivia Wheeler's pint of cider was on the bar almost as soon as she had walked into the pub; Olivia Wheeler had several male admirers and they made noises in soft Dorset drawls about how she could not possibly have a granddaughter this old. One of them, Graham, offered Emma a drink.

'Not our scrumpy,' Gran said. 'It'll lay her out.'

Wine would be undrinkable here and a vodka and tonic soppy. Emma asked for a half of lager.

'We're for Mrs Wheeler,' Graham said, handing it to her. 'She's not like the other incomers and she's right mean at skittles.'

'What do you mean "for"?'

'Hasn't she told you? Neighbours want rid of her hens, complain about the noise a liddle cock makes in the morning. They say there's a danger of this salmonella they go on about on the telly. Think it'll jump over the fence at them or some such.'

'She didn't tell me.'

He was on the skittles team, he said, and introduced Emma to his nephew Jan – Jan? Oh, John, of course – and instructed him to take care of 'our gahst' during the match.

John was less forthcoming than his uncle and blushed wildly at the shouts and whistles from his mates as he led Emma into the skittle alley, but was stout with it. ''Tis Mrs Wheeler's granddaughter,' he said, and further ribald comment was amputated by an elbow in the ribs.

Emma was astonished. Mum didn't know about this. Did Aunt Julie? She suspected not and felt privileged to be allowed a glimpse of Gran's other life. She watched as Olivia inspired the White Horse to victory over the Three Sheaves.

'She's our secret weapon!' John roared. 'She's our bloody Stealth Bomber so she is. We ain't never had a run like this before!'

Elation overcoming his shyness, he grabbed Emma's

hand and led the charge to the bar for celebrations. Olivia Wheeler was chaired in by her team mates, they bending their knees to prevent their star player from hitting her head on the low lintel though it could have been in reverence. Graham wrote the score up on the chart.

'Castle next week,' he remarked. 'They buggers are good, but we'll do 'em.' He called to the landlord for cider for Mrs Wheeler, but she stopped him.

'I must feed my granddaughter,' she said, and led the way out. Emma felt obliged to give a few royal waves as they went.

'You've seduced them, you witch,' she said as they crossed the road. 'How? And when did you learn to play skittles?'

'I just picked it up. I've got an eye for it.' She shrugged modestly. 'I'm only part of the team.'

'You're the queen-empress of it,' Emma said.

They went into the cottage, the smell of the casserole drawing them into the kitchen. Emma laid the table while her grandmother dealt with the oven. She staggered as she came upright with the dish and almost dropped it on to the draining board, where it hissed.

'Only my legs,' she muttered as Emma darted to her aid. 'They get tired on match nights.'

The rest of her was tired, too. She was over sixty-five, though it had seemed hard to believe at the White Horse. They ate their supper and Emma could not bring up the past, not the past she was interested in anyway. After they had eaten Olivia wanted to see the sword. Emma brought it to her in its decorated scabbard.

'I gave it some spit and polish,' she said as Gran took it.

'That was kind of you.' She fingered the tasselled handle. 'They have to hold them up, you know, otherwise they drag on the ground. One hand to salute with, one to hold the sword, and what happens if you need a third?

This all but caused disaster once. The admiral's wife tripped coming up the gangplank, your grandfather leapt forward to help and they both nearly landed in the drink.' She pulled the sword out and examined the chased blade.

'It's good it's going back into the Navy,' Emma said softly. The scourge of the Three Sheaves had turned into an old and possibly lonely woman, and Emma was filled with pity for her. 'Shall I help you upstairs?' she asked.

Olivia Wheeler replaced the blade with a sharp click. 'No, you shall not!' she snapped. 'When I'm that decrepit I'll go into a home or, better, do myself in so you won't feel obliged to visit me.' She stood, leaned the sword against a chair and bent and kissed Emma's cheek. 'I'm glad you're here now, however. Good night, darling. Watch a video if you like, but don't stay up too late.'

Emma sat and listened to the creaks above her head as her grandmother moved between bathroom and bedroom. Wind tugged at the cottage's eaves and upon it were borne shouts: revellers departing from the White Horse, presumably. Emma wondered about a video and got up to see what was on offer. Several James Bond movies recorded from the television and a batch of tapes promising the greatest sporting moments of each of the last five years. Emma shook her head at them and was selecting a book to read when the grandmother clock made important noises in its innards preparatory to issuing eleven chimes. There were no other clocks: this had to be the one mentioned in the will. Emma waited politely for it to finish and opened its door, for she remembered vaguely that there was a brass plaque inside. There was.

'15th October 1913. From the inhabitants of Bagshot.'
Emma closed the door and stood back.
'What the hell is that about?' she asked the clock.
It winked ticks at her and said not a word.

*

No liddle cock crow woke her, but the phone ringing then the sound of a radio or television did. Gran might have an eye for skittles, but she was going deaf.

'Did you sleep well?' she said over *Breakfast News* as Emma arrived in the kitchen. 'I was going to bring your breakfast up. Have you heard about this terrible rape? It's the water. It's been getting worse since privatization.'

Or that's what Emma thought she said. She could not begin to respond. In any event, the scourge of the Three Sheaves was in fine fettle this morning. She turned down the television and into the blessed near silence said, 'Al rang. He knew you were bringing the sword yesterday and is desperate to show it off to his pals. He could meet us in Exeter for lunch. It wouldn't take us long to get there in your car, would it?'

'No,' Emma said, thinking what a selfish shit Al was for not realizing Gran might want time with the sword and its memories.

'You don't mind, do you? Wouldn't you like to see Al?'

'Of course I would.' Emma was the selfish one. Gran wanted to dub her grandson with the sword which had, after all, been lying neglected in the attic at home. The truth was that she didn't want to share her grandmother with Al and his affected Dartmouth slang, not even for the period of lunch, but there was another revelation to savour: time, a world full of it. Before she would have been at the office for hours by now, already frazzled and unaware that proud pied April was outside dressed in his fickle trim. It was sunny, but a cruel wind pinned the daffodils to the grass and whistled through the open back door. Gran opened it in the mornings whatever the weather. It prevented her from catching colds, she said. 'I'd like to see Al,' Emma said more warmly.

'He'll ring back to confirm. If you answer the phone remind him to wear his uniform.'

'To honour the occasion?'

Gran put a plate of scrambled eggs in front of her. 'A bit of ceremony does no harm.'

The silver fork Emma picked up had the same crest as her mother's signet ring. The clock in the sitting room chimed nine briskly, as though urging Emma to get on with what she had come for. The silver and the clock. Emma wondered which pieces of china Gran had bought from the cats' home in Guernsey.

How was she going to introduce the subject? Now she was here, it presented quite a problem. You don't extract skeletons from cupboards using a pickaxe. Time, she reminded herself. There was plenty of it.

She felt further ashamed of herself when she saw the look on her cousin Alistair's face as he was handed the sword. His cheeks turned scarlet and his eyes ran over the accoutrements planning more spit and polish for them than Emma had ever dreamed of.

'It's been in a few places, hasn't it? Through a world war. Great!' he said, unable to stop himself admiring it. 'Thanks, Gran. I'll take the best care of it, I promise.'

'Why not try it on?' Emma suggested, since he was obviously longing to.

'I can't in public until I'm commissioned.'

Emma glanced around the almost empty hotel lounge. 'We won't tell anyone,' she whispered.

He buckled it on and stood before them, bringing his right hand up in a snappy salute. A proud young man of the Royal Navy wearing his grandfather's sword.

'Young man, she calls him,' Olivia said as Emma steered the Porsche out of Exeter. 'How much younger is he than you?'

'Two years,' Emma said, as if Gran needed to know. 'He seems much younger, though.'

'Because he's growing up at a sensible rate. A natural rate,' Olivia added significantly.

'Okay, okay,' Emma said, taking the point.

'It was sweet of you to let him drive your car.'

'There wasn't much traffic around. I thought it would round off his day.'

'And it did.' She put a hand on Emma's knee. 'You're a much nicer person now. I wouldn't have let you be present if I'd given the sword to Al three months ago. Not if you'd driven it specially from Scotland, I wouldn't.'

'Ouch,' Emma said. Then after a pause: 'And last night? Would you have taken me to the White Horse three months ago?'

'No. Three months ago my team mates would have seen something in your face which would have made them uncomfortable . . . or, rather, me uncomfortable for them.'

'Was I that horrible?' Tears were contemplating making an appearance and she bit her lip to hold them back.

'Not horrible. You couldn't be that. Impatient, though, and contemptuous when things weren't going as fast as you wanted or weren't up to your perceived standard. It's London, I suppose.'

'Why?' Emma was hoping for one of her grandmother's batty explanations to cheer her up, but was disappointed.

'There are too many people,' Olivia said. 'You can choose friends who have everything in common with you, even down to jobs and lifestyle. You have no opportunity to learn tolerance, let alone exercise it.'

'There's truth in that,' Emma said. 'It's one of the reasons why people live in cities, after all. And what's the matter with that? In the country there are feuds and quarrels because people who don't have much in common have to live together. Aren't you having trouble with your neighbours over your hens? Graham said they wanted you to get rid of them. Where's your tolerance exercised there?'

'They'll learn,' Olivia said comfortably.

She dozed then, and Emma steamed the Porsche through Devon and into Dorset. She enjoyed the power of the car, the competing glances from male drivers. Perhaps she wouldn't sell it. Perhaps she would use it to be generous to Cousin Alistair again so he could refer to its bow and its stern and bring it safely alongside in another car park.

Beyond Beaminster she saw a signpost to Chard St Sebastian and recklessly accepted its promise of a short cut. She soon found herself in a maze of tiny, high-banked lanes, any signposts there were denying knowledge of the existence of Chard St Sebastian. Emma crept round blind corners, the windscreen wipers working against a sudden April shower, and decided to go at the pace the surroundings determined and enjoy it. The banks were crowded with primroses and − she stopped and let down the window − yes, violets.

> Violets by a mossy stone:
> Half hidden from the eye.

The poet was right. Emma had once read a lot of poetry, and learned it for the pleasure of it.

She slid the car on. Gran was right, too, however much it hurt. Had Brian plunged off a decent main road on impulse (which he wouldn't have done: journeys were planned beforehand, and conducted with Emma sitting in the passenger seat, map on her lap, Post-it notes with the details of the route attached to the relevant pages), but *had* he done so he would have been in a raving fury by now. In fact something similar had happened when they had been on their way to stay with people in Oxfordshire, though it had not been impulse which had led to their predicament but an honest mistake in navigation by Emma, and Brian had indeed exhibited raving fury.

What Brian, with a fastidious wrinkle in his voice,

would have called an agricultural smell became evident as Emma and her sleeping grandmother passed a conglomeration of farm buildings and then, around another corner, the image of Brian at his most unappealing was reinforced by the presence on the road of a herd of black and white cows. Exactly this had happened before. Brian had roared his engine, roared at Emma for misdirecting them, roared at the cows and developed a furious sulk about whose road it was.

It was the cows', now as then, and they knew it. They ambled along the shining lane in their conversely purposeful way, pausing every so often to wrap a tongue around a tasty morsel that took their fancy. Emma stopped the car, turned the engine off and waited while the cattle flowed slowly past. The sun had come out but the showers were elsewhere, for a rainbow arced in the sky ahead. She twisted her head and looked up and around. The sky was full of rainbows; she seemed to be in the middle of one and another ended luminously in the branches of an oak tree not far ahead. She was at the centre of the soft, fractured light and felt her heart expand at the beauty of it, the rarity.

Had she ever loved Brian? The notion suddenly seemed preposterous, a joke. The last cow nuzzled the Porsche's wing mirror thoughtfully, and Emma grinned at her.

'Hello, Number Three Six Eight,' she said. 'Isn't it a lovely day?'

Gran awoke, as if by instinct, as they entered Chard St Sebastian, Emma having been given directions by the man in charge of Three Six Eight and her companions. Olivia poked at her grey hair, sat up and settled her pearls around her neck.

'I'm sorry,' she said. 'I can't think what came over me.'

'Post-match exhaustion?'

'Perhaps.'

'Do you practise every night?'

'Good gracious, no. It would blunt the natural skill, the appetite to win.'

'So we won't be going to the pub.'

'Not unless you insist, darling, but don't you want to ask me about my father and the will you found?' Emma braked, more sharply than she intended to, and Gran added, 'Don't be surprised. Your mother and I do talk, you know. Have you brought Daddy's albums?'

'They're in the boot.' Emma eased the car into the driveway and parked it there. She turned to Olivia. 'Gran,' she stuttered, 'I – I didn't come here only because of that.' She wanted it to be the whole truth, and it was now.

Olivia reached out and touched her cheek. 'I'm delighted,' she said, 'by any excuse my grandchildren can find to see me.'

After supper they sat side by side on the sofa, the album open in Olivia's lap. The clock ticked steadily and the logs in the fire scented the air with wood smoke.

Gran turned the black pages over, studying each photograph. 'They're so familiar,' she said. 'But, really, a bit shocking. If you had yourself photographed with two rhino heads these days you'd be lynched, and rightly.'

'Do you remember Africa?'

'I don't think so. Photographs can invent a memory as well as reinforce it, can't they? I remember the photographs.'

'So does Mum.'

'She and Julie were shown them every time we went to see him. They aren't quite the same, though. She changed them after he died.'

'Who is "she"? Why?'

Gran's attention was caught by the picture of Race Week. 'Missed that, didn't she? Ah!' H.G.A. looking like

24

Ronald Colman. 'He was lovely. The best father a child could have had. I expect it was because he never quite grew up himself. He treated me as an equal, a partner, and we had such fun together on Anglesey. Never Nick, just Daddy and me.' The fire settled. Olivia took a log from the basket beside her and tossed it into the embrace of the golden glow. The clock chimed a half hour. Emma waited.

'He taught me about the countryside,' Olivia said. 'The country ways. In those days it seemed nature was divided into friend and foe. Some things you shot or trapped or poisoned to protect the things you wanted to shoot at other times. Except for foxes, which had another death reserved for them. Was it bad?' she inquired of the fire. 'I don't believe so. There wasn't the mobility then. You didn't have millions of people able to leap into fast cars, pursue a day of what they call "traditional country sport" and zoom back to town in time for dinner. I hate this word *leisure*,' she said so explosively that Emma jumped. 'They go on about the leisure industry. It's a contradiction in terms, isn't it?'

'I suppose it is,' Emma said. 'But people need leisure, Gran.'

'They're making the country into one of those theme parks, a playground for townies. I read it somewhere and it's true. I'm glad I'm old.'

She was silent, then, until Emma prompted: 'Your father . . .?'

'He never poisoned or trapped, but he always carried a gun on our walks. A rabbit for the pot – not ours; my mother wouldn't eat them – meant one less at the crops and the vegetable gardens people relied on. He taught me to shoot when I was – what? – ten or eleven years old. Mummy was furious with him, but he was convinced a girl should be able to defend herself against a charging elephant. I believed him, naturally, and added my little

25

voice to the discussion. I remember . . . I remember most clearly feeling *devastated* for him when she told him that Anglesey wasn't Africa. I think he thought it was in some strange way, and I suspect I did too. He never grew up, you see? Such fun,' she repeated, sighing. 'Then it went wrong. Everyone blamed him. I blamed him. It was his fault, wasn't it?' Her voice had risen and Emma was shocked to see tears in the scourge of the Three Sheaves' brown eyes. Shocked but surprisingly unembarrassed.

'How did it go wrong?' she said gently.

Olivia shook her head. 'I can't say. Even now I can't. Not everything.' One hand was gripping the album so tightly that the thick paper was being crushed and the photographs were in danger. She grasped Emma's forearm with the other. 'You had a happy and secure childhood, Emma. Thank God for it. Thank Him every day.'

What happened? Emma longed to ask but, hoping to dissipate her grandmother's distress, said instead, 'What about Mo? Who was she?'

Olivia's fierce grip relaxed. The photographs were undamaged, though Emma's arm was sore. Surreptitiously she rubbed it.

'Mo?' Olivia said. 'She was my friend.'

'And the will? Gran, it seems so horrible. Why?'

The clock chimed nine question marks. Gran, her normal self after her outburst, turned another page.

'I don't know why. Who can see into someone else's brain? Your grandfather said it must have been guilt, but shouldn't you expiate – is that the word? – guilt before you die rather than take it with you? . . . Here's Nick. She put him in, notice, and not me. It wasn't so bad for him. Mummy adored him but she really didn't like me very much.'

'Nick was your brother. I'd forgotten.'

Olivia inserted a fingernail under the photograph and eased it from its moorings. Beneath it were different captions and scars to show that other pictures had been there: 'Self, Moppet, Mutali', 'Nell, Moppet'.

'The writing is different,' Emma said.

'I told you: she went through it and altered it.'

'Your mother did? What for?'

Olivia regarded her, her grey head on one side. 'This fascination with your great-grandfather. Laura thinks it's therapeutic.'

She used the word as if it had four-letter associations, and Emma laughed. 'Perhaps it is. Something to do while I think what to do next.'

'You should find a nice young man, marry and have babies. Or have babies and then marry, which is how they do it these days.'

'I've had enough of men for the moment, thanks.'

'I see,' Olivia said. 'Very well then. You should start at the beginning, and it began in Africa. He first went out there before the war – the Great War I mean, of course – and was wounded and came home.'

'But went back?'

'Oh, good heavens, yes. Africa was his life.'

Part II

I

Major Harold George Albert Wittering leaned on the ship's rail and breathed deep. Africa filled his nostrils and went to his head like champagne. Home! There had been times during the past fourteen months when he had wondered if he'd ever see this continent again. Discharged from the King's African Rifles in December 1918, he had gone to England on long leave, suffered a bout of influenza and then several of malaria and, to cap it all, the war wound along his ribs which he had considered long since healed (apart from occasional stabs of pain which he assumed he would have to live with) had begun to itch and suppurate and eventually, with the help of a doctor, had ejected a sliver of shrapnel. The cumulative effect of this had left him infuriatingly weakened and entirely at the mercy of his Aunt Caroline in whose house in Dorking – Dorking! – he had convalesced. The only good thing had been pretty Jilly Fletcher, the daughter of a neighbour, but even that had turned sour when Jilly decided to marry a respectable stockbroker and stay in Dorking rather than risk life in unknown Kenya as the wife of Harry Wittering, passed fit by the Colonial Office and appointed District Commissioner at Fort Richard. 'Miles from anywhere,' he had told the fetching Jilly, hoping to impress her, 'and the land below Mount Kenya alive with game.'

Home now, and never mind about Jilly and Dorking and poor, wet, cold England with its ungenerous skies. Harry took another breath and turned to the man standing beside him.

'Isn't it grand?' he said.

'Grand?' Jack Soames repeated, incredulity in his voice. Mombasa from this distance, with its pink, buff and ochre-coloured buildings dominated by a huge old fortress seemed a cut above Port Said and Aden, but *grand*? And the nearer they got to their berth the worse the smell became: a mixture of rotting fish and soot from the funnels of their ship and of the tugs that were guiding her in. On the quay was a swarm of gibbering black men, their bare backs gleaming. 'It's different up-country,' he said to Harry, 'isn't it?'

'Good God, yes,' Harry replied. 'Mountains, cool air and as much land as you can buy. You'll be Farmer Jack in no time.'

'Don't think I'd put it quite like that,' Jack muttered. Lord of the manor was more what he had in mind, with plenty of cheap labour to keep one in a style that was no longer possible in England.

'Never mind how you'd put it,' Harry said. 'You can be your own man here.' The ship bumped against the quay and hawsers were thrown and made fast. Harry searched the crowds below and, to Jack's astonishment, recognized one black face among the many. 'Mutali!' he shouted. 'Mutali, Mutali!'

A native in shorts and a ragged shirt waved his arms aloft, a white grin on his face. 'Bwana Wittering!'

Harry spoke to him and the man waved his hands again and began working his way back through the mêlée.

'I know it works,' Harry remarked to Jack, 'but I'm always surprised none the less.'

'What works?'

'The post, the system. I sent a letter to Mutali in the back of beyond telling him when I would be arriving. He, who reads not a word of English, takes it to someone who does and here he is. We'll be all right now. He'll meet us in the customs shed with porters ... Unless,' Harry added, for once ashore there was a division between government officers and settlers that did not exist aboard ship, 'you are being met?'

'No,' Jack said. 'I'd be grateful for your help.' He was wondering if he had made a mistake. Being a pioneer was glamorous in England, but this was far from glamorous. Harry Wittering was a good chap, one who could hold his drink with the best of them, and Jack would need him until he reached Nairobi where, he hoped, he would find soul-mates.

Yet was Harry Wittering a good chap? Jack Soames watched with distaste as he shook the black man's hand as though they were equals and jabbered away with him in some heathen language, laughing at something Mutali had said and slapping him on the back. He came to his senses, however, and Mutali distributed the luggage among the porters (not carrying anything himself, Jack noted, apart from a flat case containing the guns which Harry had bought in London and showed off to anyone on the ship who cared to admire them) and soon had it and the two white men on the Nairobi train. It was suffocatingly hot and only slightly less so as the train moved off, its slow pace scarcely stirring the boiling air.

Jack removed his hats – he had been warned to wear two as protection against the sun, though Harry made do with one – and fanned his face. 'I half expected you to invite the fellow to share our compartment,' he said.

Harry pretended surprise. 'Mutali? Oh, no. He prefers the native carriages. To him we Europeans smell unpleasant, you know.'

He's a damned nigger-lover, Jack thought, his suspicions of the past few hours confirmed; and Harry thought: are all the new settlers like this? Bad luck for Kenya if so.

It was some time before Harry could travel to his new home, for the self-important bureaucrats in Nairobi kept delaying him with bits of paper which wanted stamping, signing, counter-signing and the small print read in fourteen different positions. After a week of argument Harry took himself off to Thika for a few days to collect the luggage and – most important – his dog Nance from Louis and Lucy Fanshawe who had been taking care of both in Harry's absence. Nance greeted him hysterically and then sulked at him for deserting her. Harry took her on his knees to cajole her out of it and accepted a gin and tonic from a servant.

'Lord, but you've been doing some work here,' he said to his host and hostess. 'The place looks as good as it did pre-war.'

'We're in exactly the same position as we were in 1912,' Louis said. 'Half the land planted and years until we can expect the coffee bushes to bear. It's heartbreaking when you think about it.'

'So we don't,' Lucy said cheerfully. 'We just thank providence that we have a super headman and a fantastic set of boys. It's their work you're admiring, Harry.'

These were the sort of settlers Harry liked, the sort Kenya needed. It did not need, Harry was sure, the ones he had seen getting drunk in the bar of the Norfolk Hotel every night (and lunchtime and afternoon) for the past week, who shouted at and hit the native servants when the mood took them.

'Has Nance forgiven you?' Lucy asked him.

'I think so. She's in wonderful condition. Thank you for looking after her.'

'She's been no trouble. We'll miss her. Louis, you can show Harry our present to him now.'

'A present for me?' Harry said, intrigued. 'Why should I deserve a present?'

'He's made for you. The Thompsons bred him and when Lucy and I saw him we said instantly, "That one's Harry's." He's round the back.'

Mystified, Harry followed, Nance at his heels. Louis opened the door at one end of the stone-built stables and out danced a tawny-coated dog, half Rhodesian ridgeback, Harry reckoned, and half a variety of other breeds. Already he didn't mind. The dog greeted everyone, Nance included, then sat and met Harry's gaze with yellow eyes that had the look of an eagle in them. I've been waiting for you, they said. Where have you been?

Harry bent to stroke him. 'But – good heavens!' he said, noticing. 'He's only a puppy.'

'Six months old,' Lucy said, smiling. 'He'll be as big as a pony.'

'But braver,' Louis added. 'Were we right, Harry?'

'Oh, yes. Yes!'

'We've called him Mac.'

Harry had reckoned he'd get away with Nance in his room at the Norfolk but Mac was another matter. There was no question of leaving him with the Fanshawes until the government clerks had tied the last knot in their red tape. The dog was Harry's and knew it, and he cost a fortune in bribes over the next three weeks as every theft from the kitchen, every scratch on the furniture and any dropped tray was blamed on the six-month-old giant who, it was claimed, could easily be mistaken for a lion. Harry regretted not a cent – especially when, on a walk outside Nairobi taken to relieve both his and the dog's frustration, Mac met a real lion and faced it with such courage that Harry feared for his safety. Harry was not carrying a gun – an idiocy he also put down to frustration – but luckily the lion was well fed and too lazy to argue.

At last the Indian clerks reluctantly admitted they could find no more objections to Major Wittering taking up his post, and on a red road made slick by the first of the long rains he made his way north to Fort Richard. The fort, which had been no more than a wood and thorn palisade, had long disappeared and Fort Richard now consisted of Kikuyu *shambas*, a *duka* owned by an Indian and his ever-extending family, the District Commissioner's bungalow and a Roman Catholic mission.

'That should please you,' Harry said to Mutali. 'You can nip off to Mass every two minutes.'

Mutali hunched a shoulder at him. 'The priest there is a fool,' he said.

'Oh?' Mutali's conversion to Roman Catholicism had been the nearest he and Harry had come to a falling out during all their time together, before and through the war, and there was an agreement that it should not be discussed. This was too interesting to let by, however. 'Why is he a fool?' Harry asked.

Merely recalling the encounter made Mutali furious and he spilled the tale out with such venom that Harry, his Kikuyu still rusty, had difficulty understanding the whole. The Bwana had been kind enough to lend Mutali the truck so he could bring his two wives, their children and various livestock here. He had been having a quiet smoke with the head boy and the cook (presumably relishing their awe and respect that he should be entrusted with the truck; presumably, also, about to enter delicate negotiations about how many goats it would be appropriate for Mutali to accept in exchange for his recommendation to the Bwana that he should continue to employ these two individuals), when the madman had appeared, having been informed by Father O'Donnell in Nairobi that he was about to gain a new parishioner, and had told Mutali that he would not allow – not *allow*! – Mutali to have two wives.

36

'I see,' Harry said, trying not to laugh. 'Does Father O'Donnell know you have two wives?'

Another tirade, and the answer was probably no. Mutali, as the Bwana was aware, had taken an unworthy job while awaiting the Bwana's return. It had been necessary for one wife to remain on the reserve and oversee the welfare of Mutali's cattle and goats while the other had been in Nairobi with him.

'So what did you tell our new neighbour?' Harry said.

'I told him,' Mutali said with dignity, 'that I was a Catholic in Nairobi but had not yet decided if I wished to be one in this district. I explained how everything had changed. There is no war any more and I am an important man. Is that not true, Bwana?'

'Undoubtedly.'

'We have this big district to run, you and I.'

'We have.'

'Would the Bwana like his sundowner now?' Mutali said, satisfied all was as it should be.

'Yes, please.'

'I will inform Jomo.'

'We're keeping him on then, are we?'

'He is a good boy, and the cook as well. Bwana Lee had a wife and she taught him many fine English recipes . . . *Yorkshire pudding, dumplings!*' he sang out in English. *'Steak and kidney pie.'*

The next morning the young man who had been acting DC in the interregnum gave Harry the briefest of briefings, said Mr Lee had left quantities of notes, bade farewell and departed for Nairobi before the rains made the road impassable. Harry wandered outside and gazed around him. The garden was colourful enough now but it would be a riot after the rains. The clouds cleared for a moment and revealed Mount Kenya in the distance, its peaks even here on the Equator white with snow. On

Fort Richard's main street – its only street – the illusion of some sort of civilization created by the garden vanished and for the first time Harry could think of Jilly Fletcher without a pang. Had he really intended to bring a Dorking-bred girl here? Love must have sent him barmy. He needed a wife like Lucy Fanshawe or Mrs Lee, his predecessor's, who had resolutely taught her cook to make dumplings.

A single, enormous drop of rain extinguished the burning tobacco in his pipe. He looked up at a cloud the size of Great Britain and laughed.

News of Harry's arrival quickly spread around the district and, the rains notwithstanding, many people came to Fort Richard from the surrounding areas wanting to test the mettle of their new DC. They had to get past Mutali first.

'An elephant on your maize?' Harry heard him cry. 'And do you think the Bwana does not know that your maize is not planted yet and the elephant are in the forest? Let me tell you this, my friend: when there is an elephant on your crops the Bwana will come and measure the spoor with his special tape and inform you to within a pound how much his tusks weigh . . . Lion? My friend, this Bwana has shot so many lion that they know about him. All over Africa the lion know this Bwana and fear him.'

And so on. Harry hoped the people were not disappointed when they saw him in the flesh. As it turned out it was Mac who impressed them most and a rumour began that the dog could understand every word that was said and told his master if anyone lied. Mac, seven months old and his yellow gaze disconcerting even to those who knew him.

The summons Harry had been dreading came on the morning of the third day in the form of an invitation from Father Patrick to have dinner at the mission. It was brought by a pious boy wearing what had been an immaculate white shirt when he had set out but was grey, soaked and spattered with red mud when he arrived.

'Take it off,' Harry said to the shivering child, who shook his head and said in English with a noticeable Irish burr, 'No, sir.'

If the father insisted on his converts wearing clothes, why on earth didn't he provide them with waterproofs or umbrellas? Harry wrote an acceptance, resisted adding a recommendation that the boy be given a hot bath on his return (he shouldn't antagonize the only other white man for miles around before he'd even met him), and gave the envelope to the boy who slid it under his sopping shirt and scuttled away.

That afternoon the rain cleared and Harry and Mutali rode out on the two horses Harry had bought (along with other pigs in pokes) from Mr Lee. Nance kept close but Mac ranged ahead – out of fearlessness or foolishness Harry could not decide. His coat blended as a lion's would do into the bush, though not for much longer: already the new grass was responding to the rain and growing. When it was at its full lushness the herds of zebra, gazelle, and wildebeeste would be drawn to these grazing grounds and leopard, lion and cheetah would not need so much disguise to stalk and take their prey, so plentiful would it be. So it had always been in Africa and so, Harry hoped, it would continue.

Mac put up a lone Thomson's gazelle and chased it into the path of the two horsemen. Harry raised his rifle and brought the Tommy down. His horse shied at the sound of the shot and so did Mutali's, but Mac, who had slowed down as the gazelle speeded up and thus not come into the line of fire, trotted to the body and sat. Did I not do well? his yellow eyes said. Is this what you require me to do?

'You are a prince among dogs,' Harry told him. The sensible conclusion was that Mac had slowed when he realized he was outpaced, but his expression indicated otherwise. Harry dismounted. 'No more corned beef, eh, Mutali? Steak casserole tonight.'

'Tonight you are eating with the priest,' Mutali reminded him severely. 'And I do not think these horses are any good. The DC who sold them to us did not tell the truth as to their suitability for our purpose.'

Harry searched among his Swahili and Kikuyu vocabulary for a word approximating 'pomposity' and failed to find one.

'Never mind,' Mutali continued, of the opinion the Bwana was in some way embarrassed at having been cheated, 'I will train them to behave.'

Harry drove himself to the mission that night accompanied by Ndwetti, one of the outside boys, in case the truck got stuck in the half-mile of mud that passed for a road. Mutali had refused to go anywhere near the priest.

He was a young man, not much older than Harry, and Harry was relieved to be offered a healthy slug of Irish whiskey. Over dinner they discussed the weather, the state of the road and Father Patrick's plans for expanding the mission and building a hospital and school. Money for the work was being raised by the good people back home in Cork, he said, and some nuns from a nursing order would be coming out as soon as suitable accommodation was built for them. He himself, he added, ran a dispensary of sorts but was not able to – er – the women.

'Quite so,' Harry said tactfully.

'Mrs Lee took fine care of that side of things, I understand,' Father Patrick said. 'I was sorry not to have benefited longer from her experience. You are not married yourself, Major Wittering?'

'No.' So the man was a greenhorn, then.

After dinner the priest provided a more than decent brandy and they both settled down with their pipes before the fire in Father Patrick's study.

'Naturally,' the priest said, 'I wished to make your acquaintance, Major Wittering, since we'll be working closely together to be sure, but you must know why I was particularly anxious to see you tonight.'

'I do not,' Harry said, thinking, Blast him, just when I was beginning to relax.

'It's your boy Harold.'

'Harold?' Harry said. 'I haven't got a boy called Harold.'

'You call him Mutali. Harold is his Christian name. Evidently he chose it to honour you.'

And blast Mutali, too.

'He seems to have turned from God entirely,' Father Patrick went on. 'Several times in the past few days I have been into your compound. He will not speak to me, he flaunts his wives and he will not make them cover their – er –'

'Bosoms.'

'Top halves. Will you use your influence over him, Major Wittering, and at least make him talk to me?'

Harry prayed to his own God for strength to keep his temper. How dared this black-robed fruit bat of a man come proselytizing in Harry's own compound? 'How long have you been in Africa?' he asked, pleased his voice was calm.

'Five months,' replied the priest. 'But time, the long or short of it, means nothing when God's work is on hand.'

'Before you change something shouldn't you know the nature of what it is you are changing?'

'I don't follow you,' the priest said stiffly.

'You want to change these people's religion, but you want to change their culture too.'

'What culture? They have none!'

'Of course they do! It is different from ours and perhaps requires a new definition but it exists, it's practical and it suits them and their climate. What do you expect Mutali to do with his second wife? If he felt like pleasing you he would send her back to his relations on the reserve, but it wouldn't stop her being his wife. He has a responsibility for her which he can't abandon on your say-so, and if he did her father or brothers would have something to say on the matter.' Harry gestured with his pipe. 'It's like dropping a stitch in a piece of knitting. It doesn't leave one neat little hole, it spreads out and affects the whole.'

'I don't think I'm needing a lecture from you, Major Wittering,' Father Patrick interjected.

'You need one from somebody, Father. Go and talk to the priests who have been here for years. They will tell you to bend. And,' Harry continued, 'since I *am* giving you a lecture, hear this: you must not force the women – any of the people – to cover themselves, especially during the rains. They have no means of drying their clothes properly, and even sweat turns cold. So don't do it. Or not' – Harry smiled, hoping to lighten the atmosphere – 'until the citizens of Cork can send them several changes of clothing and airing cupboards to keep them in.'

'Have you finished?' Father Patrick asked, sarcasm in his voice.

Harry stood up. 'Yes, I've finished. It's good advice, Father. Consider how bad it will appear when your converts die of pneumonia and remember who has to investigate suspicious deaths, for you can be sure that is how I will regard them.'

'There is no need to threaten me, Major. I will pray for guidance on what you have said.'

'Good man!' Harry said.

'Father Brendan of our order, who founded this mission, died of pneumonia. Do you expect me to avoid the same fate by going around naked?' But his eyes were twinkling.

Harry laughed. 'No, Father. You stick to your culture and let these people stick to theirs.'

'You are changing them,' the priest pointed out. 'You the British.' He shook Harry's hand. 'But that's a discussion for another evening.'

'When you come and dine with me.'

'I'd like that, Major.'

'Harry.'

'Harry, then. Good night and God bless you – or is that not permitted?'

'It's permitted,' Harry said, chuckling.

'How was the madman?' Mutali asked the next morning, drawing back the mosquito net and putting Harry's tea on the bedside table.

'You are not to call him that. He is a fine priest and I've promised him your soul.'

'Bwana!' Mutali gasped.

'Don't be a fool, Mutali. Your soul is your own to do with what you want, but I will hear no criticism of Father Patrick. Where's my shaving water?'

'It is ready. We have lost a chicken in the night.'

'Well, find it,' Harry said irritably, turning Nance off the bed. Until kennels could be built, wild animal and *siafu* ant proof, the dogs had to sleep inside and their sojourn at the Norfolk had led them to believe this also meant in Harry's room.

'I have done so, but it is dead. These people are fools if they think they can steal from us.'

'They are bound to try it on at first. Who are they?'

'Two young men just circumcised. Their fathers are rich.'

Truly Mutali was astonishing. When they'd been chasing the Germans all over East Africa and the supply lines were nonexistent, or headed in the wrong direction, Mutali had always managed to produce food from somewhere together with the life history of whoever he'd bought it from. His many talents made up for what Harry's fellow officers had regarded as over-familiarity.

'I have,' Mutali said, pre-empting Harry's next order, 'sent messengers for the others of their age set. So you can *read the Riot Act*,' he added in English.

Which Harry did, and to a large audience, for everyone was amazed that the thieves should be discovered so quickly and unerringly and considered it proper that the Bwana should hold the boys who had dared the thieves equally to blame. The detection they put down to Mac, sitting by his master on the verandah, who they claimed had the powers of a most superior witch doctor; something that would not please Father Patrick, whom Harry invited to partake of the chicken.

2

The rains ended, and the rolling land – now a sea of
green lapping against the forests on the lower slopes of
Mount Kenya and, in the other direction, to the Aber-
dare Mountains – filled up with game: huge herds of
zebra, buck, gazelle, wildebeest; giraffe striding lan-
guidly around, needing only to bend an elegant neck to
find a mouthful of succulent leaves; elephant flapping
great ears. One raised a questing trunk in Mac's direction,
realized he was not a lion and ignored him. Mac
was scared of nothing, apart from a rebuke from Harry
when his eyes would cloud over in embarrassment and
shame.

But the end of the rains also improved the road to
Nairobi, and along it was borne a stream of red tape
confirming Harry's worst fears about Kenya's new status
as a Crown Colony. He shoved the boring letters into the
drawer of the table in the room he affected to call his
office and, after due preparation, set out to do what he
had been longing to do: travel around this district of his
and rediscover the Africa he had not seen properly since
the outbreak of war.

'I'll miss our evenings together,' Father Patrick said as
he hosted a farewell dinner. 'These past months have
been stimulating.'

Two more dissimilar men could not have been thrown

upon each other's company in such a remote place. They had argued, shouted at each other, and once Father Patrick had stormed out of Harry's bungalow and begun walking back to the mission on foot, refusing to accept a lift when Harry and Mutali caught up with him until Harry invited him to identify the two sets of eyes beyond the truck's headlights.

'Jesus, Mary and Joseph!' the priest said, scrambling in.

'*Simba*,' Mutali told him.

'Are they lions?' He began to laugh. 'Well, and I wouldn't be the first Christian to go that way, would I?'

For they had that most important thing, a sense of humour in common.

Harry's safari was an impressive affair consisting of several Wakamba porters (for the Kikuyu reckoned that only women should carry loads) and including such specialists as the boy whose job it was to fill Harry's bath and another who would cut grass for the horses since the *syce* in charge of them considered such an activity beneath him.

'Really, Mutali,' Harry complained, 'I'd hoped to travel light.'

'It will not do for the people to see their new DC ride out of the bush like a vagrant,' Mutali said.

He had wanted to take the truck, but this Harry had forbidden. Transporting petrol was difficult and dangerous and horses were better suited to the terrain. Mutali agreed reluctantly and, ever suspicious of the inhabitants of Fort Richard (he'd never forgotten the chicken, though not so much as a button had gone missing in mysterious circumstances since), he took the truck to the mission compound, built a rondavel to shelter it, removed the rotor arm and presented it to Father Patrick for safe keeping. Harry had no idea what the relations were between Mutali and the priest, whether Mutali went to

Mass or not, for after that first evening the state of Mutali's soul had not been mentioned, but Mutali's laconic comment when Harry inquired why he was taking such excessive precautions indicated that Father Patrick was not making significant inroads into the minds of the people hereabouts.

'We're taking Mac with us,' he said, as though it was an explanation in itself.

Mac was now eleven months old and found this safari a terrific adventure, in the first few days often causing porters to drop their loads and run as they mistook him for a lion, though they laughed at themselves and cheerfully picked up their loads and carried on (careful to pick up everything: losing something was not the same as stealing it but you could not be sure how the lion-dog would interpret it). Then when Harry was satisfied that Ndwetti was competent enough to find the way and set up camp, he, Mutali and Mac would follow four or five hours behind, Nance often cadging a lift on the pommel of Harry's saddle, and arrive to find the tents up, Harry's bath ready, the cook sweating over his fire and the headman from the village Harry had come to visit waiting ceremoniously to greet him.

Could a man be paid for doing this work?

There were times, however, when Harry earned every last shilling. One evening he was sitting outside his tent, Nance on his lap, Mac lying at his feet, a glass of whisky on the table at his elbow, and was grappling with an unexpected attack of homesickness. The bundle of letters brought by messenger from Fort Richard included one from Aunt Caroline which enclosed a photograph of Jilly Fletcher outside an English church on the arm of her brand-new husband. He was struggling to read Aunt Caroline's impossible writing by the light of the lamp – it was about the WI, the church fête and the flower show

and it seemed to Harry at that moment to be very precious
– when three exhausted natives were brought before him.
They came from a distance far off, they said, had heard
the Bwana was here and run and run to find him. Their
village was beset by a devil of a she-lion who took people
– men, women, children – from their fields or grazing
land by day and from their huts by night, and would the
Bwana come and shoot it, please?

Even allowing for exaggeration this seemed serious.
The three men were without doubt terrified and the effort
they had made to reach Harry spoke for itself. He ordered
them to be given food and water and, with Mutali and
Ndwetti, decided on a plan of action. Harry had only
tracked one man-eater before, and that had been in the
company of someone of great experience. He remembered
the old white hunter's first rule: go after the bugger with
the fewest number of men possible, only those you can
trust absolutely. The last thing you need is to have to
worry about the other chaps' safety.

'Your man-eater,' the old boy had concluded, 'knows
three rather important things: one, that you're more cunning than he is so all his wits are about him; two, that
you're not half as strong as he is and your claws and
teeth don't amount to much; and, three, he likes the way
you taste.'

Hey ho, Harry thought, visions of church fêtes in Dorking gone, here's a lark. Himself, Mutali and Mac, then –
because Mac would follow anyway and no one would be
able to, or dare to, stop him – four guns, ammunition, food
and water. They would have to take the horses for without
them they would never be able to keep up with the three
natives. Food for the horses, too, to supplement the grass.

'I will see to it,' Mutali said.

'It's going to be dangerous, Mutali,' Harry said.

'Why? It's only a lion. We will shoot it, come back
here and continue with our business.'

He grinned and disappeared into the darkness beyond the lamp. Harry turned to Ndwetti.

'You're in charge of the camp here, and any man who does not do his duty you tell me about when I get back. All right?'

'I would like to come with you, Bwana,' Ndwetti said. 'I could carry a gun but I'm afraid I do not know how to shoot.'

He meant what he said although he was shaking with fright at the prospect. Harry smiled at him. 'You are of more use here. Look after Nance for me, will you?'

Ndwetti nodded and bolted before Harry changed his mind.

Food, water and sleep had restored the three natives who had brought Harry the summons and the next morning, in pre-dawn darkness, they led the way at a loping run out of the camp and across the plain. Their stamina was extraordinary and it was only Harry calling a halt that forced them to stop, first an hour after sun-up when tea was brewed and later for a few hours in the shade during the heat of the day, when Mac and the horses needed rest even if the men did not. The sun was directly overhead, a man's shadow scarcely an inch long.

They camped that night in the open, Mac sharing Harry's bed and mosquito net and making sleep difficult for them both. Harry had worried about Mac's pads being damaged by this forced march, but was reassured: it was like sharing a bed with four wads of wire wool.

They reached the village in late afternoon and the scene that greeted them proved that the three native runners had not exaggerated anything. The torso of a boy had just been found, freshly killed, the legs gone and the head a few yards away. A lion was using this village as a larder, coming along and selecting a meal when it felt like it. Would it come back to its kill, as lions normally did, with so much meat available on the hoof, as it were?

Harry was short of sleep but didn't fancy the idea of a quiet night's rest here. He and Mutali fed and watered their horses and then asked if a thorn fence could be provided to protect them. While this was being done, Harry examined the area around the pathetic corpse. It was on low ground, away from the village proper and was overlooked by a small hill.

'What do you think?' he asked Mutali.

'We build a *boma* up there,' Mutali said, pointing, 'and keep watch. I have brought our most powerful torches.'

'Well, make it a most powerful *boma*. This animal has no fear.' Harry summoned the headman who arrived accompanied by his witch doctor. 'I would like a goat, please,' he said.

'What for?' the headman asked.

'As bait,' Harry explained, 'to attract the lion.'

'The government must pay.'

'The government will pay. Now get me one, and I want thorn for a *boma* here.'

'It is all used up for the *boma* for your animals.'

'Get some more, then.'

'My people fear to go into the bush. The lion –'

'My man and I will guard them with our rifles.' He took a gun from Mutali and cocked it. 'All right?'

'All right,' the man said sullenly, eyeing the gun.

'I do not think I like it here,' Mutali commented as the headman went off followed by the witch doctor, the feathers on his headdress fluttering, the bones around his neck rattling.

'Neither does Mac.' He was guarding the gear Mutali had removed from the horses and lifting a lip when anyone came too close. There was no laughter in this village and the people seemed, like the headman and the witch doctor, unfriendly and unco-operative. Perhaps it was fright. It couldn't be much fun being a lion's larder.

They did, however, produce thorn and made a strong, protective nest into which Harry, Mutali and Mac crept at nightfall, taking their belongings with them, of which they would certainly have been deprived had they left them outside until morning. They cut holes for guns and torches in the front of the *boma* while thorn was piled behind them to protect their backs. It was dark before the villagers moved off and Harry and Mutali began their vigil.

A low growl from Mac woke Harry out of his light doze, and Mutali's hand on his arm. Harry touched Mac and thought, distractedly, something not right. Mutali turned on the torch and revealed the scrawny goat the headman had provided and overcharged for bleating piteously, straining at its rope. Mac growled again and Harry realized that two things were wrong. He pulled his gun from the thorn, whipped it around (hitting something on the way) and fired one shot, two.

Chaos. Something or one was badly injured or dead. It was not Harry although there was warm wet stuff around, sticky and probably red, and a weight on his legs and stomach which made it hard to breathe.

'Mutali?' No answer. Harry kicked at the weight and groped for the torch on his side of the *boma*. He switched it on. Mutali, his eyes glazed, was holding a hand to his jaw.

'Oh, Bwana,' he muttered. 'What happened?'

'Mac?' Harry said. '*Mac?*'

A whine, and Mac licked his hand. Harry swivelled the torch around to find him and incidentally discovered what the weight on him was. The head of a huge lioness was lying on his stomach. The claws of one great forepaw were raking Mac's haunches; the other paw, mercifully, had been caught up in the thorn and put out of action before it could reach Harry. Beyond the lioness was clear starlight.

'Bwana!' Mutali gasped, taking in the evidence.

'They were removing the thorn, not putting it on. I wondered why they took so bloody long. I'll hang the bastards, I'll bloody well hang them!' He realized he was speaking in English and continued in Kikuyu: 'Mac. Get this thing off Mac and me.' He was panicking. Calm down. He shone the torch into the lioness's eyes. Dead, definitely. They were safe – apart from a murderous village, and they were a day and a half's ride away from help. Mac now, though . . .

Somehow they rolled three hundred pounds plus of man-eating lioness out of the way and Mutali held a torch while Harry inspected Mac's wounds.

'Not too bad,' Mutali said.

'Provided we can keep infection from setting in.' And how was a dog with wounds like this going to run alongside the horses for upward of forty miles?

Mutali had turned and was scrabbling in one of the saddle bags. He handed Harry a box.

'What is it?' He squinted in the dark, for Mutali's torch was pointing at the roof of their fragile shelter.

'Our first-aid box. I brought it with us, naturally.'

'Naturally. You deserve a medal.' Harry opened the box and found disinfectant powder. 'Sorry I nearly knocked you out,' he added.

Mutali felt his jaw and glanced at the lioness. 'I'd prefer to be hit by your gun than make a meal for her,' he remarked.

'It was Mac who warned me. He was looking and growling in that direction . . . Are you all right, old boy?' he asked his dog. 'This might hurt.' Mac wagged his tail and suffered his wounds to be dressed. 'And the goat,' Harry said. 'It knew the danger was from here . . . Is my flask around, Mutali?'

Mutali found it and passed it over. 'Not too much,' he said softly. 'We need our wits with us in the morning.'

'Yes,' Harry said. It was just past midnight, six hours until sun-up and deadly silent. No one from the village had come to investigate the shots. Take only the fewest number of men with you, the old hunter had said; the ones you trust utterly. Your man-eating lion is cunning. And even more so when actively helped by hostile natives. Harry drank some brandy and tried to marshal his thoughts. He turned his head and looked at the back of the *boma*. It was obvious now – even apart from the hole the lioness had made in the thorn, it framing Mutali over a small fire he was making – how thin a screen had been protecting them from the rear. They had not thought to look behind them. Why should they? Check. He'd check everything twenty times over next time he went after a man-eater.

What of the human element? Harry suspected the witch doctor: when his spells had failed to remove the lion, he'd hit upon the idea that the beast needed white man's meat or some similar mumbo-jumbo, having heard (for the bush telegraph was amazingly efficient) that there was a supply of it in the area. He and the headman, who had ordered his people to attempt what was effectively murder, should be arrested and made an example of to show that His Majesty's district commissioners could not be sacrificed to lions on whim. But how? Harry could pretend not to have noticed the faults in the *boma*'s construction, ride away with Mutali and Mac (Mac – how?) and return at some later date with a squad of police, but the way he had been set up here was too personal. He couldn't send runners for the police every time there was a spot of local difficulty, and the news that he was weak would rapidly spread. No. It would not do. Subdue the ringleaders and make a show of reprimanding and forgiving the other villagers. Harry could not believe they were all hostile; he had always found the Kikuyu a friendly bunch and these poor sods had been existing under the most horrible pressure recently.

The shock was wearing off and as it did so Harry became aware of a tingling in his lower limbs which quickly sorted itself into a series of agonizing pains. *Siafu* ants? It was all they needed. He played the torch over his legs and realized that a branch of thorn had been between him and the lioness and had been driven into his legs by her weight. Lucky it wasn't higher up and damaged his marriage prospects. There was a great deal of blood around, for one of his bullets had hit the lioness in the throat. She had been dead when her claws got Mac. Before he could think about it he grabbed the thorn, using his hat to protect his hands, and pulled.

His oaths brought Mutali to his side. Cautiously Harry removed his trousers and Mutali, with exquisite delicacy, extracted the remaining thorns and dressed the cuts with the powder from the first-aid box. He then produced for Harry clean trousers and shirt and exchanged the flask for a tin mug of sweet tea.

'I dub you a knight,' Harry said. 'From now on you are Honourable Sir Mutali, Order of the Boma. Let me look at your jaw.'

There was no cut but a lump the size of a hen's egg. Harry anointed it with witch hazel and gazed into his man's eyes.

'My Honourable Sir Mutali, how much scouting did you do in the village after we arrived?'

Mutali gave him a lopsided grin. 'Enough, Bwana.'

'To work, then.'

As the sun shoved its red disc above the horizon, Mutali fired a shot over the village. 'Get them out,' he told the boys he had roused from their sleeping huts. 'You know what to tell them.' He reloaded the gun. 'Go!' he snapped, and they did.

Mutali checked the horses then went towards the remains of the *boma*. 'They must come this way,' he said to the boys he had appointed as stewards. 'No one must pass behind the *boma*, understand? We have had enough attacks from that direction since we have been here.'

They smiled sheepishly and nodded. Truly Mutali could find no malice in them and he treated them as he did his own sons. He walked on, one gun on his shoulder, the other cocked and ready in his hand. He would go to mass when they returned to Fort Richard, he decided; someone had to be thanked for their deliverance last night. Christianity was a sensible precaution and the Kikuyu gods, or those who claimed communion with them, had not been helpful to Mutali in the last forty-eight hours.

He joined the Bwana and Mac in front of the *boma*. On one side of the Bwana was the headman and on the other the witch doctor. Inside the *boma* the headman's wives – whom he had kept beside him in his hut in the hope that the man-eater would take them and not him – were chattering. The villagers were gathering on the area below amid whispers of rumour or speculation. Mutali wondered at the Bwana allowing the witch doctor to dress up in at least some of his paraphernalia. He might yet cast his bones and produce a spell; it seemed an unnecessary risk.

But Harry had considered the man so pathetic when woken and taken from his hut that he would not present him to his people in that state, even though the official government line was that witch doctors should be discouraged and even banned. It was the sort of thing a missionary would do. Harry hoped he and Mutali had worked everything out correctly. Otherwise ... what? The chances were they would not get away from here alive. The people were gathered now. Harry nodded to Mutali, who fired a shot into the air, and when the echo died Harry began his speech.

He was, he said, a friend of the people of this village

and not an enemy. If the people here needed his help they could ask for it, and that help included shooting dangerous lions for them. They only had to send a message to him and he would come. He was among the Kikuyu and the other people of this region for no other purpose than to serve them and to teach them the ways of their government in Nairobi, and to do that he had a mandate from His Majesty King George the Fifth, the King-Emperor who was the sovereign of them all.

There was a concerted, drawn-out 'Aah!' and a rustle of interest.

And, Harry continued, warming to this and rather wishing he had a solar topee and a red tunic. 'And what does the servant of King George find when he comes to the aid of the people he has been commanded to help?' Another rustle, this one – Harry hoped – of embarrassment. 'He finds,' Harry went on, 'someone with an intent to kill him. Someone who believes his magic is greater than that of King George. Someone who has cast many spells but was unable to rid the people of the lion that was tormenting them. These two men' – he waved an arm at the headman and the witch doctor – 'told you that if I could be lured to this place and the lion killed me then it would go away and trouble you no more. Didn't they?'

Mumbles and a few confident shouts that this was true.

'My friends, no amount of magic can kill a lion. These do.' He patted his gun. 'And you are fortunate that this lion did not kill me for then your torment would have continued.' He gestured to Mutali, who began removing the thorn covering the body of the lioness. 'As it is,' Harry said, 'I have killed your lion and you will be troubled no more. And if you are,' he shouted over the sudden bedlam as the crowd rushed forward, 'you summon me . . . All right?' he said to the headman.

'Yes, Bwana.' Harry scrutinized the shining, plump,

black face for guile but could see only relief there – that and a longing to join his people in their spontaneous dance around the lioness and see for himself the beast that had caused them such misery. Harry let him go and confronted the witch doctor, kept from escaping in the mêlée by Mutali. No one else stood by him: even his apprentices had gone.

'My friend,' Harry said, 'do not consider attempting such spells again. You have powers which I do not dispute, but when they involve threatening my life – anyone's life – I will dispute them and the result will always be the same.'

Mutali stepped away and the witch doctor fled. Harry gazed after him. 'Will he survive?' he asked Mutali.

'No,' Mutali replied baldly. 'Listen.'

The headman, a politician to the ends of his toes, was making a spirited effort to save his face, saying he had been misled and announcing a feast from his own storehouse tonight to celebrate the victory of King George over the devil-lion. He hoped, he added, eyes swivelling ingratiatingly, that the Bwana would consent to attend as guest of honour.

'I must leave for my camp before sun-up tomorrow,' Harry said. 'Can I rely on porters and guides to escort me after a night of feasting?'

At least twenty young men declared that the Bwana could count on them. Harry took the view that this meant they were safe in the village now and accepted the invitation. He and Mutali desperately needed sleep and Mac's wounds time to scab over, harden and convince him he would have to be carried back. Also Harry should trace the pugmarks of the lioness. The state of her teats indicated that she had cubs and, if old enough, they could have accompanied her on her hunts and learned her tricks. Harry tried to remember if a man-eating lion was likely to be part of a pride. Weren't they loners? He removed his hat and wiped his forehead. He was stupid with lack of sleep and drained adrenalin.

'This way, Bwana.' Mutali led him into a cool hut, Mac hobbling after. It contained a camp bed shrouded by a mosquito net which had to be a mirage. He lay down and discovered that it was not.

'Honourable Sir Mutali,' he muttered, 'you need sleep too.'

'Soon. We want that skin, Bwana, do we not?'

'By God, we do.'

He awoke three hours later and was confronted by the head of a female lion. Confused for a moment, he groped for his gun, then saw that the head was attached merely to skin and upon it Mutali was asleep attended by buzzing flies. Mac also awoke, stretched and whined.

'Well, it's bound to hurt,' Harry whispered, examining the dog's wounds. 'You stay here. Stay with Mutali.'

Mac slumped on the skin and Harry went outside. A warrior squatting there and apparently on guard stood up.

'Bwana?' he said, his eyes on the guns Harry carried.

'Why are you here?'

'To ensure that you sleep in peace,' the young man replied. 'There is much preparation for the feast tonight. Much noise.'

Harry decided to believe him. He and Mutali could have been murdered in their sleep, after all. 'I wish to see your headman,' he said.

The warrior let out a low call and another appeared and led Harry towards the centre of the village. The place was transformed from the one they had come to yesterday. Women called out to Harry as he passed and he quickly gained a tail of inquisitive children. He entered the headman's compound and the chief, warned of his coming, hurried forward to greet him, his face one huge smile.

'I want the price of that goat back,' Harry said as he was invited to sit in the shade of a wild fig tree, the *mugumu* that was held in respect by the Kikuyu, 'and you know, don't you, that I should fine you many cattle and goats for what you tried to do last night?'

'Yes, Bwana,' the man said smoothly, 'but you also know that it was not my fault. I was under a spell and could not help myself. Now I am rid of it and am, like the Bwana himself, a true servant of King George.'

'Where is your witch doctor?' Harry asked.

The man's gaze met Harry's. 'He has run away,' he said.

'If you have had him killed I will do worse than fine you. I will arrest you and lock you up.'

'He has run away,' the chief repeated. 'What else could he do when you proved that his spells were useless? Never mind. I have appointed another one who has modern ideas and would like, please, a magic gun from you. And now –' he clapped his hands – 'I want to show you how busy my warriors have been this morning while you slept. They have been doing the King's work and killing devil-cubs for him.'

Four dead baby lions, no more than three months old, were laid before the headman and Harry. They had been killed, slowly and painfully, by repeated spear thrusts as they lay in their den.

If Harry had found them they would have died quickly by gun; or he might have taken them back with him and passed them on to a zoo. If he had not found them they would have died of starvation.

Why, then, were these little bodies so depressing? Harry had not felt this way even when looking at the child the cubs' mother had killed and whose legs she had fed to them.

It was, he realized as he set off for camp the next morning, because in those dead lion cubs he had seen a vision of the future in Kenya. Already the Kikuyu, the dominant tribe, were making demands of the colonial government, saying they had been cheated of their land by the white settlers. They had died in their thousands during the Great War and believed, not unreasonably, that they were owed something. It was their country and at some point they would own it and Harry – though he could not express his views aloud for to most Englishmen it was heresy – considered such an outcome inevitable and just. The trouble was that the glories of Kenya, the plains of game, the great cats, the elephants, were to the Kikuyu a nuisance. A nuisance which preyed upon their herds, demanded more than its fair share of grass and raided crops. The lion cubs had not been killed because they might grow up to be like their mother; they had been killed because that meant four fewer lions and a good job too.

The sun came up. Mac, agreeing he could not travel on his own, was being borne along on a makeshift litter by two young men who walked fluidly across their land. Another bore the lioness' skin on his head and the rest had come along simply for the adventure. They saw the sun rising and began to sing, and Harry's heart lifted. So what if it did not last? He was here now.

3

They arrived back in Fort Richard nearly four months later, the land parched and aching for the short rains which would soon begin. The village seemed to have grown in their absence. At first Harry thought it was his mind comparing it to the places they had visited in the past months but quickly saw that it was so in fact. The Indians had expanded the *duka* and there were many more native *shambas*. The reason for this was soon obvious: Father Patrick had been busy during the dry season and his hospital and nuns' quarters were nearly finished. The *shambas* belonged to the labourers.

The priest shook Harry by the hand. 'Welcome home,' he said. 'I've missed you.'

He was different from the pallid zealot Harry had argued with during the long rains. As he showed Harry around his building site he bantered with the workers, swearing at them in a mixture of Kikuyu and Swahili (though perhaps he didn't know it was swearing) and had evidently given up any notion of insisting on what he would once have referred to as decent clothing. He himself had abandoned his cassock, during the daytime at least, and wore instead a shirt and trousers bought from the Indians, something which might have passed for a clerical collar but not attached to anything, and his broad-brimmed black hat.

'You look perfectly dreadful,' Harry told him. 'Let me lend you some decent gear. We're about the same size.'

Which was more than could be said of the priest and his trousers, which reached halfway down surprisingly hairy calves. Truly Africa had got to him.

Father Patrick eyed Harry's specially tailored and, in the priest's view, dangerously short shorts. 'What does it matter how I look when I'm working?' he said.

'You let the side down.'

Father Patrick laughed. 'So we've both jumped over the fence and will be spatting at each other from the opposite side. Is that it, Harry?' He slapped him on the back. 'Come to dinner tonight. Your household must be in fair chaos and I want to hear about your adventures.' He broke off. 'Is that your dog? By all that's holy, when is he going to stop growing?'

Mac, whom Harry had left with his meal, was trotting down the road in search of his master and being given wary glances as he came.

'What happened to him?' Father Patrick asked, noticing the scars on the dog's back.

'Ah,' Harry said. 'Now there's an adventure to tell you.'

They were inventing new laws in Nairobi every second, it seemed. Harry could no longer avoid the complaints of the clerks in the capital about his dilatoriness in filling out their forms and, swearing fearsomely, he settled down to the paperwork. He found any excuse to get away from it, however, and seeing that the opening of the hospital would ensure the growth of Fort Richard, whether Harry wanted it or not, he decided it should do so to some kind of plan. He pegged out a route for a road crossing the main one and, for fun, designated a large area, which no one laid claim to and in the centre of which grew a wild fig tree, as the market square. He had some trees felled and saplings transplanted so the road, when it was a road, would be shady.

'You'll be giving it a name next,' Father Patrick said, amused by Harry's civic industry and aware what the motives for it were. 'And were you quite sober when you designed it? It looks like it was made by a drunken snake.'

Patiently Harry explained that was because it had to skirt around cultivated land and since he had no official budget he'd had to keep compensation down to a minimum. It could be straightened out later, he said; he was merely establishing the principle of its existence.

'It's a fine wide highway,' Father Patrick soothed. 'Congratulations.'

Harry was planning further improvements. The Roman Catholic church and the people of Cork had so far taken a lead in the undeclared battle for Fort Richard with their hospital, church and school, not to mention the doctor and nun nurses who would soon be appearing, and Harry had written to his Aunt Caroline asking if she could persuade the worthies of Dorking to adopt the village in a similar fashion. A growing population would need a more reliable source of water than the river, and how about, he had said to his aunt, Dorking paying for a well or two?

Harry's concern was not foresight. Father Patrick's labourers had not come as temporary residents; they had brought with them wives, children and other relatives and more turned up almost every day, having heard rumours of healing or of work. They offered their wives to do the latter and also expected them to clear and cultivate land for gardens and bear many children. Traditionally Kikuyu men did nothing apart from prepare for wars, fight them, have long discussions about bride prices and how many goats should be paid as compensation for some injury. Their attitude to work occasionally made

Father Patrick grind his teeth and utter most unpriestly things. The Kikuyu did not see the completion of his hospital as an end in itself, something to be striven for in return for wages, but rather as a hobby to be tinkered with when they felt like it.

'What's the matter with them?' Father Patrick exploded. 'Don't they want the money?'

'No. It's refreshing, isn't it? . . . Don't worry,' Harry said, his turn to soothe. 'The British government had the same problem when they built the railway. It's why they shipped Indians over here.'

But people were working, even if the labour force was interchanging, and being paid in coin. The money was spent at the Indian *duka* or by the new arrivals (who initially worked hard for Father Patrick) on surplus produce from the older inhabitants' gardens. And this started happening in a gratifyingly short space of time in Harry's market square. It would not be long before Fort Richard could call itself a town.

'Thanks to you,' Harry said gloomily to Father Patrick.

'Oh, surely not! It's our position as well.'

'In the middle of nowhere.'

'In the middle of nowhere there must be somewhere.'

'At least,' Harry said with perverse satisfaction, 'you'll have to dress properly when the nuns come. They'll report you to the Pope if they see you going about as you have been doing.'

'I know,' Father Patrick said, and Harry thought he sighed. After a pause the priest went on: 'It's been great these nine months, Harry. I've been wanting to thank you for the help you've given me.'

'Get away with you,' Harry muttered. 'We've been a help to each other.'

On the table between them were the remains of an approximation to a traditional Christmas meal prepared by Harry's cook. They were having it early because Harry was spending the festive season in Nairobi, meeting Louis and Lucy Fanshawe there, going to Race Week and generally, he hoped, living it up and learning to speak English again and not Kikuyu, Swahili or Irish. He would be escorting Father Patrick's doctor and nuns back, provided their ship arrived in time. Father Patrick was speaking again and Harry dragged his mind away from visions of the bright lights of Nairobi and listened.

'Could you contrive to be as stern and fierce with the newcomers as you were with me?' the priest was saying. 'The nuns will be shocked by the women – and the men, I dare say. I've gained many converts by being lenient about the matter of dress and by excusing polygamous marriages so long as the men understand they must not marry again.'

He stopped talking. Harry was bashing his head on the table top.

'Harry, what's the matter?'

'Have you ever been caught between a rock and a hard place?'

'No, but it must be very uncomfortable.'

'It is,' Harry said. 'Believe me, Patrick, it is.'

He went to Nairobi armed with the latest head count of the population of Fort Richard and demands for money to embank the river, build a proper bridge over it and buy land for roads, arguing that if these were planned now it would cost much less later – later meaning next year, at this rate – when there would be protracted negotiations about the value of standing crops and all manner of other things. The Indian clerk examined a ledger at length, closed it and declared there wasn't a problem because the land belonged to no one and therefore could not be bought.

'It belongs to the Kikuyu, you idiot,' Harry said, but

he got his budget, was promised a visit from an engineer and told that his request for an assistant would be considered. 'Someone,' as Harry told Lucy Fanshawe, 'with ambitions to be a town clerk. I certainly haven't.'

'Forget about it now,' Lucy said. 'Let's have fun.'

Twice a year the white settlers of Kenya abandoned their struggles to make this wide-skied, high land straddling the Equator grow things it was not intended to and went to Nairobi for Race Week. The racing wasn't up to much but no one cared about that. It was a chance to meet and let off the steam of frustration produced by this beautiful but intractable country which, just as you had what was undoubtedly a bumper crop, threw up a weevil, a swarm of locusts, a blight or a killing frost and you were back to where you started but with a larger overdraft. Something, however – perhaps it was in the rarefied air – always led you to continue, to believe that next year would be different.

'They are like fishermen, don't you think?' Harry said to a new arrival in Kenya, the daughter of an official, pretty but hardly sparkling.

'In what way?' she asked.

'It's the biggest ones that get away.'

'I don't understand.'

'Haven't you noticed how it's the best crops that fail and never the minnows? As it were,' he stammered on.

'Oh. Yes. I see.'

She laughed obligingly at his feeble joke and he gave up on her.

'Why don't you divorce Louis and marry me?' he said to Lucy Fanshawe as they were dancing later.

'Darling Harry, it's sweet of you to suggest it but I happen to be rather fond of Louis.'

'Think of me, Lucy,' Harry begged, 'there in Fort Richard with six nuns.' For they had arrived along with the doctor and were holed up in a convent until Harry was ready to escort them north.

'I do think of you, constantly,' Lucy assured him, 'and the moment I find a suitable girl I'll send her to you straight away.'

'Thank you, Lucy,' Harry said. 'I know your judgement will be impeccable.'

'We matched you up with a dog, didn't we? After that a wife should be a doddle.'

The nuns, in spotless white habits and attended by a convert Kenyan wearing a patterned cotton pinafore dress, drove to Fort Richard in a truck, another example of the munificence of the citizens of Cork. Ndwetti was at the wheel of the new machine for Mutali claimed he did not feel well, yet when Harry suggested he be seen by the doctor he reacted in horror.

'It's not that sort of ill,' he hissed, climbing into the back of Harry's truck and finding a place among Mac and the stores Harry had purchased. 'I do not wish for these female priests to know that I am . . . what I sort of am.'

'You'll be uncomfortable,' Harry pointed out.

'So will the white birds, and they are not used to it as we Kikuyu are. I will stay here out of sight.'

Harry knew Mutali was attached to his adopted religion by a highly elastic thread, but even so his attitude seemed extraordinary. He hardly appeared during the journey and dropped out of the truck as soon as they forded the river, preferring to walk the mile or so to Harry's bungalow rather than risk being carried into the mission compound. If the doctor, who was riding in front of Harry's truck and not minding Nance on his lap, thought his behaviour was odd he didn't say anything. He was an elderly, frail-looking widower who had spent many years in the Belgian Congo; he had, he said, been giving the nuns lectures on the sea voyage so they would be prepared for what they saw in Africa. Harry was intensely relieved.

Mutali's explanation was forthcoming that evening, although by that time he had two things to fear from his religion. He didn't mind telling the Bwana; it was only in the presence of the white birds and the black one that he needed to be reticent. It went like this . . .

The Bwana had been good enough to allow him to visit his relations on the reserve near Nairobi when he had no need of him, and the relations had told him – correctly, Mutali said defensively – that a man of his status, a man who was the right arm of a district commissioner and who was paid in coin as well as owning many goats and cattle – should reflect that status in the way he lived.

'Should he not?' Mutali demanded.

'I'm sure he should,' Harry said, sipping his whisky and soda. 'But how?'

'Bwana, by the obvious means! I must take another wife.'

Harry spluttered into his drink. 'I see,' he said, wiping his moustache free of debris with his handkerchief.

'Surely you understand it is essential? Jomo is a good boy as head boys go, the cook Kigorro is a good boy. Each of them has two wives and think it strange I should be the same when it is so evident I am different.'

'Quite,' Harry said. 'Have you – er – selected the girl?'

Mutali gave a report of her lineage which Harry could not follow, it being stuffed with names he didn't know and relationships he could not begin to grasp. 'You see how it is, don't you, Bwana?' Mutali concluded. 'How important it is for me to have a third wife?'

'My Honourable Sir Mutali,' Harry said, 'have as many wives as you like. I only wish I could find one. What is the other reason you fear the good Father Patrick?'

A sly smile crossed Mutali's face. 'My second wife, the one the fool said could remain my wife as long as I did not touch her, is pregnant.'

Harry could contain his laughter no longer.

Harry's bridge was built and the river given a rudimentary embanking so it did not flood the settlements extending in that direction during the rainy seasons. His roads were established and, though the worst kinks were straightened out, retained eccentric bends which he insisted gave Fort Richard charm. There was Dorking Well, Caroline Well and – sentimental idiot that Harry was, but none of the girls Lucy Fanshawe introduced him to at Race Weeks had come as near to accepting his proposal – Jilly Well. The market square was busy every morning and the Indians' enterprise expanded further to include a garage which sold petrol and boasted the services of a mechanic. Some English people built a hotel which gun-happy Americans and Europeans used as a base for safaris.

It was altogether too crowded here. Harry left Fort Richard in the care of the assistant he had at last been sent and took off on a semi-permanent safari of his own around the outlying villages of his district.

Unbelievably there were disputes about land in this place where one horizon ended in snow, another in the lesser mountains of the Aberdares and the others lost in a haze. White settlers had bought farms – or things they intended to be farms – and were astonished to find Kikuyu villages upon them; the Kikuyu were equally astonished to be told that the country which had been theirs since first their ancestors had walked upon it belonged to a maniac with a face the colour of a baboon's backside.

They liked Harry, however, and trusted him. He would laugh and joke, but he listened to what the people had to say and attempted to make compromises. He spoke their language and didn't shout and wave his arms around as the red-faced ones did. He shot the lions, leopards and cheetahs that took their cattle and goats; he knew which elephant to bring down to turn a herd away from the crops and did not, as other white men sometimes did, kill so many that every other animal in the bush was drawn to the putrefying carcasses while the elephants' gold, their ivory, was taken away.

News came from Nairobi of a Kikuyu man who was calling upon the others of his tribe to rise up and take what was their own. The young men of Harty's villages rattled their spears and muttered among themselves until Harry told them that he understood how they felt. The country was theirs and the British government would realize that eventually, but now was not the time. If any government official, or white settler, had heard him he would have been had up for sedition, but none did and the warriors nodded wisely in agreement and put their spears away.

They called him Bwana Lion-Dog because of Mac, now fully grown and truly of formidable size, the scars on his haunches white among the tawny coat.

4

Harry returned to Fort Richard to sit out another rainy season and soon found himself in the grip of a depression. Father Patrick was in Ireland for a much-deserved break from Africa and Harry's assistant John had a mild but debilitating dose of jaundice. Harry sent him off on sick leave and was left with only the paperwork for company and, sometimes, the doctor whose many virtues included being teetotal. Father Patrick's replacement, who was going to remain as a permanent addition, was not of a sociable nature. These days the rainy season did not cut off Fort Richard from the nagging clerks in Nairobi for it now boasted a telegraph office and a row of poles stretching from here to the capital. Harry – and his household – came to dread the arrival of the smartly uniformed Indian boy and everyone learned some wonderful English words.

Mutali was practising some of these one morning. He had been married to his third wife for over two years, but as long as Father Patrick was here he hadn't quite had the temerity to bring her and her baby son to Fort Richard. When he heard that the priest had left he had sent word to her and she was now in a *shamba* behind the DC's bungalow. Mutali reckoned that by the time Father Patrick returned her presence would be established and – especially now there were so many people in Fort Richard

– go unnoticed. He had not, however, reckoned with Father Patrick's paperwork (much more assiduously attended to than Harry's) and with the officious nosiness of the new man. Father Benedict had Mutali's name on a piece of paper and as soon as he and the Bwana returned had come looking for him and found him in the wrong hut with the wrong woman and a child of the wrong age. Today he had appeared yet again and Mutali had informed him he was a 'bloody pettifogging paper-pusher' and added, for good measure, 'Blast and damn.'

The priest reeled away and Mutali, pleased with the effect of these excellent English words, was rehearsing them as he strode around the compound trying to calm his temper. He could not understand the priest's attitude, and did not comprehend why the number of wives a man had was anything to do with his being Catholic. A woman needed a husband; it was intolerable that she should remain unmarried, shameful for both her and her family, and she should marry a man who could pay a good price for her. Many Kikuyu men had been killed in the war the white man fought against the other white man and it was only sense that the ones who survived, and who could afford it, should take the women who otherwise would have no husbands. How could the priest say that was a sin? Mutali had asked if the war that had caused this situation was a sin, and Father Benedict – whose Swahili was not as fluent as Father Patrick's – had not made a good answer. When he talked about hell Mutali thought he had been there in the war, where men went because they had sinned and where Mutali was destined to go after he died because he had married a third wife. Wives meant children, too; without children the network of kinship created by your ancestors would melt away and there would be no one to turn to for support during a dispute. It was like building a hut without walls.

'Bloody pettifogging paper-pushers,' he muttered again and was interrupted by Jonas, one of his sons, who came flying outside.

'You are to prepare the truck, the Bwana says,' the boy shouted breathlessly. 'The Bwana has to go and see the Governor in Nairobi.'

'The Governor? Are you sure?'

'Yes,' Jonas said. 'He is saying "*bugger*".'

It must be serious, then. Mutali loaded the truck with petrol cans and drove it to the front of the bungalow. Harry hurried down the steps from the verandah, a small case in one hand, his only decent suit over his other arm. Jomo ran after him carrying a pair of shoes.

'What do we know about the state of the road?' Harry asked Mutali.

'It's bad, but we've seen worse.'

'Ndwetti had better come, then. And someone else.'

Jomo took a rapid step back and Jonas an eager one forward.

'Not you,' Harry told him. 'Your big brother, I think.'

Jomo went to summon him and Harry, noticing Jonas's disappointment, went on: 'Take Mac to the kennels, will you? Help George look after him and the others until we get back.'

Jonas in charge of Mac the lion-fighter! He reached out and took hold of the great dog's collar. Upon an English command to Mac from the Bwana the boy and the dog walked off, each believing he was in charge.

They arrived in Nairobi the following afternoon, weary and filthy. Harry washed and changed at the Norfolk Hotel and presented himself at Government House only to be told by Jeremy Boggis-Twiston, the Governor's aide-de-camp, that he hadn't needed to bust a gut to get here.

'But I got a telegram. It said ASAP. I thought a war

had started or I was being given the boot,' Harry said, aggrieved.

'You are recognized, I believe,' said Boggis-Twiston, 'as being *unconventional* but effective.'

'Thanks a lot. What's this about, then?'

'I'll leave it to the Governor to inform you. Shall we say ten thirty tomorrow morning?'

'Prat!' Harry fumed as Mutali drove him away. 'Stupid bloody prat!'

'*Stupid bloody prat,*' Mutali repeated in English. 'What is that, Bwana?'

'The idiot Boggis-Twiston.'

'Is he like a *bloody pettifogging paper-pusher*?'

'Yes.'

'Like the new priest, then.'

'Is that what you called him?'

'Is it not true?' Mutali countered.

'Yes – no! Mutali, if you want to learn English go to the classes at the mission.'

'I like your English better,' Mutali said darkly. 'After all, do you not speak my Swahili, my Kikuyu?'

The most notice the Governor had paid to Harry so far was the extension of his hand and a curt nod when he had passed through Fort Richard while on his way further up-country. Today, however, the handshake was warm, the greeting friendly.

'Sit down, my dear chap, sit down!' he said jovially. 'Coffee?'

'Thank you, sir,' Harry said, sitting and wondering what the hell this was about.

He was given a cup of coffee and stirred in sugar while the Governor seated himself in the chair opposite.

'You know a fellow called Pritchard, I believe,' he said when the servants had left the room.

'Colonel Pritchard? Yes, used to during the war.'

'He's General Pritchard now and is down in South Africa. Remembers you well. Says, so I'm told, you're the best damn shot between Cape Town and Cairo.'

'Really, sir?' Harry had kept Johnnie Pritchard and his men in meat for a while when game had been scarce, it having fled from the noise of the guns; Johnnie had been grateful, but to dub Harry Africa's best shot was, surely, an exaggeration.

'It seems,' the Governor went on, 'that he's recommended you to the Governor General of South Africa, who is anxious to go on a decent safari before he leaves the continent. Do you know who that is?'

'Prince Arthur of Connaught, isn't it?' Harry ventured.

'His Royal Highness Prince Arthur of Connaught,' the Governor corrected. 'He and Princess Arthur plan to break their journey home here. Think you can do it?'

'Do what, sir?' Harry asked, confused.

'Take their royal highnesses on safari. I gather,' the Governor added, a twinkle in his eye, 'that you make something of a profession of it in any case. You could manage a couple of royal passengers, couldn't you?'

'I – I suppose so,' Harry stuttered.

'Good chap!' the Governor said, putting his cup down. 'They are arriving in August – Boggis-Twiston will give you the details – so you can spend between now and then making sure there is plenty for them to shoot. The honour of Kenya is at stake.'

'Quite so, sir,' Harry said, gathering that the interview was over and standing up.

'Good chap,' the Governor said again, and dismissed him.

Jeremy Boggis-Twiston was lurking in the corridor outside. He pounced on Harry and bore him to his office where he showed him a schedule which must have been modelled on that of Colonel von Lettow, whose activities during the Great War had led the King's African Rifles a merry and macabre dance around East Africa. The six central blocks were each labelled 'safari', and the two on either side were divided into seven columns and extended down the page in blocks marked 'morning', 'luncheon', 'afternoon', 'evening' and so on. Harry was presented with a copy of this document, instructed that he must not on any account intrude upon the two side blocks with his safari and told he would be kept *au fait* with the latest developments as and when these happened.

'All right,' Harry said, folding the paper and shoving it into the pocket of his suit jacket.

'And one more thing,' Boggis-Twiston said, wincing at the cavalier treatment of his precious schedule. 'I've done some checking up and find there's no proof that you speak Swahili. Kikuyu yes, Swahili no, and it is essential to the safety of their royal highnesses that you speak the *lingua franca* of the region.'

'But everyone knows I speak it like a damned native,' Harry protested.

'Everyone *here*, Major Wittering,' Boggis-Twiston said, tittering, 'but not his grace of Devonshire,' naming the head of the Colonial Office in London. 'It must have been an oversight, only revealed when your name was put forward for this weighty task. No –' as Harry was about to tell him what he could do with his weighty task. 'It is easily remedied if I *myself* deal with it. All you have to do is go to a designated examiner and he will sign a certificate and forward it to me.'

Harry let out a stream of Mutali's choicest oaths.

'Sorry, old chap, didn't get that,' Boggis-Twiston said.

'Just as well.'

'Be a *good* fellow and play the game, won't you?' Boggis-Twiston begged. 'Roland Gaffney's nearest –'

'Gaffney? That old soak?'

'Well, perhaps he is but they don't know that at home. He's *designated*, you see . . . I'm told,' he went on, slightly

76

sheepishly, 'that a bottle of *amber* liquid helps. Not, naturally, to say you need help, but –'

'Could you get me designated?' Harry said, interested now. 'It sounds exactly my sort of job.'

'One could *consider* it, of course,' Boggis-Twiston said, 'but you'll need your certificate first.'

'I surrender,' Harry said, and was at last allowed to go.

He climbed into the truck and had a think. To the hotel to tell Mutali and the others that they could go and visit their relations, then lunch at the KAR mess, perhaps. Roland Gaffney lived on the road to the Ngong Hills. Harry would buy the whisky Boggis-Twiston said he needed, endure Gaffney's examination and his reminiscences about the days when the railway was being built and then see if he could get supper and a bed at Karen Blixen's farm.

'But is it not a great honour,' Karen asked him, 'to be selected as white hunter to members of your royal family?'

'I suppose it is,' Harry said, for the first time thinking about it. He did not tell her about General Pritchard's recommendation. There were plenty of other men who could lay claim to being the best shot in Africa.

Karen got to her feet to trim a lamp. She paused and listened to the night. 'Rain!' she said. 'Isn't it a beautiful sound? Shall we dance to the rain, Harry?'

She grew coffee, as the Fanshawes did, and the failure of the rains meant disaster. Unlike the Fanshawes, however, whose farm was at a lower altitude, another disaster lay in annual wait for her: frost. Every year it hit to a greater or lesser degree and every year she believed it would not. She was a woman of extraordinary courage. During the war – which was not her war since she was Danish – she had taken charge of ox wagons carrying provisions and ammunition through the Masai Reserve to the border. Now she ran this farm on her own, having split up from her husband.

'I'll dance to the rain with you,' Harry said. 'You'll have to be the orchestra, though, because I can't sing in tune.'

She invited him to escort her to a do at the Muthaiga Club in three days' time, which was why he was still in Nairobi when Boggis-Twiston summoned him. He seemed rather uneasy as he told Harry it was about his Swahili exam.

'You mean I've failed?' Harry asked.

'Oh, good Lord, *no*!'

'What's the problem, then?'

'How many bottles of whisky did you give Gaffney?'

'Two.'

Boggis-Twiston shook his head mournfully. 'Over-generous. You've passed, old chap, but they won't wash it in London. One bottle would have done, top-*hole*.'

'For Christ's sake, Boggis-Twiston –'

'He's given you a hundred and twenty per cent. Signed the certificate and everything.'

'Oh, Africa!' Harry howled, and slithered in the truck back towards the Ngong Hills.

'I thought I was doing you a favour,' Roland Gaffney said plaintively. 'What mark do you want?'

'Ninety-five per cent will do.'

'You should have told me before.' He got out a blank certificate, filled it in and signed it, and Harry delivered it in person to Boggis-Twiston.

'A very good result,' the ADC said. 'Congratulations, Major Wittering.'

5

Prince and Princess Arthur of Connaught arrived and after a week of being fêted by Kenyan high society they were driven by car to where their white hunter waited with horses and various attendants to escort them to their first camp in the bush.

Harry had been introduced to the Prince and Princess at a reception at Government House and had spent a couple of hours with them one morning, during which time he could practically feel Boggis-Twiston's anxiety emanating from his office as his precious schedule was threatened. Harry reminded the royal couple of the precautions they should take in the bush and showed them the map Boggis-Twiston had insisted he prepare and which the ADC had carefully traced for his files.

The Princess looked at it and laughed heartily. Harry had done his best, but even using extensive imagination their proposed route was merely arbitrary lines meandering artistically across blank spaces, and it would be altered day by day according to where the game was.

'Don't explain,' the Princess said. 'I understand. What an adventure it's going to be! And for heaven's sake, Major Wittering, light your pipe. I can see you are longing to do so.'

Harry took to her immediately and suddenly found himself looking forward to the safari which, during the past months, he had been regarding as an unpleasant duty, something to be endured like a visit to the dentist.

His enthusiasm was tempered a little by the Prince. For him the safari was not about adventure or landscape: it was about killing, and he even had a list of the heads he hoped to bag. 'I came to Kenya in '09 with my parents,' he said. 'I've always remembered the game here. South Africa's has nothing on it. It was primitive going then. No bridges, hardly any roads to speak of.'

'We're a bit more modern now,' Harry said, 'but it won't be like staying in a hotel.'

'Don't you worry about us,' the Princess said. 'We can rough it.'

And indeed they were delighted when they rode into the camp, enchanted by the little village of tents pitched among a cluster of trees, by the boys lined up to greet them, by the ingenious washing facilities and by their French chef in his open-air kitchen, his saucepans and exotic implements hanging on a screen of woven wattle. The Princess took photographs of everything while her Scottish maid Kirsty organized her tent and noisily bossed the Prince's valet.

A fire was lit before dark fell and the Prince and his doctor sat around it sipping their drinks. As the valet and maid served the first course of dinner a herd of elephant obligingly made an appearance, ambling in silhouette across the last of the sun.

'Ah, the simple life!' the Princess sighed. 'There's nothing like it.'

Simple? The chef's soup caused explosions among the tastebuds on Harry's tongue. The second course must have started out as salmon in a tin but something extraordinary had been done to it. The meat was buck – Harry had shot it that morning – and had been transformed. The fourth course was a chocolate pudding and the meal ended with biscuits and cheese followed by brandy and coffee.

Encamped some distance away were over a hundred porters ready to move everything to a new location when required. The chef's equipment alone needed six men to carry it. In addition to the specialists Harry normally had with him were taxidermists who would cure the skins and heads of the animals they shot so they would not rot or fester. There was a farrier carrying a spare set of shoes for each of the horses and a portable anvil. The horses themselves were in a thorn enclosure and more fires ringed the camp, each with a pile of wood beside it. Following as closely as it could and in touch by daily messenger was a truck in case – God forbid – there should be an accident to a royal personage which the doctor, for unthinkable reasons, was unable to treat.

If this was simple, what the hell was complicated?

Not Princess Arthur of Connaught. Harry's first impressions of her had been right and if he needed further confirmation it came from Mac. The great dog treated other people with civility, even those he knew well. His affection was given only to Harry and his place was always at Harry's side unless he was hunting under Harry's orders. Harry was, therefore, astounded on their second night to see Mac by the Princess's chair, leaning against her and behaving for all the world like a dowager's lapdog.

'Well, I'll be damned!' he exclaimed. 'Mac, come here and stop making a nuisance of yourself.'

'He isn't.' The Princess gently pulled one tawny ear. Mac yawned and closed his yellow eyes. 'He's a lovely boy. Where did you find him?'

'Some friends gave him to me.'

'And the scars on his back. What happened?'

'A lioness. A man-eater.'

She indicated the chair next to her and Harry sat down. The Prince, satisfied after a gory day, had retired to his tent to dream of more killing tomorrow and the doctor, too, had gone to bed.

'Tell me,' the Princess invited.

He did so and afterwards, because she was so comfortable to be with and so responsive a listener, he dared to ask her about herself.

'Oh,' she said, staring into the fire, her brandy glass in one hand and the other still resting on Mac's head, 'I'm just your ordinary minor member of the Royal Family.' And there crossed her face – unless it was a trick of the firelight – a look of what Harry thought was intense sadness.

She had been, before her marriage, the Duchess of Fife, Lady Alexandra Victoria Alberta Edwina Louise Duff, though none of those names pleased her and by her family and friends – and Harry, that night, became included among the latter – she was called Diana. She was thirty-three years old, the mother of a son and a great-granddaughter of Queen Victoria. She had married – 'been married to', she said, a certain bitterness in her voice – a cousin, for Prince Arthur was a grandson of the old queen, and she was a niece of his present majesty, the one Harry served, King George V.

It was long after midnight when at last they stopped talking. The sounds of the night invaded the camp site, and they stood for a while listening.

'Hyena,' the Princess said. 'People always say it's a hideous noise, but I don't mind it.' She sighed. 'I love this life. I wish I'd been born a nomad.'

'I wonder if you'll feel that way in six weeks' time.'

'I'm sure I will,' she said. 'Good night, Harry.'

'Good night.'

Harry went to his tent and sat on the bed, his head in his hands. Was he going completely round the bend? He was falling in love with an older woman, a married woman and a woman who called the King 'uncle'. In the face of such danger the sensible thing to do was flee, but that was impossible; to avoid being in her presence equally so.

Very well, he told himself, you must keep yourself under control, not let your feelings show and don't get in any deeper. Simple, really.

It might have been had Princess Arthur, in her tent on the other side of the fire, not been thinking much the same.

Such undercurrents aside, the safari was a success from the outset. The game behaved like clockwork and turned up as though by royal command. The Wakamba porters marched into camp each evening bearing bloody animal carcases, chanting of the brave feats they had achieved and of the feast of meat they would have tonight. Prince Arthur ticked things off his list and wrote up his game book with enthusiasm.

'Johnnie Pritchard was right,' he told Harry. 'He said you'd be the man for us and he dashed well hit the mark, eh?'

There was jolly chat and laughter around the fire after dinner, but the Prince and his doctor would declare themselves ready for bed after an hour or so and Harry and the Princess would stay up and talk. Harry tried to convince himself it was because he wasn't tired – and he could scarcely leave Diana alone – but he was past fooling himself. How could it do any harm, though? Nothing could come of it, apart from a bruised heart.

Two and a half weeks into the safari something approaching the unthinkable happened, though it could not be considered Harry's fault. Prince Arthur's horse – being ridden too hard and without proper attention – put its foot into a pig hole and dislodged its royal rider, causing what the doctor feared was a fractured right wrist. The Prince was unable to use a gun and riding was uncomfortable and, since they were not far from Nyeri, he decided he would make for civilization while he could. Harry assumed the safari was at an end, and part of him could only be relieved, but Princess Arthur persuaded her husband to allow her to continue with Kirsty and the chef. The doctor, however, would accompany the Prince.

'But what if something happens to you?' Harry said to Diana when they were having tea after their arrival at the hotel in Nyeri.

'I never get ill,' she said. 'And if I do Kirsty can look after me.'

'I was more concerned about injury.'

'With you and Mutali and Mac to protect me?' She patted Mac's head and gave him a titbit from her plate. She spoiled him dreadfully, and he thought she was wonderful.

After a barrage of telegrams to and from Government House, Lord Francis Scott appeared and took the Prince and his attendants off to stay at his huge stone house at Deloraine. Diana and Harry rode back to their camp. She dismounted from her horse and turned to her white hunter.

'Now!' she said, her eyes alight. 'Now we can have fun!'

That day she shot her first buffalo, but did not kill it outright. As it crashed away into the bush Harry grabbed her arm.

'Into the tree ... Mutali, get her up. *Quick*, man!' Never before had a royal princess been so unceremoniously treated. She scrambled into the branches of the tree, pulled by Mutali, pushed by Harry, who tossed the gun she had been using to Mutali and checked his own.

Diana looked down at him. Her hands, gripping the

branch of the tree, were white-knuckled. 'I know a wounded buffalo is the most dangerous thing there is. Shouldn't Mutali go with you as well?'

He grinned at her. 'We might forget which tree you're in if we leave you here alone. Don't move. All right?'

'All right,' she whispered.

His tracker called to him: blood, lots of it. Harry gave his frightened princess a reassuring smile and, with Mac, turned away.

The blood left a trail as wide as a road. The beast was close by, dying and – as Diana had said – extremely dangerous. Mac crept along, legs stiff, hackles up. He and the tracker indicated, at the same moment but in their different ways, a thicket ahead. Harry caught a glimpse of something that might have been a horn but could not risk a shot for fear of wounding the animal further. It had been a horn, though; the buffalo saw them and charged. Harry made sure of it with a bullet through its brain.

As soon as he was in sight of the tree, Diana slid from it before Mutali could assist her. She ran to Harry.

'You've been gone for nearly half an hour. Oh, I was so worried, and when I heard that shot –'

She was trembling. He held her, feeling strangely relaxed about doing so, until she had calmed down and then took her to see her kill.

'But I didn't kill it,' she said.

'It would have died. I simply finished the job more quickly. Back to camp now? Enough for one day?'

'Lord, yes,' she said, shuddering.

'You've lost your nerve,' he said. 'I should make you shoot another one straight away, like remounting a horse after a fall.'

She stared at him. 'It wasn't shooting the buffalo that frightened me. It was the danger I put you in. If you'd been killed or hurt –'

'Well, I wasn't, was I?'

'No, thank God.'

'Why aren't you married, Harry?' she asked that night. 'You must get lonely on your own.'

Lions were hunting in the dark beyond the camp, far away but at times the roars were disconcertingly loud. Harry checked his gun and watched for alarm signals from Mac.

'I don't get lonely out here,' he said, 'but sometimes in Fort Richard I do. I'd like to get married and have children, but it's not easy to find a woman who's prepared to commit herself to a life in Africa.'

'Will you stay here, then, for ever?'

'For as long as they'll have me.'

'You'll find a wife. She'll be a lucky woman.' She was silent for a while and then turned to him. 'I love you, Harry,' she said. 'You know that, don't you?'

His heart leapt within him, shouting, No! Yes! But all he managed was a stuttered, 'Diana – I –'

'It's been given to us, this piece of time. We'd be fools not to take it.'

'It's too risky. Kirsty . . .'

'She won't say anything, and what could be more risky than what you did today?'

Not having done it, he wanted to say, and getting you hurt – or worse – by a wounded buffalo; and the Prince your husband finding out about what is going to happen (if it was) and wreaking royal revenge. Never had it occurred to him that his love for her would be rewarded in this way, and he felt inadequate, scared, elated . . .

'Harry?' the Princess said.

'I . . . Prince Arthur –'

'Has kept himself happy with a succession of mistresses for years.' She leaned forward. 'I want to live,' she said. 'Live a little before I return to the half life in England.'

'Is it that bad?'

'You can't imagine! South Africa was a three-quarter life, perhaps, but from now on . . . You're free, Harry. Let me share that for a while.'

'Go. I'll come to you.'

He couldn't believe he'd said it, but she stood up and a short while later the lamp was lit in her tent. Harry went round the camp going through the before-bed routine and trying to sort out his feelings. He couldn't refuse her, he didn't want to refuse her; as she had said, they had been handed this piece of time. He would cope with what he had to when it was over.

In his tent he undressed and put on pyjamas, dressing-gown and safari boots, told Mac to stay and then went outside again.

'Bwana?'

It was Mutali drifting in the night.

'What are you doing, Mutali?'

'Keeping watch, Bwana.' A white flash of teeth. 'I watch, Bwana, but I see nothing.'

'Lions are out there,' Harry said, deliberately misunderstanding him.

'I see nothing and I speak nothing,' Mutali said, his voice chiding and slightly offended. 'I guard your secrets, Bwana, as you guard mine. Good night, Bwana.'

He vanished. Damn him, Harry thought, and then: what the hell? He was to be trusted.

He scratched on the flap of Diana's tent and slid inside. His princess, similarly attired to him, was finishing her brandy. She gestured to the boots.

'See? I've remembered your lesson. Never do *anything* improperly shod.' She put down her glass and held out her hands.

'Two people, Harry. Two lovers.'

'No more,' he said, 'and no less.'

*

An idyll followed, twenty-four days which both would remember for the rest of their lives.

'What about Kirsty?' Harry asked one night. 'She must suspect something.'

'She's been with me since I was seventeen. She's as loyal to me as Mutali is to you.' She touched his cheek. 'We're in an oasis of time, Harry. Forget everything else.'

'Is that a royal command?'

'It is,' she murmured.

'Then I'd better obey it, hadn't I?'

She would – might have – found him amusing in a primitive kind of way had she met him in London or at a reception in Cape Town or Pretoria. She would, given the chance – and that was unlikely – have discovered his charm and sense of humour to be considerable, but altogether she would not have given him a second glance.

But here in the great, wide spaces of Kenya he seemed to be a colossus, a hero. He joked with the natives but never lost his authority over them. She loved him for the way they most obviously loved him, and she could not forget her vigil in the tree with Mutali when they were waiting for the shot that would tell them Harry had dispatched the buffalo. Mutali had been at least as anxious as she had, wanting to be with his master, and when Diana had used the one native word she knew – 'Bwana?', the interrogative heavy – he had replied tersely in English, 'Bwana bloody damn good.' 'Yes,' she had said, and the Princess and the Kikuyu had smiled at each other and needed no more words.

She fell in love. Like many others she had been bitten by the Kenya bug, the desire to be in this high, beautiful land, but she could not succumb to it. She was a slave to her birth, and Harry had become, for her, the spirit of Kenya and its freedoms.

She cried in his arms on their last night in the bush.

'I can't believe it's over,' she wept. 'Over for ever.'

'You might come back, mightn't you?'

'Yes. I suppose I might.'

'I'd better go to my tent now,' he said gently.

'Not yet. A little while longer.'

The next morning the porters set out for Fort Richard. Kirsty and the cook hitched a lift in the truck, for they were now close to the road, and the Princess, Harry and Mutali were left with their horses in a deserted camp site. The Princess bent to say goodbye to Mac and he forgot himself enough to give her a large lick. She stood and turned to Mutali.

'Honourable Sir Mutali, thank you,' she said, and she presented him with her field glasses which he had ferociously coveted from the moment he had first been allowed to use them. He put the case in his saddlebag and hung the glasses reverently around his neck. Never before had Harry seen him at loss for words. 'I will send you a special tag to put on them to remind you who gave them to you,' the Princess said. 'And if,' she went on, 'it was anything to do with me you'd be a real knight.'

Harry translated and Mutali smiled shyly and shuffled his feet.

'Well, then,' the Princess said with forced cheerfulness. 'To horse!'

She stayed that night at the English-run hotel in Fort Richard.

It was over. Boggis-Twiston was there.

Nairobi was ready to fête their royal visitors again. The first evening at Government House Harry had the shock of seeing the woman he had held in a cramped camp bed while lions coughed and roared in the bush around them, who had performed a version of the cancan wearing the feathers of the ostrich she had shot, had laughed and kissed him when she had brought down an elephant – that same woman appearing as a princess of the House of Windsor on the arm of her husband while every other woman in the room curtseyed and every man bowed. She was distant now, unattainable. Harry, from his seat so far below the salt that he would need Mutali's field glasses to get a decent view of his lover, experienced an earthquake in his stomach. The finality of it was appalling. He wanted to be at home in Fort Richard arguing with Father Patrick and never having witnessed this.

Diana led off the dancing after dinner with the Governor, he scarcely daring to touch that body, then with Lord Francis and then – to a sycophantic spattering of applause – with her husband.

Boggis-Twiston searched out Harry as he was leading Karen Blixen off the dance floor. He had been compelled to include Harry on the invitation list and, trying to mask his contempt of Harry's borrowed white tie and tails (they were Louis Fanshawe's and had begun life in Savile Row, but had lost the battle against years in Africa), he informed him he was summoned to the royal presence.

Karen looked up at Harry's strained face as he took her to her seat. 'Perhaps she would like to see how her morning coffee is grown,' she said softly. 'On my farm it is peaceful, isolated.'

'The Princess, you mean? You must ask the Governor's wife to take her.'

It was pretty unconvincing, but he could do no better. And more was to come. Denys Finch-Hatton brought Karen a drink.

'I hear you did royalty proud,' he said. 'Not bad for a government wallah.'

He was one of the Colony's foremost white hunters and the son of a duke. Harry wished Johnnie Pritchard had recommended him to the Connaughts, a better choice than Harry in every way, for then he wouldn't be in this turmoil.

'One does one's best,' Harry said, attempting a smile and rejoining an agitated Boggis-Twiston. 'I couldn't leave a lady alone,' he said as the aide-de-camp began to reprimand him. 'Not even for a summons from a princess.'

'Actually,' said Boggis-Twiston sulkily, 'it's from the Prince.'

'Oh,' Harry managed, thinking: they can't chop one's head off these days, but, oh Lord, what else can they do; and when will this end?

But Prince Arthur could not have been more friendly.

'Harry, my dear boy,' he said, waving him to a chair beside him. 'Diana had a wonderful time. Dashed silly of me to have taken that tumble – entirely my own fault, you warned me often enough.'

'How is the wrist, sir?'

'Much better. All but mended. Still can't handle a gun, though. Dashed nuisance. Did Diana really shoot that tusker whose trophies she keeps showing off?'

'Certainly she did, sir. A beautiful shot.'

'She says you saved her life more than once.'

'Her life was never in danger, sir.'

'Because of you! Dashed fine, I call it.'

The Governor was looking at Harry as though he was the school's star pupil and even Lords Delamere and Scott were noticing his existence.

'Ah,' the Governor said, and he would have patted Harry on the head if he could, 'we have the best here in Kenya, your highness, and we choose the best of the best when it comes to something like this.'

'Harry,' the Princess said, interrupting the Governor and relieving Harry of his embarrassment, 'we did everything in the bush except foxtrot. Shall we repair that omission now?'

'Wasn't that rather close to the bone?' Harry said when they were on the floor.

'Why? Who would suspect? And if you dared look at me you would know that I'm not gazing at you soulfully, however much I want to do so.'

The other dancers avoided their space and were staring, albeitly discreetly, at the sight of the King's niece dancing with a mere district commissioner. Harry glanced at his partner and saw she was wearing her most regal and disdainful face. He tightened his arm around her waist and she reacted as though electrocuted.

'Don't,' she whispered. 'Harry, please.'

'Can you bear this? I'm not sure I can.'

'We have to.'

'I was thinking of going back to Fort Richard tomorrow.'

'Stay! You must until I leave. Promise you will.'

He did, cursing his weakness.

She found excuses to see him each morning when she was alone in her private sitting room in Government House. Her films had been developed: which photographs would he like copies of? She wanted to see how his had turned out and select some for herself. Her waterbuck head had been declared a record: what did this mean? He saw her most evenings in her other guise, for invitations were sent to him at the Norfolk Hotel where he was putting up. If he was good enough for royalty, white society reasoned, he was good enough for them.

But the old thief time was about his business and demanded that the last farewells be said.

'I'll write,' the Princess said. 'Will you write back?'

'Of course I will.'

'Goodbye, then, my dearest Harry. Think of me when you're up there on your travels.'

'It will seem empty without you.'

'Not when you've found the wife you're searching for. Find her, Harry, and be happy.' She gave a sad smile. 'But don't stop loving me – as a friend.'

'A friend? It's rather too late for that.'

'It's too late now for anything else.'

Was he being dismissed? A cast-aside toy? A welcome anger rose in him, something to counterweigh the pervading misery, but then tears welled in her eyes and she turned her face away.

'I'm trying to make it easier for you.' She swallowed a sob. 'I've known love. Thank you for that.'

6

He could not have got himself more hopelessly embroiled if he had taken a degree in it. The woman he was in love with was married, a member of the Royal Family and, as though those two weren't enough, several thousand miles away.

She wrote him friendly, newsy letters and he replied in kind, not knowing if her mail was opened by a secretary and not, in any case, wanting to expose his heart to further pain in such a useless case. It was healing – a bit – when she sent him an article in the *Illustrated London News* about an exhibition of royal photography. Harry's photograph was captioned 'My White Hunter' and that of Mac 'My Hunting Dog'; the possessive articles were difficult to ignore.

But he had to. The long-term solution was to fall in love with someone else, he decided, but this was easier said than done. There were plenty of girls around: the Connaughts' attention had not gone unnoticed and it did wonders for his social life. He was invited to stay with the Scotts at Deloraine and with other settlers in the grand houses being built in the White Highlands, and the guests often included young, pretty, female ones. Those Harry found himself attracted to never seemed to be attracted to him; and one who initially he thought would suit him very well showed him that the feelings were mutual so promptly that Harry retreated with more speed than politeness, wondering – not for the first time in his life and certainly not the last – at the perverse power women had over him.

The Fanshawes teased him about his new friends, saying he was becoming too posh for poor coffee growers like themselves, but nothing really changed Harry. He still went around his district with Mutali and evaded the boring bureaucracy of his job. He rejected another appointment and his request to stay on as DC at Fort Richard was granted. He deceived the powers that be by spending his long leave in India rather than going to England or somewhere that would provide a change of climate, thus also evading a meeting with Diana for he still did not trust his heart.

When he returned to Kenya life hotted up. Harry had known Lady Idina Gordon when she had lived there for a while with her second husband, but now she had returned married to a third, Josslyn Hay, eight years younger than herself and heir to the premier earldom of Scotland. They had left England in a storm of divorce and scandal which caused a flutter even in Nairobi.

'We do not know them,' Jeremy Boggis-Twiston said. 'They have gone *straight* on to our blacklist.'

Lord and Lady Francis were apt to condemn by association. 'I would hope,' said his lordship, 'that no chap I held in esteem would contemplate attending their parties.'

Harry did not know if he was held in esteem by Lord Francis Scott, but it did not much worry him. He disappeared up-country and reappeared at will and could not be considered part of any of the sets the Europeans had created. Sometimes, anyway, it was impossible to avoid Idina's parties for they happened in the most unlikely places – Harry and Mutali came across one on the escarpment where three vehicles had got stuck in the mud – and, in limited numbers and for a limited time, they could be the most enormous fun. Besides, Idina and Joss had a constant flow of visitors, first to their bungalow and then to their luxurious mansion Clouds, and Harry, ever the optimist, continued his search for his one true love.

'You need a wife,' Idina told him as she entered his bedroom at Clouds one night, 'but you are going the wrong way about it.'

'What's the right way?' Harry asked nervously as, casually, Idina began to undress.

'You're too eager.'

'Am I?' He didn't feel eager at the moment. He was not one of Idina's fans and would have been happier at the prospect of a female hyena in his bed.

'You're so amusing when you're not trying to attract a woman but become like a silly wobbly jelly when you are.'

'Can a jelly be eager?' he said, hoping to distract her.

'It's difficult, but you manage it . . . Damn, I meant to bring some champagne.'

She wandered out wearing only her slip and did not return. Instead Joss Hay and Raymond de Trafford appeared with a bottle of whisky and an unaccountable desire to play poker.

Mutali, hiding among the bougainvillaea in the garden the next morning, caught Harry's signal and waylaid him after breakfast with the news that he was wanted: elephants were trampling maize fields and a leopard had attacked a woman.

'I have to leave,' Harry said to Idina. 'Work.' In fact he was miles out of his district, but Idina wouldn't consider this.

'You're like a will o' the wisp,' she complained. 'Here one moment and gone the next.' She sipped a cocktail, for after breakfast was noon. 'Now remember what I told you last night.'

'I'm an eager jelly of a will o' the wisp. Every word, Idina.'

'And I wish you would tell your boy he is *not* allowed in the house.'

'He's not my boy, he's my right-hand man.' Mutali, followed by one of Idina's long-suffering Somali servants, was making his way to Harry's room to pack. He would find Idina's clothes there, and Harry hoped he would not pack those as well: he sometimes tended to be over-literal.

'The elephant would have done,' Harry told him as they drove away. 'The leopard was a bit much.'

Mutali grinned and offered Harry a flask. 'For your *hangover*,' he said, the English word a perfect imitation of Harry's pronunciation. 'I do not wish to be beaten as those men are.'

Harry should have reprimanded him for his implied criticism of his white masters but he could not be bothered. Joss and the others treated their servants worse than they did their horses and dogs and anyone who said otherwise was lying. Harry had an attack of distaste for these people who had come to this glorious country to use it for the pleasures forbidden or frowned upon at home. It was a familiar feeling, one that often visited him as he left the parties at the houses in what they called Happy Valley, yet the urge that drew him there was one of excited anticipation. Now he was longing to be back in his bungalow (yes, and he must reply to Diana's last letter), but a few days ago he had wanted only to sit at a crowded dining table among people who spoke English, even if they talked of nothing but who was sleeping with whom.

A jelly, was he? Damn Idina!

He stopped the truck and took the flask Mutali was offering him. 'You drive,' he said. He climbed into the back of the truck, drank some of Mutali's revolting brew, rested his head on Mac's flank and slept.

7

Eleanor Dickins stepped down on to the platform, let go of her companion's hand and smiled her thanks at him.

'Are you sure you're being met?' he asked.

'Quite sure.'

'I'll wait, just in case.'

'Please don't let me hold you up. You've been so kind.'

'No trouble,' he assured her. 'Really.'

His name was Denis Farmer. She had met him only briefly on the ship, and on the train from Mombasa he had progressed from helpful through solicitous to openly admiring. Nell was grateful to him, but no more. Her face and clothes were covered in dust, and the excitement of the journey, of seeing the animals she had read about in books, of seeing Mount Kilimanjaro in the dawn, had distilled into a fervent desire for a bath and a bed. She hoped Daisy would appear soon. At school she had been famous for her tardiness, and obviously nothing had changed. And would she find her in this chaos? Luggage was being removed from the train and she was about to ask Mr Farmer, as a final favour, to organize porters to separate hers when a familiar screech rose above the ambient noise.

'Nell! Nell!' Daisy Davidson, plumper after five years and the birth of a child, flung her arms around her old school friend. 'How gorgeous to see you, and how brave of

98

you to come out all on your own. Were the officers on the ship delicious?' She rushed on, saving Nell from having to answer, 'Where's your luggage? Ali will deal with it.'

The tall, turbaned black man behind her stepped forward.

'The trunk and the case,' Nell said. They had already been appropriated by a squad of half-naked natives to whom Daisy's servant gave orders. Nell turned to Denis Farmer. 'Thank you so much for everything. I'm quite safe, as you can see.' She shook his hand firmly and turned away even as he opened his mouth to speak.

'What a dreadful little man,' Daisy said, guiding Nell through the space in the crowd cleared by her servant while the porters followed. 'Who on earth is he?'

'An importer of something, I think he said.'

'Trade!' Daisy exclaimed scornfully. 'Never mind. You won't encounter him again . . . Here's our motor car. Eric let me have her to come and meet you. Isn't she a beauty?'

Nell agreed she was, though Daisy's driving of her was terrifying. Horn blaring, she gave minimal attention to the road and talked non-stop.

'We're going to have the most super time,' she gushed. 'There are loads of men here, some of them frightfully wicked. I'll have to fight to protect your virtue, Nell.' She giggled. 'You've got some catching up to do, what with baby sis married. Imagine spotty Celia getting married!'

'She's not spotty now,' Nell said, but Daisy had scored something of a hit: Celia, three years younger than herself and with a safe, kind husband.

Perhaps there was some catching up to do, and perhaps Kenya was the place to do it. Nell was twenty-five years old. She and Celia had been orphaned by the Great War and by the influenza epidemic after it. They had been left more than comfortably off, and Nell had used her money to travel and generally have a merry time while Celia had used hers to net herself Donald.

Africa, however, was by far the most adventurous of Nell's journeys and she was looking forward to getting closer to those beautiful animals she had glimpsed from the train – and about which Daisy had written with such enthusiasm that Nell was here now. So graphic had been her descriptions that Nell half expected her, Eric and daughter Katie to be living in a grass hut and was almost disappointed when Daisy drove up the drive of a thoroughly modern house; and certainly disappointed on discovering that the biggest cat in the vicinity was an incongruous Persian. Daisy's letters had implied they lived in fear of leopards under the beds.

'Oh, we do,' Daisy said when challenged. 'It used to happen all the time. And snakes. You must watch out for snakes.' Daisy hugged her. 'Nell, darling, if you want to see animals then Eric will arrange something, but first there's Race Week. Human animals, male and lots of them.'

For once Daisy was not exaggerating. The people who flocked to Nairobi for Race Week were as wicked and colourful as she promised. Nell considered herself worldly and tried to hide her shock at the tone of their conversation, but could not help blushing the first afternoon at the Muthaiga Club when Josslyn Hay, a big, blond and handsome man, took her chin, looked her in the eyes and said, 'A virgin. What a pity,' then wandered off.

Nell was beached, feeling gawky and hopeless. Daisy, her adored Eric forgotten, had her head close to Raymond de Trafford's, and he was an out-and-out rake if ever Nell had seen one.

Joss's wife, Lady Idina, patted her sympathetically on the knee. 'My dear, what a ghastly bore for you,' she said, and as Nell was about to – what? Deny it? – added, 'Don't argue, my sweet. Joss always knows.' She straightened a ring on her finger and stretched out her hand to admire the effect. 'I think,' she said, 'I have just the man for you. You do want a man, don't you?'

Nell was searching for a response when a diversion was caused by a young woman striding out of the club and over to where they were sitting under some trees. She was about Nell's age and had a strangely flawed beauty; she was evidently in a furious temper.

Lady Idina Hay introduced Nell to the newcomer. 'Alice de Janzé, Nell Dickins. What riles you, Alice darling?'

'They're making me send Samson home. The stupid secretary says I can't have him here. Why not? What harm can he do? I bought him the sweetest collar and lead and was going to take him to the races tomorrow. It's just not fair. Is it?' she demanded of Nell.

'I'm sure it is not. Who is Samson?'

'My lion.'

'Perhaps,' Nell suggested, utterly out of her depth but determined to find the bottom, 'they think he'd frighten the horses at the races.'

'He's only a baby. Harry's arrived,' she said to Idina. 'I wanted him to tell the secretary where to get off, but he said no. He said I should never have taken Samson to begin with and he'll end up in a zoo. I won't let that happen to him. I won't, won't *won't!*'

'Ah, Harry,' Idina said, a sideways glance at Nell.

As she spoke, a tall, dark-haired man, pipe in mouth, came out of the club and strolled towards them.

'Idina, are you well?' he said, bending to kiss her cheek.

'Revoltingly.'

'Daisy?'

'Very well, thank you.' She paused and then said: 'Harry, this is Nell Dickins. She's staying with us. Nell, this is Major Wittering.'

'Delighted to meet you,' Harry said.

'Have my chair, Harry.' Smiling slyly, Idina stood up and drifted away.

Harry sat down. 'How long have you been in Kenya, Miss Dickins?' he asked.

'Four days.'

'Not yet acclimatized, then,' he said, twitching an eyebrow in the direction of the rest of the party.

She took his double meaning and laughed, suddenly feeling relaxed. 'Not quite.'

'So you haven't seen anything of the country?'

'None, apart from Nairobi. Daisy and Eric have promised to take me after Race Week. Are you in the army, Major Wittering?'

'Not any more. It's a wartime handle I can't seem to get rid of. These days I'm a district commissioner. Rather dull, I'm afraid.'

'It doesn't sound dull. What does it entail?'

He told her and she listened, enthralled. This was the Kenya she had been expecting, a country of wild places where encounters with dangerous beasts were everyday occurrences. He spoke modestly about his exploits, which impressed her; she suspected he was very brave.

'Do you really sleep in a tent in the . . . the bush,' she said, careful to remember the right word. 'Don't you get frightened?'

'The animals prefer to stay away from people, though there is the odd rogue.'

'And you shoot those?'

'If I can. It's part of my job.'

'You make it seem a boring routine.'

'Oh, it's not boring. At least I don't find it so.'

Not since that first night with Diana, beside the camp fire, had Harry felt so immediately at ease with a woman. Nell Dickins' clear, hazel eyes were upon him as he spoke, her lips parted to drink in his every word. He lost track of time until Daisy exclaimed at it and declared they must find Eric and go home to change.

Harry stood as Nell did. 'Will you dance with me later?' he asked her.

'Yes. Yes, please. I'd like to.'

The two ladies made their way across the lawn to the club, and Idina clapped her hands.

'Excellent, Harry,' she applauded. 'Not a wobble in sight.'

'Harry Wittering?' Daisy said, inspecting the clothes in Nell's wardrobe. 'What do you want to know about him?'

'Nothing. He seems nice, that's all.'

'He is nice, darling, but I'm afraid he won't do.' She pulled out a dress and held it against her. 'I wish I were thinner. This would look divine on me. We try to keep up with the fashions but it's hard being so far away. Did you get it in Paris?'

'Yes. Why won't he do?'

'Who? Oh, Harry. Well, he hasn't any money for a start and he's not a member of the Muthaiga Club, although he behaves as if he is. People make a fuss of him because the Connaughts did when they were here and he'll always find someone to take him in –'

'Daisy,' Nell interrupted, 'I haven't a clue what you are talking about.'

'The Muthaiga's frightfully exclusive. The Nairobi Club's the place for government officials.'

'Isn't Eric a government official?'

'No! He's a sort of consultant. He came as a settler. When the farm gets going we'll build a house and live there.'

Nell gave up on the complexities of colonial class.

'And another thing about Harry Wittering,' Daisy went on. 'He disappears with that servant of his and no one sees him for months.'

'He's doing his job, which is more than anyone else around here seems to do.'

'But it's Race Week! Eric works frightfully hard most of the time.'

'Consulting.'

'Being consulted,' Daisy said crossly. 'Anyway, you don't want to marry a DC and live shut away in Fort Richard – or worse.'

'I've only just met him,' Nell protested.

'He's been after a wife for years,' Daisy said. 'He's famous for it.'

Nell wore one of her Paris creations, and the knowledge that she was in the latest fashion made her sparkle. She was a pretty young woman new to the Colony and never short of a partner – men assiduously introduced by Daisy and considered by her to be more eligible than a mere DC who had, it so happened, once snubbed her. Harry, however, out-manoeuvred her and managed to dance frequently with Nell, appearing at her shoulder with his charming smile and the cocked eyebrow which seemed to indicate a shared joke, an understanding.

'If it wasn't so funny it would be sad,' Lucy Fanshawe commented to Louis.

'Why sad?'

'Harry's smitten.'

'Let's hope she's smitten back. It's time he settled down.'

'With a girl from London? Louis, be serious.'

'You came from London.'

'And we came out here together. We made the decision together.'

'Lots of women have married men here and managed perfectly well. Anyway, Harry isn't married yet. You are overreacting, or,' he added shrewdly, 'jealous.'

'Jealous? Don't be absurd!'

'It isn't absurd, my love. We're fond of Harry and in our heart of hearts we don't want him to change. We want him to be our friend and like he's always been, no matter what might be best for him. True?'

'Yes,' she admitted after a while. 'I suppose it is.'

Harry took Nell's stole from her and put it around her shoulders. They went on to the verandah. The scent of frangipani crept towards them through the pre-dawn darkness while behind them Josslyn Hay could be heard organizing teams for a polo match.

'Good heavens,' Nell said faintly. 'Doesn't anyone ever sleep?'

'I'll take you back to Daisy if you're tired.'

'Funnily enough,' she said, sounding surprised, 'I'm not. It must be this cool air.'

'And the altitude. Even, possibly, the scintillating company. The sun will be up soon. Shall I show you a real African dawn?'

'What? Now?'

'Real Africa isn't far away. I can promise you zebra, gazelle, antelope. Perhaps lion or elephant, if we're lucky.'

'Oh, yes, let's go!' she said. 'But first I'd better tell Daisy.'

'Send her a note.' Every second in Nell Dickins' company made Harry more certain she was the one. Daisy Davidson had not been fond of him since the time he had refused to play games with her at a house party at Clouds (games which would not have reached the goal posts, so to speak, since she was notoriously faithful to Eric) and her hostility to him had to be overcome or counterbalanced. Daisy took vicarious thrills from attaching herself to the edge of Idina and Joss's set, and though Nell might get used to their kind of loose talking and living she was for the time being (Harry was sure) made uncomfortable by it.

Well, Harry would make himself comfortable to be with. He felt confident and determined and not in the least bit jelly-like as Nell wrote her note and he summoned a boy to deliver it. He would do what he was best at and not try any fancy tricks. The first and most powerful recruit to his side was the beauty of his adopted land. It had acted before and caused him a great and enduring pain. It owed him something now.

And how it repaid him with that dawn! A misty pink that rose to a slashing gold and then a clear pale violet as day rolled back the night. Only a few miles out of Nairobi and here no lion or elephant, but yet more luck: a family of rhino, the father with a horn on him that must have been a record. He stopped and turned, catching wind of their presence, and Harry picked up his gun.

'No,' Nell whispered, her hand on his arm as the rhino, his short sight revealing nothing to him, turned away again and trotted after his wife and child.

'Only in case he charged,' Harry said, putting the gun down. He had no desire, not this morning, to shatter paradise.

And the creatures of paradise seemed to know, just as they know whenever a predator not in hunting mood is among them. Zebra lifted their heads as the truck passed and grazed on peacefully, their tails twitching around their striped rumps. White herons picked ticks from the backs of buffalo. A pair of young wildebeest tested the mettle of their horns.

'Over there, under that tree,' Harry said, pointing and handing Nell the field glasses. 'Got it?'

A single, spotted cat sat gazing over its domain, its proud face held high. Not it — a she! At her feet three tumbling cubs.

'Is she a leopard?' Nell asked, entranced by the sight.

'A cheetah. It's said they're the fastest animals in Africa. You should see one run!'

She lowered the glasses and looked at him. 'Would someone shoot her?'

'I'm afraid so. She won't hunt with her cubs and it's not easy to distinguish her sex without them, even if people wanted to. Her skin is valuable.'

'And the rhino?'

'In definite danger. It's a miracle he's survived so close to town.'

He thought of Prince Arthur of Connaught: if he'd found him a rhinoceros with a head like that old man's he'd have had even more praise heaped upon his own.

'Harry?' Nell's hand on his arm again, and feeling so right.

'Yes?'

'Let's keep them a secret. Make them our secret?'

'Our secret,' he said, a hundred miles off the ground.

They arrived back in Nairobi at ten o'clock in the morning, the sun two hours from the zenith and hot. Nell, her stole in her lap, had fallen asleep but woke as Harry parked outside the Davidsons' house.

She gave him a drowsy smile. 'Sorry,' she said.

'You need your beauty sleep.'

'I'll never manage the races.'

'Please try to, but if you don't I'll see you this evening.'

'Another dance?' she said, yawning as he helped her out of the truck. 'I'd rather have another African dawn.'

'Would you, Nell? Would you really?'

'It was the most wonderful experience. Thank you, Harry.'

He saw her safely inside and drove to his hotel. Mac greeted him, smelled the bush on him and stared accusingly.

'This is it,' Harry told his dog. 'Mac, my dear fellow, this is *it!*'

'All right!' Daisy wailed a week later. 'All right! I admit he's frightfully attractive, but that's not the most important thing in a man.'

'What is?'

'Money. Position. Harry Wittering has neither. Besides,

the wives of DCs are the dreariest things imaginable.'

'I expect that depends on the individual DC and his wife. Anyway, I'm not thinking of marrying one.'

'He's thinking of marrying you. Don't,' Daisy pleaded, 'go up-country with Harry Wittering. He *always* proposes.'

'Then I shall say no.'

Eric and Daisy's idea of showing her the country was to travel by motor car up the Rift Valley as far as Lake Naivasha. Daisy and Nell would stay with friends while Eric made one of his two annual visits to his farm, which was presently being worked by a Boer couple. Harry Wittering, on the other hand, offered a journey to Fort Richard and a two-week safari on horseback. As far as Nell was concerned, the choice was obvious.

Except she was no horsewoman.

'Poor Nell,' Harry said, helping her from the saddle the first evening, 'are you very sore?'

'Yes,' she said, rubbing the affected part. 'But it's been worth every single ache. Was I dreaming it or did you say I could have a bath?'

'Of a sort. It should be ready for you.'

'What bliss!'

As that other woman had been, Nell was astounded at the comfort of safari life. Her stiffness wore off more rapidly each day and soon she rode her horse with confidence. She could think of nothing more glorious than waking in the morning and going outside to see zebra streaming through the haze, giraffe, their legs and bodies blending with the trees and scrub while their heads stood out against the giant backdrop of Mount Kenya. On the other side of the remains of the night's fire Harry would be consulting with Mutali and Ndwetti about their day's route, and from the kitchen area came the smell of fresh-ground coffee.

And, like that other woman, Nell fell in love.

And wished what Daisy said was true. Far from proposing to her Harry had not even attempted to kiss her, treating her with the utmost respect as he had done since they had left Nairobi and driven with only the briefest of halts to the hotel in Fort Richard. The following morning he had presented her with a black woman, the mission-educated wife of one of his 'boys', to be her maid, realizing she might feel awkward with only male servants. For all this, for his sensitivity and the respect, she had been grateful until now.

Now she wanted –

It must be another attribute of the altitude, she told herself; that or loose morals were catching.

She wanted to be taken in Harry's strong arms and kissed.

He knew when she changed. There was something about her smile, in her eyes, in the way her hand lingered in his as he helped her from her horse.

They had climbed a tree and were sitting astride a broad branch overlooking a water hole. Below them, unaware of their presence, was a herd of elephant. The serious business of drinking done, the calves and adolescents were playing and Nell was watching in delight, her fists pressed to her mouth to prevent her gasps of wonder escaping. She had taken off her hat and her short-cropped glossy brown hair was moulded to her head. She watched the elephants and he watched her.

She loved his Africa. Only Diana could have been more at home in it.

Perhaps she sensed his gaze upon her, for she turned to him.

'Nell, my dear,' he said.

'Harry?'

He leaned towards her. She met him halfway. Her lips were soft, responsive, then she drew back.

'All right?' he asked.

'Your moustache tickles.'

'Help! Shall I shave it off?'

'I like it.'

'Can it tickle you again?'

Below them the matriarch gave a shrill trumpet. Splashings, squeals of calves. Silence.

Too soon, too soon: 'Bwana?'

Mutali returning with the horses.

As much contentment as Harry had ever known: Nell by his camp fire, their love open, without guilt or shame and with a future. They made plans. It would be a Nairobi wedding; since neither had parents alive there was no point in going to England. Daisy's woman could make Nell's dress.

'Daisy won't be pleased,' Harry said.

Nell smothered a yawn. 'I don't expect she will, but never mind.'

'Tired, my little Nell? To bed with you.'

'Yes . . . Harry, I – I –'

He understood immediately. 'My love, I wouldn't dream of it until after we're married. Some of us in Kenya have principles.'

She put both arms around his neck, pulled him towards her and kissed him. 'Maybe I was going to say mine have vanished.'

'Were you?'

'No.' She rubbed her cheek against his. 'Thank you.'

'Thank *you*, madam, and good night.'

When she had gone to her tent Harry lit his pipe and poured himself another brandy. 'I said so, didn't I?' he remarked to Mac. 'I said she was it.' He stretched out his legs, tilted his chair back and gazed up at the mass of stars. He felt his happiness reaching to the very farthest one. 'And thank you, Africa,' he murmured.

8

Daisy greeted the news of Nell's engagement with resignation, but in no time her grasshopper brain had turned it into an excuse for a party, especially welcome in the dull aftermath of Race Week.

Lucy and Louis Fanshawe came from Thika to attend it.

'Congratulations, dearest Harry,' Lucy said, kissing him. While Harry was asking Louis to be his best man she moved on to Nell. 'And every joy to you. He didn't manage to put you off, then, by traipsing you through the bush?'

'I adored every moment of it.'

Her eyes were sparkling and her glances at Harry proved that the bush was not the only thing she adored. A great weight left Lucy and impulsively she gave Nell a hug. 'Take care of him. He's our best and oldest friend.'

'I will,' Nell said.

'What did you think of Fort Richard?'

'It isn't like London or even Nairobi, but it wouldn't be, would it? Still, Harry's bungalow will keep me occupied. It's what you might call bachelorish.'

'It certainly is, and much in need of a feminine hand.' The two women laughed, but Lucy hoped Nell appreciated how remote Fort Richard was and how few of her own kind were there. And she hadn't seen it rain in Kenya yet.

In truth, Nell had been disconcerted by Fort Richard. What had been on the outward journey a curiosity was on the return one the place she had committed herself to live. She consoled herself, however, with the thought of the nearby hotel and the fact that she would accompany Harry on his travels. Love would surmount any problems, and if she had feared she was making a mistake the letter from Celia waiting for her in Nairobi dispelled her qualms. Celia was pregnant, giving Nell more catching up to do.

'I have to marry you or be a maiden aunt,' she had teased Harry.

'Whatever excuse you need, my little Nell.'

Lady Idina Hay, to celebrate the success of what she considered her matchmaking, organized a dinner at the Muthaiga Club. Smiling wickedly, she offered Clouds as a venue for the wedding. 'There's a C. of E. chap somewhere,' she said, as though she had temporarily mislaid him.

'Thank you, Idina, but I must decline,' Harry said. 'No self-respecting priest would go within spitting distance of Clouds without bell, book and candle at the ready.'

Alice de Janzé sighed. 'Heavens, Harry, are you becoming a prude?'

Harry put his arm around Nell's shoulders. 'Definitely,' he said. 'How's your lion?'

'It's so sad. He's too big to sit on my lap now. He scratched one of the *totos* rather badly, but it was only in play.'

'I hope the *toto* enjoyed the game.'

'You've always been against Samson.'

'Have you got a cage for him?'

'No. He's a wild animal. You said so yourself.'

'One who hasn't learned to hunt for himself and isn't

afraid of humans. Contact me, Alice, when he gets too much to deal with – preferably before he kills a *toto*.'

'You're so masterful,' Alice marvelled, 'since your engagement.'

'Am I masterful?' he asked Nell as they danced after dinner.

'Yes, Bwana, sir!' She sketched a salute, then became serious. 'A *toto* is a child, isn't it?'

'Yes. You're learning, Nell.'

'Her lion hurt a child. Could it kill one?'

'Easily – but only, recall, in play.'

'The DC in her area should shoot it, shouldn't he? It's a rogue.' She looked up at his astonished face and laughed. 'I have been listening to you, Harry, from the moment we met.'

'And learning more than I'd realized. Nell, my darling, you've just gone to the top of the class.'

The icing on Harry's cake arrived. It was a letter from Diana in response to the telegram he had sent her and was everything generous. Nell was the lucky woman Diana had assured Harry he would find and she wished them both all the happiness in the world. A parcel from her contained a silver coffee pot with a matching cream jug and sugar bowl, which pleased Nell and, incidentally, gave her a warped idea of what life in Fort Richard would be like. Her memory of the place was already blurred and in her mind the white population had grown to provide lady guests for morning coffee served from a silver pot.

And Harry had forgotten how Kenya produced her killing frosts, her blights, her swarms of locusts to ravage a promising crop.

It would be some time, however, before he discovered what was in store for him.

For several weeks after their wedding they travelled

around the district and everywhere the natives greeted them with dances and displays, pleased that their DC had found a wife at last. Nell loved watching Harry at work and was never bored by the travelling when each day brought something new: a pair of crested cranes dancing, fantastic in the haze; the gift of a half-grown tame mongoose which made a home in Nell's saddlebag and developed a liking for sweet tea until one night it disappeared and was never seen again.

'It would have eaten hens anyway,' Harry said, 'or been accused of it and cost us a fortune.' To console her he brought her an ostrich egg. 'Fried, boiled or scrambled?'

'How about poached?'

'That could be a problem . . . Oh, Lord!'

'Whatever is the matter?'

'Listen.'

A distinct tapping came from within the giant egg.

'Could I have a tame baby ostrich?'

'No,' Harry said.

'Then you'll have to put the egg back in the nest because I might not be able to resist the dear little thing.'

'Dear little thing, indeed!' Harry said, but obeyed and Mac was nearly kicked by an irate ostrich parent.

He taught her Swahili in the evenings and in the nights everything he knew about love, the narrow camp bed making invention a necessity.

'The only thing I miss,' Nell said, 'is a decent mattress.'

She didn't mind the ticks and the other discomforts of the bush, and she was now an accomplished rider. Harry bought her a horse from a farmer he knew, a chestnut mare with Arab blood in her, and she enjoyed the extra mettle, the lighter handling.

She was the perfect wife Harry never dared hope he would find.

*

They returned to Fort Richard for the short rains. The sewing machine Nell had ordered from England had arrived. She began making curtains and when Harry wasn't swearing over his paperwork he attempted to design a double camp bed which would, he was convinced, make his fortune.

'But whichever way you view it,' he complained, 'you need a brace in the middle.'

'And there go the knees again.'

In the house she was turning into a home, a fire alight, Mac and Nance lying on lion skins before it, the rains seemed cosy. They had each other and didn't need anyone else.

Christmas in Nairobi, Race Week time again.

'Golly, you both look well,' Lucy Fanshawe said, embracing them, and to Nell: 'I've always said you have to be mad or madly in love to survive here. Which are you?'

'Oh, madly in love,' Nell said.

After Race Week the Witterings were invited to Gilgil, to Clouds. As a veteran of two Race Weeks Nell considered herself unshockable, but she could not avoid gaping in disbelief when one of the other guests produced a silver syringe after dinner and casually injected herself. A lot of shouting and slamming of doors went on late at night after Harry had taken his wife to bed and locked them both in.

'What was in the syringe?' Nell asked.

'Heroin, I'm told.'

'And what are they up to now?'

'What we are about to do,' Harry said, 'but odds on it's not with a lawfully wedded husband or wife.'

Nell's so-far robust health began to fail her early in the New Year. She felt tired, dispirited and sick and no amount of aspirins or the 'simply marvellous' tonic Daisy had pressed on her made any difference until, at last, she realized what was the matter with her.

'Harry,' she said one morning after another bout of sickness, 'I must be pregnant.'

'Oh, my little Nell!' he breathed, his reaction as dia-metrically opposed to hers as it could possibly be.

She hoped she was mistaken, but the doctor at the mission confirmed her diagnosis. She was no longer allowed to ride nor even to travel in the truck unless the road was relatively smooth. She wished she could, like her sister, miscarry – for Celia had – but the thing inside her was not letting go, was determined to come into the world and spoil everything.

Then the long rains began: day after day, week after week of water pouring from a dull grey sky. The bunga-low no longer seemed cosy and she had no energy for home-making. The material for the curtains grew mildew and the sewing machine rusted until Harry cleaned it and put it away.

'I might want to use it,' Nell snapped, 'and you've covered it in oil.'

'I was worried it would be ruined. Sit down, Nell darling. You're supposed to rest.'

'I never do anything but bloody well rest. There isn't anything else to do! How long does this go on?'

'Until . . . until June, usually.'

'Oh, my God!'

When the sun came out she sat on the verandah and watched the garden steam. The hotel closed during the rainy season, and Nell didn't blame it, but even if it were open she probably wouldn't be allowed there. The road to it wasn't smooth at the best of times and Harry fussed and fretted over her so; he was a hopeless expectant father, hopeless indoors generally.

'I'm sorry, Nell,' he said. 'What can I do?'

'No, I'm sorry,' she said, suddenly full of remorse. 'It's

this baby. It's come between us already, and it always will. We won't be able to go on our safaris when it's born unless we take the truck. Nothing will ever be as wonderful again.'

'It will be,' he insisted. 'We'll have our baby to love.'

'I'll never be able to love it. Never ever.'

Worse, if it were possible, than the rains was a discovery Nell made in herself: she could not stand black people near her. It had never bothered her before and she had got used to the custom of there being only male house servants, but now she could not bear an African in the same room as her.

The doctor said it was unfortunate, but women got strange notions when they were pregnant.

'Be patient and it will pass,' he said.

Harry patted her hand. 'And, darling, please try to hide it. It would hurt their feelings dreadfully.'

'What about my feelings?' she raged. 'If you had any consideration for them you'd take me to Daisy.'

'When the roads are better,' he promised.

The only other visitors, apart from the doctor, were the wife of a Calvinist missionary who, having given birth to five children in Africa without the aid of doctors or hospitals, made it plain she thought Nell was making a fuss of nothing, and Father Patrick who was not at ease with women who had no respect for his calling and to whom the platitudes of his faith were no comfort.

He was worried for Harry, though, for he could see things his friend was blind to and tried to give him some advice. 'Stop flaffing around her so much,' he said. 'Can't you tell it annoys her? And you should stand up to her more, be firmer with her.'

'How can I when she's so ill and it's my fault?'

'Not easy, Harry, but try it.'

Father Patrick had seen the blight, the killing frost: Nell was making Harry jump through hoops and beginning to despise him for doing so. She was falling out of love with Africa and out of love with him.

And the result of her suffering was a baby girl and not the boy she had promised herself.

'She's lovely,' Daisy said. 'Not quite as lovely as my darling Katie, naturally, but a close second.'

Nell shifted in her bed. 'She'll have to be bottle-fed. She's done enough damage to me already.'

But Harry was jelly-like in his adoration of his daughter, knew he was and did not care.

'She's got a cap on today,' he crooned. 'A little mob cap for my little Moppet.'

Nell's irrational fear of the natives vanished as quickly as it had risen and, after she had recovered from Olivia's birth, she was able to ride her chestnut mare again. They were short, circular hacks, though, and nothing like the wandering rides through the bush where a makeshift bath awaited her at a new camp site. She had been right: nothing would be as wonderful again, and she could not love her baby.

Harry engaged an Indian *ayah*, the widowed sister of the owner of the *duka*. Olivia was well looked after and didn't need her parents, but Harry would not contemplate leaving her and spent hours gazing besottedly at his daughter as she slept in her mosquito-netted cot.

'She's not a toy to be played with or dumped at our convenience,' he said, and considered he was being firm.

It was he who made the arrangements for Olivia's christening in Nairobi. Daisy Davidson and Celia (*in absentia*) were godmothers, Louis Fanshawe godfather and the party afterwards was held at the Norfolk Hotel. None of the Happy Valley set was invited, for Harry feared that any hint of scandal might blight the life of his little Moppet – whose crying had him tangled in knots of anxiety, convinced she had malaria or worse; whose every smile cast him into transports of delight – and scandal was what they had been up to, and in no small measure.

Alice de Janzé had left her husband and gone to France in search of Raymond de Trafford. He had told her that he could not marry her, whereupon she had shot them both on a train. Not successfully in either case, and the darling judge – they understand that sort of thing in France – had let her off, but the boring colonial government had declared her *persona non grata* in Kenya and thrown her out as an undesirable alien. The men of the Happy Valley set said, predictably, that she might be an alien but only an octogenarian eunuch would consider her undesirable. Joss and Idina had split up and there was going to be a deliciously juicy divorce case.

'I wrote to you about it,' Daisy said to Nell. 'Don't you remember? And the Prince of Wales is coming here. You know that, don't you?'

'We do,' Nell said. 'We are bidden to Government House on several occasions. Harry knows a cousin of his.'

'Princess Arthur. I'd forgotten. You'll stay with us, of course.'

'May we, Daisy dear? We have to bring the baby – we have to take her everywhere – and they wouldn't like her night-long screaming here when the place is full. The *ayah*'s thoroughly reliable, but Harry won't believe it.'

She tried to keep her tone light. Daisy had warned her about being the wife of a DC and she did not want to prove her right. Anyway, she loved being a wife – she did! It was being a mother that made her feel dreary.

The Prince of Wales arrived. Nell and Harry were asked for by name and messages of congratulations on the birth of their daughter were relayed from Princess Arthur. An aide was sent to fetch the silver mug the Prince had brought with him, at his cousin's request, as a late christening present for Olivia.

Nell did not need to sing the song that everyone was singing. She had not danced with a man who'd danced with a girl who'd danced with the Prince of Wales; she had danced with the Prince himself, a number of times. One night in the Muthaiga he objected to the records being played and, helped by his partner, threw them out of the window of the ballroom. Everyone thought it a huge joke but Harry looked on disapprovingly, fatherhood having made him nearly pompous.

'What kind of a king will such an idiot make?' he asked Louis Fanshawe. 'It's a disgrace.'

The Prince went on safari with Denys Finch-Hatton and the Witterings retired up-country. Harry's Aunt Caroline had died and obligingly left him a legacy; he acquired a Model T Ford in which he, Nell, Olivia and the *ayah* travelled followed by the truck containing Mutali and his two sons, Ndwetti, Mac and the other dogs and the camping gear. They went by road or established track and Harry always made sure they were within a day of either Nyeri or Fort Richard in case something happened to his Moppet and she needed a doctor.

'How could anything happen?' Nell said wearily. 'You never let her out of your sight.'

'The bush is a dangerous place, especially since she's beginning to crawl.'

The outlying areas of Harry's district were now the business of Harry's assistant and these . . . picnics were the merest shadows of Nell's honeymoon safari. The magic was gone. Nell wondered if it would return if Olivia was, somehow, not there and even considered the possibility of sending her to Celia to bring up, but she knew Harry would not allow it though in all else he was desperate to please her. He urged her to spend the rainy seasons with Daisy, which she did, and each time she returned to Fort Richard she felt she was going into oblivion. The only manifestation of civilization was the hotel, but dinner or drinks there was worse, in a way, than staying in the bungalow which she could not call home. The people they met were either embarking on or finishing their African adventure. To them it was finite; to Nell it was infinite and any concept of adventure had vanished the moment she learned she was pregnant. There were Race Weeks, odd visits to the Scotts and to the Fanshawes – Lucy also the mother of a daughter – and with that Nell had to be content. Lucy and Louis were doing well with their coffee growing and lived in comfort; they had neighbours and, compared to Fort Richard, were within reach of Nairobi and its excitements, limited though those were. Nell thought about persuading Harry to stop being a DC and become a farmer instead, but quickly rejected the idea.

She was tired of Kenya and she was homesick. She was a wealthy woman and did not need to live like this. Let the Fanshawes and the others scrape at the mud of Africa. Nell determined to remove Harry from the place and return him to England. Just over two years after Olivia's birth, when Harry's long leave was due, she discovered herself – in spite of her best efforts – to be pregnant again and issued an ultimatum: this child would be born at home and be brought up there; if Harry did not agree he would return to Africa alone.

9

Harry, gaunt and wild-eyed, rushed to Nairobi to beg Daisy Davidson to plead with Nell on his behalf. She was Nell's best friend, and responsible for bringing her out here to begin with. Daisy, big with importance and gossip, drove with Harry back to Fort Richard and remained cooped up in the DC's bungalow with Nell for a whole afternoon while Harry was fed liquid consolation by Father Patrick.

'I didn't realize she was so unhappy,' Harry kept saying. 'I should have, but I didn't.'

Daisy emerged and reported total lack of success. Harry, drunk with Father Patrick's whiskey, distress and uncertainty about his future, took the two women out to dinner that night at the hotel. Poor Harry: another mistake. A large party of Americans was there ready to set out on safari the next day, the women wearing dresses with a style about them which even Harry could recognize neither of his companions had.

He set out to return Daisy to Nairobi the next morning, hoping viciously, selfishly, that the American women might have stirred something in her, but she returned his barbs with others, more wickedly poisoned, of her own.

'Well,' she said at last, 'of course I'm happy wherever Eric is.'

He left her at her house, not knowing that she had Nell's instructions to book a passage for her and Olivia on the next available ship. He went to the administrative offices and assured a sandy-haired Scotsman that he was only going for his long leave, that he would make his wife change her mind and they would all come back. The man's eyebrows were bushy and almost pure white and Harry found himself fixated by them. He had a terrible headache (a delayed hangover, perhaps) and he was sweating in spite of the ceiling fan.

No. This wasn't a hangover. He had to get out of here. He bade farewell to the eyebrows and somehow managed to find the main doors, which he almost fell through.

It was God's judgement on him, he realized. He should not have deceived the bureaucrats about his last long leave. He should have gone to England then, seen Diana, seen Aunt Caroline for the last time . . . God's judgement. He had spent his aunt's legacy to him on worldly show.

That was Father Patrick talking, but he wasn't here, was he? He was in Fort Richard among Harry's crooked streets.

He heard Mutali's soft, anxious voice, and then a sharper one, accented but speaking in English.

'It's all right, Harry. All right. I'll take you home with me.'

It was only a bout of malaria. When he next came to his senses Karen Blixen was standing at the foot of the bed and Mutali, grey-faced, was seated beside it bathing Harry's forehead with cool cloths. Tears were running down his cheeks.

'Honourable Sir Mutali,' Harry said, 'I am not dead yet.'

'Bwana, these tears are of relief. It was so very bad.'

'How long?' Harry asked, sitting up.

'Three days.'

Karen reappeared with a bowl of soup on a tray. 'Go,'

she said to Mutali. 'Farah will show you where you can sleep.' Mutali disappeared and Karen put the tray on Harry's lap. He felt weak but ravenously hungry, and the soup was delicious. 'I telegraphed your wife,' Karen said.

'Thank you.'

'Is she really making you leave Africa, Harry?'

For a split second he thought that was part of his delirium. Knowing it was not made his appetite vanish.

'What else did I say?' That was the worst thing about malaria: you gave away secrets as you sweated. And what the hell had he told the eyebrows?

'Nothing much,' Karen said, briefly touching his hand. 'I tried not to listen and I don't think your Mutali understood. I too will have to leave here.'

'Karen, no!'

She shrugged. 'The price of coffee has fallen and the well of money has run dry. Africa has broken many hearts, Harry, and it does not hurt her. Only us. Our hearts.' She smiled sadly at him. 'Now drink up your soup. We need our strength for the times to come.'

He stayed with Karen for another four days, gathering that strength and rehearsing the arguments he would go through with Nell. Of course she needed a period in England, he would say; of course the new baby would be born there. But Harry's life was in Africa. His job was here, his career. He wasn't trained or capable (or had the inclination) to do any job in England. Surely she would see that.

Lucy Fanshawe turned up on the fourth morning and Karen directed her to where Harry was sitting on the verandah.

'Why didn't you tell us?' Lucy said, looking distressed.

'A bout of malaria is hardly news, Lucy.'

'No, I meant about –' She stopped, utterly at a loss. 'We saw Nell last night . . . at the Norfolk,' she stammered. 'She said you were here and had been ill.'

'Nell's in *Nairobi*?'

'She was having dinner with Daisy and Eric.' Lucy gulped. 'That's what you didn't tell us . . . I mean, it was a farewell dinner.'

'Oh.' Harry didn't move, but he seemed to shrink inside his clothes. 'Oh,' he said again.

'Harry, dearest,' Lucy said, wanting to spare him the pain; but old friends should not lie to each other, or dissemble. 'Harry, she and Moppet are leaving on the boat train tomorrow.'

Nell arrived with Moppet that afternoon, in Harry's truck which was driven by Ndwetti.

No, she said, she hadn't planned it to be quite like this, but the *Arundel Castle* had a cabin available and, you know – almost gaily – once one had decided upon something one wanted to do it as soon as possible. Didn't one?

Harry agreed despondently that one supposed one did.

And, truly, it was amazing, Nell went on, how very little there was to pack from the bungalow in Fort Richard. She'd got news of the sailing from Daisy and twenty-four hours later had been ready to leave – well, earlier, really, but Ndwetti had said it was not sensible to leave in mid-afternoon so she'd had to wait until the next morning.

Harry's logical arguments failed before this *fait accompli*; and, also, crawling over him was his daughter, who was asking him if his illness had been like hers (it hadn't – she'd had a mild dose of flu), and telling him how she and Mummy were sailing on a boat 'home', and he'd be coming later, wouldn't he?

'Yes, Moppet,' he said, kissing her cheek, and she kissed his back. 'I'll be in England soon.'

'For our long leave?'

'That's exactly it, my Moppet.'

Nell stood up. This pregnancy suited her. She wasn't

nearly as ill as she had been when carrying Olivia and altogether looked very like the young woman he had first met on the lawns of the Muthaiga Club four years ago.

Harry had not then, though, seen the steel in her as he did now.

'Not "our" long leave, Olivia,' she said. 'It's Daddy's.' She put on her gloves and, before she pulled down the veil of her hat for the dusty journey to Nairobi, gave her husband a challenging look that jolted his guts. 'Understand?' she said lightly, the difference between the eyes and the voice saying everything: Africa or your daughter and the unborn child. Me? I don't much mind.

Olivia, as very young children can do before their methods of communication get confused by too much vocabulary, assimilated the undercurrent and began to cry and cling with extraordinary strength to her father's leg. He picked her up and carried her to the truck. As they reached it Nell turned towards him.

'We'll be at Celia's, Harry. We'll expect you there.'

Moppet's arms were like a monkey's around his neck. He kissed her again and promised her he would see her soon and she quietened and relaxed. As a reward Harry was invited to the Davidsons' for supper that evening.

If he really behaved, he asked himself as the truck drove away, would he be allowed to stay the night, to wave them off at the station tomorrow? Or even – good grief, was this expecting too much? – accompany them to Mombasa and see them safely aboard the ship?

He was too angry and frustrated to feel upset, but then he discovered Mutali's eyes upon him.

'Bwana,' his man said. 'Bwana, is it true what Ndwetti told me? You are going away from this place for ever?'

It was true. It had to be. Nell's clinical departure left no room for doubt, and if there was a chink under the door of that room a letter from Nell for him at Fort Richard –

written before she had ordered Ndwetti to prepare the truck – shut off the last bit of light. It began, 'Harry, I know you are thinking you can change my mind', and ended, 'you will not!', the last word underscored several times.

As she herself had said, it was amazing how little she had taken with her. The bungalow was hardly altered from his bachelor days, apart from the bedroom that had been Moppet's which still had Harry's sketches of giraffes, elephants and other animals in a frieze around the wall, but none of her dolls or toys. The sketches, lacking the magic of a child's imagination to bring them to life, looked tawdry and ridiculous. Harry, embarrassed, tore them down and used them to light the fire.

'Susie would have liked them,' Lucy Fanshawe said. She and Louis had accompanied Harry back, worried about how thin and ill he was, about his state of mind. Louis was of the opinion that Harry should give up on Nell, divorce her for desertion and return to Africa.

'You belong here,' he said. 'Harry, my dear fellow, what would you do in England?'

'Something or other,' Harry said distractedly. 'I can't divorce her, Louis. I can't. There's Moppet and the new baby . . .'

How had it gone so horribly wrong? Africa had given him the perfect wife and Africa had driven her away. It had also given him a daughter, who already he achingly missed. It had defeated Karen Blixen and killed many good men. It was about to spit out Harry, a minor casualty.

IO

The hotel in Fort Richard had begun organizing safaris, seeing more profit in this than in merely being a setting-out point. Its English owners jumped at the chance of employing Mutali, Ndwetti and the other experienced boys, and one of their white hunters confided to Harry that he had already attempted to poach Mutali. Tears came to Harry's eyes when he heard what the man had been prepared to pay for Mutali's services; Mutali who, unlike many Kikuyu, knew the value of coin money, had, according to the white hunter, rejected the blandishments with startling promptness.

'Made me feel a bit of a rotter,' the man said.

'You were being a thorough rotter,' Harry said, but took comfort in knowing that Mutali already had the respect of his new employers.

Mutali himself, however, was unimpressed. He knew white men were different from Kikuyu but this was incomprehensible. If a wife ran away you went and found her, brought her home and gave her a good thrashing to prevent her doing such a thing again. He loved Bwana Lion-Dog very much; he would have – and nearly had on several occasions – died for him if required; but he was ashamed for the Bwana that he was being subdued by his wife and meekly following her. He was like the huge, fierce bulls the white men brought out from Europe and which they controlled by a ring through their noses, insulting the animals' strength and power.

Mutali's outrage kept his distress at a distance until there were only five days to go before Harry's ship sailed from Mombasa. He summoned Mutali to the room he called his office. He had a duster in his hand and was using it to wipe the wooden stock of one of the pair of rifles he had brought with him to Kenya in 1920. He showed Mutali the brass plate he had screwed to the stock of each gun.

'You can't read what they say,' Harry said, 'but I want you to know.'

Mutali peered at the brass plates as though looking at them could tell him the message there.

'These are now your guns,' Harry went on. 'I have explained to Bwana Safari that this is so and he will keep them with his other guns at the hotel until they are needed when you lead safaris with him. But they are yours and he knows that.'

'Bwana!' Mutali gasped. 'No! They are yours!'

'I give them to you, Mutali, in return for all you have given me.'

'But I haven't given you anything,' Mutali said in agitation. 'Bwana, I cannot –'

'Listen to what it says here.' Harry pointed to the plate on the rifle he was holding and translated what was engraved. '"To Honourable Sir Mutali of the Kikuyu people who served his King and Country with honour and bravery."' Harry picked up the other rifle and continued. '"From his friend and companion Major H. G. A. Wittering, KAR, who will never forget him."' He then showed Mutali the rifles' case on which there was another plate with the two inscriptions run into one. In a daze Mutali repeated the words in Kikuyu after Harry and resolved to go to Father Patrick and learn them in English.

'Can I borrow one of your rifles, Honourable Sir Mutali?' Harry asked, a crooked smile on his face.

For the last time Harry and Mutali rode out together. The Fanshawes had taken Nance back with them to Thika, there to end her days. She was ancient, wheezy and warty, but they had wanted her. Harry had told Mutali and the hotel people that they could have the other hunting dogs and Mutali's son Jonas was to be in charge of them. Mac, however, could not be included in the general term 'other dogs' and Mutali wondered what the Bwana planned to do with him.

He discovered today.

Mac, as that first time long ago, put up a Thomson's gazelle. Harry shot it and Mac, as that first time and countless times since, trotted to the kill and sat beside it. Harry rode over, dismounted and went to his dog. He knelt in front of him and gazed at him. One proud yellow eye gazed back. Harry ran his hand over the empty socket of the other eye, lost in an argument with a leopard, over the great head and down the neck and back, over many battle scars with minor beasts until his haunches where the four long grey streaks were.

'You were hardly more than a puppy then, were you?' Harry whispered.

Mac licked his face as though in agreement.

Harry stood up, rested one hand on the dog's head while with the other he raised the gun.

Mac was ten years old and one-eyed. He was slowing down as a hunting dog and would not be anyone's pet. The quarantine required before he could be free in England would be cruel.

'Goodbye, Mac,' Harry said. 'Goodbye the best dog a man could have had.'

The sound of the shot was still in the air when Harry mounted his horse and rode away. Mutali, shocked beyond measure, stared down at the two bodies. The

Bwana never left a gazelle dead, unused and unexploited, but Mutali understood why he had done so today.

It was right Mac should have a companion when the vultures and hyenas came.

Many people were at the station in Nairobi to see Harry off, and Father Patrick insisted he had business to attend to on the coast and accompanied Harry on the train.

'It's a tedious old journey,' he said. 'I'll be glad of the company.'

'Yes,' Harry said weakly. He was grateful but he felt detached, as though the train was the ship and he had already left.

No. Not yet. They stopped to take on water and a face appeared in the window of their compartment.

'Mutali!' Harry exclaimed. 'What are you doing?' They had said their goodbyes. Why did it have to be prolonged? 'You'd better come in,' Harry added and opened the door.

Mutali was at his most dignified. 'It is my duty to be with you, Bwana,' he said. 'Who else is to stop those Mombasa porters cheating you and perhaps even robbing you?'

'Only you, Honourable Sir Mutali,' Harry said, overwhelmed. 'Only you.'

Who cared what Harry's fellow passengers thought when they saw a white man and a black one, both in tears, hugging each other?

The ship left her mooring and tugs nosed her bows out of the harbour towards the Indian Ocean. Because of Father Patrick's tall, cassocked figure Harry knew where in the crowd Mutali was long after he could see individual faces. He continued to wave even after this marker, too, was indistinguishable; then, abruptly, stopped and turned away from the rail.

Part III

'Your mother and aunt may remember more of his stories,' Olivia said, 'but that's enough for tonight.' She looked at the clock. 'Lord, is that the time? I'm for my bed.'

'Wait! I want more. Removed from Africa he – and you – ended up on Anglesey. Right?'

'Right.'

'Where it all went wrong. Why? How?'

'Go to Anglesey, darling, if you want the whole story. There are still people alive who know it – better than I do, probably. I only have my own view, and the hurt.' She patted Emma's shoulder and stood up. 'You discover the truth for me.'

'Who, Gran? Who's on Anglesey?'

'Three very old ladies, two within spitting distance of their telegrams from the Queen, but as sharp as saucers none the less.'

'Tacks, Gran. Saucers aren't sharp.'

'They are if you break them.'

On which note she left the room.

Breakfast News, the sound of what could have been a stampeding herd of elephants conjured from Olivia's tales of Africa and the high voices of children at the bottom of the garden awoke Emma the next morning. Downstairs the television was on in an empty kitchen and outside the elephants proved to be John and his uncle throwing logs from a handcart into the woodshed. They stopped work and gave Emma a bright good morning, Graham explaining that Mrs Wheeler's stock of wood was getting low and these April and May nights could be fierce. Clearly he was taking no chances with the health of the White Horse's star skittle player.

The children's voices rose in altercation with a woman's and as the noise faded Olivia walked up from the hen run. She had a look of glee on her face which made her appear thirty years younger.

'They came through a hole in the fence,' she said. 'I gave them each an egg to take home. They were thrilled to bits.'

'You've subverted them,' Emma hissed. 'Gran, honestly!'

'Listen,' Graham urged, and the four of them huddled together as they heard male anger erupt. A door slammed, a voice shouted, 'Mrs Wheeler!' and the top of a bald head appeared above the fence.

'Like an egg itself,' Graham gasped. 'Boil it up and it 'ud be good enough to eat.'

'Hush,' Olivia admonished, and went to meet her adversary.

The conversation was conducted in low tones. A piece of paper was taken from Olivia's cardigan pocket, read by the bald head and passed back. Both processed down the fence and bent to examine the damage. The bald head reappeared as Olivia straightened up and, with a parting comment, vanished. Olivia positively skipped to where the others were waiting.

'He tried to say the hole in the fence was both our faults, but all the bits of it were on his side. The children didn't attempt to hide them. He said he'll sue me for trying to poison the little brutes, but I floored him with this.' She produced the paper from her pocket. It was a letter from some ministry saying her hens had been tested and declared free of disease. 'He's reported me to the council. We'll take a copy of this there later, Emma. That'll fix them. Breakfast, everyone?'

Graham had evidently eaten here before. While John finished dealing with the logs he moved about the kitchen, collecting cutlery and laying the table, putting on the coffee and supervising the toaster in a way that was totally familiar . . .

Or intimate? Emma wondered suddenly, as, her offers of help rejected, she sat at the table and watched the slow dance of two people in a small kitchen who each knew where the other would be. She looked at Graham more closely. He was tall and burly and, in fact, rather attractive. Older than she had first thought but still, surely, well short of her grandmother's years. They couldn't . . . could they? At their age?

'All set, 'Livia?' Graham said. 'I'll call John –' He stopped.

'I'll get him,' Emma said, and hurried outside before they could see her laughter. She wouldn't have thought anything of it, even though he'd been careful to call her Mrs Wheeler before – presumably under strict instructions – had it not been for the expression of ludicrous horror on his face.

John was wrestling the handcart up a makeshift ramp into the back of a Land Rover.

'Breakfast's ready,' she told him.

'Thanks.' He chucked the planks that formed the ramp alongside the handcart and fastened the tailgate.

'Do you live with your uncle?' Emma asked.

'Yes. He's my great-uncle really. My gran's brother.'

'Is he married?' It was crudely put but she had to know.

John fiddled with the chain on the tailgate and glanced

at her out of the corner of his eyes. 'Has been. Twice. One died, t'other buggered off. 'Tis him and me and our farm. Do okay.'

'What about your parents?'

'Motor smash. Long time since.' He gave the Land Rover's back tyre a friendly kick and went over to Emma's Porsche. 'Now there's a car,' he breathed.

'Want a go in it?'

'Bloody 'ell, could I?'

'If you've passed your driving test.'

'Oh, I done that.' His reserve vanished into a huge grin and he bounded through the side gate calling out his news.

His excitement made breakfast less awkward than it might have been. Graham kept assuring Emma that John was a good driver and she need have no fears for her car; and Emma, who found that she did not – it was only an expensive bit of metal, and well insured – suggested diffidently that they might like to take it for a spin together. After breakfast she showed them what things did which in the car and John took it off at a brave thirty miles an hour.

Olivia was washing up when Emma returned to the kitchen.

'Men and cars!' Olivia said. 'You only need to wave a big one in front of them and they go gooey at the knees. Al yesterday, those two today . . . It's companionship,' she went on before Emma could comment. 'Nothing more. Understand?'

'Of course I do. Anyway, it's your business and no one else's.'

'I hate the idea of my family gossiping about me.'

'I won't tell tales.'

Olivia banged the coffee pot on to the draining board. 'There's no tale to tell,' she snapped.

Emma picked up a tea towel and began drying knives

and forks. It was wrong of her to have wanted to laugh. Why shouldn't two old people find happiness with each other? It wasn't the prerogative of the young – who, Emma reminded herself, were more than capable of inflicting grief as well.

'Where on Anglesey would I find the ancient ladies?' she asked, to change the delicate subject.

Olivia emptied the bowl into the sink and turned to her granddaughter. 'You're not going straight away, are you?' she said in dismay. 'Is it because –?'

'I want to know, that's all.'

'Lady Firling is in a home. The other two live in a guest house in Rhosneigr owned by one of Annie's grandchildren. Actually, it's more of a bed and breakfast, I think. I've got the details somewhere.'

'I'll phone and book myself in, then.'

'When, darling? Not too soon, please.'

Emma gave her a hug. 'After I've seen you and the White Horse wallop the Castle. If,' she said, 'I won't be cramping your style by staying that long.'

'Emma,' Olivia warned.

'Not a word, I promise.'

2

Say what you will, Emma thought as she parked the Porsche outside the Sea View Guest House, a flash, fast car gives confidence. She had felt it last night when she had stayed in a hotel near Shrewsbury for the first time ever on her own, and even more now with her peculiar mission on hand. A man appeared, gave the car an appraising look and then transferred it to Emma as she stepped out.

'Got here, then,' he said, and removed her one bag from the boot. 'Good journey, was it?'

'Yes, thank you. I've never been to Wales before. It's so beautiful and empty.'

'Not in summer it isn't. Wall-to-wall trippers it's then. Park her round the back, I should. The salt'll get at her paintwork else.'

Gooey at the knees. Gran was right. Emma returned herself to the driver's seat and took the car to where the man indicated. At least the natives were friendly, she reflected. She could not suppress ridiculous panics of whether she had enough toothpaste, money, clothes. The road signs in Welsh, the people's accents when she had stopped for petrol, then crossing the bridge over the Menai Strait to Anglesey compounded the notion that she was in a distant country away from familiar shops and banks.

She parked the car, locked it and walked back towards the guest house's entrance. Sea View, but only just. The tide was out and the water a distant blue strip. The sand was empty and inviting, the nippy wind exhilarating. Emma took a deep breath of freedom. Wall Street had opened two and a half hours ago and she didn't give a damn.

The man had been watching her and smiled as she approached. 'It's a fine sight,' he said. 'Never the same two days in a row.' He extended a hand to her. 'Rhys Jones, and welcome.'

They went inside and a middle-aged woman hurried along the corridor towards them.

'Elunid, my wife,' Rhys murmured, and Emma's hands were taken and warmly pressed.

'The two old ones are that excited. Will you take tea with them? You'll want a wash first. I'll show you to your room.' She bustled Emma up the stairs, still talking. 'Mrs Wheeler said you want to chat about her childhood here. They'll love that. They're for ever on about those days, and we've heard it all before, see?' She flung open a door and ushered Emma into a large room with the eponymous sea view and containing a double and a single bed. 'It's our best one,' Elunid said. 'Makes no difference. We're half closed this time of year and there's only our regular staying.'

'I hope I'm not inconveniencing you,' Emma slid in.

'Oh, no! One half's closed but the other half's open, isn't it? Here's Rhys with your bag. You come down when you're good and ready and I'll make tea ... Wait, now. There's something you'd like to see.' She dragged Emma to the window. 'The house that looks like a castle. Got it?'

'Yes.'

'Near it is the cottage where your great-grandmother's sister lived. Lived and died.'

'Really?' Emma said, interest quickening. She could go there later, an excuse for a walk along the beach.

'Really. And now I'll leave you.'

Elunid went out and Emma opened the window and leaned into the wind. The patterned curtains brushed her face as she gazed out.

She had roots in this place she had never been to before.

Annie Jones and Gwen Llewllyn seemed entirely composed of wrinkles. Annie was nearly blind and Gwen deaf, and they sat in identical armchairs on either side of the fire in the sitting room of what Elunid referred to as the grannies' wing. The walls and the tops of chests of drawers and tables were covered with framed photographs, and Emma was startled at how many she recognized: there were some of H.G.A. and Nell, duplicates of the photographs Mo had sent Olivia from Canada, some of Emma's Aunt Julie and her own mother and of their various offspring, Emma included, which were in Olivia's sitting room in Dorset. Emma was beginning to think her mother and grandmother had been playing tricks with her, or at least had not been as forthcoming as they might. Her sense of adventure heightened, even so.

'Is she here?' Annie said. 'What's she look like? I said what's she look like?'

'Like the pictures of her. How else? Not,' Gwen said, regarding Emma out of watery blue eyes, 'like Miss Olivia.'

'Take my hand, child, and sit down. I said –'

'She's not the deaf one, Granny,' Elunid interrupted, putting the tea tray on a table at Gwen's elbow.

'What's that?' Gwen demanded.

'I said Emma's not deaf,' Elunid said, winking at Emma and nodding to a low stool in front of the fire between the two armchairs. She had made Emma ring her mother and grandmother to report her safe arrival, insisting she use the private instead of the public phone and rejecting offers of payment. She was a sweetie, and Emma had a dreadful feeling she was not going to be allowed to pay for anything while she stayed here.

'Can't I help with the tea?' she asked.

'I'll see to it. You sit down.'

Emma did so, having been captured by Annie's questing hand.

'How's your mam and your grandmam, Emma?'

'Well. They send you their love.'

'It's love from Olivia and Laura we have, Gwen,' Annie said in a raised voice to her sister.

'There's nice, isn't it?' Elunid said brightly, loudly, giving the grannies and then Emma cups of tea. 'You're not forgotten. Emma's driven all this way to see you. Two days on the road she's been, so don't you tire her, mind.'

Annie exuded a delightful, delighted laugh at such an idea, and at last released Emma's hand. Elunid disappeared and Emma, banking on the photographs and the assumption that Annie's half of the room housed those of people who were closest to her, said: 'You're Morfydd's mother, aren't you?'

'Why, yes! Didn't they tell you? My dearest Mo. It's a terrible thing to outlive your children. Two of mine gone and here's Gwen and me stuttering on.'

'How old are you?'

'Ninety-eight, child, and Gwen'll be ninety-five next month. I said you were ninety-five, Gwen.'

'Soon to be.' She poked a plate of cake at Emma. 'Have some. It's good. My recipe, see? Your grandmam liked my cake, though only ate it on Sundays.'

'Why was that?' Emma said, taking a piece.

'Wasn't allowed to other days, was she?'

There was silence as the three of them chewed cake, which was delicious. Olivia's Sunday treat, baked by Gwen. Morfydd had been in service, a maid, and Gwen must have been the cook. Emma licked crumbs from her fingers and looked at the photographs again.

'Why,' she said hesitantly, thinking the subject of Mo must be painful, 'did Mo take so long to contact my grandmother? You all seem to have kept in touch.'

'Not always,' Annie said. 'There was the war and . . . other troubles. We left Anglesey for a while, went south, and drifted slowly back. Then Mo wrote from Canada asking if I could find Olivia's address. She'd had her first operation and maybe she wanted, like, to clear the decks.'

She paused, and Emma said, 'Don't talk about it if it upsets you. Please.'

'They did a good job, those Canadian doctors. Another twelve years she . . . Anyway, your grandmam's aunt was still alive then and I got the name and address from her, and when next your grandmam came to visit her she visited us as well, see, and we've kept in contact ever since. I went on an aeroplane, you know,' she continued. 'Four times to Toronto. They paid. Saved up and sent me the tickets. Wanted me to live there with them, but home is here. Anglesey's home, eh, Gwen?'

'She's asleep,' Emma said. She removed the plate from Gwen's lap. 'Do you want me to leave?'

'Her world is so quiet. I prefer my darkness, I think. Seven-course meals she cooked in the old days. Seven courses and the table dressed that beautiful! Stay, child, if you will. Ask me more questions.'

'Who is Lady Firling?'

'Her? She's not far away. She can tell it from the other side, if she knew what was going on.'

'Tell what, Annie?'

'The story you've come to hear, child. The one about your great-grandda.'

'And Mo. Why was Gran on her conscience for nearly thirty years?'

'Ah!' Annie breathed.

'They live in the seaweed, Moppet, and under the rocks. You've got to get your net right in there.'

Harry demonstrated and his net emerged dripping from the water accompanied by the flickering crackle of leaping grey-green prawns.

'Get 'em out, Moppet.'

'There's a crab. He'll bite me.'

'Only if you put your fingers where he can grab 'em.'

Cautiously she reached into the net. The crab was burrowing downwards while the prawns were trying to escape up. She grasped the crab and threw it into the sea, then picked up the biggest prawn – by the head, as her father had taught her – and held it inquiringly, longingly, as it flipped its tail and its myriad legs worked at the useless air.

'Put it in your bag, then,' Harry said.

'I didn't really catch it, though,' she said, opening the bag hanging around her neck and slipping the prawn in before he could change his mind.

'I won't tell anyone you didn't,' he said.

She pounced on another prawn bouncing in the net. 'That makes thirteen. How many have you got?'

'A few more, but I'm stronger and have a bigger net. Are you cold, Moppet?'

'No.' She stashed the last prawn. She was a bit cold, but she wanted to carry on. The sea was no higher than her father's waist, but the rippling waves hit at her chest and chin. She took a breath, bent under the water and plunged her net into the rock crevice that had just yielded riches and shook it up through the fringe of seaweed. The magical sound of prawns trying to hop out of trouble greeted her as she tossed her hair out of her eyes.

'Bravo!' Harry cried, retrieving her floating sunhat. 'Look, Moppet, you've nabbed a whopper.'

A whopper, indeed – three or even four inches long. She took it from the net, stowed it and the lesser prawns and inverted the net to clear it of seaweed. 'There may be another there,' she said, preparing to dive again.

Half an hour later, having submerged herself several more times and increased her tally to forty-two, she could no longer deny she was cold. She was run up the beach to where they had left their bicycles and given a good rub down with a towel.

'We'll ride like the devil was behind us,' Harry said when they had put on dry clothes. 'That'll warm you. I'll get into terrible trouble if you arrive home shivering.'

'Why?' Olivia asked prosaically, climbing on to her bike. 'No one there except you cares what I do.'

Harry, buckling the saddlebag containing their catch and strapping their nets to his crossbar, cast an astonished glance at his daughter, but she was already pedalling across the ridged sand towards the dunes, her sturdy brown legs pumping like pistons. The child was right, but how awful that she could diagnose it. The entire household was obsessed with the well-being of little sickly Nicholas and seemed to consider Olivia's robust health as some kind of affront, along with what they regarded as Nick's father's lack of concern about his son. Harry loved the boy. Of course he did, and worried about his health when it was necessary to do so – for the doctors had assured him that the child's constant, niggling illnesses were not life-threatening, though (seeing fat fees in it, their faces portentous) his inability to thrive could leave him vulnerable to any passing germs or diseases – but even when Nick was well he wasn't nearly such a good companion as Moppet was. Nick cried if a wave played more than the most gentle game with him, demanded to be carried if they walked more than a hundred yards, was frightened of cows and Harry had been ordered not to regale him with stories of charging rhinos or others of his African adventures because it produced nightmares. When Harry had responded, saying Nick was growing into a namby-pamby, his mother and nurse drew themselves up in twin outrage and looked at him as though he had committed blasphemy.

Moppet was worth a dozen Nicks. She was . . . dash it, a damn fine *chap*!

She was struggling to carry her bike across the dunes and he mounted his own bike and rode to the rescue.

'I can do it,' she said.

'I know,' he said, with a heavy sigh, 'but as a gentleman I simply can't allow you to.'

He left her on the track which ran inland of the dunes and returned to retrieve his bike. The sun was going down, a red ball in a July haze, but dark wouldn't fall for a long time yet. Not like in Africa where the sun plummeted to the horizon as though committing nightly suicide, taking all light with it. Harry liked Anglesey, the gentle beauty of it, and the Menai Strait which cut it off from mainland Wales. It wasn't wild enough, though, or dangerous, and he laughed to himself as he heaved his bike over the loose sand of the dunes: the man who had returned to a tent in the bush having faced up to a lion which had acquired a taste for man-flesh, his and Mutali's guns between them and an exceedingly unpleasant death, was now taking home a couple of pounds of innocent prawns. Even after all this time he missed Africa; missed it and felt diminished.

Three young women, out for an evening cycle ride, had stopped by Olivia and Harry recognized the two Barker sisters under their wide-brimmed summer hats.

'May, my dear,' he said. 'we heard the good news today. Young Birkenshaw's a lucky man.'

'You're coming to the party, I hope?'

'Try to keep us away.' He tipped the brim of his elderly Panama hat to Claire Barker, smiling greetings, and waited to be introduced to the other girl. The three of them burst out laughing and something in the upturned, painted face of the unknown one struck a chord.

'Eve!' he exclaimed. 'It can't be!'

'Oh, but it can.'

'When did you arrive home? There hasn't been a whisper on the bush telegraph.'

'A few hours ago. An English couple were coming back and I decided to accept their offer of an escort. I wanted to surprise everyone.' She shrugged her shoulders. 'Berlin isn't as fun as it used to be.'

She had gone to stay with cousins, Harry recalled, to teach their children English and to learn German: pretty rum thing to want to do, Harry considered, but her red lips and knowing eyes indicated she'd learned rather more than the language. An exotic number, she looked, alongside her wholesome sisters.

'Well,' he said vaguely, 'I doubt if Anglesey can compete in the fun department, but we'll do our best.'

She swept him a curtsey, one hand on the seat of her bicycle to keep it steady. 'Why, thank you, Major Wittering.'

'Come on, Moppet. We must be off,' he explained to the Misses Barker. 'She's been in the sea for over an hour.'

Moppet had been gazing at Eve Barker with round,

wondering eyes which she now switched to her father, a remembered excitement in them.

'I'm to be a bridesmaid,' she announced.

'Moppet, really?'

'It's all right, isn't it?' May said. 'I know I should have asked Mrs Wittering first –'

'Of course it's all right.'

Out of courtesy he waited until the Barker girls were on their way before he and Moppet rode home through the lanes. They parked their bikes outside the kennels and went into Harry's special room, calming the mayhem of welcoming barks from the six spaniels. Olivia's mother never came in here for she said it stank of the disgusting meat Harry cooked up for the dogs – which, to be honest, it did – but Olivia liked the place. On the walls were framed certificates and photographs. The certificates proved that various of Harry's dogs had been field trial champions and were not very interesting, but the photographs were of his years in Africa and Olivia never tired of looking at them.

'Is this a man-eating lion?' she asked. A great maned cat was stretched out on the ground, its head propped up on a stick, and her father was standing over it, his pipe between his teeth as it was now as he set two pans of water to boil.

'Had three women and a man in as many weeks.'

'You forgot the children,' she accused.

'One child, another badly mauled.'

'And Mac helped you kill the lion.'

'Good old Mac.'

Her father's best hunting dog, massive in his photograph. In the albums, which were kept in the house, there was a picture of him in the *Illustrated London News*. A princess had gone to Kenya and Harry had been appointed to take care of her. The caption called Mac 'My Hunting Dog', which Olivia thought rather unfair but her father didn't mind.

'Time to get the butter, Moppet,' he said.

This was the worst bit about prawning, the moment they went into the boiling water, hopped once or twice and then turned pink and delicious. Her father insisted that her duty at the fateful time was to collect butter and pots from cook, and she scooted across the yard, round the corner of the house and through the front door. She was in the hall and making for the green baize door when a voice halted her.

'Olivia!'

Her mother, her satin dress and jewels glittering, was at the top of the stairs. She came down in a cloud of scent.

'Where are you going?'

'To Gwen, for the butter. We've been prawning.'

'Oh, Lord, look at you!' her mother said, taking in the salt-encrusted hair and the still sandy legs embellished with oil from the bicycle chain. 'Up to Nurse for a bath – now!'

'I can't. Daddy's cooking the prawns.'

'Daddy,' she said sharply – she never talked to him like this, but it seemed to Olivia that she ticked him off through her – 'seems to have forgotten the time. We're due at the Cowleys for cocktails in twenty minutes.'

'I'll tell him. I'm sure he'll change as though the devil was after him.'

Her mother put a hand to her face.

'Can I go?' Olivia asked.

The hand waved and Olivia took it as assent. Gwen, as usual, grumbled and delayed and Olivia hopped from foot to foot in anxiety until the new maid said, 'Aunt!' in an exasperated tone and produced what Olivia wanted, putting them in a basket and handing it over with a lovely smile. By now Olivia was beset with another anxiety.

'Daddy has to go out. Who'll help me peel them?'

'I will,' the maid said soothingly.

It had to be done under Nurse's disapproving eye, for to have 'that child', as she called Olivia, in 'that dirty place', as she called the kennels, she would not do with, not when the mistress was away from home. She did not like Morfydd invading the nursery, but consoled herself that the chore would be over the sooner if the maid was there and, no matter what she thought of the master of the house, his orders were not to be countermanded. The master of the house had only one fault, though because of it the nurse (as did her mistress) ascribed several others to him. At any rate, to prefer his daughter to his son was the action of a lunatic.

Nicholas demanded and was allowed to help with the prawns. He was slow about it, which was the only good thing for he ate precisely every other one, and that the bigger of the two, and when Olivia remonstrated Nurse simply said, 'Let him be.' Then he reached for Olivia's whopper, which she had been saving so it could go at the top of the pot and she would know it was hers, and peeled it. He was about to put it in his mouth when he became aware of two pairs of brown eyes, one horrified, the other containing an expression he was too young to interpret as contempt but which made him feel distinctly uncomfortable. He looked to his nurse for support but she was busy with her knitting. Morfydd shook her head at him and he dropped the giant pink comma into the pot. Morfydd's knee nudged Olivia's under the table. It signalled collusion, friendship, and Olivia smiled.

'What's so amusing, young lady?' Nurse said, glancing up.

'Nothing!' Morfydd and Olivia said together.

'Have you finished with that nonsense?'

'Nearly,' Olivia said.

'Then go and have your bath. It's way past time and just see the state you're in. How you manage it I'll never know.'

'I have to melt the butter.'

'I'll do it,' Morfydd said, peeling the last prawn and wrapping the discarded shells into a neat bundle of newspaper. 'All proper, mind. Plenty of butter and a dash of pepper on the top.'

'Thank you,' said Olivia, and skipped away to run her bath. Morfydd was a friend! And that meant two people today who had wanted her and not Nick, for May Barker had asked her to be a bridesmaid.

She told Nurse about the last news when she came in to wash Olivia's hair.

'A bridesmaid!' Nurse said. 'Well, you'd best not go up the aisle the way you go everywhere else.'

'I'll have to be dignified.'

Nurse laughed at her the way she usually did at Nick as she wrapped a towel around Olivia's head.

'Dignified? You? That'll be the day.'

Olivia understood the way things were and that she couldn't change them: Nurse loved her, in a way, and so did her mother, but they loved Nicholas more. Balanced against that was Daddy, who even if he didn't love her more he liked her more. Then there was Aunt Celia, her mother's sister. She only came to Anglesey for holidays but always found time for her niece, her godchild. Olivia had overheard her saying it was disgraceful the way Nell treated her daughter and why did she never buy her any clothes?

'She'd wreck them,' Olivia's mother had said. 'She's a disaster. She'd wreck anything.'

'She wouldn't if you gave her something decent. How can you bear to see her going around in the Cowley children's cast-offs?'

Olivia had heard the shrug in her mother's voice though not the actual words, but the next time Aunt Celia appeared on Anglesey she brought Olivia a skirt and a beautiful blouse which Olivia had taken such care of she'd only worn them four times. She'd need a special dress to be a bridesmaid in. Something very special indeed . . .

'Why are you humming?' Nick asked as Nurse left their bedroom. Olivia had to share a room with him and go to bed at the same time although he was three years younger.

'Because I'm happy,' she said.

'Why?' he whined, wanting his portion of this as well as everything else.

'Just because.' Olivia pulled the sheets and blankets over her ears, turned away from him and fell asleep.

4

'Come on,' Eve Barker persisted. 'Who's the most handsome man on Anglesey? And don't, May, say Stephen Birkenshaw.'

'Why shouldn't I? I happen to think he is the most handsome.'

'Marks out of ten for sexiness.'

'Eve!' May protested.

'Sex. You and Stephen are going to do it, if you haven't done already. Why pretend it doesn't exist?'

'It's not the sort of thing one talks about,' May said, flushing.

'Why not? It makes the world go round. In Berlin –'

'Oh, Berlin!' Eve's other sister Claire exclaimed, putting her book down with an irritated slap. 'We're not in Berlin now.'

'Don't remind me,' Eve said, sighing.

She stood and paced over to the window. Rain poured down outside, obscuring the sloping lawn and the Menai Strait below. Welsh weather. It could set in for days. How had she spent the first seventeen years of her life here and remained sane? She wondered if she would be able to persuade her mother to let her go to London and stay with Reggie and Millie. She would want to meet them, though, and that would be fatal. So far she had been impressed by them, albeit from a distance. It had been they who had decided the dancing had to stop in Berlin and intended it should start again in London, but all Mrs Barker knew of them was that they had escorted her youngest daughter from the perils of Herr Hitler's capital and brought her home. Not that Berlin was full of perils – not if you had blonde hair and a fair complexion, anyway – but Mother thought every city, most particularly a foreign one, a place of devils. It was a miracle Eve had been permitted to go there at all, and certainly wouldn't have been if her parents had realized what a timid mouse Franz Hinkel and five lusty German sons had made of Father's Cousin Hilda, and how often Herr Hinkel went out in the evenings. And to where.

Eve sighed again. The dancing had to stop in Berlin. When you weren't that interested in politics and not fluent enough in German to understand the Führer's speeches you could dance on heedlessly. The sight of shops with broken windows and scrawled graffiti was so common that you took no notice and someone always hurried you away from Brownshirts kicking a life-size rag doll on the pavement. But no language had been needed when Reggie, dark-haired and his suntan misunderstood, was beaten up and forced to drop his trousers.

'Thank God I'm uncircumcised,' he'd announced cheerfully as Millie bathed his wounds. 'But I'm not going to give them another chance to fiddle with my old man. Children, it's time we moved on.'

They had left three days later, Cousin Hilda waving them off amid tears of sudden homesickness compounded by domestic crises: Herr Hinkel had ordered her to dismiss the Jewish maid and there was no one to press Ludwig's Hitler Youth uniform.

Time to move on, indeed, except Eve had moved backwards into a cage she had never known existed, a cage with bars of sea, mountains, more sea and rigid bloody convention. Mother would never let her go to London and dance with Millie and Reggie. They were ten years older than she and, Eve realized with a start – for she had quite forgotten it – they were not married and made no pretence of being so. It would be two years until she was twenty-one and had sole control of her share of the money Grandma had left. Another two years here!

'All right, Eve,' May said behind her, humouring her and wanting everyone to be happy. 'Who do you think is the most handsome man on Anglesey?'

Eve gazed at the pouring rain. Into her mind came an image of a man she instinctively recognized was as caged as she felt herself to be, a man with a past that was at least romantic and exciting. She ignored the way he had appeared on the evening she had arrived home, dishevelled and showing unmasculine concern for his grubby, unappealing child, and cared to remember instead his presence at a party last night. Trapped in evening wear, he seemed like a wild buffalo among the placid cows of Anglo-Anglesey. Eve turned away from the window.

'The most handsome man on Anglesey,' she said, 'is Major Harry Wittering.'

And in that moment she decided she wanted him.

5

Olivia watched Morfydd pack her mother's clothes. A layer of tissue paper, a shining evening frock, more tissue paper. Olivia extended a finger and stroked the cool silk of a protruding skirt. She was never allowed to touch it when her mother was wearing it and her action now seemed imbued with wickedness, but Morfydd only paused, another dress in her arms, until Olivia withdrew her hand.

'Do you wish you were going with them?' she asked.

'I do not!' Morfydd rustled tissue paper to emphasize the negative. 'Me being a lady's maid in a royal household? I have enough trouble trying to be one here.' And it was not what I was employed to do, she almost added.

'Daddy says he's only asked to Scotland for the shooting because of his dogs.'

'And if I went I'd be treated no better than a kennel maid.'

'Daddy wouldn't let that happen to you.'

'He's a good man, your da.' Morfydd placed the last dress in the trunk and smoothed yet more tissue paper over it. She did not intend to be in service all her life but, as her mother had always said, you do any job you are given as well as you possibly can. Whoever unpacked this trunk at Mar Lodge would recognize the handiwork of a good Welsh maid. It was odd to think that some of the dresses it contained would be seen by the King and Queen – and because of Major Wittering's dogs! Altogether it was a strange old world. Stranger yet when a woman spent a fortune on clothes for herself while her daughter ran around looking like a ragamuffin and her son sat in his nursery or went on sedate excursions with his nurse or his mother wearing immaculate outfits ordered from London. It added up to something bad, Morfydd thought as she closed the lid of the trunk.

Olivia rose from the bed and went to the dressing table. There were several cut-glass bottles on it which would travel tomorrow in a little case of their own. She unstoppered one – another forbidden thing – and lifted it to her nose. She had a whiff of a divine scent and then, inconceivably, the bottle fell from her hand. Aghast she watched it go, as though in slow motion, and as it reached the floor her tears were beside it.

Morfydd, more shocked by the gush of tears and the anguish of the child than bothered about the fate of some silly bottle, was holding Olivia within half a second.

'It doesn't matter,' she soothed. 'There's no harm done. It's not broken, see?' She held up the bottle as evidence.

'But it's nearly empty and the carpet will smell and I always do everthing *wrong*.'

'No, you don't,' Morfydd said.

'I'll get into trouble,' Olivia said, 'and I try to be good.'

'I did it. How about that?'

Olivia gulped. The tears cascading down Morfydd's neck ceased and the maid could tell the child was thinking.

'Then you'll get into trouble,' she said.

'Maybe I won't. It'll be a secret between you and me. We'll give the carpet a fine old scrub and fill the bottle. There's plenty more of the same. It comes from Paris, imagine!'

Olivia pushed herself away and her reddened eyes met the maid's. 'Wouldn't that be wrong, too?'

'Yes,' Morfydd said, 'but no one will find out. It doesn't make it right, mind,' she added, wondering what her mother would have to say about such deception, yet why should the child be punished – as she would be – for an accident? It was fear of chastisement which made her fingers slippery, that and a lack of confidence in herself. A stamped-upon flower, she was, trying to unfurl her petals. The Major made time for her, but her mother and nurse had more important things to do. Nicholas coughed and the whole house sneezed.

'I'll fetch the mop, shall I?' Olivia had recovered and come to a decision. 'I know where it's kept.'

'And be found on the stairs with it? No, and we don't need a mop, anyway. Not a mop, Moppet,' Morfydd said, taking a handkerchief from her apron pocket and wiping Olivia's face with it. 'Moppet. It's your da's special name for you, isn't it? Can I call you that, too, privately, when we're alone?'

'Yes,' Olivia said. 'Yes, please.'

'My mam calls me Mo.'

Olivia flung her arms around Morfydd's neck. 'Thank you, Mo,' she whispered.

'I don't know *what* I'm going to do,' Harry complained, champing on his pipe stem. 'I simply can't think how I'll manage without you.'

Olivia cranked the handle of the mincing machine clamped to the table of the room in the kennels. A satisfactory swirl of meat fell into the tray below. 'You'll have a kennel maid who'll be treated badly,' she said.

'Will I? Will I, indeed?' Her father tamped his pipe and relit it.

'Yes. Mo says so. That's Morfydd. She's allowed to call me Moppet.'

Yet as her heart lightened at the thought a heavy hand crept upon it and laid it low again. She stopped cranking the handle. The dogs scrabbled at their kennel doors.

'I'm glad you've got a friend, Moppet, and you know Aunt Celia will take care of you . . . if you need anything.'

The things between them that were not said . . . Her father and aunt were the safety net between Nurse's temper (with Olivia, never with Nick) and the ground.

'It's not that,' she said, nearly breaking their rule. 'Daddy, I – I spilt some of Mummy's scent. I didn't mean to, really I didn't, but if she finds out she'll . . . tell you,' she finished miserably.

She didn't lie, *ever*, but when things went wrong it always came out as though she did and her mother would say, '*You* speak to her, Harry. I can't, and she never pays any attention to Nurse,' as though Olivia wasn't nine years old and couldn't understand what was being said.

Her father laid out the dogs' bowls. Smoke rose from his pipe and he spoke around it. 'Morfydd – Mo – sorted it out, did she?'

'Yes. If we're found out she'll get into trouble too.'

Harry Wittering looked at his daughter standing resolutely before him. He removed his pipe from his mouth and gestured with it. 'Carry on winding, Moppet. Don't keep the dogs waiting.'

'It would be teasing them and that's wrong, isn't it?'

He bent and kissed her, his moustache brushing her cheek. 'Yes, it is. You didn't spill the scent on purpose, did you?'

'No! It – it fell.'

'Things do, particularly when you don't want them to most.'

'Sod's law,' she said knowledgeably.

'Moppet!'

'That's what you call it. I've heard you.'

'Your ears are too big.' He tweaked them and she wriggled away to the length of her arm, her hand still cranking the mincer.

'Will you tell Mummy about the scent?'

'If she wonders where it's gone I'll say I used it. Would it suit me?'

A deception shared three ways. She and Morfydd were safe.

The bowls were placed in the kennels and the dogs were gobbling their food when a golden retriever puppy hurtled into the room. Eve Barker dropped her bike on to the cobbled yard outside and followed the puppy in.

'Major Wittering!' she said merrily. 'Meet Lulu. I want to train her as a gundog and you're the expert. Will you help me?'

Busy, the senior spaniel, raised her head and issued a warning growl as the puppy scratched at her door. Harry picked it up.

'She's a fine beast,' he said. 'How old?'

'Eight weeks.'

'You haven't made her run all this way, have you?'

'Oh, no. She travels in my bike basket. She's very good about staying put. Will you help me with her, Major?'

Harry handed the puppy over. 'Why do you want a gundog?'

'Because I'm going to learn to shoot, of course. Haven't you heard of women shooting?'

Harry smiled. 'Yes. I've heard of women shooting. Seen 'em, too.' And more than a defenceless pheasant or rabbit.

'Well then. How do I train Lulu?'

Harry turned away and began cleaning the scraps of dog food from the table top. 'You tell her, Moppet,' he said over his shoulder.

'But —' Eve began, then rearranged her face and looked at Olivia. 'Tell me, please,' she invited.

'It's just the training for any dog for the first six months. To come and sit and stay and walk to heel, and lots of praise so she wants to please you, and the lessons not long and with lots of play, too. But no tugging games 'cos it would spoil her mouth, and no ball games because it will make her chase things instead of retrieve them . . . Is that right, Daddy?'

'Absolutely.' His back was towards them. Olivia thought the smoke from his pipe might be laughing, but his voice was very serious.

'Does she have to do the "git on in there, little girls"?'

'Not in the first six months, of necessity,' he said. 'She could try it on walks, if she likes.'

'To encourage her to work,' Olivia explained.

'Is that all?' Eve asked, seeming disappointed. The puppy wriggled and she put it down.

'It's enough for now,' Harry said, turning round. 'She's only been on the earth eight weeks. She'll bring your birds to you when you're able to shoot them, and the first step is to make her obedient. She must be, already, to sit in your bicycle basket, but she'll soon grow too big for that.'

He went out and pulled Eve's bike upright. She put Lulu in the basket. 'How long will you be away?' she asked. 'Are you really going to stay at Mar Lodge?'

'The dogs are. Nell and I are mere appendages. It's only for ten days or so.'

'I never knew dogs opened such doors! Lulu,' she said, stroking her puppy's yellow head, 'consider where you might take me.' She laughed up at Harry. 'Will you be her tutor? Oversee her education?'

'Keep me posted on her progress,' he said noncommittally.

'I'll let you know how lesson one proceeds and come for instruction on lesson two.'

She wobbled away, and Harry gazed after her. He was

being flirted with. Why, for God's sake? He was over twenty years older than the chit, and married.

And bored. As bored as she was on this gentle island. But he didn't want the kind of excitement Eve Barker was – apparently – offering him, and neither could he share in Nell's that their invitation to Mar Lodge included a bidding to lunch at Balmoral. It was hard to believe that the Duke and Duchess of York, young and carefree in previous years, were now the King and Queen and Princess Elizabeth was the heir to the throne – all because King Edward had insisted on marrying his American divorcee. Harry had considered him suspect ever since he had caused mayhem in the Muthaiga Club that night, though it was amateur compared to the mayhem caused by his abdication.

Harry always said that his spaniels were the reason for the annual invitation to Mar Lodge, but the real reason was Diana. Diana, estranged from Prince Arthur although she was not permitted to be divorced or even to live apart from her husband, and who hankered after the freedoms of Africa at least as much as Harry did. They were the very best of loving friends, she and Harry, and after killing their quota of grouse would go for walks or rides together and talk about their idyll on the rolling land below Mount Kenya – not mentioning the nights, for such moments between them were gone for ever, but remembering the days: the fun, the excitement, the danger. Neither did they discuss the reasons for Harry being here and not there, just as they did not speak of the widowed Russian countess in the house party who was Prince Arthur's latest mistress. Nell had excised Africa from her mind; it was as though she had never been there and she had repackaged her husband, forgetting his more immediate past and instead choosing to present him to their friends as a former army major.

'Well, you are,' she had said when Harry had told her

it was absurd to lay claim to a rank he had held so briefly.

'I'm a former district commissioner.'

'People don't know what that is.'

They did, of course, but she preferred an ex-army officer to an ex-colonial official.

Olivia nudged him and he looked down and encountered his daughter's brown eyes. He had long since stopped asking himself if he loved his wife or not, but when he weighed his Moppet against Kenya she won every time.

'What's the matter?' he asked.

'Do you like her?'

'Who?' His mind years and a continent away.

'Eve Barker,' she said impatiently.

'I suppose so. Do you?'

'No. I think she –'

'She's going to spoil that puppy, I agree.'

Not only ears, but eyes and brain far too big!

6

Morfydd had her half day off on Mondays and every week she would take home to Annie the generous end of Sunday's joint of mutton or beef which Gwen said would go to waste if her sister's family had no use for it. Annie Jones knew that the Major's dogs would surely have a use for it and also that Mrs Wittering was aware of her weekly donation to the Joneses – Annie would have it no other way – but was not too proud to accept charity if it meant she could feed her sons with meaty broths. Her husband Dai complained, of course (he would have preferred the meat stolen), but took more than his share none the less, just as he did the mouse's share of work on the smallholding which he had inherited from his father.

Dai hated Mo skivvying for the English, and Gwen he had long considered a traitor and lost to Wales. He held every English individual personally responsible for the wounds he had received on the *Indefatigable* at the Battle of Jutland – wounds that had left him undamaged where it mattered most. Five live children and four stillborn he had sired since coming home, and much as Annie loved the ones she had she hoped God would not bless her with any more. It was too late, wasn't it?, but if He did then another girl please. The first daughter was conceived in pre-war innocence, the second in immediate post-war optimism, the sons and the poor dead ones amid drink and resentment on one side and resignation on the other. Dai the Grump they called him, and they didn't know the half of it. Already he was taking Dan off to his meetings and Annie could feel the boy moving away from her. Boys did that; it was natural and right – but not in the direction Dai was leading Dan. Annie Jones was as Welsh as Anglesey itself, but the war with the English had been lost hundreds of years ago and there was no profit in trying to fight it again, not with guns and bombs as Annie feared Dai and his group were planning.

'With words,' she said to thirteen-year-old Dan. 'The Welsh have always been good with words. Talk the leg off a sheep, we will.'

Dan had given her a small, patronizing smile, shaken his head slightly and turned away. And was talking of leaving school and the island to find a job, no longer seeing his sister Megan's achievements as anything to be emulated. Megan was Annie's pre-war daughter, who was a teacher in far-off Aberystwyth and travelling on the Continent this summer to broaden her mind. She was due, next year, to take over the village school when the present headmistress retired. Annie didn't want Dan to be a teacher, not necessarily that, but she was impressed by Megan's views on education. It unlocked doors, she said, and every child could find the key if there was the will and wit to do so. Dai was showing his eldest son a different door entirely, and would lead his other three – if he didn't come to his senses before then – the same way. He and his friends would make an *Indefatigable* out of Anglesey: an explosion in the sea and those who survived as mutilated as he was. They had said, the men down in London who made the decisions, that Great Britain had won the Battle of Jutland; if it had then pray for Germany. There were wives there too, as heaven knew.

Annie talked it over with her post-war daughter. Mo

was not clever with books as Megan was, but she had a natural intelligence and a vision of the wider world put into her head by her mother as Annie, seeing her own world curtailed by pregnancy after pregnancy, thrust her dreams upon her.

'I'll try to talk to him,' Mo said.

'School's a waste of time,' Dan asserted at supper that night, and his brothers listened since he received no cuff from their father.

Mo cleared away Dan's plate. 'School's the best use of time at your age,' she said.

'You left quick enough.'

'Mam and Da skimped the brains on me to share out among the rest of you. Plaid Cymru wants intelligent, educated men not simple boys.'

'It's not the Plaid, it's –' Dan began, then burst out, his voice humiliatingly childish: 'It's *secret!*'

'Nothing,' Mo said, with just the right amount of light dismissiveness, 'Gareth Evans does is secret, and our da's not far behind.'

'Now, girl,' her father warned, trying to get to his feet to face her but his injured leg robbed him of authority. 'Don't you bring your fancy ways in here.'

'Since when has the truth been fancy?'

'You work for the English,' Dan said. 'The English who steal our land and take the profits from it to spend in London while the Welsh starve.'

Mo returned his plate to him. 'If you're starving, eat the fat and potatoes you left while the rest of us have our pudding.'

Dan pushed the plate aside. 'It's for the pig,' he muttered.

'And that's to starve after you do? I didn't know you cared for it so much. The world is grey, Daniel Jones, not black and white. There are good Englishmen and bad Welshmen. And Major Wittering,' she added, 'owns no

167

land or even the house he lives in. He's stolen nothing from us and puts food in your belly in return for your aunt's and my honest work. Remember that.'

Dan fled from the table in turbulent fury, but the smaller boys had, perhaps, taken the lesson in. They ate their gooseberry pie garnished with cream from their own cow with relish. And noted that their father did too.

After supper Mo and Annie settled down with a companionable pile of mending and darning. The little ones were in bed, Dai had gone out and Dan had not yet returned. There was no purpose in worrying. He would have to come home, for there was nowhere else he could go.

'It's what I said made him run off,' Morfydd said. 'I'll be out and find him if he's not back soon.'

'He can take care of himself,' Annie said, more for her own comfort than Morfydd's.

Morfydd took up a shirt of Rhys's and thought of another child whose clothes were more worn than this was, and less carefully mended. Annie's children at least started the day looking tidy and well cared for. 'Mam,' she said, 'could I bring Olivia for a visit this week? She's that lost and lonely with the Major away and she'd like to see the calf and the piglets.'

Gwen's gossip had not featured the daughter of the house and Annie had been aghast at what she had learned from Morfydd. Her kind soul stirred as she exclaimed, 'No need to ask, Mo! Bring her. Tell me the day and I'll bake some buns for tea.'

'I'll have to clear it with the nurse.'

'Let her come too, and the boy. There'll be enough for everyone,' Annie said peaceably. The back door clicked and she stiffened. Dan sidled in, his hair and jacket wet. 'Raining outside, is it?' his mother said, well-rehearsed at concealing relief.

'Drizzle.'

Morfydd cast her mending aside and went to him. 'I didn't mean to upset you, Dan. I'm sorry. We saved some pie for you. Sit down and I'll bring it.'

'Not hungry,' he said, shouldering past her to the stairs.

Morfydd turned back and met her mother's eyes.

'It's not your fault,' Annie said. 'It's the way he's become.'

'Why? And how, so quickly?'

Annie shrugged, but it was in defeat rather than indifference. 'He's made the wrong men heroes,' she said.

7

Olivia missed her father, of course, but actually it seemed she would have rather a good time while he was away. Aunt Celia had taken her in Uncle Donald's motor car to the Barkers' house and they'd had a delicious morning looking at samples of cloth for the bridesmaids' dresses. May Barker wasn't getting married until the spring but Olivia's co-bridesmaid was here on holiday with her parents and it was, so Olivia understood, an ideal opportunity to get the girls together to see what suited the two of them. Olivia was invited to tea later in the week as the grown-ups had decided the children could entertain each other. Olivia was doubtful because she mistrusted girls who wore pink ribbons in their hair and said 'Go away, you dirty thing' to friendly retriever puppies, but was willing to give it a try since it meant another trip in Uncle Donald's Bentley. Two, in fact, as Aunt Celia – more even-handed than her sister – had said it was unfair on Nick and promised to take them both for a day out.

And it was Aunt Celia who had told Nurse there was 'No question, none whatsoever!' that Olivia should be allowed to go with Morfydd to see her farm, and 'Nonsense!' when Nurse muttered about Morfydd gaining for herself an extra half day off. She bent to talk to Nick, who was wondering whether tears were appropriate.

'Where would you like us to drive to on Friday? It's up to you to decide.'

'Carnaervon,' he said immediately, his face clearing. It was his favourite place, apart from London which he claimed to remember, and the only town within sensible reach.

'Carnaervon it is, then,' Celia said, marvelling at how two siblings could be so utterly different.

Morfydd marvelled, too, as Olivia steered her bicycle in a figure of eight in the lane and drew alongside.

'A calf and piglets. What else?'

'The cow, the sow, hens, ducks and a dog.'

'I haven't seen a proper dog for five whole days.' Harry had only taken two spaniels, but the others were staying with a friend of his; Olivia could have taken care of them but Nurse would not accept the responsibility, she said.

'What's proper?' Morfydd asked.

'Not a puppy.'

'Clip's not a puppy, but he's not like your da's dogs.'

'Really?' Olivia dismounted from her bike and pushed it along beside Morfydd. 'What is he like, then?'

'Black and white and hairy.'

'You're teasing. Daddy's dogs are like that, or brown and white.'

'Clip's nose is pointed.'

'Then he must be a collie. Is he?'

'Partly. Perhaps.'

Olivia was silent as she thought about this. 'Never mind,' she decided. 'I'll love him anyway. I love all dogs and I love the whole of today. It's an adventure, isn't it? Better than going to Carnaervon.'

'We're only visiting my mam,' Morfydd said, worried about the investment of expectation the child was making.

'And a calf and piglets. Piglets! Do they wear vests like in *Winnie-the-Pooh*?'

'Moppet –'

'A joke. I know they don't.' She remounted her bike. 'Have we far to go?'

'No. There's my brother Rhys.'

Out in the lane, he was, shading his eyes against the sun until he was sure who it was and then running towards them. Morfydd could feel Olivia tense, but before she could do anything about it Rhys was upon them.

'A bicycle!' he said breathlessly, gazing at it and ignoring his sister's greeting.

'Want a ride?' Olivia offered, understanding the coinage. Rhys ran with the big gang of boys at school, the one led by his brother Dan which routinely terrorized the girls during break time if they dared stray from the tiny patch of worn grass that was their playground.

Rhys did not recognize Olivia, however, as, his eyes still on the machine, he thrust his hands in his pockets and rocked on his heels. 'I might want one,' he said cautiously. 'But it's a while since I've ridden a bike, see?'

'Oh, you never forget,' Olivia said, letting go of the thing so he had to take it.

'Try the back field,' Morfydd suggested. 'Neither you nor it can come to harm there . . . and mind that shirt!' she called after him as he scampered the bike up the lane and through a gap in the hedge amid a scatter of chickens.

'Are they yours?' Olivia asked, her bike already forgotten.

'They are, the daft creatures.'

'Gwen says we eat their eggs.'

'So you do. We'll collect some later on and take them back with us.'

'Do we pay for them?'

Morfydd ruffled her hair. 'We do,' she said.

Annie was like her sister Gwen, grey-haired and broad and smelling of baking, but unlike Gwen she was outgoing and full to the brim with affection. Olivia was perfectly astounded to have herself clutched to a large, pinafored bosom and to be given, for no reason she could think of, a great, smacking kiss. In fact she found it rather embarrassing. Fearsome Dan was there, skulking around the kitchen, but when Mo told her mother about Rhys and the bicycle he brightened and made for the door, followed by his two younger brothers.

'Take care you don't damage it!' Annie shouted into an empty space, and to Morfydd she said: 'What if they do? It would be dreadful.'

'I haven't damaged it, and I wreck everything,' Olivia said, wanting to put Annie's mind at ease: the bike would keep the boys away.

Annie gazed at her. 'You speak Welsh,' she said.

'At school. I'm not allowed to at home, but I'm not at home now.' All the Welsh on Anglesey were bilingual, and could write in both languages too. Her father said it was good to know languages, but Nurse called Welsh heathen and ugly.

Annie fingered the frayed collar of Oliva's blouse and gave her a push. 'I'm sure you don't wreck everything,' she said in English. 'Off you go with Mo and see the calf and the piglets, and later there'll be hot buns to eat.'

She would not have believed it if she hadn't witnessed it herself: that a nine-year-old child whose mother was staying with royalty and wearing a different gown every night was dressed in tatters Annie would be ashamed to put on her children, even for an afternoon on a mucky farm.

And the child as sweet as a nut and willing to do anything to please, so thankful to be allowed to give the pig her swill and thrilled when old Clip waved his tail at her . . .

But the shame of it when the boys returned Olivia's bicycle, the saddle raised to way higher than was safe for her to ride. The smaller boys ran away laughing, but Dan stood his ground and raised a spanner against his mother's fury.

'I'll fix it, Mam,' he said mildly, and did so, knowing that the comfort of Olivia's day was gone although she kept saying it was all right and what was the fuss about? He had calculated how it would be, having learned to hate the English and their works, no matter how innocent and already damaged these might be.

Harry and Nell came home and quickly September came too. Back to school. Previously the Welsh Olivia put on like an autumn coat when she arrived and shed when she left had ensured she did not stand out. Now she was targeted by Daniel Jones, and bullied and teased. She lost her temper and yelled that she had been born in Africa, but it made no difference. She was still a nasty little English girl. One day she surprised herself and Dan by returning his sly pinch with a volley of punches, done in full view of the teacher, and was rewarded with two hundred lines of 'I must not fight in school'. These she completed by torchlight in bed – luckily she no longer shared a room with Nick – for she could not begin to explain to Nurse how she had come to receive such an ignominious punishment. Then Nurse caught a cold and Morfydd came to fetch Olivia from school. Wanting to see the junior teacher over whom her sister Megan would be presiding in a year's time and with whom Morfydd had attended this same school, Morfydd wandered into the playground and discovered her brother and his friends taunting Olivia. She knocked a few heads together and had them hanging shamefully before her as she berated the boys.

'If you must exercise your strength – and I'm not saying you should, mind – then do it with a worthy opponent. Cowards. *Cowards*!' And to Olivia as they walked away: 'Why didn't you say what he was doing to you? Moppet, why not?'

'Couldn't,' Olivia said, shrugging but enormously relieved.

Morfydd well remembered the etiquette of school which dictated you suffered a broken nose rather than earn the title of tell-tale. 'You could have given me the whisper, Moppet, and I'd have chanced to be passing before. Next time, eh?'

'Yes,' Olivia said, and was grateful that Dan's only revenge was to ignore her the next day.

Morfydd, though, for the rest of her life would worry about what she had said to Dan that day had cost them all.

Saturday. Olivia and her father were out mushrooming and they met, having scrutinized every inch of the field they had walked, and compared baskets.

'You have done well,' Harry said admiringly.

'We need lots more. Gwen dries them and we eat them right through the winter.'

She was about to climb the gate and investigate a promising gleam in the next field when he caught her arm.

'I've been wanting to talk to you, Moppet. Are you happy at school?'

'Happy?' she repeated, and considered the concept. You went to school; were you supposed to be happy there? 'I don't think so, but it doesn't matter.'

'Of course it matters! You could go to Nick's school, perhaps,' he said. It was run by two English spinsters and considered more suitable for delicate Nick than the village school – and Nick was not going to learn a nasty heathen language. Harry hadn't concerned himself with his children's education before now and had been astonished to be accosted by the maid Morfydd as he pottered around in his room in the kennels. She had been nervous but determined, and forthright as she saw the expression on Major Wittering's face change from a general wish not to be disturbed to a genuine anxiety about his daughter. 'Or,' Harry said, 'perhaps you should go away to school.'

'And leave you?' Olivia cried, dropping her basket of mushrooms and launching herself at him. 'Don't make me, please! I like school, really I do. I'm very happy there.'

And, curiously, it turned out to be true. Her lines for fighting had given her status. Dan continued to ignore her and his brother Rhys brought an apple for her on her birthday.

'It's from my mam,' Rhys said.

And somehow the boys' playground wasn't frightening any more.

Another walk; the mushroom season was over and there was a light frost on the ground. Harry had three rabbits and a pair of wood pigeon in his bag, and two young spaniels had been learning their business. Harry stopped walking and pulled his watch from his waistcoat pocket.

'Another minute,' he said, and called the dogs and ordered them to sit. 'Now,' he said quietly. 'The eleventh hour of the eleventh day of the eleventh month. Let us remember the fallen.'

He removed his cap and bowed his head, and the child beside him did so too. Busy lay down in the ensuing two minutes, but there was no other movement or noise. Even the wind seemed to share the silence.

'And a prayer, Moppet. A prayer for no more war.'

After a while he replaced his cap and Olivia asked: 'Might there be another war, then?'

'Herr Hitler's heading that way, I fear, in spite of what our masters in London think. He's giving himself a dress rehearsal in Spain.'

'Will you join up?'

'I'll have to do something. It's one's duty.'

'Aren't you too old? And then there's your wound from the last shower.'

'Shower!' Harry said, laughing.

'It's what you call it.'

'I know. It seems funny coming from you, though.'

'But it's not funny, is it? War.'

He dropped a kiss on her head. 'No, it's not funny. It's the most serious thing there is.'

A yellow fireball streaked across the field and erupted among the spaniels. Olivia's heart sank. They often met Eve Barker and her dog when they were out walking and, although Olivia had to admit she was training Lulu well, she did not like the woman. She was always a bit too nice to Olivia, asking her opinion on Lulu's progress and then not listening when Olivia gave it, instead turning to Harry and talking of other things.

'The gun you recommended I buy has arrived at last and I can't wait to try it out,' she said gaily. 'If you'll teach me how to load it and aim I can begin practising. Except how *do* I practise? It would be awful to injure birds because I couldn't kill them outright.'

Olivia kicked at a frosted clump of grass. It had been beautiful before and now it was dirty and ordinary, and she was glad. 'Why do you want to kill birds?' she said. 'It's much nicer to look at them, unless you're like Daddy and shoot for the pot, or magpies to protect the songbirds' nests, and you never, ever miss.' She was flabbergasted by her impertinence and anger and faded into silence to commune with it alone.

'Well,' Eve Barker said, with a brittle laugh, 'it's a point of view, I suppose.'

'I've been wanting to teach Moppet to shoot,' Harry said, as though he had heard none of this. 'You can have your lessons together. How about that?'

And thought, relieved, that he must have mistaken Eve Barker these past three months, for she clapped gloved hands together, declared his idea was splendid, called her obedient puppy to her and waved goodbye.

8

He was, though, being stalked by a creature more dangerous than any he had encountered in Africa, and one with infinitely more cunning and patience. At some point during the next year predator and prey reached stalemate, looked each other in the eyes and swapped roles. It took Harry a while to appreciate this, however. Diana was once more on his mind, for Prince Arthur had died and she was now a widow. Harry had written her a letter of condolence and received a brief thank-you note in reply. She was in mourning and had been swallowed up by her extensive family. She seemed as lost to, and distant from, Harry as she had done when they had returned from their safari so many years ago. There had been no visit to Mar Lodge this year for Nell to boast about, and perhaps there would not be again. Harry had not realized how much he had cherished those few hours alone with Diana in the wild beauty of Scotland, and his heart felt unexpectedly vulnerable when he had thought it forever unassailable.

It was as hopeless a cause as it had ever been. Diana was far away in London and Eve — as a reward, she said, for the sentence she had served on Anglesey — was allowed to go there too, to visit friends she had known in Berlin, and Harry discovered that he missed her. Missed her presence and the recklessness it vaguely promised, and resented – as he was designed to do – that Anglesey, including him, was lightly compared to a term in prison. She was to be gone for a month, and that was extended to five weeks. Her mother shook her head at the round of parties that preceded Christmas 1938 and wondered, sighing, if Eve would be home for the festive season, then focused her attention on her less unpredictable daughters: May, married in the spring and with a baby due in the New Year, and Claire newly engaged to a satisfactorily rich and well-connected young man.

Nell, too, was discontented. Her soul belonged in the south and she considered Anglesey a halfway house between there and Africa. She had forced Harry into the big leap; only a small step remained. Christmas was fun on the island because people came and opened their holiday houses, but it was also a reminder of the long, dark months before Easter and the summer. January and February on Anglesey were equated in her mind with the rains in Fort Richard. She could get away, of course, but that would mean a parting from Nick who, she now said, should be at a 'proper school', but she rejected absolutely the idea of his boarding; and Olivia's education was belatedly used in the argument to take them south.

'She's eleven years old, Harry. She can't stay at the village school for ever, speaking Welsh. I'm sure our friends think it strange.'

'I'm sure they do,' Harry said, trying not to sound sarcastic. 'How about the new place in Llangefni? The Cowleys seem pleased with it.'

'How would she get there every day?'

'That can't be an insurmountable problem, Nell. I could take her, or we could arrange something with the Cowleys.'

'It would be an awful nuisance.'

'We're not moving south. There's going to be a war.'

'Of course there isn't! You men are all the same.'

'Hitler has got to be stopped, and it's a fool who says the German people will do it on their own.'

'I'm bored of Anglesey,' she said.

'So am I. I always was. It's you who insisted we leave Kenya, remember.'

'It was killing me.'

'London would kill me, Nell. Don't ask me to live in or near a city. Please don't.'

'You don't care about me or Nick. Think of him, at least.'

'Oh, God help me!' he said and went to the kennels. The dogs, sensing a mood, tucked their tails down and curled around him anxiously. 'It's all right,' he told them. 'It's not your fault.' He realized he was gripping his pipe so tightly between his teeth that his jaw was aching.

Olivia appeared in the doorway. 'Daddy –' she began.

He went to her, somehow thinking her agitation was due to the row he'd had with Nell. 'Darling, I'm sorry. It's the talk of war. It's making everyone edgy.'

She twisted out of his arms. She was already tall. She was wearing his old shooting coat against the cold and the wind and it didn't look ridiculous on her.

'Rhys is here,' she said. 'Mo and Gwen are frantic. Dan's been arrested by the police.' She grabbed his hands. 'You'll help, won't you?'

Relieved to have something constructive to do, he hurried with her to where Rhys and Mo were waiting hopefully outside the coach house where the Witterings' motor car was kept.

'Where is Dan?' Harry asked Rhys.

'Bangor,' he said, gulping. He couldn't cry in front of the Major and Olivia; he was thirteen and thirteen-year-olds didn't cry, but there'd never been a portentous visit from Morgan the Police before, not one where he refused a cup of tea because the news he brought was so bad and his mother had wept for the shame of it.

'*Bangor?*' the Major said, suddenly sounding cheerful, as though the whole thing was a grand adventure. 'Then we'll need rugs and coats, won't we?'

Morfydd flew to the house for them, and Rhys's mind was distracted by being invited to crank the motor's engine so the Major could get her out and ready to move. Morfydd reappeared with an assortment of warm clothing, Gwen accompanying her.

'Mrs Wittering –?' Gwen asked.

'Tell her to expect us when she sees us,' Harry said. Mo and Rhys climbed into the back seat of the car and Olivia into the front. They set off. 'What has Dan done, do you know?' Harry called over his shoulder.

'Tried to blow up the Menai Bridge, by all accounts,' Morfydd said.

The car swerved as Harry tried to contain his surprise. In the back seat Rhys gulped again. Olivia gasped.

'I see,' Harry said calmly. 'Should we pick up your mother and father? Perhaps they ought to be there when we get Dan.'

'Da's off and Mam has to stay with the little ones,' Rhys said in a high voice.

They rattled along into the December dusk, the noise of the motor making much conversation difficult and Rhys, in spite of his anxiety, began to enjoy his first ride in a car. He even achieved a laugh when they reached the Menai Bridge and the Major made a pantomime of inspecting it and pronouncing it undamaged.

He was all seriousness, however, when he parked outside the police station and they went inside. The others were shown into a side room while Harry discussed Dan's case with the station's inspector.

'Three boys with not much more than fireworks,' the man said. 'The thing's built like a castle, as you know, and they wouldn't have made a dent in it.' He straightened papers on his desk. 'It's the intent, isn't it? The intent. It was murderous.'

'Who are the other boys?'

'They're from here in Bangor, and that's another worry.'

Harry thought about it. 'Because it indicates organization?' he said then.

'*An* organization,' the Inspector said heavily. 'How else would a boy from the island and two from here get together in a caper like this? Your lad's the youngest so we could argue he was influenced, but against that he's travelled the furthest and made the most effort.'

'Is he frightened?'

'He is at the moment, I'm told,' the Inspector said with a slight smile. 'We could get a magistrate to frighten him more – him and the others – but that could have an opposite effect and make them heroes to their mates.' He straightened pens this time, and it seemed to decide him. 'A warning,' he said. 'The others will have to wait until their fathers come off their shift, but we'll have young Daniel in here now. A major and an inspector. It's more brass than he'll have seen in his young life.'

Dan knew Major Wittering as a friendly man – English and therefore the enemy but friendly none the less – and one who gave out threepenny bits when the mood was on him. A soft touch. He did not know that once he had been the representative of a colonial government and in charge of a swath of Kenya, dispensing punishment and justice to many thousand people and enforcing it through personal authority. Dan was faced with that authority now as, after a lecture from the policeman with a lot of silver on his uniform, he was released into the Major's custody and told that a full report of the incident would be sent to Constable Morgan and his superiors at Llangefni. He had been scared on his own in the cell and had thought, while the policeman was speaking, that he would be spending the next five years there. When he understood he was going home his relief was followed by triumph and contempt. He and the others were fools to have been caught, and to have gone for such an ambitious target, but these people were fools to dismiss what they had done as a childish prank. Their bombs weren't big enough, but they knew how to make them: it was only a matter of acquiring the ingredients. Then he caught the Major's eye and had the uncomfortable feeling that his mind was being read; quickly he assumed a penitent expression and the Inspector stood up.

'I hope, my lad, I won't be seeing you again,' he said.

'No, sir,' Dan said, registering and storing the fact that the man was English. Why should he have power in Wales?

He avoided the Major's gimlet gaze after that and even murmured 'Sorry' as his sister greeted him with a sad, 'Oh, Dan –' Already he felt the fire in him, and then he heard, but dared not acknowledge, John and Dylan's defiant singing from the cells downstairs. He would have liked to have joined them, but reckoned that would have got him back in the cells and he was of more value free.

Have to keep his head down, wouldn't he, for a few months, be a good boy and give Morgan the Police no bother until the old fool's attention was taken by something really serious – the poaching of a brace of his lordship's pheasants, say – and Dan could get to the meetings again, get active. His bloody almighty lordship didn't realize anyway the barns on his estate were host for local meetings, and neither did Morgan the Police. Best kept that way, too.

He was glad of the darkness as he was thrust into the back seat of the Major's car between Morfydd and Rhys. Even Major Wittering couldn't read his mind in the dark, could he?

Nell was already dressed when Harry arrived home, having dropped Rhys and Dan at the Joneses' place and reassured Annie that her boy was not a criminal; his father was still not there. Harry warded off Morfydd's thanks, kissed his daughter good night and shot upstairs to change into evening dress. Nell followed him into his dressing room.

'I had to help, Nell,' he said. 'I'm sorry if it's going to make us late.'

'It won't – not very, anyway. What happened? Gwen was incoherent.'

As Harry changed he told her about the events in Bangor. 'There'll be more trouble,' he concluded. 'Young Dan has a look in his eye.'

'Poor Annie. It's dreadful to worry about one's son.'

'Mind you,' Harry said, taking up his hairbrushes, 'you have to admire his pluck, however insane his plan was. These nationalists have a point. It's their country, after all.'

'That's what you always said about the Africans.'

'It's true. No one will rejoice more than I when they get their independence, believe me.'

She sighed. 'I believe you.'

'But until that happens one can only do one's best. Govern them and treat them with respect – that and feel privileged to be allowed to share their country with them.'

'Harry, you are not in Kenya now.'

'Oh,' he said. 'I'm not, am I?' He hadn't been for more than eight years, and still he was ambushed by a notion that he was on an extended home leave. Absurd! This one must have been spawned by a recent letter from the Fanshawes, containing the familiar tales of locusts, of a disaster in the *shambas*, of the price of coffee. Lucy and Louis were surviving the Depression, but only just. Harry stared at his image in the looking glass: your English gent togged in ridiculous gear about to attend a party where he would see and chat to people he had seen last night and would do tomorrow.

'What we were talking about earlier,' Nell said. 'About going to England. Not London,' she pleaded, 'but somewhere closer to it.'

He had forgotten their quarrel and was astounded that it could be revived like this, and heading down the same road.

'Nick –' she began.

'Can go to the village school,' Harry said wearily, 'when he's too old for the Misses Ramptons' establishment. Or he can board at somewhere suitable among others of his so-called class.'

'No!'

'Why? And why isn't what's good enough for your daughter good enough for your son?'

'Boys are different. Nick's different!'

'I compromised before,' Harry said. 'I left my life in Africa for you and exchanged it for Anglesey. I left my job, so now I have to train and sell dogs to get by. Make me compromise again and I'll shoot myself.'

'You don't need to sell the dogs. I have enough –'

'Don't say it. *Don't!* I think it a thousand times a day, and I die a little each time I accept a cheque. My only dignity is that my dogs are the best and most expensive in the country, and I will never have to beg my wife for money to buy tobacco with. No more, Nell. Let's go to this bloody party.'

Eve Barker had come home at last, and she was there. She had learned to fly, she said, and it was the greatest fun. She had piloted Freddie's plane home . . . Oh, this was Freddie.

He was an utter idiot, all hair oil and wet lips and stupid loud laughter. What could Eve see in that? And Harry recognized, with a shattering mixture of elation, relief and fear, jealousy within himself.

9

'Oh, yes,' Lady Firling said. 'She knew what she was doing and didn't mind the damage she caused. She cast the fly upon the water over and over again with nothing to show for it, until he moved a bit, moved once more, nibbled at it and –'

'And what?' Emma said as Lady Firling broke off.

'Angie's here. My hairdresser. I do like having my hair done once a week. It makes me feel years younger.'

It was the second visit Emma had paid to Claire Firling, née Barker, Eve's sister. She lived in the house, now an old people's home, that had once belonged to her family. No, she had said. She did not find it disturbing. It had hardly changed – though the bathrooms were better and the place much warmer, thank God – and it was nice to be among the friendly ghosts. It was better than the place being turned into holiday flats, which had been the fate of other big houses on the island – like the Witterings' house – or pretentious hotels.

Lady Firling was in the plot along with the other people Emma was seeing here on Anglesey. They were playing tricks on her, as had Emma's mother and grandmother. Annie, Gwen, old Rhys and his sister Megan would get to a point in their story then say she'd have to talk to someone else. Elunid had told her it was only because they so enjoyed the rarity of someone eager to listen to their ramblings, but Emma had her suspicions about Elunid too.

Emma's mother had said it was therapy, Emma recalled. Perhaps it was, and if so it was working. She had never felt healthier, more relaxed and more motivated in her life. She had looked at herself in the mirror that morning and had hardly recognized the person there: pink cheeks and shining eyes and hair but, Lord, her jeans getting harder to zip up each day.

'I must stop eating!' she'd exclaimed to Elunid downstairs.

'Dear me,' Elunid had responded, sympathy in her voice. 'Listening's hungry work, isn't it?'

And had watched, amused, as Emma downed a kipper and three thick slices of toast and marmalade. Emma realized now that a half-eaten Danish pastry had appeared in her hand. Oh well, she could hardly return it to the plate.

'Be a darling and wheel me over, would you?' Claire Firling said. 'I expect you think it odd that someone my age should care about her appearance, but it's that which keeps me going, I'm sure.'

'I don't think it odd,' Emma said, swallowing the pastry. 'You look amazing, anyway.'

Her stupid legs, as Claire called them, had given up on her but she sat in her wheelchair like a queen, the epitome of fading – but far from faded – elegance.

'We haven't finished, have we?' she said as Emma delivered her to the hairdresser. 'When will you come again?'

Emma stood outside the house Eve Barker had once lived in and gazed down at the Menai Strait. Already she loved Anglesey and felt at home to a degree she would not have believed possible ten days ago. The tiny area contained an astonishing variety of landscape, from the windswept west around Rhosneigr with its bleak dunes and pale sand, to the east where the sand was reddish in the curved bays embraced by rocky headlands beyond which, to the south, the mountains of Snowdonia occasionally deigned to appear. Parts of the south-west of the island could have been transported from Sussex, and the north – though Emma had not yet penetrated there – from, according to Elunid, who said Emma need not worry about exploring Holyhead, any of England's run-down ports. The people, too, were a variety. The language was Welsh and the English accents Home Counties or northern.

Dismissed by Lady Firling ... Where next? She had been as far as the gates of the house her grandmother had lived in as a child but had been intimidated by the 'Strictly Private' sign. Old Rhys, however, Morfydd's sister, Annie's son, had said no one was living there now, would not be until July or August and there was nothing to stop Emma having a snoop around.

Emma got into the Porsche and drove up the drive her great-grandmother and grandfather, as friends of the Barker family, must have known well. Had Harold George Albert taken the fly dangled before his nose and swallowed it? Things were beginning to fit into place.

The lane beyond the sign was rutted and had grass growing down the middle of it. After a short while a high brick wall appeared on the right behind some trees. It continued for about two hundred yards then took an abrupt ninety-degree turn away. Beyond it was the house, the lawn in front of it studded with daffodils. The lane ended in a yard at the far side, and Emma parked the car there and got out. There was no sound except for the wind, bringing with it a dashing of rain. Emma hunched her shoulders against it and other presences, marched through a pair of open wrought-iron gates to the front door, pressed each of the four bells there and knocked loudly for good measure.

No response, of course, apart from a distant bleating of sheep. Emma peered through one of the huge windows to the left of the door. The room she could see had been divided; it must have been part of her great-grandparents' drawing room or dining room, but the furnishings in it now were utilitarian and on one wall hung a fishing net complete with floats and decorated with shells. The window on the right revealed a similar room, similarly furnished.

The yard was rimmed with outbuildings used as garages, and for storing garden machinery and beach paraphernalia. One had once been the kennels where field trial champion springer spaniels had lived and where, also, H. G. A. Wittering had a room to which he fled when he wanted to be alone. Impossible to say which building it had been.

The rain began to fall harder. Emma returned to the car for her waterproof jacket and hat, then went to investigate what was behind the wall she had seen as she approached.

It was a garden, a secret garden, entered by another wrought-iron gate, semi-neglected, its lawns more like rough-cut fields and the daffodils and narcissi growing there seeming out of place. Emma wandered along pathways, the trees and shrubs overhung with roses, feeling the peace and the enchantment of the place envelop her and imagining how it would have been before the war, in summer and under the sun. Garden parties here, the ladies in hats and long dresses – she was getting a little hazy about the fashions of the thirties, but never mind – and the gentlemen in white flannels and striped blazers. One young woman casting a fly on the water . . .

She turned a corner and stood for a moment, bemused, unable to take in what was before her: a bright green all-weather tennis court, its surface spattered with last autumn's leaves, surrounded by a high, chain-linked fence. Beyond it was a summerhouse type of thing made of hideous red wood.

'Oh, go to hell!' Emma said out loud, a surge of real anger rising in her as the spell of the garden was broken. Then: 'Idiot!' she said, laughing at herself as she turned back towards the gate. 'Complete, total idiot!'

It was six o'clock and still raining when Emma reached the main road. Too wet for a run along the beach at Rhosneigr, exercise which made her fitter but no slimmer. A sign indicated Menai Bridge to the right, the town developed around the Anglesey side of the bridge which, fifty-odd years ago, three boys had tried to blow up. That story wasn't finished with.

She would go to Rhys and his sister Megan's bungalow, then.

Rhys's wife had run the guest house until a few years ago when she had died and Elunid and young Rhys had taken it over. It was more of a hobby than a business, Emma gathered – for such places were marginal with so many holiday cottages and flats available – but more than either it was a home for Annie and Gwen, and would be for as long as they had breath in their bodies and Elunid the energy to take care of them.

'And when they die she'll have us in there,' old Rhys had told Emma. 'She'd mother a stone, that one, a stone or some horrible wet thing from the sea,' and had added, his head shaking sadly, 'Such tragedy she couldn't have children of her own.'

It was Rhys who had intervened about Emma paying for her room and board. The rate for bed and breakfast was advertised, but Emma ate other meals and could not discover the cost of these. There was no restaurant and no menu.

'I must pay,' Emma said as Elunid, near to tears, had wailed, 'But you're family, almost. As good as.'

'If you won't let me I'll move somewhere else.'

'You wouldn't dare!'

'How could you stop me?'

'Dad!' Elunid had appealed, and Rhys had looked into the two sets of agonized eyes and smiled.

'You must take her money, Elunid,' he had said. 'Where's the point in having a customer go elsewhere?'

'And I will,' Emma stated doggedly.

Rhys suggested Elunid work out a flat daily rate, which she had done, hating it, and Emma left the money on the dresser in the kitchen each morning. It meant frequent journeys to the bank for cash and in retrospect Emma wished Rhys had arranged she pay by weekly cheque, but she did not dare renegotiate with Elunid; and neither did she trust her to bank the cheque.

Emma overtook a tractor and resisted the car's urge to go faster on the empty, rain-slicked road. Rhys was a bit generous with the whisky at this time of day and Megan was sure to produce nuts and crisps – apologizing for the arthritis that denied her the ability to bake anything more substantial – and there was Elunid's supper to look forward to.

If this was therapy she could cope with it. She wanted to know more – everything – but she would need a new pair of jeans.

10

Annie went to visit her daughter in the cosy quarters above the schoolhouse. She brought with her a cloth-covered dish containing rabbit stew.

'Major Wittering gave us three. It'll only need a bit of heating up, and here's potatoes and turnips to go with it.'

'Mam,' Megan said, with great affection, 'I'm grown up now. I can look after myself.'

'It still seems strange, you here and us just up the lane. Not right, somehow.'

'A cup of tea for you?' Megan said, taking the dish and then filling the kettle.

'Thank you.' Annie sat herself in one of the two chairs about the fireplace. 'It's nice here, isn't it? Peaceful.'

'I'll come home for supper, Mam, the nights I'm not busy marking. I've told you that.'

'And I've told you it's not good the boys should muddle their sister with their teacher.'

'I won't let them! I'm a professional. It's why I went away these years, to stop such things being said.'

'They say fine things, Megan. They say the school's transformed.'

'It's gone modern, is all.' Megan, teapot in hand, opened the door and listened downstairs to her two youngest brothers in the schoolroom. 'They never did painting

192

before,' she said, closing the door, 'Imagine that! And no proper games.'

'Painting!' her mother said.

'It develops their creative side. I don't forget the basics, mind, in English and in Welsh. It's a wide world these children will be living in.'

'Rhys is at his books so much it's hard to get him away.'

'Yes, and who's his teacher?' Megan said. 'There's no muddle in my head, Mam, or in his. Or in the little ones', either.'

'You don't want to be mixing with us too often,' Annie said, not meeting her daughter's eyes as she took the cup of tea she was offered.

'Mam, our blood's mixed and there's nothing even you can do about it,' Megan said, exasperated; and, after a while: 'How's Dan? Have you told Da yet?'

'No.' It was two weeks since the appalling incident at Bangor and there had been no gossip about it. But if the talk should begin Annie did not want her schoolteacher daughter any nearer to the disgrace than she had to be. Annie had kept her distance during Megan's first term here, so things could settle down and Megan establish herself, and had been looking forward to a closer relationship, but Dan had scuppered that for the time being.

Annie had been trying to avoid exploding with pride these past four months at the comments about Megan. Megan had been shocked at how lax Miss Edwards had become and no fewer than six of the children from the school would be at the grammars in Llangefni next term, Megan having faced up to the people in charge and yelled at them that it wasn't the children's fault their teacher was old and they hadn't passed the exams. So what if they had to go in at the wrong time and at the wrong ages? They wouldn't be behind the others, not for long anyway, because she'd give them tuition until they caught up. The authorities had been no match for her and Megan's 'grammar class' had been the talk of the village.

And consider how it would change if Dan's escapade got public! Annie tried to think of it as that, but Morgan the Police was regularly at his lordship's estate where Dan was working (temporary, he said, a curl on his lips; a man had a right to a wage, and what could he do when there was no choice of where to get it . . . yet) checking up on him and taking everything most seriously.

'No,' Annie said to Megan. 'I haven't told your da. I'm frightened he'd laugh, see, and praise Dan. I'm frightened,' she continued after a pause, 'he was there, that afternoon.'

'Mam!'

'He wasn't home, was he? And he's never asked why the attention to Dan.'

'And he hopped away, I suppose, on his one good leg and the healthy young 'uns stood and waited to be arrested.'

'Major Wittering brought Dan home in his motor. Next morning Dan's bike was there in the shed. It was his half day, and he'd gone to the bridge from work.'

'And he rode his bike to work,' Megan said, sighing.

'He'd ride it to bed if he could.' It was his pride and joy, saved up for and slaved over and polished every Sunday.

'Can Da ride it, though?' Megan asked.

'Not fast, maybe, but fast enough. He'd figured out that a grown man arrested among boys would make the police see the whole thing differently. Or Gareth Evans had, more like.' She drained her cup and stood up. 'It's why you should stay away from us, Megan. There'll be more trouble and it'll affect your standing here, and everyone saying how good you are.'

Megan took the cup and put it down. 'I've been meaning to tell you,' she said conversationally, 'I've opened an account at Jones Brothers in Llangefni. You and Rhys had better go in on the bus and buy his uniform for school. Everything on the list, now. I don't want my brother short. I'm paid well and don't have much use for my money.' She smiled. 'Not when my mam brings me my supper and I can go home whenever I'm hungry.'

'Oh, Megan,' Annie whispered.

Megan put her arms round her. 'One bad apple doesn't taint the whole barrel,' she said. 'I know the saying and maybe it's true of apples but it isn't of families. You're respected in spite of Da and so am I, I reckon, even though I've not been home long. Rhys is off to the grammar, and there's no need to tell me how hard he's working for I see the results every day, and the little ones are copying him, not Dan. I see that too. The stars in their books last term weren't a present from their sister, you know. They were given to them because they deserved them.' She shook her mother's shoulders. 'I'll be buying more uniforms for the grammar. Saving up already, I am.'

Annie brought out a handkerchief and blew her nose. 'It's right what you say, Megan. I should count my blessings, for I have plenty of them. Except' – again she blew her nose – 'didn't Jesus say that the shepherd weeps more over the sheep that goes astray than he prides himself on the rest of his flock?'

'Something like that, He said.' Megan sat her mother back down in the chair. 'But sheep are silly old things and probably don't notice or care if the shepherd is proud of them or not.'

Annie stared her her. 'You're saying I'm not proud of my other boys?'

'You just warned me to be their teacher and not their sister. You said –'

'I remember what I said. And thought. You're a wise woman, Megan Jones. Wiser than I'll ever be.'

'And who brought me up, Mam?' Megan said.

Olivia was to attend the private girls' school in Llangefni and Rhys had already begun at the grammar. A few days before Olivia's term began Harry Wittering strolled down the lane to the Joneses' smallholding, a pair of spaniels at his heels and six pigeons in his game bag.

'Oh, you're so good to us!' Annie exclaimed. 'Come out of the cold, Major, and have a cup of tea, won't you?'

'Thank you, Annie. I'd like one.'

That was the thing about Major Wittering. He had stayed with royalty, but you weren't embarrassed about inviting him into your own home. His spaniels lay down outside to wait for him – Clip too lazy to raise a bark at them – and he removed his cap and entered the kitchen, saying 'good morning' to the two boys and pretending not to notice Dai's shuffling exit.

'Actually,' he said, 'it was Rhys I wanted to see. Is he around?'

'Outside somewhere. Emlyn, Hughie, find Rhys for the Major, will you?'

They ran out. 'Rhys isn't in trouble, is he?' Annie asked, suddenly anxious. She couldn't see how for his time was used up with his books or on the farm, but nothing was certain these days.

'Good Lord, no,' Harry said with a grin. 'I want to ask him a favour.'

'Oh!' she said. He was so handsome and kind she felt quite fluttery.

Rhys appeared and the Major said he had a spot of business to discuss with him. Taking his tea, he led Rhys out and they walked around the yard deep in conversation, Rhys listening and nodding until the Major shook him by the hand, clapped him on the shoulder and brought his empty mug in to Annie.

'Many thanks for that,' he said. 'Just the ticket.'

'And thank you for the pigeons,' she said, but he'd called to his dogs and walked away. 'Well, and what was that about?' she asked Rhys.

'He's worried about Olivia on the bus and her getting home these dark nights. They'd send someone to meet her, he said, but the bus arrives all hours and better to have her escort already on it.'

'What did you say?'

'I said yes, Mam.' His voice had the slightly tired, patronizing tone Dan's had, but the reason for it was very different.

'Do you get paid?' Dai grunted from his chair, having sidled back in.

'No, Da,' Rhys said steadily.

'Exploitation then, isn't it?'

Rhys raised a quietening hand at his mother as she was about to speak. 'It is not. I could see he was half wanting to pay me but didn't know how to bring the subject up. And I was glad he didn't,' he said over Dai's hoot of derision. 'It shows more respect for me.' He smiled at Annie and shrugged. 'I was going to do it anyway. Already planned to, reckoning it'ud be Morfydd waiting at the bus stop in the cold and dark.' He glanced at his father. 'There's a man in the family now, Mam,' he said.

II

Europe was heading for a war and this was, surely, no time to be falling in love and discussing a future.

'It's exactly the time,' Eve said. 'If we don't discuss it and do something about it we might not have a future.'

'But I've got a past,' Harry said. 'I can't simply chuck that over the side and let it drown.'

'Nell doesn't love you. You know that. She's got money so she won't be destitute.'

'There are two children, Eve. They're people, not pawns in a game to suit you and me.'

'They won't be destitute either.'

'Nick won't, perhaps, but Olivia ... it's not money that makes children secure. It's love.'

'Perhaps we could get custody of her.' Eve found this agonizing tedious and unmanly, and had no desire to begin married life with a Harry encumbered with a daughter whose brown eyes already had too much suspicion and accusation in them, but if it was the price ...

'How?' Harry groaned. 'I'm the guilty party. I'd never be given custody.'

There were times when he couldn't think how it had gone this far with Eve. It had begun as a flirtation, a diversion. On weekdays they would meet – by appointment and not, as for the past year, by apparent accident –

and go for walks together. She carried a gun as a kind of disguise, though cheerfully admitted she was no sort of shot.

'Perhaps I'm no sort of a teacher,' he had said. Except Moppet was pretty good with a gun – but then she had a natural eye.

Moppet. He gave a shudder of panic. She was not threatened by this, was she? No! He would not let her be. What was 'this', anyway? He and Eve did no more than walk and talk.

And she was so easy to talk to, so understanding, this third woman in his life. She encouraged him to tell her about Africa, his adventures there, his love for the wide spaces of Kenya and his hopes for the country.

'Why did you leave?' she had asked one day.

'Nell, the children . . . it's no place for them.'

'But aren't there lots of white women and children out there?'

He had hunched his shoulders and turned into the bite of a February gale. A clatter of wood pigeons rose from a field of kale, put up by Lulu, and Harry didn't even raise his gun.

'You want to go back, don't you?' she said to him over the wind. 'You're unhappy. Anyone can see it.'

He had turned back to her. 'I'm in prison, Eve. And now Nell wants me in chains as well, and I think the key to my cell is entirely lost.'

'It's not lost,' she had said gently. 'We'll find it, Harry.'

And that had led to the first kiss, and nothing was innocent any more.

Their affair had hurtled on, as Europe did, towards conflagration. Eve found ways around the preposterous difficulties of two lovers meeting on an island where they were both well known with an ingenuity that had Harry reeling between admiration and damnation. She seemed to think the solution was simple: he would divorce his wife and marry her. He could contemplate divorcing his wife – he supposed he could – but it would mean divorcing his children. Both of them . . . Moppet, his companion and friend.

No. He could not do it.

'Why can't we carry on as we have been?' he said. 'Well, not quite. Moppet's summer holidays begin soon and I won't be so available.'

Eve suppressed a sigh. Patience, she told herself. Don't nag; his wife does that.

'Oh?' she murmured. 'So you're available now, are you?'

He groaned again, this time in passion and not anguish, but still managed to register: we're safe. The dogs are outside the barn and will bark if someone approaches. Remember to listen for a bark.

War was declared, though nothing much changed on Anglesey. Harry tried to join up but the army did not want a 44-year-old major, ex of the King's African Rifles, with a bullet scar across his ribs.

It will be over by Christmas, everyone said, but it did not begin. A winter of waiting.

The dogs never barked.

Morfydd was about to start a scandal, too, although a minor one by comparison to the others brewing. She was on her way home one March Monday, leaning grimly into the wind, when she looked up and saw a man in a service greatcoat standing in the lane before her.

A German! she thought. Come the easy way round. But he smiled at her, threw his cigarette away and said, 'You seem to be over-burdened, ma'am. Can I carry one of your bags for you?'

It was English, but she couldn't quite grasp it and said stupidly, 'Pardon?'

'Rabbits!' he said, relieving her of one bag and peering inside. 'They'll want skinning and jointing. Can I do it?'

She grabbed the bag back, convinced he was a thief as well as a German.

'Sorry, ma'am,' the man said, extending both hands as though to show he wasn't armed. 'But here I was, walking down this track and missing home and female company like you'd not believe, and then you come along looking as downcast as I feel.'

He ran his words together; she could only understand about one in ten as he followed her down the lane talking non-stop. She tried to open the gate, encumbered with her bags, and he unhitched it for her.

'Any chance of a cup of tea?' he said. 'I've discovered that, since I got to England. Everyone gives you tea. I've learned to like it,' he added quickly. 'It's great stuff.'

'Got to England?' she repeated. He *was* a spy then, although his smile was most engaging. He had closed the gate, but behind him. He had invaded the Joneses' territory.

He smote himself on the forehead. 'Wales. I'm in Wales, right? It's not the same. Steve told me that.'

'Who are you?' Mo asked, deciding to be overwhelmed.

'Ma'am, forgive me.' He brought his heels together and saluted her. His eyes were as grey as the sea and his hair the colour of the sand on Rhosneigr beach. 'Flight Lieutenant Max Johnstone of Toronto, Canada, currently serving in the RAF. You want my ID?'

'Canada!'

'Here to help the old country in her time of need.' He produced his identity card for her inspection. 'So now will you tell me your name?'

'Morfydd. Morfydd Jones.'

'Morfydd. That's beautiful. Morfydd, fair maid of Wales, will you give me a cup of tea and let me skin your rabbits?'

'But why do you want to do that?'

His face changed suddenly. 'To remind me of simple things, maybe. I don't know.'

'Yes, you do.'

He shrugged. 'Weekends camping with my dad. Safety, security, I guess. This war doesn't seem to be happening yet, but it will – and soon.'

'And you're wishing you hadn't come and joined it.'

'No! I'm not a coward, Morfydd. I just want us to get on with it. Waiting is hard.'

'And you're a long way from home,' she said. 'My mam will make you a cup of tea, and you can skin the rabbits.' She had fallen in love, and it was ridiculous as well as utterly certain. 'I wasn't downcast,' she said. 'It was the wind swiping at me.'

'I wasn't either,' he confessed. 'Well, perhaps a little. It was kind of Steve to invite me for our leave, but he and his wife don't want me around and – wow! – does their baby scream!'

'Steve . . . Stephen Birkenshaw?' Morfydd said, her heart snapping shut and not liking it.

'Right. You know him?'

'He's one of the grand families around here.'

'Is he? His house isn't grand.' He grinned. 'Not big enough for that baby, anyhow.'

'Wait till you see where his parents live,' she said gloomily.

'We're going there tonight. It's a hooley to raise money for a Spitfire. Steve and I are the stars of the show since we'll be the guys who will fly it.'

It was double-Dutch. She could only understand the first sentence.

'My employers will be there,' she said.

'What are their names? I'll introduce myself.'

'Major and Mrs Wittering. I'm their housemaid, Max,' she said, convinced he would open the gate, walk off down the lane and she would never see him again.

'Fair *house*maid of Wales,' he said. 'When do I get my cup of tea?'

He appeared the next morning and, bold as you like, knocked on the front door. Morfydd opened it and stepped back, her jaw dropping in shock and consternation.

'Hi there,' he said, walking into the hall and gazing about him. 'No, it won't do,' he murmured. 'Not grand enough for me now I've seen the real thing.'

'Max!' she whispered, and at the same moment a door opened behind her. She froze.

'Good morning, Flight Lieutenant Johnstone,' Mrs Wittering said.

He winked elaborately at Morfydd and turned. 'Morning, ma'am. Major Wittering invited me over.'

'He told me. You're interested in spaniels, aren't you? He, and they, are at the kennels.'

'I can't wait to see them. Maybe your maid could show me the way.'

'Yes, of course. I'll see you later. I'm sure Harry will bring you in for a drink.'

'Which way are the goddamned kennels?' he asked Morfydd when they were outside.

'Over there.'

'Then let's go here. Is anyone else around?'

'No one that matters.' Gwen was out and it was the gardener's day off.

He hustled her through the gate into the walled garden. 'Listen, we're leaving this evening. Can you get away this afternoon?'

'I'm rolling bandages for the Red Cross.'

'Get out of it, can't you? Morfydd, I know it sounds crazy but I've fallen for you. We must have more time together.'

'Yes,' she said, accepting these two statements as facts.

203

'So can you get out of it?'

'Yes,' she said again. She'd have to, wouldn't she?

'We'll meet at your folks' place. Three o'clock, okay?'

'Okay.' She'd learned that word yesterday and was pleased she had remembered it.

'Now, tell me about spaniels. What the hell do they do?'

He was extraordinary. Not even Annie could stand up to him.

'And what lie did you tell Mrs Wittering?' she inquired when Mo arrived home, Max already there.

'That you are unwell, Mam.'

Annie let out a faint, resigned sigh and Max leaped towards her. 'Are you ill, Annie?' (He called everyone by their first name, as though he had known them for ever.) 'Shouldn't you be resting?'

'But where are you off to?' Annie said, finding she had been led to a chair and was actually sitting down. 'What if Mrs Wittering sees you?'

'We won't let her,' Max said. 'Anyway, isn't she rolling bandages, or does she just send the maid to do it?'

'She's there,' Morfydd said.

'Bye for now,' Max said to Annie, leading Morfydd out.

He had wangled from Major Wittering an invitation to stay whenever he wanted to.

'How did you do that?' Morfydd asked. The world seemed to be spinning the wrong way, or she was spinning faster than it. She had heard of people being swept off their feet but had never before believed it happened.

'I told him the truth: that I didn't know anyone in Britain and I loved this island and its people. Okay, so that was an untruth. I love one person on this island.'

'It's not possible in twenty-four hours!' And that's a second lie in one afternoon, she told herself.

'Twenty-four hours?' Max said, smiling down at her. 'It took me less than five minutes.'

'Whatever did the Major think of you?' Morfydd asked him later.

'He's a nice guy. I got him into a corner so he had to give me the invite, but he must have been suspicious.'

Harry was. The young Canadian flier was willing and eager, but he didn't know a spaniel's arse from its tits. He had been one of two men under thirty at the party the previous night and the only one unmarried. Eve – to make Harry jealous, perhaps, to force him over the brink – had monopolized him all evening.

Flight Lieutenant Johnstone took up Major Wittering's offer and appeared several times over the next few weeks from his base far away on the Kent coast of southern England. He used his considerable ingenuity and charm to get north, hitching on aircraft being delivered, hitching on anything, he said to Morfydd, that moved. He was an ideal guest, Nell Wittering decided (not noticing the absences of her maid), happy to spend his time wandering around the countryside.

He was not wandering with Eve, Harry knew. There were two sets of lovers seeking privacy in one small corner of one small island, one pair innocent, the other dishonourable.

'But why do we have to be secret?' Max kept asking.

'Because I'm a maid,' Morfydd insisted.

'I don't understand. I'm a man, you're a woman. What else is there?'

12

In May the war began. Max was in action across the English Channel, first as the retreat of the British Expeditionary Force began, then as it was evacuated from Dunkirk. He managed some scrawled notes to Morfydd (this was safe as it was she who sorted out the post) but it was a time of great anxiety for her. For the whole country, of course, as it seemed the army would be lost and Germany would overrun Great Britain as it had continental Europe, but Morfydd had something extra: if Max was killed she would not be told. There would only be a name in the casualty lists. If he was badly injured and unable to talk, or lost his memory, or . . .

'Hush, Mo,' Annie said, holding her daughter close.

'There'd be a lifetime of silence,' Morfydd wept. 'I don't even know his parents' address in Canada.'

But Max survived and came to Anglesey looking older, graver and stuffed to the brim with decisions. He had brought a ring for her and, yes, he had thought about how she would worry and had made arrangements. They would be married as soon as there was time, and until then she was better off here. She could leave work —

'No. I must keep busy,' she said. 'But I should do something for the war.'

'After we're married and I've moved you somewhere

more accessible. Away from what's coming but not too far away from me. And I'm going to tell Nell and Harry about us.'

'Max, no!'

'I have to be able to phone you, Mo. Talk with you. That's not a lot to want, is it?'

'Oh,' she said. 'No, it isn't.'

She wouldn't stay in the room while he did the deed, though, and perhaps it was just as well. Harry was stunned and Nell said, '*What*? Engaged to Morfydd? This is outrageous!'

'Why is that, ma'am?'

She paced around the drawing room. 'You come here, posing as a house guest, and all the time you . . . I don't know how you behave in your own country, Flight Lieutenant, but that sort of thing simply isn't done.'

'I've seen some pretty outrageous things in the past few weeks, Nell. Treaties broken, international borders violated, helpless refugees strafed from the air —'

'By Germans, Flight Lieutenant. Germans.'

'Okay, but falling in love with a girl can hardly be called outrageous. I'm sorry if it's not "done",' he added, smiling slightly.

'The girl you speak of is our housemaid.'

'She needn't be,' he said, gazing round the room, the furniture polished, the summer flowers picked and arranged by Morfydd. 'She could go home to her mother, or to May Birkenshaw's. It might be good for both of them since their men will be in the same danger. The RAF will be in the front line now.'

Nell snorted. 'May Birkenshaw will hardly think a Welsh maid a proper companion.'

'No? Her nanny has left and she could use help with her baby.'

'Stitched up, Nell,' Harry said, tapping his pipe out in as ashtray. 'We need Morfydd more than she needs us.

Let's have her in to congratulate her.' He shook Max's hand. 'And congratulations to you, Max.'

'Go to May's,' Max urged Morfydd. 'She'd welcome you.' He had been horrified by Nell's reaction. Her country was about to be invaded and all she was concerned about was whether something was 'done' or not. She had told him it was 'inappropriate' that he and Morfydd should spend the night under the same roof – meaning, he supposed, that he would sneak into Morfydd's room or she into his; and, okay, he agreed: that was not *done* – so when she had washed up after dinner Max escorted Morfydd home.

'I'll be all right,' Morfydd said. 'I'd rather be in the place I know.'

Max put his arm around her shoulders. 'Happy?' he asked.

'Happy? Yes!' She felt like a piece of delicate china, precious and protected. 'But you, Max, up there in the sky. You take care.'

'Nothing can harm me,' he said. 'I have a lock of your hair to defend me.'

He took her inside and explained her presence to Annie, who wept in delight and even Dai seemed pleased at his prospective son-in-law, then walked back and found Harry in his room at the kennels.

'I'm sorry about this,' he said awkwardly.

'Not your fault, old fellow,' Harry said, offering him a brandy from the bottle he kept there. 'Not a lot one can do when love gets her tentacles around one, is there?'

At last Harry was given something to do. He was put in charge of the Local Defence Volunteers, soon afterwards named the Home Guard, and if there was a better drilled bunch of misfits in Wales or England they didn't believe it.

'It's pointless, though,' Harry said. 'What sensible German is going to come here so we can nab him? I feel so useless! There must be something else.'

'You've tried, Harry. You can't do more than that,' Eve said.

'Perhaps we should have some sea exercises. It would redress the balance in the troop. Stop the landlubbers laughing because the fishermen don't know an oak from an elm.'

'The Home Guard can't go to sea,' she said.

'How do you know? In war anything can happen.'

The talk of war had been on her side; its reality was against her. He seemed to think that the issue of his divorce and remarriage had been set aside until Hitler was defeated, especially since Nell had at last agreed that she and Nick were safest where they were and the chains of the soft south were no longer a threat. He was not bored any more. Was so busy, in fact, that they scarcely met except in public.

'I've been thinking,' she said, 'that my German could be of use. To the Ministry,' she added vaguely.

'In London?' he said, shocked.

'I ought to do something for the war effort.'

'Yes, but can't you do it here?'

'Join you on your fishing boat, Harry?'

'Eve, you can't leave. Me.'

'But you can't leave your wife, you say.'

'It's not that simple. I've got my men to consider now. The scandal . . .'

'You love me and I love you. It's the only thing that matters.'

'A damn great war matters. Don't you see?'

It was closer than he thought. That evening he, Olivia and Rhys Jones arrived at the hall where the Home Guard mustered and found the walls daubed with anti-English slogans and the pathetic amount of equipment Harry had managed to acquire sabotaged.

'Dan,' Rhys said in a strangled voice. 'It's got to be Dan. What does he think?' he cried. 'That Hitler's going to stop at the border and leave Wales alone? When I fight it'ull be Wales I'm fighting for, and when I see Dan I'll hammer that bloody fact into his head.'

Rhys was fifteen and big with it. He wouldn't have to fight yet, and Harry prayed he never would, but he was anxious to do his bit and claimed to be too old for the Scouts. Harry had invented the rank of cadet for him and Olivia; they ran messages and made themselves generally useful.

'Don't let the rest see,' Rhys begged. 'Please, Major. I'll clear up the mess.'

'You can't be sure it's Dan, Rhys, and I'm afraid you can't clear it up yet. But we won't meet here. Wait for the others outside and tell them we'll muster on the beach for . . . Oh, I don't know. Think of something.'

'A training run?' Olivia suggested.

He smiled at her. 'That'll do. You go too.'

They went and Harry inspected the damage in detail. It was violent, unnecessarily so. He put his hands to his face and rubbed his eyes. Decisions, decisions. Why couldn't Eve be satisfied as his mistress? It was she who had started the whole business, after all. Had she done so planning to remove him from his family? How could he leave them? Yet Eve's talk of leaving him had shaken him to the soles of his boots. Rhys was worried about Dan's activities reflecting on his family; Dan the renegade. Eve was wanting to turn Harry into a renegade and cause suffering to innocent people. Thousands of innocent people suffered in war, but this was to be done as a result of love. It was most confusing, and Harry wished it would go away.

One decision had to be taken, though. There was no

alternative and it meant a trip to Llangefni tomorrow. This could not be reported over the phone.

The former inspector at Bangor Police Station was now in charge at Llangefni.

'I'm very glad to see you,' Harry said, shaking his hand. 'It makes a hard task easier. I didn't think this was something for the local plod,' and he told the Inspector what had happened.

'You think it was Daniel Jones?' the man said when Harry had finished.

'His brother does.'

'A lot of damage, you say.'

'And a theft.'

'A box of dummy detonators.'

'For training. We don't have the real thing. Anglesey's hardly the front line, Inspector, but if the Germans pay us a visit we'll scare them to hell with our dummies.'

'I'm scared to hell about a lad who steals detonators.'

'Dummy ones.'

'He didn't know that, did he? It's why he took them . . . The intent.'

'Yes,' Harry said. 'Murderous.'

'Where is the lad?'

'He lives at home and works on an estate near by. His father's not up to much, but the rest of them . . . Why, you couldn't hope for a more honest, hard-working bunch. One sister's the school teacher, for heaven's sake, and the other is our maid. A lovely girl.' Harry paused. 'Will you have to search their place? I think it would break the mother's heart. Dummy detonators aren't worth much, are they?'

The Inspector moved an ashtray an inch northwards. 'We'd better visit the scene of the crime. We can't do anything without evidence.'

'I padlocked the doors and hung "No entry" signs,' Harry said. He smiled wryly. 'Or my cadets did.'

Olivia had tried to argue with him, had wanted to help Rhys clear up the hall, until Rhys had said sharply, 'It's an order from the Major, Cadet Wittering!' Harry had taken advantage and ordered him not to tell his mother or confront Dan; relieved, Rhys had agreed, not realizing why Harry needed the time. Rhys hardly saw his brother these days anyway and hiding something from his mother was not wrong if it was war business.

The Inspector and his detective constable found no evidence. The fingerprints on the damaged items belonged to Major Wittering, and the excitement over a footprint was short-lived as that proved to be his as well.

'I had no idea it was such a science,' Harry said, wiping fingerprint ink from his hands. 'I wouldn't have touched anything had I known.'

'Whoever did it knew, didn't they?' the Inspector said.

At least there was nothing to hide now, and Morfydd blessed Max for that as what came to be called the Battle of Britain began. Mrs Wittering made no reference to Morfydd's fiancé, but the Major invited both her and Gwen into the drawing room to hear the news on the wireless each evening. Morfydd was grateful for his thoughtfulness but found it an appalling ordeal: the English voice always sounded cheerful, saying our boys had shot down several enemy aircraft with a loss of 'only' so many of ours. Only meant fathers, sons, husbands, lovers. Only could be Max's Spitfire.

Max phoned her whenever he could and after the first few times she forgot her diffidence and embarrassment and spoke to him freely. Charlotte Jenkins at the telephone exchange would be listening anyway, so who cared about Mrs Wittering? The calls came at all times of the day and night and Morfydd, without fully realizing what she was doing, made answering the strident ringing her monopoly. One day she collided with Mrs Wittering in her dash to get there and hardly registered the furious, 'Well, really!' as she picked up the receiver, heard Charlotte's 'Go ahead, caller' and then Max's voice.

He sounded even more strained than usual as he told her he was fine, no problems. She had no idea, of course, what he was hiding, what the wireless glossed over with its 'only': the empty places at the tables in the mess, how Max had flown back to base and crash-landed, one wing of his plane on fire and oil leaking into the cockpit. She had a notion that he'd been in the same trusty Spit these weeks and had been promoted through merit, and he wanted her to go on believing it. He wanted her, his maid of Wales, untainted by the hell. But this afternoon he couldn't hide everything; he was too tired and too upset, and he forgot the procedure about official notification.

'Steve's gone,' he said.

'Oh, Max, no!' she whispered.

'His radio was out. It must have been. He was chasing a Me and there was another on his tail. I was screaming at him, screaming and he paid no attention . . . Well,' he went on, having taken a shuddering breath, 'he got the Me he wanted and I got the one that did him.'

'Don't let any bloody Me get on your tail, Max,' Morfydd said.

'I won't. Don't worry.' Except they were all so damned tired and the bastards were everywhere in the sky. 'I won't,' he repeated. 'Time's nearly up. Tell me you love me, Mo.'

'I love you.'

'And I love you.'

Morfydd put the receiver on the rest and turned away. Her employer was still in the hall.

'Morfydd,' she said, 'I'm prepared to put up with so much. Rather a lot, in fact, but I consider this . . .'

She went on about standards and how we shouldn't let the war and the Germans alter those. Mo wondered if she should leave here. She could find another job, easy, or go home to Mam whom she wanted to be near during these desperate days, wanted it most awfully. But Mam had no telephone, and the telephone was a lifeline. Or a deathline.

'I don't believe you're listening to me, Morfydd,' Mrs Wittering said.

'Steve – Stephen – Birkenshaw is dead,' Morfydd said. 'Dead, and my Max will be next.'

'Oh, my God!' Mrs Wittering said, going to the phone. It had become a well-worn routine, this rallying around the bereaved. So many of the laughing boys had gone, the ones who in the golden days before the war had arrived by plane at summer parties for the fun of it, had joined up because it was bound to be a jolly adventure.

Who would rally around Morfydd when the time came?

Olivia found her in the garden later, her face as white as the apron she was twisting with agitated hands.

'It's not Max, is it?' she said, sitting on the seat beside Morfydd and unscrambling her hands from the apron. Olivia knew about Max, though her mother thought she didn't, and considered it the ultimate in romance. She knew about romance, too, because she and Rhys had seen films about it in the picture house in Llangefni; after one of them Rhys had wondered if it would be romantic to kiss. They had experimented and decided it was not. Obviously you had to be old; as old as Mo was.

'No, it's not Max,' Morfydd said. 'Moppet, it's Stephen Birkenshaw, and him with a young wife and baby.'

Olivia had not cried about the war before, not about the young men who had landed their planes in the field on the other side of the drive, scattering the cows and sheep, but she cried now. She had been bridesmaid at Stephen and May's wedding and had worn the most beautiful frock she had ever owned in her life.

A shout. Her father's voice. She stumbled towards him and he held her, his moustache tickling her cheek and the comforting smell of tobacco enveloping her.

'Where's Mo?' he asked.

She gestured to where Mo had stood up and was smoothing the crumples in her apron. Harry set his daughter aside and went to her. 'May is here and wants to see you. Will you talk to her?'

'I've realized,' she said dully, 'Max shouldn't have told me and I shouldn't have told Mrs Wittering until ... until it was verified.'

Verified. These words she'd learned.

'The telegram came. Mo, my dear, please talk to May.'

She was in the drawing room and, weeping, she flung herself at Mo. 'Stephen told me about you and Max. I should have insisted you come to me, but ...'

But a Welsh housemaid and a patrician's daughter could have nothing in common, not in normal circumstances.

'Nell says you had a telephone call from Max. Did he see what happened?'

'He said he thought Steve's radio was out,' Morfydd said, and related what Max had told her.

'So he took one with him,' May said, sniffing. 'It's something. And Max downing the one that did it.'

She began to cry again in Morfydd's arms. Her mother moved forward to take over but her father stopped her, glancing quickly at Harry and briefly shaking his head. They both knew Stephen's radio had nothing to do with it; it was the heat of battle and fatigue, but best to blame equipment in this case. Eve also tried to catch Harry's eye, wanting to show him that life should be grabbed when it could for it was so easily snatched away. He was talking to Olivia, however, who was crying too. Why? What did she have to cry about?

Gently her parents detached May from Morfydd.

'Will you come and see me?' May said as they led her away. 'Max, too, when he's here next. I have to know everything.'

'If he comes.'

'Yes. Perhaps one should fear the worst. But they can't kill them all, can they?'

Somehow Morfydd kept going, every day seeming like a year and every three-minute phone call passing in an unfair instant. Mrs Wittering made no comment but her disapproval was obvious.

She awoke to the fact that her daughter would soon be thirteen and was really quite pretty, and had an attack of disapproval about how much Olivia went around with Rhys and her role as cadet in the Home Guard. She dragged her to one of the Red Cross afternoons. Olivia was hopeless, becoming even more so as her mother, shrugging, said lightly to the assembled matrons, 'All thumbs, I'm afraid. She couldn't sew to save her life. Harry's turned her into a complete tomboy.'

Olivia had long ago stopped trying to please her mother, but was bored by the way her faults were laid at her father's feet.

'I can shoot,' she said. 'It's more likely to save my life than sewing, isn't it?'

Nell tittered, the other ladies at the table laughed and Olivia was not taken there again.

13

The *Indefatigable* came to Anglesey on an early September day in 1940 with three explosions which would distort and destroy lives.

The headmistress's son had been killed and Olivia had been given an unexpected half holiday. She was walking home down the lane, and walking towards her was one of Harry's young spaniels.

'Hello,' Olivia said. 'What are you doing here?'

The spaniel wagged her tail in an embarrassed manner and indicated that she was only . . . well –

'Hunting on your own, and that's not allowed,' Olivia said. 'Where's Daddy?'

She climbed on to a gate and searched the surrounding countryside. Busy was lying outside a barn.

Busy wouldn't bark at Olivia, would she?

Olivia, breath rasping, her satchel banging on her back, ran down the drive and shot through the gate into the walled garden, her one idea being to hide. Morfydd was there picking flowers; she had thought she had heard the telephone but Mrs Wittering had not called her to the house. Couldn't be Max, she reassured herself, then forgot about it when she saw Olivia.

'What is it?' she said, rushing towards her. 'Moppet, what's the matter?' The child could hardly speak, then it came out in a rush.

'Mo, I saw Daddy and Eve . . . They had no clothes on and they were . . . No clothes. Daddy and Eve Barker . . .'

'Olivia!'

She turned, the tears running down her cheeks. Her mother was standing by the open gate.

'You are a liar,' she said. 'You always have been. Go to your room at once.'

Olivia fled.

'And you,' Mrs Wittering said to Morfydd, 'had better pack your things. I was coming to find you. There was a phone call. Wing Commander Johnstone has been shot down and is in hospital at Chelmsford. I'll take you to the station.'

Mo had been expecting it. Rehearsing how to be brave. 'How bad is he?' she asked, her tongue seeming like iron in her mouth.

'Alive, at least. Hurry now.'

They both paused, however. In the distance but coming closer was the sound of police sirens and ambulance bells.

'Car crash, I expect,' Mrs Wittering said as the noise faded away again, but an instinct in Morfydd knew this wasn't true. The sounds belonged to her in some way.

She shook the feeling off as she packed her few things, told Gwen — what had happened to Max, not the rest — and asked her to tell Annie. And Moppet, she added. Poor Moppet, but Morfydd was torn in two. There would be time to comfort Moppet later, comfort each other perhaps. Max had been shot down.

It was kind of Mrs Wittering to drive her to the station, explain where Chelmsford was and give her money. She scarcely heard the words as she took the notes, their significance only sinking in when she waited on the platform.

'Your work recently has been unsatisfactory. We will not be wanting you back. This is in lieu of notice.'

When the train reached the Britannia Bridge she looked back at her island. A column of smoke was rising in the air over to the left. She could not tell precisely where it originated, but again the feeling that it belonged to her was overwhelming. Again she shook it off.

'What does "in lieu" mean?' she asked the soldier sitting in the next seat.

'Instead of, doesn't it?' he said, and another passenger nodded.

That means I've been given the sack, Morfydd thought dimly.

An hour later Annie arrived at the back door of the Witterings' house, trailing her two youngest children and wailing about Dan and Dai and murder. Nurse was collecting Nick from his school and upstairs Olivia had fallen into an exhausted, nightmare-filled half sleep. In the drawing room Nell was confronting her foolish, weeping husband.

'Really, Harry,' she said. 'I've known something has been going on between you and Eve Barker, of course, but to allow yourself to be seen by Olivia . . .'

Nothing could have punished Harry more, nothing would as much as removing Olivia from him as Nell could, with honour, now do. She, Nick and Olivia could leave this bloody island and – as soon as the threat of an invasion had passed – go and live somewhere civilized.

It was, she considered, perfect.

Part IV

I

'Very interesting,' Olivia Wheeler murmured. 'I hadn't realized you were going to write it down.'

'Have I got it right, Gran?'

'You could have, I suppose. What had Dai and Dan done?'

'Killed a policeman who'd gone to investigate the theft of rifles and other equipment. Lobbed a bomb at him. I must say,' Emma went on, 'the police were pretty inefficient. Why hadn't they been keeping an eye on the group after the dummy detonators were stolen?'

'I daresay they had, but it's not easy to trail someone in empty countryside. You tend to get noticed.'

'That's a point,' Emma admitted.

'What happened to Dai and Dan?'

'Dai and the others were hanged. Dan was too young but was killed later in a prison brawl. Don't you remember? It was why the family sold up and left Anglesey after the trial. The shame, Annie said.'

'We'd gone by then, I expect. We left almost immediately and – well, you are right about that – my world had exploded that day.'

'You mean the rest isn't right?'

'It's a good story, darling. You're not altogether fair on my mother, though. Daddy treated her shamefully.'

'She treated Morfydd shamefully.'

'Things were different then. You really couldn't have a house guest having an affair with a maid. Not a public one, anyway.'

'You don't know, do you? That phone call was from Max. He had been shot down but he was fine. He asked Nell to tell Morfydd to stop worrying as the war was over for him, at least for a few months. His elbow had been smashed and they weren't sure he'd regain full use of his right hand.'

'Oh,' Olivia said blankly.

'She let Morfydd believe it was much worse. She let her travel all the way to Essex – and it was the first time she'd ever left Wales – thinking he was dying. To get rid of her. And,' she added, as her grandmother was silent, 'it was not an affair. They were engaged to be married.'

'I did think she had deserted me,' Olivia said. 'Disappearing when I needed her most.'

'That's why she felt guilty.'

'It was hardly her fault that I'd gone,' Olivia mused. 'Though it is true I felt betrayed. By Daddy most of all, but her as well.'

'She had Max to worry about, and her father and brother. By the time that was over you had left Anglesey and your aunt was off somewhere. Mo had lost you. And then she married and went to Canada.' Emma paused. 'Did you feel guilty?' she asked.

'Me? What about?'

'Well, what you had seen precipitated your mother leaving . . . didn't it?' Emma's voice trailed away. She was prying and had no right to.

Olivia stood up and went to the sink to fill the kettle. Outside John was mowing the lawn and Graham was coming to supper later. It was nice to have a future when you were eyeball to eyeball with your three score years and ten. The past, though.

She switched on the kettle and turned back to Emma. 'I put it out of my mind. Years later I wanted to ask Mummy if she would have divorced him anyway, but I never got round to it. I suppose I was terrified of the answer being no.'

'I expect it would have been yes,' Emma said, wanting to comfort her.

'I expect so. They didn't have a lot in common.'

'What about Eve Barker, Gran? Was I unfair on her? Her sister certainly didn't like her.'

'No, you weren't unfair on her,' Olivia said.

'Why didn't you all tell me everything before?'

'You were so determined to make a mystery out of it and we didn't want to disappoint you. Or perhaps you're disappointed now?'

'No way. It's been great. Anyway, there are lots more mysteries left.'

The will. The clock . . .

Emma had spent nearly six weeks on Anglesey. She had begun to put what she was finding out down on paper almost as a joke, but it had quickly become an end in itself. Her, her pens and paper at a table in the room overlooking the sea, emerging for Elunid's meals or to run along the beach at low tide, or for a walk through the dunes to the house once owned by her great-great aunt Celia.

Lots more mysteries.

'Well, darling,' Olivia said, 'it seems to have done you good. Your mother said she's never seen you looking better and I agree.'

'I'm fat,' Emma groaned.

'No. Just right,' Olivia soothed. She poured water into coffee mugs. 'Very interesting,' she said again. 'What are you going to make up next?'

'Gran –!'

'If you're writing a story you should do it properly,

with a beginning, middle and end,' her grandmother said severely.

'Tell me what comes next, then.'

'Darling, you don't need my help. Your imagination's done a wonderful job so far.'

'In what way?' Emma asked, outraged.

'The Africa bit. Where did you get that about Mutali and the rifles, for example? I didn't tell you.'

'H.G.A.'s papers in the attic at home, actually. Mutali wrote to him quite often.'

Pathetic scraps of letters they were, dictated to an Indian scribe and full of unlikely flowery phrases. In one of them Mutali, for some unknown reason, had made the scribe copy out the inscriptions.

Emma's grandmother, however, was not deflected by a trifling piece of fact. 'It's a thorough muddle,' she said. 'And you've forgotten entirely about . . . What year have you reached?'

'Nineteen forty.'

'There!' Olivia said, triumphant. 'You'll have to go back ten years. I mean, you must put him in, mustn't you?'

2

A group of boys was playing cricket on a bare-earth pitch under a brilliant tropical sky. The boundaries were marked by a frangipani tree, the front rank of a huge army of rubber trees, a rough road and the back of a whitewashed line of low buildings in which the plantation workers and their families lived. The audience were a family of monkeys and a pet mina belonging to Victor, the son of the plantation's chief clerk. Victor was mad about cricket and had taught his bird to speak the language of the game. Its commentary sometimes caused irritation ('Fine shot, sir, fine shot!' when the bat hit empty air) but more often hilarity, never more than now when Robert hit a sweet sweep for four and then, upon an authoritative shout of 'Out!' from the perch beneath the frangipani, philosophically shouldered his bat and left the crease.

'You walked, you walked!' Victor cried as Robert realized his mistake and turned back.

'I wasn't concentrating.'

'You should have been.'

'Meat of the bat,' the mina said, moving the length of its tether along the perch. 'Six?' it inquired. 'Leg before wicket. Wide ball.'

'It's too hot to play,' a boy said, and they flung themselves down in the shade of the frangipani.

'Silly mid-on,' the bird said. 'Caught behind.'

'I'm thirsty.' Victor clicked his fingers and three of the smaller boys – eight or nine years old compared to Victor's towering twelve – ran off. They were going to climb palm trees and collect king coconuts. Robert felt he should be the one to give the order since his father was the owner of the whole plantation, including the palms, but Victor had always led the group. Besides which, he was two years older than Robert.

Victor lay back and put his hands under his head. 'At your school in England,' he announced, 'you'll play cricket once, twice, thrice a day.'

'Will I?' Robert said, sighing.

'You will be forced to. In between you will learn history and geography, but cricket is the most important thing. I wish I were going to school in England. I would meet Jack Hobbs and he would offer me a place on the team. When I am a little older,' he added modestly.

'You can go to England instead of me,' Robert said. 'Really, Victor, you can.'

The three boys returned, their arms laden with coconuts. Robert took his penknife from his pocket, hacked the husk from his nut and made a hole in the top. The juice was cool and refreshing. Robert didn't know much about England, the place he was supposed to regard as home, but he was fairly sure there were no king coconuts there. He did not understand why he had to leave Ceylon and go to that strange land.

'To learn to be a man,' his father said.

'But Victor will be a man and he doesn't have to leave Ceylon.'

'He's not British, like you.'

'Can't you make him British in my place? He would so like to go to school in England and play cricket with Jack Hobbs.'

'Listen to your voice!' his mother said. 'The sooner you

are among your own kind the better. You spend too much time with the natives.'

'They are my friends.'

'The sooner the better,' his mother said firmly.

Victor's assertions that he was going to a cricketers' paradise sustained him; his mother kissed his cheek and his father shook his hand, patted him on the shoulder and told him to behave himself. They both thanked the couple who were to look after him on the voyage and departed down the gangplank. Soon afterwards the ship was detached from its moorings in the harbour at Colombo and Ceylon vanished into a haze.

The full extent of Robert's loss did not hit him until the ship arrived in Southampton and he was handed over to his father's sister and her husband – or that's who they said they were, but what proof did Robert have? He was very un-British and unmanly as he clung to the last of what he had known of home. Mrs Smith unravelled him from her and spoke kind, reassuring words; in spite of these he ended up with Aunt Susan and Uncle Clive on a train to London. He looked out of the windows and saw strange flat fields, things he was told were sheep and others he recognized as cattle. There were no palms or rubber trees, no flame of the forest; the birds he could see in the grey sky were a grim black or a boring pale grey and white, and already Robert thought the country where peacocks roamed, where there were hummingbirds and bulbuls and paradise flycatchers, was a distant dream.

He understood that his aunt and uncle were trying to be kind to him, so he tried to reciprocate. He found the journey across London from one station to another on the underground railway terrifying rather than exciting. The people were too big and loud, their clothes drab and harsh, their hair a bewildering mixture of colours. He was taken to the station hotel for tea, which tasted revolting, and he was completely confused by the white-skinned waitress.

'You'll get used to it,' Aunt Susan said.

'Yes,' Robert said faintly.

She was enormously tactful about the tears he could not help leaking out of his eyes.

'Really you will,' she said, and held him to her padded bosom. He resisted at first then found it rather nice, and, since she didn't seem to mind, he stayed there – not knowing, of course, that she would far prefer a child who cried than one who gazed about him with uncomprehending and too composed eyes.

Another train journey and they arrived at Yarmouth. It was cold and enveloped in an unfriendly dark, but they said it was beside the sea. The thought of seeing it the next day relaxed him enough to enable him to sleep in the room they said was his – a small room with miserable windows and a quantity of dark furniture in it. They laughed at him when he demanded to know where the mosquito net was but opened the windows at his request. He closed them when he felt the chill air. He slept, and when he awoke his feet seemed disinclined to belong to the rest of him. No one brought him a cup of fragrant Ceylon tea, and nor had anyone thought to unpack his luggage.

He rummaged in his suitcase, his teeth chattering with cold, put on as many clothes as he could find and went downstairs. A maid was polishing the banisters and, instead of putting her hands together to bow and acknowledge him, she looked him up and down and grinned.

'Well, aren't we a one?' she said, and gestured to a door. 'Breakfast's ready in there.'

Robert had been taught to treat servants with disdain coupled with respect, a dichotomy natural and understood by the Singalese. He did not dare, however, order this woman to unpack his belongings – something which any guest in his parents' house would expect to have been done last night – for already he was realizing he had come to a very strange land.

His aunt was in the dining room and his uncle looked out from behind his copy of *The Times*, gave an explosive sort of grunt and disappeared again. Aunt Susan put some grey stuff in a bowl and presented it to him.

'What is this?' he asked.

'Porridge.'

He pushed the bowl aside. 'I would like some fruit, please.'

Uncle Clive put his paper down. 'Robert, old fellow,' he said, but his voice was gentle, 'I'm afraid porridge is what you have for breakfast in England, and that's an end to it. Don't be difficult, hey?'

Robert ate the slimy grey stuff. He didn't want to be difficult and his aunt put syrup on it so it didn't taste too bad. Uncle Clive went off to his office and Aunt Susan told Robert that he could accompany her on a shopping trip, but first she took him upstairs and helped him change the bizarre clothes he had dressed himself in.

'It's August,' she said. 'It really isn't cold. And Robert, dear, you must make your own bed. We don't have an army of servants like you are used to.'

'I don't know how.' Tears were threatening again, but he managed to hold them back and concentrate while his aunt showed him how to tuck the sheets and blankets in.

Susan Young was a kindly woman and sensitive with it. She thought it was frankly cruel of her sister-in-law to send her ten-year-old child halfway around the world to face a new life on his own. Surely she could have abandoned her husband and her gay parties in Ceylon for a few months and come with her son? But she had not, so it was up to Susan to make the transition as untraumatic as possible. Her own son was twenty years old and just about grown up, but Susan remembered the cruelties small boys practised upon each other at boarding schools. Robert, with his understandable ready crying and his disastrous sing-song accent, would have a rough time unless he was ready to stand up for himself. Susan had four weeks to prepare him for the ordeal.

She was a very nice woman. Robert might not have been fortunate in his mother and father, but he hit the jackpot with his aunt and his cousin Douglas whom Susan summoned from where he was staying with university friends. Between them they transformed Robert from a little lost thing who wept as though his heart was breaking that first morning when he saw the sea, which he had convinced himself would be like home and the sand a blinding white and not a dirty grey, to a confident enough individual as ready as anyone could be given his upbringing so far to face the rigours of an English prep school. Douglas had been there himself so was able to give him lots of tips. Robert began almost to look forward to it, though was horrified to discover there would be no cricket until the distant summer. He wrote Victor a furious letter.

Lots of the boys cried under their bedclothes in the dormitory after lights out on the first few nights of term, missing their parents and their homes. Robert missed his Aunt Susan who already seemed more of a mother to him than the woman in the photograph on his bedside table sitting on a verandah thousands of miles away, her face half hidden under a wide-brimmed hat. He missed his cousin Douglas, too, who had slipped him a ten-shilling note as he left with his parents and said, 'Have a jolly time, old chap. Remember what I said. Chin up.'

Robert was teased and beaten, but no more than other boys, and he was not bullied for he did indeed remember Douglas's advice. He quickly achieved a nickname, Rubber Ball, having been unwise enough to boast about what his father did.

It was a small price for acceptance. He coped, he did a bit more than that and succeeded. House prefect, school prefect, cricket captain, swimming captain: young English gentleman.

Ceylon was a colourful, warm memory and faded from his mind, though occasionally incidents in England triggered something of the past: a sudden whiff of spices from a shop in Soho which stopped him in his tracks and had him sniffing the air trying to recapture it; staying with a friend at his parents' house where peacocks paraded on the terrace and their screeches invaded his sleep at dawn and he awoke confused; a black and white photograph in a book of a Buddhist monk and instantly he made the robes a vibrant orange, the bare shoulder and face a smooth brown, the eyes dark, dignified and at peace.

He saw his parents once. He was by then at Charterhouse and playing for the school's first eleven. The plantation was being sold – something to do with the Depression, Robert understood – and his father came to England to negotiate with Dunlop. His mother accompanied him, interested, apparently, in seeing what her son looked like in the flesh six years on.

She should have been proud of him. He was tall, broad, not handsome but he had a nice, honest face and a head of curly hair the same colour as her own. He was not an academic genius but passed exams by doggedness and he was good at games, which was far more important anyway. He stroked a four for his fifty and lifted his bat to acknowledge the cries of 'Well done, Rubber Ball' – the name had followed him from his prep school – and saw Aunt Susan and Uncle Clive arrive with another couple. He did not recognize them, but he knew who they must be. Not surprisingly his concentration faltered and he was out soon afterwards.

They claimed him, and he found it extraordinary. The woman hugged his resisting body, kissed him and called him 'darling', and the man appeared delighted with him and the innings just completed, clapping long after everyone else had stopped and seemed ... *proud*? Robert moved around them so he could greet the two people who in every way apart from the biological were his real parents and was shocked to feel from them a distancing, a kind of mental handing over.

Robert was allowed out from school to have dinner with them all that night at a hotel. The stranger who was his father talked to him man to man about the reasons why he had decided to sell the plantation and explained that he would be employed by Dunlop to manage both 'our' spread and the two adjoining ones.

'The time for the small chap is over, you see,' he said.

'Yes, sir,' Robert said. He remembered the plantation as being enormous, but supposed everything was relative.

They were staying for three months and expected him to spend his summer holidays with them at the flat they had rented in London. They discussed his future, which was to be in rubber. He looked helplessly at Susan, who gave him an encouraging smile and once more ordered Douglas to the rescue. He came to Charterhouse and took Robert out to tea.

'They are your parents,' he said. 'You can't change that.'

'It's just that they appear after all this time and seem to think they own me,' Robert said.

'Well, they do in a sense. Your old man has paid for an expensive education to give you the best possible start in life. Do you think he was wrong to do that?' When Robert did not reply, Douglas continued: 'Naturally he was not. Seeing you must have proved to them both that they were absolutely correct.' He hit him playfully on the arm. 'You've turned out pretty well in my opinion. Now eat your strawberries and cream and stop fussing.'

Douglas was right. Robert could not possibly regret the person he was now. The idea was ridiculous. It was odd to see his mother and father on Founder's Day instead of Susan and Clive, but now the shock was over he could recognize how exotic and glamorous his mother was and it was fun to notice that the other boys thought so too. He had never before realized how much younger than his father she was, but when he came to think about it this explained the ten-year age gap between himself and Douglas, for he knew Susan was only two years older than her brother.

He enjoyed escorting his mother around London, to the shops and sights. She needed his help to find her way around, to deal with taxis and the currency, and he grew more mature almost by the day. Quite often, too, he went with his father to the Dunlop offices and began to believe he would like to spend some time there getting to know the ropes before returning to Ceylon to work alongside his father. His memories of the place were enhanced by his mother's constant, 'Darling, you *must* remember. Surely you do!' He asked after Victor, but he and his family had moved away. The two boys had stopped corresponding years ago.

Yes. A couple of years at head office, and then ... home. He went to see his parents off, and this time his mother cried and his father gripped his shoulder in emotion. He understood: they had done their duty by him and were fearful he would not do his by them.

He left school, wondered if he should go and fight in Spain and decided not to. He was a cautious sort of fellow and not inclined to dispose of his life for a principle or a people he knew nothing about. He moved into Douglas's flat in London – Douglas was a barrister and doing well – and began his apprenticeship in the rubber business.

He liked the work and looked forward to getting to the

other end of it, to the raw product dripping into coconut shells from taps in the rubber trees, to the frangipani and the palms and the peacocks in the wild. As time went on, however, he realized that this was going to have to be delayed for he would soon be required to put his life on the line for his country.

A friend came to stay and the two young men discussed the imminent war.

'The way I see it,' Geoffrey said, 'we join the Reserves and do our training now. Mind you, it will mean we get called up first.'

'I'd join up anyway the moment war was declared,' Robert said stoutly.

'And me, but by my method we can choose our service and get in as officers. Train together, perhaps.'

'I'm for it,' Robert said. Geoffrey's presence would ensure that he would be called Rubber Ball for the duration, but never mind. 'Which service?'

'The senior one, naturally,' Geoffrey said.

'Lucky it's short,' Olivia commented. 'It will be thoroughly confusing.'

'Why? There's a hint there.'

'True, I suppose.'

'Now I've caught up with myself, where did you go when you left Anglesey?' Emma asked.

'To school, of course.'

'Where?'

'Does it matter?' Olivia went into the house, leaving Emma on the tiny patio, and re-emerged with a small case which she opened to reveal a set of darts. 'Want a game?'

The dart board was on the woodshed door. Gran was determined to star on the White Horse's darts team, but was being coy about revealing herself until she was sure she could live up to the high esteem in which she was held because of the skittles. Graham said she was coming on well.

Emma had learned a bit about the game during her stay on Anglesey, for Rhys had a dart board and was something of an ace. She scooped the three darts from the case, hefted them and wondered what kind of inscription they would have on them if they served their mistress as well as H.G.A.'s guns had served him; and to whom Gran would give them if so.

Silly meanderings. Emma only seemed to be half here these days, her mind in other countries, other times. She threw the darts: a one, a double twenty and a fluke bull. She went to pluck the darts from the board and turned to hand them to her grandmother.

Olivia took them, replaced them in the case and reached out to smooth Emma's hair away from her face.

'Darling, I'm being stupid and selfish,' she said. 'I'll tell you, but it could get repetitive and boring. It was a bit like what happened to Robert – something which might have been bad but turned out good. I even had the tendency to a sing-song accent.'

'I've been meaning to ask you about that. Do you remember any Welsh?'

'Not a word. Odd when you think I spoke it fluently until I was thirteen, but I can still pronounce the name of that village.'

'The one near the Britannia Bridge? It's the longest place name in the UK. Llanfair something.'

'Llanfairpwllgwyngyllgogerchwyrndrobwllllantysiliogogogoch.'

'Good heavens!'

'But I shouldn't bother to write it down. It looks even more ridiculous on paper than it sounds.'

Part V

I
____

Olivia adjusted her hairband and wiped her hands over her hair in an attempt to smooth it. There were no mirrors, so she could not tell if she had succeeded. She rubbed at a chalk mark on her dark blue tunic, took a breath and knocked on Reverend Mother's door.

'Come.'

She went in, curtseyed and waited for Reverend Mother's black-veiled head to look up from the desk. When it did the light reflected from the utilitarian glasses. A white frill surrounded her face and Olivia always found the bare flesh of her neck rather shocking. Nuns shouldn't have flesh in the same way as they didn't have hair.

'Ah. Olivia.'

'Yes, Reverend Mother.' Olivia bobbed another curtsey.

'Your father has written to me with a somewhat unusual request.'

She waited. Olivia stared at the crucifix on the wall behind Reverend Mother and tried to empty her mind, make her face a blank mask. To ask what the request was or to appear eager would invite a lecture on the proper comportment of young ladies.

'On balance,' Reverend Mother said, satisfied, 'I have decided to accede to it.'

'Thank you, Reverend Mother.' Olivia worked it out: accede meant assent, didn't it?

Reverend Mother smiled. 'Don't overdo it, child. I am very pleased with your progress so far but there are times when it appears unconvincing. Now,' she went on briskly, 'you are not to take this as a privilege for yourself or think that rules will be bent or broken for you at the drop of a hat. Your father is going away, is he not?'

'Yes, Reverend Mother.' Or should she have said no, in answer to the previous comment?

'He has asked if he may take you out to luncheon on Saturday.'

Olivia gasped with joy. She could not help it. Reverend Mother chose to ignore it, or to take it as appreciation of her generosity.

'He will collect you at eleven o'clock and I want you back here no later than five. Is that understood?'

'Yes, Reverend Mother.'

'You may go.'

Olivia had been at the Convent of the Sacred Heart for six weeks. She had arrived so shellshocked by what had happened, by the abrupt flight from Anglesey, that the strangeness of the place had scarcely registered. But that same strangeness had also institutionalized her to the extent that now, as she left Reverend Mother's office, she could feel real gratitude at being allowed to leave school for seven hours to see her own father before he left for Africa.

She was secure here in the convent. From the moment she got up in the morning and put on the uniform from which no deviation was permitted to the time she folded that same uniform on the chair beside her bed in the prescribed way her life was regulated. Girls were allowed long or short hair but the style was censored (the hairband Olivia wore was on the orders of Mother Eliot) and no experiments were allowed, for to care about your appearance – beyond being clean and tidy – was to fall towards the sin of pride. You never talked or ran in the corridors and you curtseyed when you passed a nun as she floated along, hands in sleeves, rosary beads clicking softly. If you broke the rules you were punished before the whole senior school every week at exemptions, when each girl's name was read out and the summary of her behaviour given, from 'excellent' to the expel-worthy 'unsatisfactory', and you collected the relevant card from Reverend Mother.

Olivia was an outsider – as the only Protestant in the senior school she was bound to be, and she had arrived after term had begun – but she did everything she could to be like everyone else. She crossed herself as she passed the chapel doors and helped pick the flowers to be placed before the statues of Jesus and of Our Lady. She recited the Hail Mary before each lesson and other prayers afterwards. She asked if she could attend Mass instead of sitting on her own in the classroom, and she put on her white veil and gloves and tried to get her tongue around the Latin in the missal Reverend Mother had lent her. The priest preached about the fiery pit that awaited her along with all other Protestants, sinners and heathens, but she did not believe him. Instead she believed that, whatever else was confused and had gone wrong, she belonged.

The nuns had not, of course, eliminated naughtiness, bullying or the girl in the class no one liked, and some of them displayed temper, spitefulness and other secular failings, but everything had soft edges and nothing hurt. The girls were always supervised and close friendships were forbidden, so there was neither time nor opportunity to do anything to excess.

Except be unhappy, and even that was not allowed. It, too, had its edges blurred. Within the convent walls, within the embrace of the Roman Catholic Church, the world and the war might not have existed. Heaven only knew what purposed Nell to send Olivia there – convenience, perhaps; perhaps to wound Harry still further, for he disliked religion for what it did in Africa – but it was the best thing she could have done.

And Harry was wounded. He had an interview with the Reverend Mother, who seemed nice enough and assured him Olivia had settled in well, but he winced as his daughter, her hair scraped back from her face, entered the visitors' parlour and dropped him a curtsey.

'Moppet!' he said, appalled, and, ignoring the disapproving glare of the old nun who had come in with her, went to her, hugged her, removed the offending band and fluffed out her hair. 'That's better,' he said smiling, though he was close to tears.

For Olivia the smell of tobacco was almost unbearably nostalgic. The nun unlocked the front door and they hustled each other out before either could do anything unseemly.

'You're not wearing the dress I sent you for your birthday,' Harry said as they got into the car.

'No. I'm not allowed to. It's very pretty, though,' she added politely.

'I want to buy you your Christmas present today. Will you be allowed that?'

'It depends what it is,' she said, a first smile, as shaky as Harry's had been, appearing. His voice, teasing and loving, was so beautifully familiar. He took his pipe from his jacket pocket and put it into his mouth. 'Shall I fill it for you?' she asked.

'Oh, yes *please*, my Moppet,' he said, as if he wanted nothing more in the whole world.

He handed her the pipe and his tobacco pouch and watched out of the corner of his eye as she pulled out the strands of tobacco and carefully filled the bowl.

'How long will you be in Africa for?' she said.

'I don't know for sure. I'm only glad the Colonial Office has found me something useful to do.'

'A DC again?'

'No. Less exciting than that, I'm afraid.'

'Will you see Mutali?'

'I hope so.'

Gradually the convent girl receded and something like the old Moppet emerged. Something like: he had destroyed the old one for ever.

They went to a fun fair which they happened to pass by, then he took her for the most lavish lunch the George at Stamford could provide under wartime conditions. In the afternoon they went shopping. He did not know how long he would be away and the world was a precarious place these days; he wanted to buy her something she would not grow out of, would not leave behind as she grew older. Jewellery, perhaps, but she said the only jewellery they were allowed – he was getting bored with that horrible word – to wear at school was a plain gold cross.

'Or a Child of Mary medal,' she said. 'But of course I'm not allowed those.'

'Why?' Annoyed anything should be denied his daughter.

'Because I'm not Catholic,' she explained patiently.

'Oh.'

'I would like a gold cross, Daddy. Please.'

He bought one for her, wondering what his old friend Father Patrick would say when he heard. If Harry told him. Anyway, he reflected, better he gave it to her than one of the popish friends she chatted about. Why was Harry haunted by the Roman religion?

He returned her to the convent at five minutes to five, but stopped her getting out of the car immediately.

'You will write to me, Moppet, won't you? If you lose

245

the address, care of Government House in Nairobi will reach me.'

'Of course I'll write. Daddy, will the ship be safe?'

'As houses. Don't worry.'

'Can I have my hairband back, please?'

He had confiscated it and produced it for her. 'Don't put it on yet,' he said.

She fiddled with the cheap, gaudy things she had won – or he had won for her – at the fair. 'Daddy . . .' she began, not wanting to hurt him.

'You aren't allowed them.' He removed them and, twisting around, placed them on the back seat.

They got out and he rang the convent bell. It jangled away into secret places Moppet knew but he would never. Bolts creaked.

'Goodbye, darling Moppet. Take the greatest care of yourself.'

He turned away as the door opened so she would not see his tears; thus he did not see her put on the hairband.

In spite of what her father said, she worried about the sea voyage and prayed for his safety. She thought he had gone to Kenya to do war work and did not know about the divorce proceedings. She thought he would return and live with her, her mother and Nick again, if not on Anglesey then in the house her mother had taken near Fotheringhay where Mary Queen of Scots had been beheaded – an act of unparalleled villainy, according to Olivia's history teacher, for she had a rightful claim to the English throne and would have rescued the country from the heresy of Protestantism. The house was quite nice, from the one time Olivia had seen it, although it was a long way from the sea, and there were outbuildings which could be converted into kennels for the dogs. Most of the girls' fathers were away from home, after all.

She looked forward to the Christmas holidays with

some misgivings, having come to rely on the structured days, but her father had left for her the most wonderful surprise.

'Busy?' Olivia said, her eyes on stalks. *'Busy?'* as the spaniel recognized her and greeted her. 'Oh, Busy!', her face in the silky ears.

'I didn't tell!' Nick crowed. 'I wanted to and it nearly popped out once on the way, but I didn't.'

'Have you been looking after her?'

'Yes, and taking her for walks every day.'

Olivia, forgetting that the last time she had seen Busy was outside a barn on Anglesey, glanced at her mother, wondering how on earth she had been persuaded to have a dog, let alone allow it to live inside, for there was a basket in the kitchen with a water bowl beside it.

'I don't mind dogs in small numbers, so long as they are clean and don't smell,' Nell said. 'We couldn't let Busy go to strangers, could we?'

Olivia's joy was enough reward for Nell making the concession to Harry. He had been uncharacteristically cold and utterly determined when he told her that it was disgraceful of her to torment their daughter in the hope of tormenting him.

'That awful school,' he had said. 'How could you, Nell?'

'She's happy enough there,' she had said defensively.

'You must be disappointed, then.'

No, she wasn't disappointed but Harry had touched upon her motives and she was ashamed. Busy was no trouble.

'You'll have to take her out with your gun and feed us all, won't you?' she said to Olivia.

'My gun is here?'

'Upstairs in your room.'

And upstairs, too, were the toys won at the fair, arranged on the chest of drawers with a care and humour that could only belong to her father. She wept in happiness and loss.

At school news of the war was filtered to the children in measured doses. Here outside the convent Olivia was exposed to the full horror of it. Cities were being bombed and Britain was holding off Hitler by a miracle or, as Olivia was now inclined to believe, by God's help. Her father was on the U-boat-infested seas somewhere between Liverpool and Africa.

To take her mind off things, Olivia taught Nick to shoot – though carefully rationed the ammunition Harry had provided – and how to work Busy. Nurse put up a terrific argument but Olivia told her that Nick knew every one of Daddy's safety rules and she had learned to shoot when she was Nick's age.

'He's not to go out by himself.'

'Naturally not,' Olivia said. Her tone of voice would have earned her a reproof at the convent; but the place had also instilled in her an almost nun-like stand-offishness and Nurse was unnerved. 'Graves has promised to take him,' Olivia added.

Busy, former field trial champion, had once opened royal doors; that of the neighbouring sporting farmer had been child's play to her.

'I've got to get rid of Nurse,' Nick said one morning as they stumped across a frosty field. 'Olivia, you can't imagine the awfulness of her, the ragging I get.'

He was at a prep school near by. He would insist on boarding, he said, if it wasn't for Busy; both he and Olivia couldn't be away.

He hit upon a solution two days later. He and Olivia were in the village shop and a woman there was complaining about the shortages, about staff difficulties, and, to cap it all, her nanny was going to work in a munitions factory.

'A flighty youngster,' the woman said. 'I should have employed someone older and steadier.'

The shopkeeper emitted sympathetic noises and Olivia saw Nick's eyes widen. Before she could stop him he stepped forward.

'Excuse me,' he said, 'is a nanny the same as a nurse? I only ask,' he went on rapidly, 'because we've got a splendid nurse at home who's very old and perfectly longing to take care of proper children.'

The woman looked down at him. She must be a very nice mother, Olivia decided instantly, for her complaining expression turned into amusement.

'And what is a proper child?' she asked.

'One not like me,' Nick said. 'I'm far too old to have a nurse.'

The woman put her head on one side. 'Don't I know you?' she mused

Nick extended his hand. 'My name is Nicholas Wittering. How do you do?'

'Very well, thank you. I'm Mrs Falkirk.' She took the hand and shook it. 'What good manners you have. Did your nurse teach them to you?'

'Yes,' Nick said gloomily. 'I expect so.'

'I've met your mother. I think I might call upon her.'

She did, that very afternoon. Gales of laughter came from the sitting room, the like of which Olivia and Nick, slinking in the passage outside, had never heard before. They retired as Nurse was summoned and were innocently playing Snap when she puffed her way up to the nursery ('Nursery,' Nick had said. 'See what I mean?'). Somehow they both managed to keep a straight face as Nurse told them that there were poor little children who needed her help and that, because of the war, she was required to go to their aid.

'But don't worry,' she said to Nick. 'I shall see you every day. Master Giles Falkirk goes to the same school as you.'

She went out to pack her things and Olivia and her brother fell into an exquisite fit of giggles.

She could not believe she had once thought her brother soppy and a bore. She was as thrilled as he was when he unwrapped the Christmas present from their father. It was a gold Rolex watch, far too big for his skinny wrist, and he drove everyone mad by asking them if they wanted to know the time. For Olivia there was a pearl necklace, and she discarded the cross on its chain and wore the necklace and the dress Harry had given her for Christmas lunch.

'Where's Olivia?' Aunt Celia said, pretending to search for the familiar tomboy and then kissing her niece. 'You look lovely,' she said. 'Very grown up.'

The convent claimed her and laid its tentacles upon her. Her father arrived safely in Kenya and wrote her several letters, many of which she was not permitted to read. Reverend Mother felt obliged to write to him to tell him that the topics he covered and the language he employed were hardly suitable for the consumption of a thirteen-year-old girl, though in fact Reverend Mother found the letters riveting. They were about the scandalous murder of Lord Erroll, formerly Josslyn Hay – he who had diagnosed Nell as a virgin on her arrival in Kenya – and she had known his mother in the giddy days before she had taken the veil. Lord Broughton had been charged with the killing and all Nairobi (and Reverend Mother) was avidly awaiting the trial. Still, it would not do. And as for Major Wittering informing his daughter that a bitch had whelped . . . !

Major Wittering's reply, which came several weeks later, was full of outrage that Reverend Mother should read his private letters to his daughter and inquired sarcastically if she read Olivia's to him.

'You must explain to him that this is the way we do things here,' Reverend Mother said to Olivia.

The children had to leave the flaps of the envelopes of every letter they wrote unsealed and all incoming ones were read. Olivia no longer thought about it and fumbled in her explanation of why it should be so.

'It is done to protect the minds of the children under our care from unsuitable influences,' Reverend Mother said. 'Now go and write it again, child.'

Other girls might have received a harsher scolding, but Reverend Mother was easy on Olivia, treating her firmly but kindly. Olivia's friends dreaded a summons from Reverend Mother and often emerged from her office in floods of tears to spend hours in the chapel in penitential grief. Not so Olivia. She was not on the whole disobedient and the full wrath of the nuns seldom descended on her, and they were reluctant to let it do so. They were advancing stealthily on their prey.

2

Eventually Aunt Celia told Olivia about the divorce, since no one else seemed inclined to.

'But – but that's a sin!' Olivia exclaimed.

'Lots of people get divorced,' Aunt Celia said largely. 'I will be soon, too.'

'Don't you want to be married to Uncle Donald any more?'

Her family was full of sin, and she would have to do a lot of praying for them. Reverend Mother had said God would hear her prayers even though she was not Catholic. Two years of stalking had almost succeeded, the only obstacle now being her parents' consent to her conversion.

'Well,' Aunt Celia said after a while, 'we don't always get what we want, do we?'

Donald had left her because she could not bear children; after her miscarriage she had failed to conceive again and he had fallen for a younger and fertile woman.

'Don't worry,' Olivia told her. 'You are still married in the eyes of God.'

'You have understood, haven't you? In the eyes of the world your mother and father aren't married any longer.'

Olivia was fifteen years old and had to accept it, but she could not help hoping and prayed to God to put it right.

*

She thought her prayers were answered when her father returned to England. He had been gone nearly three years and was amazed how tall she was, how pretty.

'Wait until you see Nick,' she said. 'He's ginormous.'

'I can't wait, actually. We're going to see him straight away.'

'But –'

'I've got permission to take you out for the day ... though why I should need it I have no idea. Hurry along and change, Moppet.'

Oh, to be called Moppet again! She went outside to report to the nun overseeing Saturday morning games and met Linda Lacey.

'Golly,' Linda said, 'you look as though you've found a five-pound note.'

'My father's here,' Olivia said and then recalled that Linda's father was dead. They had been praying for his soul – his and those of other girls' fathers. 'I'm sorry, Linda.'

'You're lucky. In spite of everything you're lucky. Remember that, Olivia.'

Linda was going to be a nun. She maintained she had received her vocation with her First Communion and had not doubted it since. Once a week she offered her Mass up to the cause of Olivia's conversion, which was incredibly generous of her when her father's soul was in purgatory.

Olivia went to change into what the girls called civvies, half thinking she was dreaming. But no: her father was in the visitors' parlour with Reverend Mother.

'Back by supper-time, child.'

'Yes, Reverend Mother.'

'She was trying to persuade me to let you convert,' Harry said as they drove away.

'Daddy – '

'When you are twenty-one, Moppet, you can do as you please.'

I'll convert, God, she promised, if he goes back to Mummy.

But he had been married to Eve Barker for over a year.

'Oh, Harry,' Celia said. 'When will you learn to be strong and face up to things?'

'Never. Will you tell them? Say it happened recently.'

'But they'll realize you were planning it when you saw them.'

'Please, Celia.'

She sighed in Anglesey and he heard it at his hotel in Stamford.

'Very well,' she said. 'It will take some arranging to get down there. There is a war on, you know.'

Celia made her way south-east with some difficulty, wondering whether to tell both children together or separately. Brother and sister were close, but the news would hit Olivia hardest. Other children's fathers were dying and this could hardly be classed as high tragedy, but the magnitude of individual hurts could not be compared.

Celia had to meet Reverend Mother first and explain. She did not know that it was a tricky time for the nun. She would not have Olivia under her control for very much longer, for she was leaving at the end of this school year, and was aware of the pact Olivia had made with God, although, of course, she deplored it for no mortal could do any such thing. Olivia was reaching an age when, Reverend Mother thought, she could convert without her parents' permission, but what her father had done might make her less inclined to defy them. On the other hand, so long as she did not blame God, it could provoke the opposite. Truly the mind of a child not brought up in the Faith was a morass, and it was frustrating so nearly to have a soul for Jesus.

In spite of this, however, she could not deny Olivia's aunt access to her, and Celia for the first time witnessed the convent girl on her home ground. Long hair, by now, pulled back and tied in a single thick plait, the ugly uniform, the curtsey.

They walked up and down on the terrace, their breath causing minor explosions in the November air, while Celia delivered the unpalatable facts.

'*Married?*' Olivia said. 'Daddy and Eve Barker?'

'You have to live with it, Olivia. Worse things are happening.'

'Yes.' Such as death. There were things to do about death, though; rituals to be observed.

Olivia had invested three years of prayers in this, her only selfish petition to the Catholic God into whose arms she had been thrust. She had been told that God did not grant wishes at whim, that humankind had free will but everything that happened was nonetheless God's will. His Church directed that marriage was a sacrament and could not be undone. Olivia had prayed that her father would live with his wife and children again, and it seemed peculiarly capricious of God to make it His will that her father broke God's own law and married for a second time – and Eve Barker at that.

Olivia became, by her lights and those of the school, naughty. She was stripped of her prefect's ribbon for persistent talking; she stopped plaiting her hair and instead wore it in a ponytail. She could not be reprimanded for vanity since the style was suitably Puritan, but the ponytail had a jaunty and defiant swing about it, as Olivia well knew. She began to ask awkward questions and put them to the nuns with feigned, wide-eyed innocence.

Please, Mother (curtseying), was God having a difficult time during the war?

God never has a difficult time, child.

Yes, but how was it that the Russians, who had dismissed Him as the opium of the people, were on the side of right and good, and the Germans who had started this wicked war were Christians?

Protestants, child. Protestants.

But their Axis allies were the Italians. Rome was in Italy; Rome was the fount of the Catholic faith. The Holy Father, the descendant of St Peter the Fisherman, lived in Rome.

The Vatican City, Olivia, is not part of the Italian state.

Yes, but what of all the Catholics in Italy? How had they so abandoned their faith as to fight on Hitler's side? And –

Enough, child. You have a habit of pushing yourself forward, forming your own opinions, not thinking before you speak or listening afterwards.

Olivia took her defiance a stage further during the Easter holidays and had her hair cut and curled into a fashionable bob by Nell's hairdresser.

'Child, you do not have a Catholic soul,' Reverend Mother said, almost despairing.

'Why is that, Reverend Mother?'

At exemptions that week she was given 'fair', only one level above the dreaded 'unsatisfactory'. The senior school gasped at such a falling from grace and Olivia's cheeks burned as she took the dirty green card. 'Unsatisfactory' was a muddy brown and that card Reverend Mother did not deign to touch. You had to pick it up from the table, and there were only two or three of them (seldom awarded but a reminder that they existed) compared to the healthy piles of shades of blue – the colour of Our Lady's mantle – which were designated 'good' to 'excellent'.

All right, God, Olivia decided as she curtseyed again, moved away and deposited her shameful card on a side table. I realize this is letting us both down, but me more than You. She stopped being silly, kept her head down and reverted to her normal behaviour.

Reverend Mother suspected – rightly – hypocrisy, though, and Olivia was never again awarded the gorgeous azure card of excellence.

She and Nick met their father and . . . Eve for lunch. Olivia could accept no other description of her than her Christian name, for the other possibilities were unbearable: her father's wife, her stepmother, Mrs Wittering.

Eve found it hard to face up to Olivia's accusing, hostile gaze and turned her attention to Nick, who had not known her before except, perhaps, as one of the anonymous adult friends of his parents, and had certainly not seen her naked in a barn.

'She's not too bad,' he said to Olivia afterwards. 'In fact, I think she's rather nice.'

'I'll never like her,' Olivia said, 'and she'll never like me.'

3

Olivia left school and, at her mother's insistence, learned shorthand and typing. Nell had leased a flat in Hampstead: home at last after an adventure begun eighteen years ago when she had boarded ship for Africa, and London surely safe now that the Allies were in Europe and the war almost over. Olivia wasn't much impressed by Hampstead, and neither was Busy, but they both enjoyed the heath.

Olivia had spent years in school uniform but was longing to put on a service one before it was too late. Not wearing uniform in London made you stand out almost as much as not wearing it at school and, besides, Olivia – as her father had – wanted to do her bit. On her seventeenth birthday she offered her shorthand and typing to the Women's Royal Army Corps and in a few months was a tiny cog in the war machine. The front line of her convent innocence retreated daily before the battle-hardened conversation of the other typists and the cheerful swearing of the NCOs.

'Damn!' she exclaimed when she made a mistake, and looked around expecting Reverend Mother vengeful at her shoulder. She no longer thought of converting and the Catholic religion had been relinquishing its hold on her since she had learned her father had remarried – though really she did not blame God for that – but she could now see how it had helped her and was grateful to it.

Harry was also in London, a step away from hell he would once have considered it, doing something or other in the Colonial Office, and he met Olivia for lunch once a week. Olivia loved him – who could not?, apart from the woman who had married him first, which seemed a cruel twist – but found his guilt and anxiety about what he had done difficult to deal with. It seemed that his attention to her, the half-teasing, half-worried inquiries about whether she could spare time to see him, the way he made such efforts to find somewhere new to take her (apologizing about the food, as though that at the convent was a level to be aspired to): all this was an attempt to make everything up to her.

She knew what the solution was and, once, when Nick was home for his school holidays – Nick inches taller than her and a swaggering public schoolboy – she tried to arrange a truce. Eve should join them for lunch, she said, hoping her voice sounded more enthusiastic than the rest of her felt; they should get to know each other better.

Olivia could not believe that her efforts were greeted with such indifference and insensitivity. Eve arrived at lunch at the Savoy swathed in furs, her face made up so it showed the world a distant mask.

'How sweet,' she said, raising painted eyebrows at Olivia's army uniform. 'Are you winning the war for us? . . . Harry, darling' (leaning against him, tucking her arm through his and holding his hand). 'I'd adore a gin.' And kissing him when the waiter brought it, leaving a touch of red on his moustache.

See? her cold eyes said. He's mine, and there's nothing you can do about it.

Olivia had intended to be friends with her, truly she had. It did not matter that her father released himself from his wife's hold, pulled out his handkerchief with definite irritation, wiped his mouth and moustache and then devoted himself to his son and daughter. The lunch was scuppered before it had begun.

On a chilly April morning Olivia went into the kitchen and was surprised not to be greeted by Busy eager for her early run on the heath.

'Come on, lazy-bones,' Olivia said, shaking the lead at the spaniel curled up in the basket. 'Walk time.'

Still Busy did not move. Her busy days were done.

Harry said he would find her a puppy, but Olivia said no. London was no place for a dog and they'd had problems keeping Busy adequately fed. There was truth in that but the other reason, the real one, was that Olivia did not want to be tied to Hampstead by anything. Nothing could replace Busy, and an attempt to try could wait; life would not. The war would be over soon and it had occupied six of her seventeen years. There were things in the world to be discovered.

Germany surrendered three weeks later and Olivia and a group of friends went into the streets with the rest of London to celebrate. There had never been a night like it. Church bells rang out and strangers hugged each other. There was a smile on every pallid, war-ravaged face, smiles and laughter and pure joy. Somewhere in Piccadilly Olivia was parted from her friends and found herself surrounded by boisterous tall men.

'Olivia!'

She heard her friend's voice, turned, stumbled and was caught and held against a broad, uniformed chest.

'Rubber Ball,' said a slightly drunken voice. 'What have you picked up?'

A curl fell across the man's forehead as he peered down to examine his trophy. He grinned.

'Something rather interesting, I believe,' he said.

Part VI

I

'Well, isn't that charming!' Olivia exclaimed admiringly.

Emma was not to be distracted. 'It must have been a whirlwind romance between you and Granddad,' she said.

'Must it?' Her grandmother appeared startled at the idea.

'Yes, since Mum was born the next year . . . Unless – Gran, you didn't!'

'No, of course not,' Olivia said laughing. 'It was a proper white wedding and Daddy gave me away weeping buckets. It's the thought of a whirlwind romance. It didn't seem like that. I suppose at the end of the war everyone was longing to get on with life. As you so rightly say.'

'Did Granddad ever go back to Ceylon?'

'Occasionally with the Navy, and we went once for a holiday. His parents left there after independence.'

'And came to England? That must have been a shock.'

'It was,' Olivia said, remembering her mother-in-law's whining about the cold and the lack of servants.

'Serves them right after what they did to Robert. It seems a cruel way to treat a child,' Emma reflected.

'Yes and no. I'd say you described the dilemma perfectly.' Olivia gazed at her granddaughter with the manner of a teacher whose dimmest pupil has managed, against the odds, to answer a question correctly. 'There weren't passenger airlines in those days,' she went on. 'Robert had to have an education, so what choice did his parents have?'

'Not to have been colonials to begin with.'

'Careful, Emma,' Olivia warned. 'You're in danger of being hoisted on your own up a creek without a paddle, or whatever the saying is. You've written . . . yes, quite movingly . . . about how my mother forced my father to leave Africa. If she hadn't done so the same would have happened to Nick, and perhaps to me as well, as it did to Robert. No question about Nick, though. A boy had to be given an education and what do you think Daddy was if not a colonial?'

'Oh.' Then rallying quickly: 'But H.G.A. approved of Kenya being independent.'

'Did he? And didn't Robert's father of Ceylon?'

'You tell me.'

'He thought it a shocking waste of a decent country.'

'There you are, then.'

'Am I? If you say so, darling.'

'Gran, I don't think you're being awfully helpful.'

'I'm trying to be, honestly I am. It's . . .'

'What?' Emma prompted.

'How can I put it? You've been very clever in the way you've excluded my father from the worst excesses of the white people in Kenya, and it is true he did want independence for the natives, but you have fuzzed the lines somewhat.'

'How?'

'He wanted independence when the time was right. In no way did he think they were ready for it when, say, India was, although he did think that the Mau Mau rebellion was waiting to happen, that in many ways the white settlers asked for it. He was a liberal, but there's no doubt that he agreed with colonialism in its every part.'

'I haven't said he didn't.'

'Cleverly fuzzed, darling. You've made him acceptable to the 1990s though his attitudes were pure 1920s and '30s. That business of him only shooting things when necessary . . . Is there an animal in his photograph albums actually alive?'

'I know,' Emma had to admit. 'Mum said the same. She once asked him if he felt guilty for killing so many harmless, beautiful creatures and he became quite upset and angry. But I've got to make him sympathetic, haven't I?'

Olivia raised a questioning eyebrow. 'It depends what for,' she said. 'I suppose.'

'Karen Blixen's ambition was to shoot one of every type of animal in Africa, and she wasn't the only one. The rarer the type the more pleased they were. It's attitude, as you say. It seems inexplicable now.'

There was silence for a while.

'What happened to Douglas?' Emma asked at last.

'Robert's cousin? I never knew him. He died on the Burma railway.'

Were there tears amid the euphoria at the end of the war? Yes, of course there were and for a long time afterwards. Robert had taken her to meet his uncle and aunt in Yarmouth. It was over three years since Douglas had been captured by the Japanese and there was no reason as well as every reason to hope until the dreadful news came. Some time afterwards a haunted, wizened object of a man had made his way to Yarmouth with a last message from Douglas to his parents. He died well, the man had said in an attempt to comfort, his appearance belying his words. Only later was something approaching the true suffering of the prisoners on the railway revealed, and Robert had followed the war crimes trials of those responsible with a desperate, pained obsession.

'I wish you could have met him,' he had said over and over. 'He was a super chap. The very best.'

If Olivia and Robert had had a son he would have been called Douglas.

'There's a headstone,' Olivia said now to her granddaughter. 'We went to see it.'

Rows and rows of them there were, beautifully kept for those who braved the Burmese visa requirements and made the pilgrimage to their loved one's memorial. It was after they returned from there that Robert's illness began.

'You do remember your grandfather, don't you?' Olivia said, suddenly concerned.

'Lots about him.'

'Really? You were only – what? – ten when he died.'

'We all went to Ireland. He built an amazing sand castle.'

'So he did. I'd forgotten that.'

'And we played cricket on the beach. He taught us how to bowl.'

Robert had wanted a holiday with the whole family before things got too bad. None of the others realized exactly how much it had exhausted him but Laura had been marvellous, keeping the children away when Robert couldn't cope and making sure they were there when he could. Because of it her elder child at least remembered Robert.

A touch on her hand, and she jumped.

'You were miles away and you looked so sad,' Emma said.

'Sorry, darling. It's not always a good idea to visit the past.'

'I haven't upset you by making you, have I?'

'No, you silly child.'

'You sound like Reverend Mother.'

Olivia chuckled. 'I doubt that.'

'Why do you think your mother sent you to a convent school?'

'I can't imagine – unless she did indeed intend me to

present Daddy with Catholic grandchildren. Certainly she had no interest in religion of whatever persuasion.'

'You might have become a nun.'

'Heavens above, so I might! That would have larned her, wouldn't it?'

Another silence. A hen gave a series of squawks from the run at the end of the garden to proclaim the fact that she had laid an egg. Smoke drifted over the fence from a bonfire next door.

'How's the feud with your neighbours?' Emma asked.

'I wouldn't have called it a feud. He's stopped making a fuss, thank goodness.' Olivia lifted the lid of the coffee pot on the table beside her on the patio and peered in. 'It's a bit cold but there's enough for another cup. Do you want one?'

'I'll make us some fresh.'

The clock in the sitting room was chiming eleven when Emma went into the kitchen. 'You shut up,' she told it. 'I've worked out where you came from, or I reckon I have.' She only needed to go to a library and check a date.

The will? It was Eve Barker's, of course. No mystery if Emma had been told H.G.A. had married twice. No mystery . . . but cats, though! And if Eve had really been so nasty, and the will was in character, then why had H.G.A. – who, even if he did shoot beautiful wild animals, was far from nasty – stayed married to her? And why had he settled on Guernsey (of all places) after the war instead of returning to Africa where he belonged? He would have been fifty years old, hardly youthful but not near retirement age. And Nick. What had happened to him?

Oh, well. Never mind. It was time to do other things.

She heard a deep voice and saw Graham's burly frame pass the window. She collected a mug from the draining board and took it and the coffee pot outside. Graham was bending to kiss Olivia on the cheek, one large hand resting possessively on her shoulder. He straightened and smiled at Emma.

''Lo there. How've you been, young Emma?'

'Fine, thanks.'

'Still writing away, your gran says.'

'Finished now.'

'Have you, darling? You didn't tell me.' Olivia took the mug and pot. 'Thank you. Graham takes sugar. Would you –?'

Emma went back inside to fetch the sugar bowl – part of the wedding present to her great-grandfather from Prince and Princess Arthur of Connaught – and felt a spasm of jealousy at the sight of two people so obviously and peacefully in love. The rest of the family still didn't know, and Emma had to prevaricate when she went home after her stays with Gran and her mother questioned her about whether Olivia was happy and how she occupied her time.

'I mean, what does she *do*?' Laura would ask. It was not surprising Olivia had finally decided to sell the house in which she and Robert had spent most of their married life, but to move so far away, and with such rapidity, to somewhere where she was a stranger . . .

'She's found lots of friends,' Emma would assure her. 'She adores it there.'

Yeah, and Mum, she's on the skittles team, drinks scrumpy like a native and has an intimate male friend. A farmer and younger than her; rather handsome, actually.

Laura would ring Julie and they would want to meet him, this man who was after their mother's honour and virtue, and he would find that daunting. He wasn't as shy as his nephew, but Emma guessed he had once been and had learned to cover it up. Now that he was relaxed in Emma's company she could see what her grandmother was attracted to. If Emma had been a few years older she might have fancied him herself.

It was up to them, Emma reasoned. If they wanted it kept secret, then so be it. It only meant Graham staying away when members of the family visited Olivia. Emma wondered why she was in on the secret. Perhaps their relationship had only just begun in the spring when she had caught them out.

She remembered the hand on Olivia's shoulder, Olivia's hand reaching up to his cheek. Their ages didn't matter.

And, yes, Emma envied them.

Olivia called her name and she went outside.

'We were about to send in a search party,' Olivia said. She spooned sugar from the bowl into Graham's mug. 'What were you doing? Mining it?'

'Thinking.'

'A sugar mine,' Graham said. 'That would be something, wouldn't it?'

'Sticky in the rain,' Emma said.

'Rain!' Graham gazed at the brown lawn, the drought-stricken shrubs. 'I dream of rain, you know that? I've forgotten what it looks like. I've had to feed my cattle on hay since the beginning of last month. Hay in August! Reckon I'll end up rearing camels like they do in Saudi Arabia and those parts. You seen 'em on the telly? They live on sand, it seems. Do me fine.'

'Is there a market for camel meat in England?' Olivia inquired.

'Might be,' he said, grinning. 'What was they trying a while back? Kangaburgers? Something like that. Camelburgers got a ring to it, hey, Emma?'

'Well,' she said. 'Perhaps. If you really can't sell your beef.'

Olivia directed a quelling glare at her swain. 'Don't tease her, Graham,' she chided, and turned to Emma. 'He loves complaining. All farmers do, I've discovered. It's their favourite occupation.'

'Watch it, 'Livia,' Graham said, the grin still in place.

'He can sell anything he raises or grows,' Olivia continued. 'And at a premium. He's organic, you see.'

'*Are* you?' Emma said.

'Organic! It's a new word, like those people who call theirselves Greens. Greens is veg and good for you, not a blamed political party.'

'But you don't use chemicals?'

'I do not. It's the way it's been on our farm since whenever. My dad'd never heard of chemicals and I don't like 'em or trust 'em. I'm a farmer, not a bloody scientist. No rep from ICI or wherever sets foot on my place, and the vet only comes when the old remedies don't work and a beast is suffering. But I do need water. Rain. The wet stuff that comes from clouds – remember it? Can't be without that.'

Emma recalled his nephew John saying that they did okay on their farm, him and his uncle. Did very nicely, she thought. An unencumbered, unmortgaged property and every health food shop in the area beating a path to their gate, no doubt. And Graham fully aware of the value of his farming policy, in spite of his rejection of labels. He was no one's fool. Gran had got her feet under a substantial as well as wholesome table.

Graham fiddled with his coffee mug and reverted to silence. He did this: outbursts of garrulousness followed by a tongue made of wood.

'Maybe you'd like to see the farm,' he muttered, glancing sideways at Olivia. 'Come for tea this afternoon, look around and maybe stay for supper. I'm no bad cook.'

Olivia waited composedly for her granddaughter's response, but only for a moment. Emma gave it without hesitation.

'It would be great,' she said, 'if it's okay with you, Gran?'

Olivia winked at her, said that would be very nice and they all stood. Emma picked up the coffee tray and tried not to watch her grandmother seeing Graham out of the side gate. They leaned towards each other talking softly (discussing times, probably), Gran giving a light laugh, Graham's arm rising . . . that possessiveness again.

Emma turned away. Jealous, definitely. Her heart was healed and seeking light exercise.

'Have you really finished your writing and all this delving into the past?' Olivia said as Emma, following her directions, manoeuvred the Porsche through the narrow lanes.

'I gave myself the summer. I must get on.'

'How wonderfully disciplined you are, darling. Get on where, may I ask?'

'Well . . . wherever it is my life is going, I suppose.'

'Not towards another nervous breakdown, I hope.'

'No. Not to one of those.'

'But back to what you did before?'

'I suppose so, if I can find a job. What else can I do?'

'I should have thought that obvious,' Gran said with some asperity. 'Turn right after this hideous bungaloid. How can anyone build something so out of place in this landscape? I know everything can't be old, but why does the new have to be so awful?'

'You're enjoying being old, aren't you?' Emma said, wrestling the topic of conversation on to a new track with an emphatic lack of finesse.

Her grandmother didn't mind. She let out what could only be described as a giggle. 'Actually, yes, I'm afraid I am. Do you mind?'

'Mind? What business have I to do that?'

'None. But I'm glad you're not embarrassed.'

'Not in the least.'

Olivia patted her arm. 'That breakdown was the best thing that ever happened to you. You realize that, don't you?'

'Yes. Yes, I do.'

'So don't throw the lessons you've learned away.'

Graham had laid out tea on a table under an apple tree in the garden of his cosy stone house. He produced scones, jam and viscous yellow cream which made eating a deliciously messy business. Emma entertained notions of a plump, apron-clad retainer in the kitchen sweltering over ovens and vats until Graham, amused, said the scones and jam had come from the supermarket. The cream, he admitted, was his own.

'Or my cows',' he amended, with the sideways glance, the grin that made Emma go weak at the knees on her grandmother's behalf. He rose to his feet and his large, rough hands quested gently among the apples above. Two dropped into his palm and he gave one each to Olivia and Emma. 'Clean the palate,' he said.

Emma bit into hers. Sun-warmed on the outside and dew fresh inside.

'Taste good, young Emma?'

'Wonderful.'

'It should do, shouldn't it? Being organic.'

His farm was like those idealized ones in children's picture books: something of everything. Geese, ducks and hens roamed free in the yard. Pigs occupied traditional sties and grunted hopefully on hearing their master's voice.

'Rare breeds, they call 'em,' Graham said, running a stick apparently kept near by for the purpose along a bristled back. 'Daft, isn't it?'

Sheep with black faces and legs, like Siamese cats, grazed in one field and in another little cows with rich ruddy coats chewed the cud while their calves – Emma cried out at the enchantment of them – played king of the castle or tag.

'They're Devon Ruby Reds,' Graham said, in response to Emma's query. 'I get letters and whatnot from you wouldn't believe where asking after them.'

'Do you keep one cow specially for milking?' Emma asked as they walked back to the yard.

'No, we take some from whoever's nearest. We don't need much, and those blokes in Brussels won't let me sell it.'

'It's a beautiful farm,' Emma said. The hedges were cut and laid and there was no barbed wire in sight. In spite of the drought the whole place was fat and content.

'Suits me,' Graham said. 'I just wish it weren't so fashionable all of a sudden and I could be left in peace.'

'Parties of schoolchildren,' Olivia explained. 'Poor Graham's besieged.'

'Had an over-sixties group ring yesterday. The teachers tell me it's a chance for the children to see how a farm used to be run and this woman says it's an opportunity for the old folk to relive their youth. Fine, but where's it leave me? I'm over sixty myself, damn it. I don't like to be mean, but it's the time, see? John and me've other things to do and these kids need supervising. You can't take liberties, 'specially not when there're cows with calves. The idea of a child getting into their field – oh my Lord! I sweat when I think about it.'

'What's the solution then?'

Graham leaned against the stone wall of a barn and folded his arms across his chest. 'I've given it some thought, young Emma,' he said, addressing himself exclusively to her. 'And what I need is a partner. Someone to do the organizing. Take the bookings for the blamed coach parties and show 'em around when they come. Someone in an apron, hey, like you was saying earlier, who'd maybe give them a cream tea. At a fiver a go I'd soon make my fortune now, wouldn't I?'

'You would.' Emma stole a look at her grandmother who was apparently fascinated by the sight of a duck preening itself. Was that a blush on her cheek? 'But where would you find such a person?'

273

'Ah. Well then.' Abruptly Graham pushed himself upright. He had emerged too far from his shell and Emma's last question had reminded him of his vulnerability. 'That's it,' he said, leading them back towards the house. 'My farm.'

'He's great,' Emma said as they drove through the dark lanes to Chard St Sebastian. 'I seem to recall John saying his second wife had left him. How could anyone leave such a kind, gentle man?'

'She was a town girl and much younger than him. She had a notion she'd like to be a farmer's wife but couldn't stand the reality. It would be boring on a farm if you didn't take an interest.'

'Would you be interested in making cream teas, Gran?'

'Mind you own business,' Olivia said placidly.

'He wants you to be, though you'd have to sort out the blokes in Brussels first.'

Silence.

'But he's also scared, isn't he?'

'It's a big step. At one's age.'

'At any age – or it should be.'

'How very moral of you, darling.'

'He's spoken to you, then, about his last wife?'

'Yes.' A pause. 'We talk about most things.'

'He's a good cook,' Emma said. Roast duck, they'd eaten, vegetables fresh from the garden and apple crumble with more of the cream. 'And he's got a gorgeous sense of humour when he's not gone shy.'

'Darling, stop trying to sell him to me as though he was double-glazing.'

'He practically proposed to you, Gran, there in the yard. "Have me, have my coach parties." He might as well have gone down on his knees.'

'Emma, shut up,' Olivia scolded. 'This is no way to speak to your grandmother. You should have more respect.' She was trying to sound severe, but Emma could sense the suppressed laughter.

'I should take him, Gran,' she advised. 'Keep him dangling any longer and he'll get snapped up by someone else. Think of it. On skittles nights there you'll be, tears blurring your eyes, spoiling your aim, while Graham's sole intent is to impress the new Mrs Wellbeck . . . No,' Emma added, after some thought. 'You'll get dropped from the team and will be alone in your cottage dreaming of what might have been.'

'As I have had cause to point out to you on more than one occasion,' Olivia said, 'you have a very vivid imagination. If I were you I'd find constructive use for it.'

'You can't be imaginative with stocks and shares.'

'Exactly,' her grandmother said.

2

The summer was over. The apples hanging heavy on the tree in Graham's garden indicated it and it was confirmed as Emma drove eastward from Dorset by the leaves on other trees turning to autumn from drought brown and tired green.

'I'd said I'd give myself the summer,' Emma told her parents. 'I have, and now I must find another job.'

'But I thought —' Laura began, and then stopped and shrugged. 'All right, but doing what?'

'Something in the City, I suppose. I'll ring around.'

'Wrong strategy,' her father said. 'Your best friends won't want to know you when you're looking for work, believe me. Send off formal applications with your CV and references.'

Brian's reference. It was a glowing testimony to Emma's extraordinary skills and abilities and should land her a directorship at least, except life wasn't like that. What Hamish had said was true. Emma had once been in a position to throw a lifebelt to shipwrecked Yuppies after storms in the City had cast them adrift on a mighty sea of mortgage repayments and school fees. She had been expected to use her influence with Brian. Some of the calls were from friends, and Emma had soon learned to be in meetings when they came and forget to return them. Distant sympathy, yes; instant help, no. A friend stopped being like a friend when he or she had been deemed surplus to requirements. Emma's case wasn't precisely the same, but the outcome would be and the gossip about her breakdown would add to the contamination. Did she really want to go back to that? Being like that?

'I could register with an agency,' she said, trying to sound positive.

'Don't you mean an executive outplacement bureau?' Hamish asked. 'Aren't I up with the jargon? Good idea, darling.'

'Right.' Emma went upstairs to her brother's bedroom, which she had commandeered to house the word processor she had bought on her return from Anglesey. She set it up and created a document: Emma, CV. The machine whirred and clicked and presented her with a blank screen, the cursor blinking encouragingly.

'Name,' Emma typed in: 'Emma Langton. Date of Birth—'

She sighed. The other files on the disc were notes . . . chapters? . . . about H.G.A, her grandmother. She had a ridiculous feeling that they would resent the presence of this intruder.

'Education: Yes. Work Experience: Screwing the boss.'

Be serious. She pressed the delete button and started again.

'Don't fuss,' Hamish said to his wife.

'I couldn't bear it if we had to go through that again.'

'We won't have to. Look at the colour of my acer.' (They were in the garden.) 'Isn't it glorious?'

'And she's hiding something about Mummy.'

'What?'

'If I knew she wouldn't be hiding it. I think we'd better go to Dorset. Mummy's being odd.'

'Hasn't she always been? In the nicest possible way, of course,' said Hamish, who was fond of his mother-in-law.

'When we rang to say Emma was home safely she said she was getting a Dictaphone.'

'Good grief! Whatever for?' This was oddness beyond even Olivia's normal standard.

'She meant an Ansaphone,' Laura said impatiently. 'I assume. What does she want an Ansaphone for? At her age?'

3

Emma had let her flat in London for six months and so invited herself to stay with a friend in Putney. Jackie Lawson was a nurse; she and Emma had been at school together and met when weekends with their parents co-incided, at parties at Christmas and Easter, but seldom recently in London. Jackie thought it significant that Emma chose to be in her unglamorous flat – which was as far as you could get from the Square Mile without being absurd about making a point – rather than with one of her high-flying friends, but kept her counsel.

The bureau which had taken Emma on had arranged several interviews for her and was reasonably confident of placing her, even in the slimmed-down City, provided she was prepared to accept a lower salary and a lower position. She must expect to work her way back up the ladder, she was told. Fine, Emma said listlessly, and dis-covered she could no longer fit into the smart clothes she had designated as her interview ones.

'For God's sake, Emma,' Jackie said, 'why didn't you try them on before? You've been complaining how you've gained weight.'

'Can I borrow something?'

'I suppose so,' Jackie said doubtfully. 'But I'm not into power dressing. Why not buy new clothes?'

'Can't be bothered. Haven't got time. Can I try these?'

'Be my guest.'

Emma appeared in the sitting room a short while later. 'How do I look?' she asked.

Jackie surveyed her. 'I might,' she said, 'if I was your future employer, offer you a job as a secretary providing you stayed in the back room. You're not doing yourself any favours, Ems. Your hair' – picking up an offending lock and examining it – 'is full of split ends. When did you last have it cut?'

'Ages ago. I can't remember.'

'Well, get it done tomorrow, and some new clothes. Regard the interview in the morning as a dry run and work up for the next one.'

'Thanks for the confidence boost.'

'Why are you doing this? You don't want the job.'

'I do!'

'You'd rather be running a guest house in Wales or communing with nature in Dorset.'

'Rubbish,' Emma said.

Her interview lasted fifteen minutes, which shocked and even humiliated her. In spite of what Jackie and the bureau had said, she had believed that she would be the one doing the choosing and being so summarily rejected was not a pleasant experience.

Okay, she would acquire the trappings.

Her hairdresser didn't recognize her when she walked into the salon, then raised his hands in horror.

'*Mon Dieu!*' he exclaimed. 'But what have you done to yourself? The fingernails, too. You have been building the roads, I think.'

'Can you fit me in, Pierre?'

'*Sacré bleu*, I shall have to.' He made a pretence of consulting his appointments book even though the salon was virtually empty, as it would be in this area at this time of day, and declared he could squeeze her in now. He was quite a pretender was Pierre. He pretended he was French and gay, though Emma knew he came from the East End and had a plump wife and three Cockney children. She and Brian had been in Bethnal Green one Saturday morning, slumming it in search of bargains, and she had seen him. Their eyes had met; they had both turned away and never mentioned the episode – which meant Emma pretended too.

Her hair was washed and she was presented, combed and conditioned, to the maestro.

'Not the style we had before,' he decided. 'Your face, it has become a leetle fuller. We need – 'ow we say? – to complement that.' He waited, his head cocked expectantly above hers in the mirror.

She smiled at his reflection. 'Whatever you say, Pierre. You know best.'

He had obviously added up her frumpish clothes, 'fuller' figure and the time she had been away and reached the sum of nine months. Let him think what he liked, the old fake.

Two hours later, manicured and with a new head, Emma emerged from the salon and summoned a taxi to take her west.

It was extraordinary what the months away from London had done to her. She had lost the capital's body language, it seemed. Once she had – presumably she had – walked along the pavements without appearing to look where she was going and automatically avoided bumping into other people. Now she stepped right when someone coming in the opposite direction stepped left, kept knocking into people and was sworn at for not giving her change to three youths – which she might have done had she not been afraid to open her handbag in front of them.

She resisted the urge to jump into a cab and direct it to the multi-storey car park in the City where she had left her car and carried on. Her sense of humour reasserted itself: power dressing; that was what she was here to acquire. She hoped it would work. She had never felt less powerful in her life.

Other interviews lasted longer than the first one, but no job for Emma Langton was forthcoming in the shrunken Square Mile.

'You don't interview well because you're not hungry enough,' Jackie told her. 'You look terrific on the outside but as soon as they peel that away they find a . . . well –'

'What?'

'A rather obvious lack of motivation in the candidate, a disinclination in her to devote herself body and soul to the interests of the firm.'

'No. I'm sure the trouble is explaining my abrupt departure from shitface's outfit and the embarrassing gap in my CV since then.'

'How do you explain it?'

'I say I had a nervous breakdown, naturally, followed by a perfectly reasonable obsession with my family's distant past. Quite ordinary, really, compared with the inmates of your average lunatic asylum.'

'Seriously, Ems.'

'Seriously, Jackie, I flannel about having wanted a sabbatical, an extended holiday, and I don't do it very well. I wouldn't offer me a job so I quite understand why they won't.'

'They don't offer you a job because they know you don't want it,' Jackie said. 'Admit it, Ems. You don't, do you?'

'No,' Emma said, sighing.

Jackie slumped in her chair, wiped imaginary sweat from her brow and held her glass out to Emma to refill with wine. 'Thank God for that! Now let's think positive. You should do something completely different.'

'Like what? I don't know how to do anything else.'

'Learn how, Ems! You're different now.'

'In what way?'

'You look different, for a start, even apart from your hair. Less of a beanpole. Sort of softer all round.'

'Nicer?' Emma said, remembering her grandmother.

'To be honest, yes, since you brought it up. More like my old friend.'

'And what do I do with this new image? Be a nurse like you?'

'You a nurse?' Jackie said, pretending horror. 'We're not that desperate. And anyway,' she added, 'it's not an image. It's you.'

'Thanks, Jackie,' Emma said. 'Your're a real mate.' She felt almost tearful with relief that she could end this charade. She didn't want to live in London again, to donate her one short time on this planet to the capriciousness of the FT Index, Dow Jones, Nikkei and the rest. She had been light years away from those few 'friends' who had returned her calls and invited her for a drink over the past ten days as they had toasted the prospect of Emma's return to the City but had done nothing to promote it happening. Most of all Emma dreaded being like them, stuck on an escalator moving at an ever-increasing speed so they had to work harder to stay in the same place. Or thought they did. You could fall off or step off. Emma had done a bit of both.

'Hey,' she said, 'let's dress up and go out for dinner tonight. My treat. Somewhere really posh.'

'Your swansong, Ems?'

'Maybe. I've got one more interview tomorrow.' She was searching through her Filofax for the number of an expensive and pretentious restaurant . . . help, not there. Brian's favourite. Awful place. This would do. Outrageous prices for the equivalent of three fish fingers and four peas, but oh so tastefully arranged. They could have a good giggle and then come home and fill up on beans on toast. She dialled the number and made a reservation.

'Not maybe. Definitely,' she said, and chucked the Filofax into the wastepaper basket.

Jackie retrieved it. 'Don't go over the top,' she said.

4

Fate decreed Emma would not attend the interview the next morning. She was driving eastwards from Putney when a motorcyclist, lane-hopping, swerved in front of her. She braked and heard the dreadful crunch of metal on metal, then saw the black-leathered rider cartwheel over the bonnet of a parked car and land on the pavement. A woman screamed. Emma sat frozen, then horror was replaced by anger as the motorcyclist, already undoing the chinstrap of his spaceman's helmet, was helped to his feet by passers-by and, evidently not seriously hurt, limped towards the Porsche.

Let him even begin to try to say the accident was her fault! Emma was power-dressed and in the mood. She put on the hand brake, turned off the engine and got out.

'What the hell do you think you were doing?' she demanded of the cyclist, ignoring the snarling and swearing of the traffic behind. 'You came straight across me. Didn't he?' she said to the passers-by. Since there was no blood they were beginning to lose interest, apart from a grey-haired man who organized others to remove the bike from the road and told Emma to get her car out of the traffic lane and park on a double yellow line.

'I want his name and address first,' Emma said, reaching into the Porsche for her Filofax. She opened it at a fresh page, whipped the pen from its slot and thrust both at the motorcyclist. He took them in one gauntleted hand and with the other removed his helmet. A lock of auburn hair fell on to his forehead and he brushed it back, leaving a streak of London grime among the freckles.

'I'm sorry,' he said. 'It's this traffic –'

'If you can't cope with it don't drive in it,' Emma snapped. 'You admit it's your fault, then?'

'Yes. I might be incompetent but at least I'm honest.'

'Oh,' Emma said, her belligerence fading before this. And then, before it departed altogether: 'I still want your name and address. And yours,' she added to the grey-haired man. 'As a witness in case he gets tricky. You heard him say it was his fault.'

'I heard him, but move your motor, will you? A sidelight broken and a few scratches. There's not a lot of damage.'

'Enough,' Emma growled, feeling further deflated. A dragon's tail of traffic was now backed up behind the Porsche, horns hooting and indicators flashing as two lanes tried to get into one. A florist's van moved away from a parking meter beyond the double yellow line and she eased the car in there, got out and returned to the two men, whose heads were together over her Filofax. She suspected male complicity and tried to make the idea of such a thing fuel her waned temper and indignation. To cover signs of weakness she inspected the Porsche. The grey-haired man was right: the damage was slight, especially in comparison with that done to the motorcycle. It sat mournfully on its stand on the pavement, the back wheel looking as though it was trying to go in opposite directions at the same time. The effect, to Emma, was like trying to meet the gaze of someone with boss eyes and, suddenly, she felt shaky and sick. It might not have been her fault, but the buckled metal could so easily have been mangled flesh and bone.

The grey-haired man handed her the Filofax and

she muttered thanks as, his civic duty done, he went on his worthy way.

The cycle rider tossed his gloves into his helmet. 'That's it,' he remarked. 'Motorcycle messengering is not for me and I'm jacking it in. It's my third accident. If one is a misfortune and two is carelessness, what does three count as? . . . Oh, Christ, look at you. You're trembling. Are you all right?'

'Yes,' she said weakly.

'Let me buy you a drink. I certainly need one.'

'I'd just like to sit down for a moment.'

'Pubs have chairs. It's the second best thing about them, the first, of course, being liquid stiffeners.'

Her fingers wouldn't work properly as she took her handbag from the car and fiddled the key into the lock. Shock. Bound to be, thinking, even for a millisecond, that you had killed someone.

'The meter . . . ' she began.

'I'll deal with it,' he said, and produced coins to feed the beast.

There was a pub on the corner of the next intersection, on the other side of the road. As they waited for the lights to change Emma emerged from her fog.

'Hey,' she said, 'I don't want a drink. I must get on.'

'You're in no fit state to drive and *I* want a drink,' her companion said, taking her elbow and propelling her across the road. He was tall and she would have had trouble keeping up with him had his limp not slowed him down.

'How about you? Are you all right?' she asked.

'Bruised. If the last time's anything to go by I'll be interesting shades of colours for a few days and then as good as new.'

The pub had a red-patterned carpet which, presumably, breweries had learned through experience masked the widest variety of stains. The bar and tables were occupied by a spattering of ten-o'clock-in-the-morning drinkers, none of them speaking to each other. Muzak blended their silences. Emma was seated at a table in a grubby patch of sunlight and left with the helmet and gloves while their owner went to wash his hands and order drinks. Beside them on the scarred table was Emma's Filofax. She picked it up, thinking how Jackie would be amused when she heard how soon it had come in handy, and found the names of the motorcyclist and the witness to the accident.

S. Birkenshaw of London SW4 and somewhere in Gloucestershire, and R. E. Carter of London SW4. Who was her present escort, though? S. Birkenshaw, possibly, since she had given the Filofax to him first. Birkenshaw. The name was familiar, but she couldn't think why.

He, or R. E. Carter, came out of the gents', caught her eye and waved at her as he went to the bar. She watched him as he waited for the barman's attention – it being an absolute law that the emptier a place the longer it takes to get served – and was astonished to find a squiggle in her stomach that told her she liked what she saw. Long and lean, even under his cyclist's leathers, he had big, strong hands, one now under his chin and the other tapping idly on the bar, a straight nose and a squarish face. The freckles added humour.

He turned to her, raised an exasperated eyebrow and rapped more authoritatively on the bar. She quickly averted her gaze and pretended to be immersed in the study of her Filofax. What was she thinking of, fancying – well, considering it – a man she had only just met (and in such circumstances!) and whose name she didn't even know? And what about her interview, for heaven's sake?

The shock was over and she was quite capable of driving. She snapped the Filofax shut, grabbed her handbag and was prepared for flight when two brandy glasses were placed on the table before her.

'Please don't go,' Emma's motorcyclist said, sitting down. 'At least not before we've been properly introduced. I'm Stephen Birkenshaw.' A freckled hand was extended and, back in the fog, she took it. He gave hers a firm shake then shaped it round one of the glasses and picked up the other.

'Stephen Birkenshaw?' she stuttered, remembering why the name was familiar.

'Ex-motorcycle messenger and entirely at your service.'

'This is brandy. I can't drink it at this time of day.'

'You've had a shock. It will calm your nerves.'

That shock was forgotten. She had another one to cope with – or did she?

'Stephen Birkenshaw,' she said again, lifting the glass and taking a tiny sip to give herself time.

'I've written it down, and where I live,' he said, pretending to be – or so she thought – offended. 'I can't remember the name of my insurance company, but there won't be any trouble. My only efficiency was admitting I'd be using the bike for what they call commercial purposes.'

'It's not that. Stephen Birkenshaw . . . ' This was incredible, impossible, but she had to ask. 'Was a relation of yours a Battle of Britain pilot?'

He had put down his glass and was groping for something in his leathers. He stopped mid-movement and stared at her. 'Yes, my grandfather. I'm named after him.'

'Then you grandmother is called May.'

He pulled out a packet of French cigarettes and a lighter. 'Was. She died a few years ago.'

But Emma knew that, didn't she? Incredible, impossible. He offered her a cigarette and she shook her head. One last question.

'Do you have a great-aunt called Claire who lives on Anglesey? Her maiden name was Barker.'

'Yes, I have and it was. For Christ's sake, who are you? How do you know this?'

'You and I,' Emma told him, 'are related by a distant marriage. My great-grandfather married your great-aunt Eve.'

'Well, I'm buggered!' he exclaimed. 'Are you sure? . . . Yes, you must be. You know all the names.' He lit a cigarette and dragged on it. 'Eve,' he said thoughtfully. 'The one no one spoke to.'

'The very one.'

'There was a scandal about a will. She was loaded, wasn't she?'

'Yes, and left it to a cats' home.'

'There was some hope she'd chuck a bit of the loot our way. Keep it in the family in spite of the quarrels at the dawn of the age. I remember. I was eleven or twelve at the time. Well, well, well.'

For the first time he looked directly at her, from head to foot. His eyes were tawny. She was glad she had been to Pierre and that her interview gear today was a gold woollen dress. She felt herself blushing and a devastating smile slid up one of the freckled cheeks.

'Fancy me bumping into you like that,' he said.

'The world is a small place,' she agreed gravely.

Quite deliberately – the cheek of it! – he stared down at her left hand, lying on the table beside the untouched brandy, and noted the absence of a ring.

'Distant cousin,' he began. 'Cousin what?'

'Emma.'

'Emma. I must phone base and tell them they won't be seeing me again, get something sorted about the bike. Stay here, all right? Don't move.'

'Were you delivering a parcel?'

He put out his cigarette and stood up. 'Good thinking. Some bastard better not have stolen it.'

'Shall I fetch it while you phone?'

'No, I'll go.'

'If it hasn't been stolen we could take it in my car.' Was that too forward of her? Why? He could always say thanks but no thanks. However:

'Thanks a lot,' he said, wincing as he worked his left

shoulder. 'The little pains begin to show themselves. Will you be okay here? It isn't exactly salubrious.'

'I can take care of myself.'

'Can you?' That smile again. 'Were you on your way somewhere important in that smart car of yours?'

'No. Nowhere important.'

'Don't move,' he repeated.

He loped stiffly away. Emma took another sip of the brandy and leaned back. She was in the afterglow of relieved tension when the systems were off alert and felt as though they would never be needed again. She should have been at her interview now, should be demanding first use of the telephone from Stephen Birkenshaw so she could explain her non-appearance, but she was not meant to get there and would not have got the job in any case.

Stephen Birkenshaw ... the smile, those bold eyes. Was he married? It was so unfair that men did not invariably wear wedding rings. How could it be that he, of all motorcyclists, had hit hers, of all cars, in an undistinguished south London street on this day and at that time? The number of coincidences was extraordinary, the odds surely several million to one. The setting up of her interview and his orders to deliver a package to this area were only the last two in a chain of events begun with her breakdown and dismissal back in March. He could have been going a bit faster, she a bit slower and an anonymous motorcyclist would have gone on his way and she on hers.

Was there power in coincidence? Some people believed there was. And what was coincidence, anyway? If her grandmother hadn't been in that precise place in Piccadilly where her grandfather was on VE night in 1945 Emma would not be here now. Yet no one considered that coincidence; it was merely meeting the person you married. Everyone's parents' meeting was the same, and those whose existence resulted from it could regard it as monumental coincidence – if they cared to.

Stephen Birkenshaw, the great-nephew of Eve Barker. Was he the light exercise her heart craved? Could be. She didn't imagine she would refuse if he asked to see her again, for she was definitely attracted, but there was something else: power in this coincidence, when she was at a crossroads wanting to continue in the direction she had been going all summer while the sensible part of her said it was foolish and a waste of time. Power, if she chose to see it that way. And she did: a sign. A road sign.

H.G.A., she said to herself, eyes closed against the sun seeping in through the windows, you're there somewhere. Thank you.

'Wake up, Cousin Emma.'

She opened her eyes. 'I wasn't asleep.'

He put a package on the table and sat down. 'Free after I've delivered this. It's not far away. Would you mind?'

'No. What about the bike?'

'The usual garage will pick it up.' The tawny gaze was on her. 'Were you really going nowhere?'

She laughed. 'You could say that.'

'It's a beautiful day.'

'Yes,' she said, wondering where this was leading.

'Would you like to go for a picnic?'

'A picnic!' A leap of excitement. 'Where?'

'Sheffield Park Gardens. It's their time of year and I've been dreaming of them.'

'*Sheffield?*'

'Oh, they're not there. In East Sussex – not far away. What do you say?'

'All right.' And then, in case she sounded ungracious: 'That would be nice,' and succeeded in sounding prim.

'Let's get on, then. Don't you want your brandy?'

'Not if I'm driving. Am I?'

'Afraid you'll have to since I'm down to one wheel. Silly to waste it.' He finished the drink, picked up his belongings and steered her to the door, the limp more pronounced than ever.

'You should have a hot bath,' Emma said, ducking under his arm into the sunny, rubbish-strewn street.

'Yes, and I'd like to change. I'm staying in a house in Clapham . . . '

'I'll take you there, shall I?' Staying. No wife, then.

'I feel I'm imposing on you.'

'Don't. I must change too.'

'Must you? You'd match the colours of Sheffield Park.'

This was definitely admiring. Ignore it. She wasn't prepared to dress to please a man she had only just met. Except her mind was scanning her newly acquired wardrobe and selecting something suitable for a (romantic?) country picnic.

'I can't walk in these shoes,' she said.

'I can hardly walk at all.'

'And whose fault is that?' Severely, to put him in his place.

'Mine, mine. Don't be cruel.'

She stole an upward glance as he was stealing a downward one. His eyes were lit with laughter. Watch out, said her head. Here's a flirt. Fine, responded her heart. Here's another one.

They delivered the package and Emma drove on to Clapham and was told to park outside an imposing terrace of houses near the common. Stephen opened three locks and went to deactivate the burglar alarm.

'The place belongs to actors,' he said as he led her into the kitchen. 'They are in LA. Want to make a coffee? I won't be long.'

He vanished. Emma, her mind absolutely empty as though waiting for the rest of the day to fill it, watched the kettle until it boiled (proving the saying wrong) and filled the two mugs Stephen had set out. She found milk in an enormous refrigerator and poured some into her coffee, leaving Stephen's black. Shortly she would know the first intimate detail about him: black or white, sugared or not.

Fool, said her head. Coffee isn't intimate. It is, countered her heart. It's what you drink in the morning.

Quiet, both of you, said the Emma who was in this strange and luxurious kitchen with a flipped-over life and a car with a broken sidelight. What will be will be. He might like tea in the mornings.

When Stephen Birkenshaw returned she was apparently absorbed in the half-completed crossword on the back page of yesterday's *Independent*.

'You are here, then,' he said. 'I thought perhaps I'd made you up.' He leaned over her shoulder and smelt pleasantly of soap and shampoo. 'Thirteen across is conscription, but it's a lousy clue. Have you got any others?'

'No.' She couldn't do crosswords even if she'd been able to concentrate.

He opened the fridge but it was not to get milk. He was examining the bottles of wine and champagne there, frowning in concentration. Emma was fairly sure what was going through his pretty head: champagne could indicate two ends of the spectrum on a first outing, either flirtatious flamboyance or a heavy 'I think you are wonderful and nothing is too good for you'. She approved when he selected a white wine, a Sancerre, courtesy, she assumed, of the actors.

'Corkscrew,' he murmured, 'glasses, napkins, knives, plates, salt and pepper.'

He found these things and a wine cooler and, wrapping them in clean tea towels, put them into a canvas bag, his movements decisive, assured. She approved more and more. He was wearing jeans, a pair of leather shoes with thick rubber soles and a white, open-necked shirt with the sleeves rolled up. His skin was honey-coloured and not the riotous pink that contact with the sun could cause in freckled people.

'How are you feeling?' she asked before her silence took on other meanings.

'Great!' He grimaced and yelped as he hefted the bag. 'Oh, you mean my injuries. Terminal. Shall we depart?'

'You haven't drunk your coffee.'

'No time. It may seem like summer out there but it's an Indian and could turn hostile.' He gathered a bottle-green sweatshirt and the suede jacket he had brought downstairs with him. 'To Porsche! If I were drunk it would rhyme with horsh and I would have made a joke.'

'I've got to change,' she reminded him.

'If you insist. Is there a delicatessen and a hole in the wall of a Lloyds Bank near you?'

'I'll drop you off.'

'But . . . where? How do I know you'll find me again?' He was serious, genuinely worried, the freckles making his face seem very young.

'It's only a couple of hundred yards away. I was trying to save your bad leg.'

'Give me the address. Help! I don't even know your surname.'

'It's not my flat.'

She tore a page from her Filofax and dictated Jackie's name and address as she drove.

'I'll come and get you.' Groaning he clambered out of the low seat, then bent and looked at her. 'I'm ever so glad you're a distant cousin,' he said.

Rubbish. Ignore it. Jeans, trainers, a softening blouse, a thick sweater and her caped raincoat in case the Indians attacked. Her interview make-up didn't suit but to remove it would not be appropriate. She scribbled a note for Jackie and left it on the table: 'Away. May be back late. Love, E.'

The doorbell rang and then the telephone. Emma stepped towards it. Never before had she resisted the call of the phone. Never. Jackie was at the hospital and could be reached there if it was for her, but it was more likely to be the bureau demanding to know where Emma was. She could tell them the truth, say she'd had an accident and was feeling shaky (nearly the truth); they would be sympathetic and reset the interview, perhaps arrange others. No. This was it. The end. She closed and locked the door and ran down the stairs, the bell still ringing in her ears, and opened the main door of the block of flats.

'Lunch,' Stephen Birkenshaw said, indicating the plastic bag he was carrying. 'Are you ready?'

'As you see.'

'I see very well. Thank you.'

'You are altogether too glib.'

'But practical with it.' From the carrier bag he produced a bulb, which he used to replace the broken one on the Porsche. 'It'll do for the moment. Don't want to get stopped by the cops, do we?'

He directed her out of London, saying they were heading for sunny East Grinstead and points beyond, then when they were on a relatively open road he transferred the contents of the carrier to the canvas bag.

'Plastic on picnics should be banned,' he said. 'Don't you agree?'

'I suppose I do, since you mention it.'

He sighed with pleasure. 'Isn't this lovely? Isn't it lovely having resigned on such a day?'

'How will you earn a living now?'

'I'm not a career motorcycle messenger. As you may have guessed.'

'What do you normally do?'

'I'm a gardener.'

'A *what*?'

'Why surprised?'

'I don't know. It seems . . . unusual.'

'Adam delved. It's the oldest profession there is. There

are millions of gardens and some of them have gardeners. That's where I come in.'

'Where do you usually live?'

'On the job.'

'And why aren't you gardening now?'

'I'm having a holiday until it rains.'

'But aren't there always things to be done? Weeding and so on? My father's for ever at it.'

'I'm not really that sort of gardener.'

Were there different sorts? She was about to inquire when he instructed her to fork right. 'Shall I give you a history lesson?' he said.

'If you like.'

'This garden we're going to, Sheffield Park, was designed for the First Earl of Sheffield by Lancelot – Capability to his friends – Brown and my mate Humph Repton added a lake or two of his own, as was his wont. That was in the eighteenth century. Earlier this century the Third Earl of Sheffield kicked the bucket and the house and gardens were bought by a man called Arthur G. Soames. Are you paying attention?'

'Yes, sir.'

'Good. Well, Arthur G. looked upon Lance's landscape and didn't think a lot of it, so he set about planting trees where Lance would have countenanced no such thing. You can see the bones of Lance's landscape, but basically Arthur G. buggered it up. Never mind. One can forgive him, especially at this time of the year, and anyway many people considered Lance himself a vandal. Now the place belongs to the National Trust. It took a right bashing in the '87 hurricane and another in January '91, but it's still a stunner . . . Turn left here. Oh, you've seen. I do like a beautiful woman who's intelligent and drives nicely.'

'I can read signs,' Emma said, trying to make her voice cold and distant. She steered through the gates, along drive and parked among other cars under some trees. 'Are we having our picnic here?' she asked, looking around. 'People seem to be.'

'No, we'll have it in the gardens.'

She eyed him suspiciously. 'Is it allowed?'

'Strictly forbidden, and quite right too. Will you bring your raincoat? We can sit on it.'

'Stephen –'

'It's okay, honest it is. I'm in the trade, see? Card-carrying, I am.'

She gave in. What was the worst that could happen? They would be escorted, chastened, off the premises. Stephen Birkenshaw needed a bit of chastening, Emma reckoned.

He had not exaggerated the gardens, however, and Emma was duly stunned. The scale of the place was breathtaking, the lakes so designed that the next came into view only when the limit of the previous one was being reached and there revealed was another land and waterscape. The trees and shrubs had been planted for their autumn colours. Crimson, scarlet, yellow, russet, burnished gold and bronze were reflected in the waters of the lakes. Stephen reeled off Latin names, dazing Emma further.

'You're worse than my father,' she said.

'Is that a compliment?' he wondered.

'I ask him the name of a pretty little flower and he replies in gibberish.'

'It's important, the Latin. It's our international language.'

'You can go abroad and speak it?'

'Certainly I can. That's my other vice.'

'What is?'

'Travelling. One more surprise. Follow me.'

Two parallel carpets of deep blue, low-growing flowers arkling like sapphires in the sun.

'Amazing!' Emma said. 'What are they?'

'*Gentiana sino-ornata.*' He grinned and shrugged. 'Chinese gentians. It's nearly three o'clock. Shall we have lunch?'

They found a secluded spot among rhododendron bushes away from the public paths. Stephen lowered himself gingerly to the ground, laid out the contents of the canvas bag and opened the wine while Emma, uneasy about breaking the rules, spread her raincoat on the grass and hovered.

'Relax, woman,' he said, reading her mind. He gave her a glass and reluctantly she sat. 'Listen,' he went on. 'Of course the National Trust doesn't want everyone having parties here, people littering up the place, dogs pissing, kids screaming and playing football. That would spoil it for everyone else. We're not doing any harm.'

'What if we're caught?'

'I told you: I'm in the biz. The NT has gardeners, not sodding security officers. I know the lads here.'

He was the colours of autumn himself, his eyes, hair and the freckles. She obeyed and relaxed, enjoyed him as he opened the packets of grease-proof paper. He'd been to the Italian deli on the corner.

'Olives,' he said. 'Have one. Or two if you're feeling wicked. Parma ham. An avocado pear which you can deal with. Here's a knife. Bread . . . much better broken than cut, some cheese and salami.'

The hands were delicate. Gardener's hands. She was beginning to like the word. He touched her arm.

'Sorry. I talk too much.'

'Bilingually.' What was happening? He was making her – slightly – witty.

'*Diarrhoeaticulus verbalis.* The plants love it but people find it tedious.'

'I don't. Which people?'

'My wife, for a start.'

'Wife?' Too quickly.

'Ex-wife. Try the avocado with the Parma ham. It's delicious.'

'Where is she?'

'The city of the angels. Los Angeles.'

'Is she one of the actors?'

'Got it. Aren't you a clever girl? We met at drama school, Rowena, me and Sam. We – Rowena, I mean, not Sam – got married when we were nineteen, which was absurd, and then I saw the light, chucked in drama and went horticultural. Very wisely she divorced me and married Sam.'

'And you are friends?'

'The best. I have a permanent room in their house, after all. Here I go again, gabbling. I don't know anything about you, apart from the fact that you're a distant cousin. You talk for a·change. What is your line of work, Ms Langton?' He held half a cucumber under her chin as though it was a microphone.

'I am – was – a sort of stockbroker.'

'Ah! Hence the Porsche. Was. Were you done for insider dealing? In that case you should be in prison.'

'I . . . I've given it up.'

He sensed something sensitive and didn't press her. Instead he drew her out about her researches into her – and obliquely his – family history.

'It's fascinating,' he said, when she had finished. He lit another of his French cigarettes and poured the last of the wine into their two glasses. 'There's a photograph at home of my grandfather with some other pilots. One of them must be Max Johnstone.'

'Must?'

'The photograph would have been of the squadron, surely. Somewhere, too, there has to be one of my grandparents' wedding with your gran as bridesmaid.' She shivered and he put his right arm around her. The suede of his jacket was comforting against her neck. 'Note how I positioned myself so my healthy shoulder is available,' he said. 'Are you cold?'

'Considering it.' The warm, summer-like day was turning into an autumn-chilled evening. 'But it's not that, it's . . . How can I explain it? Max Johnstone existed and he was a Spitfire pilot. I've seen other photos of him, later ones, but in the war he's my creation in a sense and it's weird to find – suddenly, like this – hard evidence about him. And the original Stephen Birkenshaw, though he's not a character.'

'He didn't live long enough to become one.'

'I didn't meant that.'

'I know. I understand. It's my stupid facetious tongue.'

'Are there names on the photograph?'

He blew out smoke. 'Maybe. I can't be sure. It's just part of the furniture at home. I'll ring and ask my parents, if you like.'

'Would you?'

'For you, anything.' His lips brushed her cheek, the faintest touch, and she thought she had imagined it.

His parents. His father! 'Oh, dear,' she said, 'I've realized something. I've said your father was a very noisy baby. Do you suppose he'll mind? I had to give Max an excuse to get out of the house, you see.'

'He'll probably sue you. Great one for suing, my dad.'

'Stephen, no!'

'He won't mind. Anyway it's true. Everyone's always saying what a noisy baby he was, speak of nothing else. Family lore, it is. Shall we go? It's a long drive and you mustn't fall asleep at the wheel. Fresh air is tiring.'

'You could drive,' she said.

'Me?' He removed his arm from around her, carefully extinguished his cigarette, stowing the stub in his pocket, and gathered the detritus of their picnic into the bag. 'After you made me drink most of the wine and your car already displays the signs of my incapacity on the road? No way.'

Gran's first rule of men and Porsches disproved. She stood and put her raincoat on over her sweater. 'Come along, then,' she said as he showed no signs of stirring.

'Can't. I've stiffened up. Lend a muscle, will you?' She gave him an arm and, groaning, he got to his feet. 'Look once, look twice,' he said, gazing around. 'Nothing to say we've been here apart from flattened grass. As it should be . . . Oh, Christ!' Attempting a step. 'Now I really can't walk.'

'Since I've learned you trained as an actor I don't believe a thing about you.' Emma said.

'Emma, I'm in agony, I kid you not. Fetch a wheelchair, a stretcher.'

'Can't you lean on me?'

'I hoped you'd offer. Left shoulder, right leg. Which to sacrifice? Obvious, isn't it? I can't walk on a shoulder.'

Slowly they proceeded to one of the bridges spanning, like a series of necklaces, the water that linked the lakes.

'I tell you what I can't believe.' Stephen stopped and, perforce, Emma did too.

'What is that?' she asked.

'Today. Here, now. Lance, Humph and Arthur G. They're all with us. What greater thing can you do than create a garden that other generations visit and take pleasure in? *Nyssa sylvatica*, water and a setting sun. It's positively orgasmic.' He turned to face her. 'And you, Distant Cousin Emma Langton. You're – No, I won't say it. Slowly, the way the best plants grow, don't you agree? Funny,' he added to himself, limping on, 'this usually happens to me in spring.'

Dusk descended and then dark as they travelled back to the sound of Mozart's Requiem and Strauss's 'Four Last

Songs', Brian's CDs unearthed from the glove compartment by Stephen Birkenshaw.

'I like a requiem for the autumn,' he said, and appeared to doze through it until he changed discs and asked: 'Do you mind if I smoke?'

'No.'

'You're a lovely woman. Almost as lovely as a good garden. How strange to think we only met this morning.'

The smell of his Gauloise filled the car and writhed among the highly charged music. She steered through the traffic, stopping at lights, moving on again as though at a distance from herself. The only thing she was truly aware of was the long figure in the passenger seat beside her.

'What time is it?' he said, and she glanced at the clock on the dashboard.

'Quarter past seven.'

'Will you have dinner with me?'

Shouldn't she prevaricate, say she was busy tonight and tomorrow would suit better? Nonsense. 'I'd love to,' she said.

'There's a condition.'

'Oh?'

'Please wear the dress you had on this morning. It will remind me of *Nyssa sylvatica*. Or was there more yellow in it? *Betula pendula verrucosa*, perhaps.'

'And what will you wear?'

'Anything you like. A tie? A – a *suit*?'

Horror in his voice. She couldn't help laughing. 'I don't mind what you wear. Do you want me to take you to Clapham?'

'How about a pub near you? I'll wait . . . if that's okay.'

'I suppose so.'

'Am I pressurizing you?'

'A little,' she admitted. She hadn't been through this since she was a teenager. The affair with Brian had begun with drinks after work and had extended from the office.

But how could she even think of Brian now? There was a pub down the road from the flat and she stopped outside it.

'There's a nice restaurant in Fulham,' Stephen said. 'I'll phone them. We'll go by taxi, yes? You've done enough driving today and I want to get you drunk. No, I don't. Why do I say idiotic things?' He was silent for an instant, then: 'A little pressure won't harm you, but take as much time as you need.' He opened the car door and began manoeuvring himself out. 'On second thoughts, don't. Not hours, anyway. I'll ossify over my pint and we'll miss the restaurant. Have you promised to wear that dress? Honestly, it doesn't matter if it's *Nyssa sylvatica* or the *betula*. I'll love it whichever.'

'If you don't stop talking,' she said, 'I won't have time to put anything on.'

'Best suggestion yet. Christ, I've done it again! I didn't mean it. I'm out, I'm off. See you in a minute. Or an hour. Whenever you care to appear.'

Impossible man. Impossible!

Oh, yeah, and who are you trying to kid, Emma Langton?

Forty minutes later she walked into the pub, her coat unbuttoned because . . . well, unbuttoned. He was sitting at a table near the door and stood when he saw her and gave her a smile of unaffected delight.

'No Latin,' she warned.

He raised his hands in mock surrender and winced as the movement tweaked his injured shoulder.

'Are you very sore?'

'Terribly, but the sympathy's worth it. If there's any more spare I'll have it. Shall we go? This place doesn't suit you.'

A taxi was waiting outside. Yes, he'd ordered it, he said. Limping around Putney in search of a cruising one was no way to impress a lady. How long had it been waiting? She had a pang about the expense of this and dinner. Gardeners couldn't earn a lot of money, she was sure, and he'd lost his job as a messenger. Next time she would pay, she decided. Yes, there would be a next time – more than one. She hoped.

She felt better when they arrived at the restaurant. He had chosen it, it wasn't frantically expensive but was far from cheap and he was known there. Before jealousy could take over, visions of him dining other girls there, one a night, the owner appeared at their table, shook Stephen's hand and asked where he'd been hiding himself recently.

'In the usual places,' Stephen said. 'James, this is Emma.'

'Hi,' James said and turned quickly to Stephen again. 'What you did to my garden . . . unbelievable!' he enthused. 'It's been fantastic this summer, all the tables out there booked almost every night. We've even had major punters in for lunch, which is unusual for us here. How about some champers on the house?'

'Yes?' Stephen asked Emma.

'Why not?'

It was brought, opened and poured out.

'To a beautiful woman, a glorious day and many others like it,' Stephen said, raising his glass.

'You've been having me on. You're a garden designer.'

'I'm a gardener.'

'But not the sort who weeds,' she remembered.

'Precisely. How have I been having you on?'

'You haven't. It was me getting it wrong. Why on earth were you being a motorcycle messenger?'

'Wanting to experience the rich tapestry of life. A bit rich today, though, in every way . . . No. Boredom and frustration arising from a thing called a drought. Heard of it?'

'Yes, of course.' Graham had complained about it, and so had her father. Farmers and gardeners shared the problem.

'I'm overseeing this bloody great project in Gloucester-shire,' Stephen said. 'Place called Great Magister. Run-down house and grounds being turned into luxury hotel and conference centre – you know the sort of thing. They want the garden really special, they say, as good as it once was and no expense spared. Oh, I've had such fun, Emma. JCBs to play with, underlings coming out of my ears and tugging their forelocks at me. We want azaleas and rhododendrons, the bosses say. Won't grow here, I say, not unless you import half the peat bogs in Ireland. Go ahead, they say, but I can't do that since I'm a conser-vationist. I put in yew hedges. Instant, I kid you not. We had blokes scouring the countryside searching for yew, knocking on doors and making an offer. In America, I tell them – as a lark, you understand – they buy full-grown trees like this, a hundred, two hundred feet high, dig them up and take them away on giant transporters. Fine, they say. Carry on. Can you believe it?'

'No squeeze on money, then?'

'But none. These people haven't heard of a squeeze.'

'So why is water a problem? Can't they buy it?'

'They've had to for the things already planted and the stuff waiting in pots, but there are thousands of deciduous shrubs and trees yet to go in and it would take an awful lot of water to get them established in dry soil. There's no substitute for rain. It will come. What would you like to eat?'

She looked at the menu. Langoustines followed by lamb. Stephen ordered snails and lamb.

Emma sipped her champagne and contemplated him. 'Will future generations go and see this garden?' she asked.

'I can dream.'

'The Capability Brown and ... who was the other one?'

'Humphrey Repton.'

'Repton of the late-twentieth century. Is that you?'

'I doubt it. It's different now from then. Then the aristocracy had money and were rooted in the idea of continuity. What kind of permanence does a conference centre have?

'Who can tell?'

'Quite. Drink up. I'm about to call for the wine list and stun you with my knowledge and discernment.'

'There's no need. I'm already stunned.'

'Are you? I'm so pleased.' For once the tawny eyes were grave. 'You're a bit nervous, aren't you? You've been hurt. No, don't answer and don't worry either.'

James brought him the wine list and they had a low-voiced conversation while Emma sat pole-axed, a stage beyond being stunned. You wanted light exercise, her head said, and her heart countered: call this light exercise? I'm powering a roller-coaster here.

'Do you want to see my place?' Stephen asked her, James having retired from the table.

'Your place?' Confused.

'My garden. I call it mine, although it really belongs to men in suits and keffiyehs.'

'Yes. Yes, I would. When?'

'Tomorrow. The next day, the day after. Whenever.' A freckled hand on her golden sleeve. 'Did you hear me? I said don't worry.'

'I heard.'

The first course arrived along with a bottle of white wine. The champagne was still half full.

'But I can't help being a trifle wary,' she continued, 'since you said you wanted to get me drunk.' She was feeling light-headed, but it wasn't the alcohol – yet. It was the gardens they had seen, the picnic. Him, their bizarre meeting.

'I told you not to pay any attention to that. How are the langoustines?'

'Wonderful. The snails?'

'Short on green stuff, poor blighters, and long on garlic. One way of keeping you away from me, I suppose.'

Was he serious or an incorrigible flirt? She didn't, couldn't care, not tonight. She let his absurd chatter bubble around her and laughed more than she had in the past year. Two, probably. She was astounded when she looked around the restaurant and saw they were the only people left.

'The best of things must end,' Stephen said, waving at the one remaining waiter and signalling for the bill. 'Or is this a beginning?' His glass and a cigarette were in his right hand and with his left he reached towards her. 'Meet me halfway? My shoulder . . .'

'It didn't stop you eating.'

'Naturally not. Mere food for the body.'

She gave him her hand; their fingers lay intertwined on the tablecloth. Gently he massaged her wrist. It was astonishingly sensual.

The waiter presented the bill, folded, on a saucer. Stephen put down his glass and opened it. 'Bugger this,' he said, and for an awful moment Emma thought he was going to argue about the amount or not have enough money to pay. 'Get James,' he ordered the grinning waiter, and turned the bill so Emma could read it. Everything they had eaten and drunk neatly itemized and the cost a consistent nothing. Total including service: zero.

James appeared in the empty restaurant. 'A problem with the bill, sir?' he affected.

'Stop fucking around, James.'

'I'm not fucking around. Who would these days?'

'I'm taking a girl out, sod you. It's got to cost me.'

'Sod yourself. You're not paying.'

'I'm trying to impress her, you git.'

'Surely mademoiselle is impressed by a restaurant that insists you eat free –'

'Yes, I am,' Emma said.

'Hear that? Far more, I venture, than your uncouth language.'

'It means I can't eat here again.'

'Eat somewhere else in the locale and do to their back yards what you did to mine and I'll break your legs ... Excuse me.' He bowed to Emma. 'But this is important.' To Stephen he said: 'You will plant the tubs again, won't you? You promised.'

'A few packets of night-scented stock and some bedding plants. It's not complicated.'

'It is to me. The punters were ravished. They drank champagne and proposed to each other like it was going out of fashion – which it is, come to think of it.'

'Oh, all right. I can't argue. It's been a long day.' He let go of Emma's hand and stood up. 'Thanks, mate. Do me one more favour and get me a taxi, will you?'

'You're wounded. I thought you were drunk.'

'I'm drunk and wounded.' He took Emma's coat from the waiter and held it for her to put on. 'She hit me with her Porsche,' he explained.

'A masochist! Stephen, I never knew.'

'Actually, he hit me,' Emma said.

'A sadist, then. Better and better. Ron will find you a cab. Go away and leave me in peace, will you?' He smiled at Emma. 'But bring him back again soon.'

He struggled out of the taxi and escorted her across the pavement to the door, waited while she unlocked it.

'Can I ring you?' he asked.

'Yes.'

'Tomorrow?'

'Yes.'

He kissed her gently on the cheek. 'Thank you for the day. Good night.'

'Good night.'

5

Jackie woke her, without apology, at half past six the next morning.

'Who is he?' she demanded.

'Who?' Emma yawned, sat up and took the mug Jackie held out.

'I was in the pub last night, Ems.'

'Oh. I didn't see you.'

'You only had eyes for one thing.'

'He's ... he's gorgeous. Jackie, you won't believe it.'

Ten minutes later Jackie had to, although she agreed it was extraordinary. 'What happens next?' she asked.

'That's just it. I'm in a muddle. I'll carry on, which means I'll have to go to Guernsey, but how can I walk away from him if he –? Can I stay on here for a while, Jackie? I'll pay you rent. And I'll have to do something about my flat. Get the car mended. Yes, there are things to do in London.'

'Stay as long as you like.'

Emma clutched at the sleeve of her uniform as Jackie rose from where she had been sitting on Emma's bed. 'What if he doesn't ring? I haven't got his number, or even the name of the people whose house he's staying in. I know where it is, but how would I dare go there?'

'He'll ring you.'

'How do you know?'

'I saw his face last night.'

'Do you think he's handsome?'

'No.'

'Jackie!'

'Nice-looking, though. When do I get a second viewing?'

'Soon. Soon, I hope.'

The phone went at nine. It will be the bureau, Emma thought.

The already familiar voice.

'Are you awake?'

'Yes.'

'I've been up since seven. Will you come to breakfast?'

'All right.'

'And lunch in Gloucestershire?'

'I –'

'Have you turned coy overnight? Please don't have. I've found a walking stick which Sam must have swiped from a set. Its handle is the head of a crocodile. Not a real one, of course. Carved . . . Or it could be an alligator, I suppose. I've been practising with it. I look terribly distinguished, and I've bought some croissants and some jam with a checked cloth on its lid which proves it's stuffed with country goodness. Are you still there?'

'How do you do it at this time of the morning?'

'Do what? Oh, talk. Talking is easy. Anyone can do it.'

'Given the chance,' Emma put in swiftly.

He laughed. 'Can you remember where I am?'

'The road, but perhaps not the number.'

He gave it and rang off.

Oh Lord, and where's this leading us? said head, and heart replied with certainty: somewhere rather special.

She wondered idly who would win the talking stakes when – if! – Stephen met Elunid on Anglesey.

*

He had a cottage by the gates – the back gates, he empha-sized – of the once gentleman's country estate and soon-to-be hotel and conference centre. He directed Emma to park alongside a Land Cruiser, which he said was his company car, and unlocked the cottage's door.

'Would madam care to enter?' he said and she stepped inside and looked around. The little sitting room was comfortably untidy with stacks of books and piles of gardening magazines beside the armchairs. It was lived in, homely.

'How long have you been here?' she asked.

'Over a year. They wanted the garden started before they did the major spend on the house. It was a hell of a break getting this job but a hell of a responsibility, too. Emma, I kid you not, I have sleepless nights worrying whether I've got my faguses and ficuses muddled.'

'How did you get the job?'

'Sam knew someone who knew someone. He plays smooth aristos, does Sam, and people think he's the real McCoy. He went on about how brilliantly I'd done his and Rowena's garden – fifty foot by twenty in Clapham, I ask you! – and I was, as they say, approached. No, I mustn't criticize Sam. He's appointed himself my agent and I'd be nowhere without him.'

'Have you got those things muddled?'

'Not yet. It would be a disaster if I did.'

'Why?'

'One's a beech, the other could be a fig or a rubber plant.'

'Oh, dear.'

'Quite.'

'You couldn't, could you?'

'Not those two, I admit.'

'What about your other work? The restaurant, for example?'

'Light relief.' He paced about, leaning on the walking

stick. 'Christ, Emma, I don't know. Are the money men right in believing a special garden will attract more punters to a hotel? There's an old boy in his eighties who cycles over from the next village once a week. He slaved here as a lad in the year dot and has seen the garden go to ruins. He cried one day when I showed him a magnolia I'd uncovered – literally uncovered: ivy, brambles, you name it; sometimes I think I'm a bloody archaeologist – and other plants have survived against the odds. The borders were designed by Gertrude Jekyll. He remembers her, imagine that! He thinks I'm going to recreate them in her image, but no way. She was the Isabella Beeton of gardening – take fifty labourers touch. This will be a Stephen Birkenshaw garden, stand or fall, and one thing a Birkenshaw garden won't do is rely on armies to keep it marching. But it can't take care of itself, that's for sure. They say they've budgeted for gardeners, but budgets get altered, don't they? The money could run out tomorrow and the plug pulled. In years to come there'll be a cocky young sod poking around and saying, "Stephen Birkenshaw. Who the hell was he?"'

'If the money men are right, though,' Emma said softly.

'Ah! If! Move aside Vita and Gertie, say I. Eat your heart out, Beth Chatto . . . You're a hell of a listener, Emma.'

'What choice do I have?'

'Don't hit a man when he's in a crisis.'

'You've lathered yourself into one since you've arrived.'

'I have, haven't I? Next I'll start getting nostalgic about the joys of motorcycle messengering.'

He cast the stick aside and put his hands on her shoulders. The tawny eyes were fixed on the low ceiling, the freckled brow puckered. The unaccustomed silence lengthened.

'What is it?' Emmas asked finally.

'I'm wondering if it's too soon. Is it? No, I can't help it.' He gathered her close to him, bent his head and kissed her on the lips. An instant of pure bliss before he raised his head. 'Oh, that was nice,' he said. 'Again?'

'Please.'

Longer. Sweet. Intimate, promising passion in the future yet undemanding for now. Friendly. Loving.

Loving, yes.

'It's unreal,' she murmured. 'Twenty-five hours ago I hadn't met you.'

He lifted his left arm to look at his watch. 'Twenty-six . . . Ouch, my poor shoulder. Can I have some sympathy? Another kiss? How lovely.' And then: 'Christ, woman, you'll do me in. My knees have gone wobbly. You've wrecked my last viable leg and I'll end up in a heap on the carpet and be capable of nothing.'

'I wouldn't like that,' she said.

'Wouldn't you? Good.' He grasped the walking stick. 'Come along, I'll show you my etchings, whoops I mean my garden. Can you drive the Land Cruiser? Sorry to be so pathetic but I honestly don't think I can.'

'Is it that bad? Perhaps you should see a doctor.'

His smile crept into his cheek. 'Doctors can't cure what's wrong with me,' he said.

Or with her, but she wasn't going to say it. Heart urged her to trust this, trust him, but for once in the last twenty-six hours she listened to the counsel of head.

But head was sorely tried over the next hour or so. Unwittingly – Emma was certain – Stephen Birkenshaw added an extra dimension to the ones she already found so devastatingly attractive. Yesterday in Sheffield Park she could have taken his knowledge, the spouting Latin, for glibness, but here today his authority was absolute. The men and one young woman working in the gardens greeted him with both respect and affection and all in-quired after the reason for his limp, the stick, and their reaction was uniform horror that he'd been mad enough to ride his bike round London as a cure for boredom. Tom, the middle-aged man whom Stephen introduced as head gardener, went so far as to give him a ticking off, which he received with charming penitence.

'Do daft things like that, Stephen,' Tom concluded, 'and it puts the rest of us at risk. We depend on you. Listen, I've had a thought . . .'

And they began discussing Latin.

But it was not just the affection and respect, it was the garden itself. It seemed to Emma, even at this season, to be beautiful, perfect, complete, and there was something about a man who had created, or recreated, a thing of beauty. More than that still: Stephen's freckled hand turning up a flower head so he could stare into – it seemed – its soul, clearing non-existent weeds from the base of the plant so it felt loved and would want to grow for him.

'No, you're not being fanciful,' Stephen said when she tried to explain some of this. 'Not in my book. Plants are alive and respond to care. But you are wrong about two things. A garden can always be beautiful but it's never complete or perfect. That's what makes it so fascinating.'

'What will you do about this place, then? Isn't your work here nearly finished?'

'If I'm not contracted to come back and tread on Tom's toes I'll do it for free. It's my garden, no matter who it belongs to.'

'I can understand that,' Emma said. 'Did you really transplant the yew hedges? They look as though they've been here for years.'

'Some have but lots were brought in. You recognize a yew, then. You're not as ignorant as you'd have me believe. Oh, I remember. Your father gardens.'

Gardens, but is not a gardener. Emma wondered what her father would think of that. What both her parents would think of Stephen Birkenshaw, now being a serious professional instead of a serious ... flirt? And Gran. Gran would love him.

They returned to the Land Cruiser.

'What happens over there?' Emma asked, of the activity in the distance she had noted earlier.

'Swimming pool, tennis courts. Nothing to do with me.' He dismissed the house, too, a massive affair besieged by builders' vans. 'Punters' palace,' he said.

'You shouldn't call them that. Your success depends on them.'

'Don't remind me. I can imagine it, right at this moment I can. Some self-important conferencee saying, "What's the matter with the dahlias, the chrysanths? I do so like a nice pompom." It'll be the equivalent of giving foie gras to a gorilla.'

Emma climbed into the driver's seat of the Land Cruiser. 'I won't consider you affected and overwrought,' she remarked, 'though many might. Where next?'

'Lunch,' he said, scrambling in before she left without him. 'We can see the rest this afternoon.'

'There's more?'

'The nursery with my babies in it. The conservatory. The lake. We won't bother if you've had enough.'

He had brought a cool bag with him today and had risked champagne. Also in the bag were gravadlux and a lobster, a whole one wrapped in newspaper.

'Rowena always freezes and unfreezes lobsters in newspaper. She maintains it's the only way to do it,' Stephen said.

'It's Rowena's? Should you have taken it?'

'She told me to help myself. Sorry if you'd prefer sausages, but she doesn't keep those in her deep freeze. You're not feeling guilty, are you? Remember, if I hadn't let her divorce me and marry Sam she wouldn't be able to afford gravadlux or lobsters. Or a deep freeze, come to that. Besides, it keeps me in debt to you. I still haven't bought you a proper meal so you'll have to have dinner with me tonight.'

The logic was irrefutable. Attempting to argue with him was like arm-wrestling an eel.

The gravadlux was exquisite, and they ate it at a wooden table outside.

'What is your ambition?' she asked him as he laid half a lobster on her plate, having removed, he assured her, the bits that should not be eaten.

'To make gardens,' he replied.

'In the long term, though. Isn't part of it having people being able to see them, as you said yesterday? This one won't be open to the general public, surely.'

'Certainly it will, so long as they own a couple of oil wells and can pay for a night at the hotel. One oil well will buy them a meal . . . Sorry, I'm being silly. You must have realized by now it's endemic. My ambition.' He poked the meat from a claw, dipped it into mayonnaise and chewed meditatively. 'It's got to be to make a garden that belongs to me, hasn't it? One I can play with for decades and instruct my grandchildren what experiments to make after I've gone. Trouble is it'll have to be big, as I couldn't do with a pocket handkerchief. I should be saving up to buy one instead of spending money on travelling.'

His other vice. She had forgotten.

'Where have you travelled to?'

'Usual places. India, China, Russia, the Americas. Europe, of course. I went to the east immediately after the revolutions and it was fantastic. Not quite so much fun now the singing and dancing's over and reality's set in, but it was amazing then. Can I help you? Don't be scared of attacking the poor bugger. It's dead.' He ripped the claw from her lobster, cracked the casing and gave it back.

'How long do you go for? Travelling implies more than a package holiday.'

'Three, six months. Longer. Depends on how much money I have and whether there are any jobs organized. Sam says I should stop this larking around. He recommends me to one of his thespian mates and doesn't know where the hell I am. Says I should settle down since I'll be thirty next birthday (twelfth of June. Put it in your diary), he being ever so much wiser since he's thirty already. Don't tell him, but I hanker after one more bit of fecklessness.'

'Which is what?' Emma didn't want him disappearing either. Was not in the slightest keen on the idea.

'I've never been to Africa, apart from the north which isn't the same. I want to go from Kenya southwards. Mount Kenya, snow on the Equator – the existence of which I'll deny until I've touched it – the Rift Valley, the animals in the wild.' He stopped, having seen the expression on her face. 'Christ, Emma, what have I said? I won't go if it makes you look like that. Have some more champagne, a napkin. What else can I offer you? My lobster, except I've eaten it.'

'Stop *talking*!' Emma said, recovering and starting to laugh. 'Please. For once.'

'All right, I'll try.'

'How can I begin?' She paused, wondering.

'At the beginning?' Stephen suggested, adding quickly, 'Sorry.'

'When we met yesterday I was on my way to an interview for a job I didn't want. I saw you as a sign that I should forget about that and continue with my researches into my family. Oh, this sounds ridiculous.'

'It does,' Stephen said crossly. 'I don't want to be a sign.'

'You've just been another one, don't you see? Before he married your great-aunt my great-grandfather spent years in Africa, mainly within sight of Mount Kenya. You planning to go there seems, well —'

'Significant. Meaning full of signs.'

'Do you believe that?'

'No, but to please you I'll try.' He swatted a wasp away from the debris of the shellfish. 'What does it involve, this research of yours?'

'Not much more. A trip to Guernsey, checking some things in London, talking to my grandmother and my mother, my aunt perhaps.'

'Then you write it down.'

'Yes. Honestly, Stephen, it's not important.'

'That's as stupid as saying my garden's not important. Apart from Guernsey, will you be in London until you've finished?'

'I – I don't know,' she said, suddenly nervous, remembering how love could hurt. 'I can stay on in the flat.'

The first wasp had radioed another. They both swooped in on daring low-level attacks.

'Piss off!' Stephen told them irritably. 'I'm having a serious conversation.'

'I'll clear the table,' Emma said, getting up.

'No, let them have their fun. We'll retire to the bench.'

It was on a knoll at the end of the small cottage garden and faced outwards to a distant view of Great Magister House. Stephen settled himself, the bottle of champagne and his walking stick on or alongside it, and took his glass from Emma.

'That's better. Where was I?'

'Telling wasps to piss off.'

'Don't be facetious. That's my prerogative. I remember what I was thinking, but not what I was about to say. Or, rather, how I was about to say it. Shall I, in the meantime, say what I was thinking?'

'Do.'

'I was wondering what kind of bastard he could be.

319

The one that gets you stammering and stuttering. I'd like to meet him when my left hook's operational again.'

'He doesn't get me stammering and stuttering.'

'Now you're quibbling. What he did to you does. Have you forgotten the sod? Not entirely, obviously. I want to make you. Do you suppose I can?'

'I don't consider that a fair question,' she said after a pause, not prepared to commit herself. Not yet.

'No. I'm sorry.' He ran a finger across her cheek and under her chin. 'Stay in London until it rains, won't you? We must get to know each other better. Don't look away.' He switched to West Country speech, his accent an exaggeration of Graham's. 'Oi intend to court you, maid. Court you proper.'

She couldn't think how to respond. 'Won't you get bored in London?' she asked.

'Bored courting you?' His normal voice. 'Gracious me, I hope not.'

'You could take your references to another messenger company,' she said.

'I might consider it if they can guarantee my next accident involves a Porsche with you in it. No, I won't get bored. Besides I, too, have important research to do.'

'Really?'

'I'm writing a book.'

'Are you? Why didn't you say so before?'

He gazed fondly down at her. 'Aren't you an innocent darling? So susceptible. I could tell you I'm a gardener and you'd be convinced.'

He had something to show her, he said, in the conservatory. They could skip the nursery and the lake but she had to see this. They took the remains of their lunch inside and Emma drove the Land Cruiser to the punters' palace. The conservatory was on one side of it.

'This is where they proposed in the olden days,' Stephen said. 'In the films they always have the man picking a

320

flower and giving it to the girl. What a check! I've designed a special notice, a plant with a red slash across it
and the text reading "Thank you for not plucking the
blooms."'

'What do you want to show me?' Emma asked, trying
not to be swamped by the flood of words.

'These.' He pointed with his stick to a spread of pale
pink flowers in pots, the loose umbels fully six inches
across.

'Very nice,' Emma said.

'Frightfully, though erring towards the vulgar away
from their native land. Ask me what they are called.'

'What are they called?'

'*Nerine sarniensis*. They originate from South Africa
but their common name here is Guernsey lily. Are you
going to turn white and shaky and tell me they are a
sign?'

'No,' she said.

'Would you have done if you'd admired them and
asked me casually what they were?'

She sighed. 'Perhaps. I suppose I might have.'

'If you'd mentioned – which you would have done at
some point in the future, because we'll be seeing a lot of
each other and occasionally I'll allow you to talk – that
your great-grandfather lived in Kenya, I would have said,
"Fancy that! I want to visit Kenya." Where would the
sign have been then?'

She didn't reply immediately, and then said: 'But . . .
our meeting. Wasn't that an amazing coincidence?'

'I don't agree.' He handed her his stick, took a penknife
from his pocket and opened it. 'Since it's me,' he said.
Stiffly he bent and cut one of the flowers at the base of
the stem, cut it again so there only remained a couple of
inches and stuck it behind her ear. 'Amazing luck,' he
said.

*

Emma crept into the flat at half past midnight. To the kitchen where she filled a glass with water and put the Guernsey lily in, to the bathroom to wash her face and clean her teeth. To bed, the Guernsey lily on the table beside it. She switched off the light, lay unable to sleep.

Was this how Morfydd had felt after being accosted in a lane on Anglesey over fifty years ago? Possibly. Probably. She would have to rewrite it.

6

Emma arranged a six-month extension on the lease to her flat, did her research (a bit) and was courted by Stephen Birkenshaw. Trips to Kew Gardens, to Wisley – headquarters, he said with a salute which would not pass muster with Emma's cousin Alistair – cold November afternoons when the Indian summer had gone in cinemas or art galleries. He spent some time farting around, as he expressed it, in poncy London gardens and was in telephonic and regularly physical contact with the punters' paradise at Great Magister. Emma drove him sometimes, others he went by train.

They spent evenings watching television or a video at the house in Clapham after one or the other – or both, the most intimate – had cooked a meal. Evenings at the flat with Jackie and her radiologist boyfriend, or at a pub with their hospital colleagues and Stephen having everyone in fits when he took off their medical jargon and turned it into the names of plants. Evenings at restaurants or invited out as a couple to parties given by Stephen's friends. (Where were Emma's former so-called friends? Fair weather, on both sides.)

If Emma was not driving he would always take her home. Long, loving kisses in the cab, another at the door and to virginal sleep.

'Why doesn't he do more?' Emma asked Jackie.

'He wants to be sure of you. Under the verbiage is a serious man.'

'How can I tell him I'm sure?'

'He's setting the pace, Ems. Live with it.'

Another worry hit her with the force of a bludgeon. Stephen knew now that Emma had had an affair with a man who had been unfaithful in multiples. He could have infected her. Was that why –?

'I don't expect so,' Jackie said, 'but let's set your mind at rest.'

Test negative.

'Should I tell him?'

'It would make a great seduction scene,' Jackie said. 'You handing over your certificate and saying, "How about it?" Ems, he loves you. He's an old-fashioned boy and he knows what he's doing.'

Old-fashioned. Emma remembered she was being courted and forgot the modern side of her that thought love meant sex.

Rain, what Stephen called proper rain, fell in December brought by a west wind. Londoners complained about it as they had complained about the heat, but Stephen rejoiced in it. He would start planting his babies in January, he said, so long as it didn't freeze. He would be moving back to his cottage, and the house in Clapham was for sale. Rowena and Sam would spend Christmas there and search for a more suitable London base.

'He's made the big time in Hollywood, has Sam,' Stephen said, 'and Rowena's on his coat tails. Whoever heard of a superstar living in Clapham?'

'I thought he was a superstar before.'

'Not in the same league. His television here didn't keep Rowena in fresh knickers. His real money came from voice-overs. Advertisements. Getting weepy over the cleanness of the laundry and the washing-up. It pays well but no real ac*tor* admits to doing it. Their first movie's going well in the States and when it's released here they'll have an image to protect. Belgravia or the Boltons. Somewhere beginning with B.'

'Balham.'

'I've warned you about that before, Emma.'

'Sorry,' she said meekly.

But everything seemed fraught with change. Stephen's London base was for sale. He was about to embark on his last major project at the punters' paradise, and after that where would he be? Africa, or maybe Sam would have him designing gardens in California. Emma made inquiries about flights to Guernsey in an effort to perceive a future independent of Stephen.

'You really think he's going to say goodbye, nice knowing you and disappear? You're off your trolley,' Jackie said. 'And,' she added, 'if I were you I'd start taking the pill again.'

'Should I?'

'Definitely.'

Sam and Rowena arrived and the following night – the one before Christmas Eve – Stephen asked Emma to have dinner with them in James's restaurant.

'I suppose some might consider it eccentric to want to introduce one's new love to one's ex-wife,' he remarked on the way there.

'Well, it is rather,' Emma said, stalled on the word 'love'.

'They are my best friends,' he said simply, 'her and Sam.'

She was blonde and beautiful, Sam dark and handsome. Their entrance was superbly theatrical, waiters fluttering around removing coats, James greeting them as though they were royalty, other diners staring at them, recognizing celebrity in general if not the detail of name. After they had sat down, drinks and menus had been brought and the court had receded, Rowena turned to Emma, smiled warmly and said, 'We've heard so much about you. It's wonderful to meet you at last.'

If she didn't mean it she was a brilliant actress. Emma began to be at ease, the more so when Sam said, 'The woman who's kept Stephen out of mischief for – how long?'

'Two and a half months and I wasn't in any mischief,' Stephen said. 'Christ, Sam, you've assassinated my character in five seconds flat.'

Laughter and camaraderie. Emma felt herself accepted by Stephen's two best friends.

In the cab later Stephen took her hand. 'Do you insist on going to Sven's party on New Year's Eve?' he asked.

'Insist? No. Why?'

'You could come to the cottage. Drive over from your parents' house. Yes?'

'Yes.' Would this be it, at last?

'There's no central heating so bring your thermal underwear.' He chuckled. 'Romantic to the toes of his bedsocks, isn't he? ... Dearest Emma, I'll give you your present then. Have the very happiest of Christmases.'

His parents lived in Hereford and he would be there. Eight days to wait. Eight days until she saw him again.

Some of those days at least were fully occupied. Olivia was staying, and Emma's younger brother Jonathan was home from his job in Scotland, where he did something in oil, and objecting to his bedroom being turned into Emma's office. On Christmas Day Julie arrived with her family. Surrounded by her five grandchildren Olivia seemed – well, grandmotherly and not the close friend she had become.

Emma wanted to tell her about Stephen Birkenshaw, show her the copy of the photograph he had got from his parents of Olivia as a bridesmaid at that distant wedding. She had not yet told her mother, beyond casual references to a new boyfriend. She would soon – she thought she would – share him with her family but with Gran first. He already belonged to her in a sense. Tomorrow, maybe, when Emma's large and noisy cousins would not be here.

The children, as they reverted to being at this time of year, naval sub-lieutenants or budding oil executives notwithstanding, were ordered to the pub with their fathers to get them out of the way while the grown-ups finalized lunch.

'Aren't you joining us, Gran?' Emma said, forgetting that Olivia's Dorset habits were not known here. She was given a bland smile.

'How kind of you to invite me,' the scourge of the Three Sheaves and several other pubs said. 'Perhaps I will. Just this once.'

The hypocrite! 'For a sweet sherry?' Emma challenged.

'No, darling. I don't drink sherry, sweet or otherwise. You know that.'

On Boxing Day Olivia pre-empted her. They had been to a before-lunch drinks party at which were many of Gran's former friends and acquaintances. Laura, Jonathan and Hamish left early and Emma drove her grandmother home.

'Who is he?' Olivia asked on the way.

'Who is who?'

'Don't be difficult, Emma. You've been in London, you haven't got a job and you've not been doing that other stuff because you haven't been phoning me with queries every other second. In fact you've not been phoning me at all, or at any rate not leaving messages on my machine. Something is occupying you and your dreamy look tells me it's male.'

'You'll never believe this, Gran.'

'No, wait.' Olivia put a hand on Emma's arm. 'Don't you think you should tell your parents first? You ought to. They worry about you and they can't forget where your previous boyfriend landed you.'

'This isn't the same!'

'It could seem so to them. You've said nothing, Emma. It isn't fair.'

'All right, I'll tell them,' Emma said, now ashamed. 'But, Gran, his name is Stephen Birkenshaw.'

'*What?*'

A tumble of words about luck and coincidence took them home, out of the car and into the kitchen.

'We want the whole story,' Olivia said. 'Darling, take a deep breath and begin at the beginning.'

Laura and Hamish, however, knew a little more than Emma had let on.

'Whenever we ring you Jackie says you are out with someone called Stephen who she says is good news,' Laura said. 'We hoped you'd confide in us when you were ready to.'

She had hurt them. Her breakdown seemed to belong to another person but to her parents it was still a threat.

'Mum, Dad, I'm sorry, truly I am,' she said.

She and Laura had a minor weep and Jonathan walked in, said, 'Oh, Gawd,' and went out again.

'Are you going to stay with him for New Year?' Hamish asked. 'Alone?'

'There might be other people there,' Emma muttered, expanding the tiny cottage into something which could accommodate a sizeable party.

Hamish resumed carving the cold turkey, his every motion disapproving, and Laura echoed his actions with an eloquent 'Hmm!' as she laid plates on the table.

'The nerve of you two!' Olivia exclaimed. 'As though there'd never been that time I caught an earlier train than I said I would and arrived at your – what I'd been led to believe was your' – (directed at Laura) 'flat and discovered you trying to hide Hamish's shaving gear in the bathroom cabinet.'

'Mummy, that was in nineteen sixty-something.'

'What difference does it make? Did I object? Did I get stuffy and prissy about it?'

'Actually, you did,' Hamish said, 'though you tried to be hip. As you put it.'

'I never would have,' Olivia said flatly.

'You did, you –' He stopped, the carving knife arrested in the air as he used it to emphasize his point, and turned to Emma. 'Did you say Stephen Birkenshaw,' he asked her.

'Yes.'

'Great Magister. Good God!' He put down the knife, disappeared and reappeared a few moments later with one of his gardening magazines folded open. 'Is this him?'

A colour photograph of Stephen Birkenshaw flanked by his staff at the punters' paradise.

'He's reviving a Jekyll garden,' Hamish said. 'There are regular features on his progress. I'd love a poke around. Emma, darling, could you arrange it?'

'It's not what you think,' Emma said, as she had been trying to for the past ten minutes, and added, since no one was paying attention to her anyway, 'yet.'

Hamish was giving a history of the garden while his wife and mother-in-law studied the photograph.

'He seems a bit serious,' Olivia said. It was a posed group, and he did.

Laura sighed. 'Don't get hurt again. Emma, please don't.'

Emma stumbled through a description of Stephen's courting and his old-fashioned ideas.

'He sounds a dream,' her grandmother said. 'I for one can't wait to meet him.'

'Neither can I,' Hamish said, turning a page of the magazine and scanning the rest of the article.

8

The motorcycle was parked next to the Land Cruiser. Emma nosed the Porsche into the narrow gap left, opened the door and was engulfed.

'I've missed you,' Stephen said. 'Have you missed me?'

His kiss, her returning it, made reply unnecessary.

'How did the bike get here?' Emma asked when she was released.

'I rode it. A frown from Emma, what I've always longed for. At the pace of a snail. I have too much to look forward to to play silly buggers, but I love you for caring. Come inside, woman. Where's your bag?'

He put it noncommittally at the foot of the stairs and led her to one of the chairs beside the log fire.

'In half an hour, when it's four o'clock, we're allowed tea and crumpets. In eight and a half hours it will be another year and then – I've booked us a table for supper at the pub tonight. It's only a short walk there. Walk there and weave back. Tom and his missus and most of the lads will be there and I must buy them a New Year drink. Do you mind?'

'No,' Emma said, fantasies of a firelit dinner for two receding, but she didn't mind. Being with him and his burble was enough.

'I had a much nicer Christmas than I thought I would

have,' he said. 'You see, I could talk about you to a fan of yours.'

'A fan of mine?'

'Great-Aunt Claire. My old man ships her down from Anglesey every Christmas. Her family's in Australia, but you know that, don't you? She was touched you sent her a card. "What a lovely girl," she kept saying and what could I do but agree? Stop! This was supposed to come later. Shall we have our crumpets now? You can toast them while I do the real work and put on the kettle.'

'Wasn't Clare astounded that you and I had met?' Emma asked, using her thumbnail to slide a crumpet from the toasting fork to a plate.

'Gob-smacked. Totally. And, yes, before you mention it, the word "coincidence" was used with abandon. My father loves the idea of featuring in whatever you're doing as a horrible baby, and my mother . . . No, I promised myself and I'm going to stick to it. How between now and till it's time to go to the pub? Would you like to do a jigsaw?'

'I haven't done one for ages.'

'My mother buys me two every year, one to keep me occupied at home and stop me from digging new beds in the garden for her to weed and one for these dark evenings. Have you, Emma, by the faintest chance brought with you the dress that reminds me of *Nyssa sylvatica* and our first meeting? You have? Don't blush about it. You can't be shy with me any more.'

Later she was offered a bath – which she declined, having had one that morning – and was invited to change in a minute spare bedroom. The bed was made up and a heater on. Good friends and nothing more? Her Christmas present to him, a pure wool sweater which she was longing to see him in, was in her bag. He had not given her a present and she was reluctant to give him his until he did.

They left the cottage and followed the wavering beam

332

of Stephen's torch out of the back gates of the punters' paradise, down the lane and into the noise of the pub. Stephen was greeted on all sides as they struggled through the crowd to the bar and found Tom, his wife and the other gardeners, some with girlfriends, occupying a substantial part of it.

'In a prime position,' Stephen said. 'You must have been here since opening time.'

'We've been here a while,' Tom said. 'Emma, isn't it? What will you have?'

'I'm buying,' Stephen said. 'Something special. It's organized – in theory.' A bucket with two bottles of champagne and several glasses appeared as if by magic. 'Clarrie, you're brilliant,' he said to the barmaid, and began opening one bottle as she opened the other. 'I realize you consider this poncy stuff,' he said generally, 'but it's the best and only the best will do for you lot after your work during the past year . . . here we go. Everyone got a glass? To Great Magister and the most magnificent bunch of gardeners in the world. Thank you.'

They laughed and drank, then Tom said, 'We've got our own bit of thanking to do.' He raised his glass and voice. 'To Stephen Birkenshaw. I reckoned he was too young, I'll admit that; reckoned he couldn't have the experience. I'm not too proud to say I was wrong. Here's to the boss.'

'Stephen,' they said and gave him a cheer.

His cheeks turned pink. 'That wasn't in the script,' he protested.

Tom poured the rest of his champagne into his wife's glass. 'It's not that I don't like it,' he said, 'but I prefer my pint.'

Stephen put his arm around Emma and gave her a squeeze. 'All right? Not feeling deserted? The menu's on the board.'

They ordered their food and Stephen led her to a table

tucked away in a corner of where the bar became a restaurant.

'It says reserved,' Emma pointed out.

'By me. Will you ever have faith in me, woman?'

'Sorry. It must be something to do with our first meal together being illegal.' He took her coat and she sat down. 'It was lovely just then, Stephen: you and your lads.'

'And lass. They've slogged their guts into mincemeat. It was little enough thanks.'

'And what Tom said.'

He flushed again. 'He was right. I didn't have enough experience. Emma, I kid you not, there have been moments when I've looked back at that arrogant sod who gazed on acres of wilderness and said casually, "I can sort this for you," and I've sworn at him using words even I would not use in company.'

'You've got the experience now.'

'I certainly have.'

'Why did Tom agree to work under you if he could have done the job himself?'

'He couldn't, probably. The best brickie in the universe can't necessarily be an architect. Good old Tom. He never let on he didn't think I was up to it.'

'He meant what he said.'

'I know.'

Emma reached across the table and stroked his cheek. 'Then why so sad?'

'Humbled. Relieved.' He shrugged. 'And sad it's nearly over. Don't stop. I'm about to purr.'

She had to, though, for wine appeared and then food.

They ate and talked – or Stephen did – as the noise of the diners around them rose in a crescendo to midnight. There was a hush as the radio in the bar was turned on and Big Ben chimed the hour through the speaker systems. Party poppers were fired and a strand of curly yellow fell on Stephen's head. He brushed it off, leaned across the table and kissed Emma on the lips.

'A happy New Year, dearest Emma.' He stared into her eyes, his tawny ones intent and very grave. 'This is it, for me. The biz. I love you. Do you love me?'

'Yes.'

They could have been alone, the celebrations, the songs around them in another place. None of Stephen's many acquaintances intruded on the table in the corner.

'Will you come to bed with me?'

'Yes.'

'Let's go.'

They passed like ghosts through the revellers to the bar where Stephen had left his torch. He paid. They glided out and no one noticed them. On such a night they might have run a gauntlet of ribaldry, but did not.

A mist hung about the lane stealing the torch's beam. Into the cottage, up the narrow stairs. There was a fire in Stephen's bedroom which he coaxed into flame. He switched on the electric blanket and turned to her.

'I want to remove your golden dress, your every garment and kiss your exposed skin,' he said, 'except you'd freeze to death. To hell with romance. I'm a closet Neanderthal. Take off your clothes, woman, and get into bed.'

It was too cold to consider shyness or embarrassment. As she slid between the sheets Stephen rolled in beside her.

'Oh, glory be,' he sighed and hugged her until they both stopped shivering. He kissed her and smiled down at her. 'My beautiful Emma, we must have the conversation sensible and responsible adults ought to at these moments. I have the necessary (bought specially for you, in case you are wondering if they are leftovers from previous excesses) but I also had a blood test . . . Not,' he went on before she could say anything, 'because I've been at the front line of risk but because Sam told me to when I garbled – or was it gurgled? – on the phone to him about you. Don't mess around, he said. Do it. They are very hot on it in California. Carry their own blood trans-fusions around with them. Are you still there? You are. I can feel you. Help.' A touch on her breast. He gasped. 'Speak before I fall over the edge.'

'I had a test too, because –'

'Don't say the name: It seems stupid, perhaps it was. Is. I've waited, you see, for a new year. This begins now. Day one. Is it stupid?'

'No.'

'Tears, my love. Why?'

'You're so . . . so sweet.'

'Sweet? Gracious me!'

'Stephen, I'm on the pill. I –'

'Ah! Flesh in flesh. Let's lead each other over the edge.'

She had run it through in her mind, this. How it would be. Would he talk all the time? Yes, impossible for him to stop. Nothing else, however, was as she had imagined it. The light on, the crackling fire. The gentleness, the selfless-ness, the laughter. *Laughter?*

'Why not? I'm enjoying myself,' he said.

And then no senses left aware to analyse or listen to the nonsense words. Followed by cradled sleep.

Making love with Stephen on a frosty first of January.

'Dear girl,' he said afterwards. 'My dearest girl. Stay here. I'm going to light the fire downstairs and bring you breakfast. Bloody hell, it's cold!' He leaped out of bed, put on a dressing gown and his Barbour – discarded on the floor the previous night – and a pair of sheepskin slippers. 'It's what every woman's lover is wearing this season,' he explained. 'Specially designed to make her swoon with desire. The next place I live in will be trop-ical.' He bent and kissed her. 'Do I look very ridiculous?'

'I'm afraid you do.' Mock alarm on his face. 'I prefer you naked,' she said.

'Good.' He poked the fire into life, stocked it with wood and disappeared.

Emma lay in the snug bed, listened to him thumping about below, smelled the wood smoke. This was it. The biz. Heart and head were in full accord.

He brought fresh coffee, boiled eggs and fingers of toast. Emma sat up, the blanket clasped to her chin, as Stephen put the tray on the bedside table and divested himself of his strange apparel.

'For me this will be bliss,' he said, getting into bed, 'but not for you,' and he warmed his feet and hands in ways that distracted Emma from breakfast.

'Don't,' she said at last. 'I'm hungry.'

'You are. I can hear your tummy rumbling.'

'It's rude of you to listen.'

'Sorry.'

He stuffed a pillow behind her back and placed the tray across their legs.

Not even her grandmother's hens' eggs tasted so delicious, and to follow there was more toast, rather cool but Stephen said no way would he make more though invited her to if she wished, which she did not, and Mrs Tom's homemade marmalade.

'You were a starved soul,' Stephen said, watching as she licked dribbles of marmalade from her fingers. 'Finished?'

She nodded and he removed the tray.

'Dearest Emma, are you comfy?'

'Mm. Apart from sticky fingers.' She ran them over his chest. 'You haven't any hair. None at all.'

'It's why I would never have made it as an actor.'

'Why did you give up drama?'

'I couldn't act. Emma, I'm about to divulge my awful secret. Promise you won't laugh?'

'No.'

'You couldn't be so mean. I was a child star. In c

337

film which they occasionally – the bastards! – wheel out on bank-holiday afternoons. Five-hanky rubbish, treacle wading through honey. All I had to do was wrinkle my nose and be cute and I thought having freckles and a nose was what acting meant. The fire will be burning merrily by now. Shall we get up? . . . Emma, what are you doing?'

'Trying to keep you in bed.'

'How nice. Very. I'll stay, since you insist.'

They went for a walk that afternoon, and he proposed. In, for heaven's sake, the conservatory attached to the punters' palace.

'You idiot!' she said, falling against him.

'It isn't madness. I've thought long and hard and decided you're the only woman for me . . . Oh, no! I didn't realize, honestly I didn't. Will you marry a cliché? Could you bear to?'

'Yes,' she said, certainty blazing through her. It had been kindling the first time she had been in here when Stephen had given her the Guernsey lily.

He sat her on what he referred to as a rustic bench, sat beside her. Pulled from his pocket a velvet-covered box, opened it, took out the ring.

'You planned it,' she said. 'Everything.'

'Do you mind?'

'No.'

'Take off your glove.' A cluster of three diamonds was slipped on to her finger. 'A little loose,' Stephen said. 'We'll have it fixed. Better this, though, than not being able to get it on. That would have spoiled a pretty moment, wouldn't it? Is it safe? It won't fall off?'

She tested it. 'No.'

'You've gone monosyllabic. Maidenly delight, I expect. Emma Birkenshaw to be, shall we be married in the ɔring? Will you live with me until then? Or – or will ur parents fuss?'

Emma recalled her grandmother's revelation about her father's shaving gear. 'They wouldn't dare,' she said.

'I want to meet them. Can we go tomorrow? And my parents. Would you like to have supper with them tonight? It's no distance.'

'Isn't it rather short notice?'

His smile. 'I don't think they'll be surprised. And now, my Emma, can I steal from you a betrothal kiss?'

She lifted her face to his. 'Betrothal. What a lovely word . . . But shouldn't you,' she said a while later, 'give me a flower in return?'

'You've got the diamonds. What more do you want? Blood? Oh, well,' he grumbled, 'I could spare an orchid, I suppose.'

'I was joking.'

'So was I. Come on, woman, we have some telephoning to do.'

His parents were thrilled, delighted, longing to meet Emma.

Hers, ditto him.

Gran's Ansaphone was on. Emma left no message and called Jackie.

Jackie, thrilled, spoke to them both.

Rowena and Sam were delighted, and they had a four-way conversation.

At seven o'clock, when they were ready to leave, Olivia's Ansaphone was still on.

'Try later,' Stephen said. He was wearing the sweater she had given him and was looking gorgeous. He covered it with his Barbour and they went out. 'Are you sure about driving?'

'I'm better at not drinking than you are.'

'One of the things I love about you most.' They got into the Porsche and set off. 'When do I get to meet your amazing grandmother?' he asked.

'I was hoping . . . Could we go tomorrow from home? Maybe stay the night?'

'Fine.'

'If I can get hold of her. She's probably with her friend. I could get his number from Directory Enquiries but I don't know how she'd feel about being hunted down. Or it could be skittles night. You don't know any of this,' she warned, 'when you see Mum and Dad.'

'Okay, ma'am.'

The Porsche powered through the dark. The ring or her left hand glinted in the headlights of the cars behind. The last twenty-four hours should have seemed momentous to her but she could only regard them as a culmination of the inevitable.

Stephen directed her and they turned into a drive, the car scrunching on gravel. The front door of an unseen house opened and two people were silhouetted in the light. Stephen took Emma's hand as she got out of the car and led her up some steps.

'Mother, Father, this is Emma.'

A tall woman embraced Emma and kissed her cheek. Stephen was being hugged by his father. They swapped and Emma was enveloped in tweed.

'Mother, don't cry. You are meant to be happy,' Stephen said.

'I am happy.' A sniff. 'Emma, into the warmth with you. Take her coat, Peter. This way, my dear. There is someone dying to say hello and a lot more, no doubt.'

She opened a door, and there was Claire Firling in her wheelchair. Emma rushed over and kissed the old woman.

'I wish I'd thought of introducing you two,' Claire said. 'So unimaginative of me. It didn't cross my mind.'

'We would have hated each other if you had,' Stephen said soothingly. 'Glared at each other and thought, sodding interfering cow.'

'We apologize for the language,' Peter Birkenshaw said, opening a bottle of champagne. 'We beat him, we deducted his pocket money, we forced him to wash his mouth out with soap and water but nothing made the foggiest difference. We're awfully grateful you are over-looking it and are prepared to take him on.'

Everyone laughed and Emma felt utterly at home. She had given up questioning the quirks of fate – or whatever it was called – that had led to her being here and the latest one, which decreed that Claire Firling paved the way to Peter and Judith Birkenshaw's instant acceptance of her, was beyond consideration.

Pheasant for dinner. Not the sort of thing you have oven-ready and in sufficient quantity on New Year's Day. Emma's mother would have dived panic-stricken into her deep freeze to find something suitable for tomorrow's lunch. How much of this had Stephen planned? All of it, probably. Who cared?

He touched her as they rose from the table. 'Try your grandmother again. Had you forgotten?'

She had, almost. Gran was in. Laura had rung her twenty minutes ago.

'I didn't want to leave a message,' Emma said. 'Not about this.'

'When can I see him?' Olivia said, interrupting her. 'Tomorrow night? It's darts, but they can do without me. No, silly child, how could anything be more important? Oh, darling –'

'You're crying, you fool. Stephen's mother did too.'

'That means she's very pleased. I *am* glad.'

'Do you want to speak to Claire Firling? She would to you.'

'Is she there? This is most extraordinary.'

'It is. Are you recovered? I'll take the phone to her.'

'Success?' Judith Birkenshaw said as Emma opened the sitting room door. 'Obviously. Don't try to move, Claire. I'll bring it to you. Emma, Peter has something to show you.'

Emma gave her the phone and went with her future father-in-law. 'I didn't mind taking the one out of the album and getting it copied,' he said, 'but I didn't like the idea of removing this from the frame. It's been in it for a long time.'

A photograph of a group of confident, grinning young men in bulky flying suits, a plane – a Spitfire, Emma assumed – behind them. No names, but Stephen had told Emma there would not be.

'That's my father and next to him is Max Johnstone, the pilot who saw my father die and who shot down the plane that killed him.'

Emma took the photograph. More or less as she had pictured Max. She wondered how many of the group had survived the war; those that had were greybeards now.

'Stephen says you're writing about it,' Peter Birkenshaw said.

'Not really. Just playing around.'

He raised an eyebrow at her. 'But he promised I had a starring role in it. Or at least junior lead ... My dear girl, I've made you blush. There's no need to.'

Emma was spared having to respond as she was summoned to say goodbye to her grandmother, and soon after that Stephen said they had to leave.

'I hate to think of you in that freezing cottage,' Judith Birkenshaw said. 'Why not stay the night here?'

Emma was tempted by the central heating, but there were other temptations at Great Magister. Stephen's face said he was contemplating them too.

'I'm house-training her,' he told his parents. 'She has to learn that life with me is tough.'

Claire Firling emitted clucking noises and Peter said earnestly to Emma: 'If you decide he's too much we'll quite understand. Send him back to us and we'll have another try at civilizing him.'

'Don't put her off,' his wife scolded.

'He won't.' Stephen hugged Emma and kissed the top of her head. 'Will he?'

'Did you tell them to expect us?' Emma said when they were on their way back.

'I suggested they should be prepared.'

'What if I'd said no, or I wanted time to consider your gracious proposal?'

'Then we wouldn't have gone.'

'Wouldn't it have been more . . . polite to ask me to marry you before asking me to sleep with you?'

'I had to give you a once-over, make sure we fit. That's reasonable, isn't it?'

'It's dreadful,' she said.

'Actually, I meant to ask you to marry me last night. The other came out first, it having been greatly exercising my mind. No, I'll be totally honest. My groin.'

'The conservatory –' she began.

'Emma, if I couldn't propose as midnight struck I wanted there to be some romance about it. It's a big moment in a man's life. I didn't fancy doing it over the jigsaw puzzle or in the kitchen. I'm sorry it ended up corny, but the conservatory is heated. There's a thought. Shall we sleep in there tonight?'

'We'll be all right once we're in bed.'

'Once we're in bed, Emma, we'll be a hell of a lot more than all right.'

He wore a suit the next day, for he said it was the correct attire in which to meet one's future parents-in-law. He seemed almost a stranger in it, but when Emma came downstairs he was a stranger in fact. The tawny eyes were distraught, his cheeks white.

'Whatever is the matter?' she asked.

He gripped her shoulders. 'Have you told your people I'm divorced?'

343

'No. What difference does it make?'

'I'd forgotten. So had my mother. The talk of a white church wedding. Rowena wanted one when she married Sam, and there was a terrific to-do. Some priests won't marry a divorced person and some bishops won't allow their priests to.'

'Oh,' Emma said, taken aback. She had imagined walking up the aisle in her village church on Hamish's arm and down on Stephen's.

'Dearest Emma, I'm sorry.'

'Perhaps our priest is allowed to.'

'One's stupid mistakes! Why should the thing I did when I was nineteen have an effect on you now? I wasn't married in a church last time. It isn't as though I'm trying to wangle two of those.'

'Please, darling Stephen, I don't mind. Stop worrying.'

The distress receded from his face and was replaced by tenderness. 'You haven't called me that before. Say it again.'

'Darling.'

He was nervous as they got out of the car. He straightened his unaccustomed tie, pulled down the jacket of his beige-coloured suit and fiddled with the handkerchief in the top pocket.

'They won't eat you,' Emma said.

'My previous parents-in-law did.'

The welcome was no less warm than it had been at the Birkenshaws', but less demonstrative. It is not easy to embrace a man you have never seen before and there was no Claire Firling to clear the way. Champagne there was, however, it being the drink for congratulating engaged couples as well as gardeners. Hamish also seemed nervous as he opened the bottle, poured fizz into the glasses and gave the toast.

'Please, Stephen,' Laura said at last, 'put him out of his misery and ask him to show you around.'

'Indeed I will,' Stephen said promptly. 'Is that a liriodendron I spy out there? Did you plant it?'

'Yes. It flowered a couple of years ago.'

'What I call a gardener's tree. An old boy I worked with once planted one when he was seventy. Said it would give him an incentive to live until he was at least eighty-five. They don't flower until they are fifteen years old,' he explained to Laura and Emma.

'And not always then. We go this way,' Hamish said. 'Bring your glass. Shall I lend you a coat?'

'I've got one in the car. Can I have the keys, Emma?' She gave them to him and heard him say as he and Hamish left the room: 'I'm so pleased I met your daughter. She's a marvellous chauffeur. Drives me everywhere in such comfort. Or should it be a chauffeuse?'

He was off, but guarding his language. 'Marvellous' would normally be 'sodding good'.

'Well?' Emma said to her mother.

'He adores you,' Laura said. 'He absolutely adores you.'

'And I adore him ... Not you too, Mum. Stephen's mother did, and Gran. The last thing I feel like doing is crying.'

Laura mopped her eyes. 'I must tell you about your father,' she said. 'He was out until nine o'clock last night with a torch and the Camping Gaz light perfecting his beastly garden for an inspection by Stephen. "Why couldn't she have got engaged in June?" he demanded, really quite annoyed. "It's at its best then." Dear me.' She blew her nose. 'Let me see the ring. How lovely. Have you considered the date of the wedding?'

'In the spring, but Mum –'

Laura wasn't in any way shocked that Stephen was divorced, merely remarking it would have been astonishing if such a charmer had remained single, but returned from phoning the vicar in a fury.

'He says he can do a blessing after the register office but the bishop refuses to let him perform the ceremony. When you remember the Church of England is considering ordaining divorced men as priests . . . it's unbelievable! It isn't as though Stephen has been divorced several times or has left a wife and children after years. I mean –'

'Mum, stop! You sound like Gran.'

'Don't tell her, for God's sake. She'll ring up our bishop and give him an earful.'

'Will you explain to Dad so we don't spend lunch talking about a white wedding?'

'Lunch! I'd better cook the veg.' They both stood. 'Do look,' Laura said.

Hamish and Stephen, heads close together, were pacing across the lawn. Hamish turned, waved and made urgent motions indicating empty glasses.

'We appear to have finished this bottle,' Laura said. 'Send your father in, darling, to decide what he wants to open next and I'll tell him. If he can't give you away he can't. He seems very happy with your choice of a husband, and so am I.' She kissed her. 'Are you going to live with him until you marry?'

Emma met her eyes. 'Yes.'

'Well, I suppose we can't argue.'

'Not easily, Mum. I must pack some more clothes.'

She went into the garden, interrupted the Latin and, reluctantly, Hamish returned to the house.

'Is he a gardener or does he garden?' Emma asked Stephen.

'Oh, a gardener, definitely. Thank goodness I don't have to pretend. Admiring a bed of begonias would have stuck in my gullet but I would have done it for your sake.'

'You don't get begonias in January. Even I know that.'

'I was speaking figuratively.'

'Stephen, our church says no.'

'Bugger!' he said. 'Bugger and shit!'

'That's got it out of your system. Half an hour without swearing must have been a strain.'

'I want everything to be perfect.'

'It will be. We can go to the church after the register office. It's what they do in Europe, isn't it?'

'I don't want a sodding Euro-wedding.'

'I do,' Emma said firmly. 'It will show solidarity.'

'You are a darling to make the best of it and I love you very much indeed. Kiss me.'

Hamish was waiting when this was over, a glass in each hand.

'Carry on,' he said. 'Pretend I'm not here.'

'Thank you, but I'd rather have a drink,' Stephen said. 'Hamish, I'm sorry you can't give her to me officially.'

'It's hardly your fault.'

'Of course it is.'

'Don't bother about it. Look, can you advise me on what to do with this corner over here? I'm wondering about a pond . . .'

'Getting on like a house on fire,' Emma reported to her mother.

'Hamish says he's awesomely knowledgeable.'

'No more fuss about me getting hurt?'

'None whatsoever. It's – it's –'

'It is, isn't it?'

They waved goodbye to Laura and Hamish when dusk was beginning to swamp the short day.

'They didn't eat you,' Emma said.

'They're terrific. Then they'd have to be, having been responsible for you. I'm pissed off about the church, though.'

'It can't be helped.'

'Suppose not.'

He put on a CD, lit a cigarette and relaxed.

347

'I've worked something out about you,' Emma said after a while.

'I'll listen if it's nice.'

'The only time you are quiet is in cars. Isn't that odd? They say babies are quiet in cars.'

'What are you implying, heart of my heart?'

'It was just an observation.'

'I'll tell you something about babies. When we're married you're going to throw away those pills.'

'Do I have any say in this?'

'Let's have babies, Emma.'

'You already have a few thousand,' she reminded him.

'Yes, but the way they get planted is much less pleasurable.'

'Oh, go to sleep,' she said.

Olivia had no inhibitions about kissing strange men. 'I have an excuse,' she said. 'I knew you long before you were born. Darlings, are you bored with bubbly? I did buy a bottle.'

Stephen wowed her with his smile. 'Would it be rude,' he said, 'if I told you I could murder a pint of beer?'

'Not a bit. I have some cans, or we could go across to the pub.'

'I would prefer it from a barrel. Emma, could you cope with a pub? Poor love,' he said to Olivia, 'she's been doing all the driving, and having to worry about me behaving myself. Talking of which, where shall I put our bags?' He gazed inquiringly at her. An understanding, almost tangible, arose between them.

'I'm afraid you'll have to,' Olivia said. 'There's only one spare bedroom, though with two beds. Top of the stairs to the left.' He clumped away. 'Serious at the right moments,' Olivia remarked to her granddaughter, 'and beautifully serious about you. Let me give you a proper hug. Darling, I am thrilled.'

'Graham will be at the pub, won't he, if it's darts night? I'd like him to meet Stephen.'

'That's sweet of you. He will be pleased.'

'Gran, when are you going to tell Mum and the others?'

She sighed. 'I don't know. Soon. I must, especially after ticking you off for not revealing Stephen.'

'Hey! Does that mean you and Graham –?'

'Probably. All right. Yes. It will be my third name and my initials have never changed. Isn't that convenient?'

'Wittering, Wheeler, Wellbeck. Very convenient,' Emma said laughing.

Graham was in his bold mood, or perhaps it was permanent now Olivia had let him off his tenterhook. He kissed Emma's cheek, said he was delighted with her news and replied with an enormous grin when she said she was delighted with his. He shook Stephen's hand and said a man who preferred beer to bubbly was one he could relate to, although he couldn't for long because he was called away to the match.

'Why not ask him to supper when it's over?' Emma asked.

'It will be too late. Tonight is for you two.'

Reaction set in over Olivia's fish pie – something light, she had said, since she knew they had eaten beef for lunch – and Emma's eyes began irresistibly to close.

'To bed, my love,' Stephen said. 'I'll come and tuck you up in a minute.'

He might have done, but she was already asleep and awoke next morning refreshed and fit for anything. Stephen, in the next bed, opened a bleary eye.

'Your gran got me drunk,' he said. 'Kept me talking until after midnight.'

'What about?'

'Cabbages and kings. About you, Emma. Who else? Are you getting dressed?'

'Yes.'

'Do it slowly, so I can watch.' He wriggled upright and bolstered himself with pillows. 'I hadn't realized your flat is enormous and probably worth loads of money. If I had I might have asked you to marry me sooner. What will you do with it?'

'Sell it – if I can – and buy you a garden.'

'How kind of you. Finished? Sit down. I want words with you.'

'That sounds like a quarrel.'

'It won't be if you obey.'

She put on a sweater and sat on the side of his bed. He took her hand.

'Olivia – she told me to call her that so don't think I'm being over-familiar – said that what you refer to as your research is a lot more than that. She said . . . Well, never mind exactly. How long will you need in Guernsey?'

'Stephen, I don't –'

'You are going to finish it, Emma. I'm not having you accusing me on our fiftieth wedding anniversary of not letting you. You can move your word processor into the cottage and I swear not to be jealous. I'll be out all day so I won't disrupt you, and I won't expect you to iron my underpants and cook for me, not until we're married at any rate.'

'I –'

'Be quiet. Planes to Guernsey fly from Southampton, your gran says. Book your flight in the next few days and I'll take you to the airport then go on to your home. I promised Hamish a few things – plants to be exact – and I'll bring your word processor back with me. Yes?'

'You're being very masterful,' Emma said.

'Am I? I hope so. How long will you be away?'

'Only a few days to get a feel of the place.'

'I can exist for days without you, and you can without me. This once and never more. Don't you remember,' he said, his smile on her, 'that I am a sign?'

Part VII

I

'Why Guernsey, Harry?' Diana said. 'Why?'

'Eve likes it there. The climate . . .'

The distance from her family. From his.

'Why not Africa?'

Harry put sugar into his cup of tea. 'It's a young man's country. I can't go back to being a DC and couldn't stand being a bureaucrat. I'm too old to learn how to grow coffee or cattle, so there we are.'

'In Guernsey. What in God's name will you do?'

'What I did before. Shoot a bit, breed and train dogs.'

'One island for another, one wife for another. Was it worth the effort, Harry? No, that's an unfair question. Don't answer. More tea?' She poured it, then replaced the silver pot on a silver tray.

'I'm happy with Eve, Diana.'

'Are you? Then I'm happy for you.' She took a cigarette from a silver box on the table beside her chair and he produced his lighter, leaned forward and lit it for her. 'Smoke your pipe, Harry,' she said. 'You don't need to ask permission.'

He took it from his pocket and began filling it. 'That's almost what you said the first time we met.'

She smiled. 'I know. You were so uncomfortable and uneasy. I thought it was nervousness until I realized.'

'I was uncomfortable. In those days I hardly ever wore a suit and I'd almost forgotten how to tie a tie.'

'I've adored the smell of pipe smoke ever since, and bonfires – though ones here aren't ever like the African ones.'

'No,' Harry said. 'The wood is different.'

'And the air. Twenty – what? – two or three years later and I remember it.' She stubbed out her cigarette, stood up and went to the window. 'They talk about a new order in this brave, post-war world. Do you think it will include equality for royalty?'

'I suspect that's a contradiction in terms,' Harry said, applying the lighter to the bowl of his pipe.

'I meant it literally. David is having a blissful time with his Wallis, from what I hear. It's odd that a king can abdicate for love and the rest of us can't, isn't it?'

'Put like that it does seem odd.'

She sat down again and breathed in his pipe smoke. 'It will always take me back,' she said. 'Back to Africa and the only time *ever* I broke the rules. Discretion personified, that's me.' She paused and then said, 'Things will change, Harry. They must. If you and I were in our twenties now we might have been allowed to marry.'

'Diana, my dear –'

'Yes. We are not in our twenties and you are married to someone else. I'm sorry. Let's talk of something else. Do you approve of your daughter's husband?'

'Absolutely!' he said, with as great an effort at cheerfulness as her. What with one thing and another he hardly knew his son-in-law. His Moppet married and now on her honeymoon! Harry had indeed divorced more than a wife when he had divorced Nell, or she him. 'He's in the Navy,' he added. Apart from the fact that he seemed a nice young man, he loved Moppet and she loved him, this amounted to his total knowledge of Robert Wheeler.

'Intending to stay in?'

'What? Oh, the Navy. I believe so.'

'A good career, I dare say.'

'Yes.'

An hour later he was shown out by the butler and regained the pavement, a horrible depression on him. A policeman, his face blue with cold, stood outside the door to guard against attacks from anarchists and the like . . . He thought of Diana with her half life – a quarter life now, even. Poor Diana. Her son, her only child, had died in Canada in 1943 before his thirtieth birthday under the most tragic circumstances, found frozen by the open window in his bedroom in Government House. Poor Diana, related to every monarch there was left in Europe, in her silver cage. Harry tried not to think what metal the bars of his were made of, yet Eve had once promised to release him from a prison. Guernsey, an island ramparted by cliffs nearer by far to France than England, British since 1066 and lately occupied by Germans. Harry could probably walk around it in a day, and its square mileage would fit several times into his former district.

As Diana had said, why? It had been Eve's decision. The climate, true, but there was better weather in other countries. Financially beneficial, Eve had declared. She was there now overseeing plasterers and painters in their house, having arranged to be thus occupied while Harry was in London for Moppet's wedding. Their house bought with her money.

Another island, another wife. No, nonsense. He was happy with Eve he told himself as he strode through an inhospitable February wind towards the underground station. He was over fifty, too old for adventure and lucky to have a rich young wife. Luckier in every way than poor Diana.

Louis and Lucy Fanshawe were in London with their seventeen-year-old daughter, Susie. They had caught an earlier ship than they had originally intended so they could arrive in time for Olivia's wedding, and Harry was grateful to them. They were probably, he considered, the only people there entirely on his side. On the evening of his visit to Diana he had dinner with them at the Dorchester Hotel where they were staying; evidently the war had been profitable for them. Susie, who was Harry's goddaughter, moaned at him about the weather, about the reason for their coming to England.

'You tell them, Uncle Harry,' she said. 'I'm to be foisted on Granny and finished. How absurd when I was never started, apart from being able to read and write – just.'

'They want you to be a well-behaved and demure English girl,' Harry said.

'They should have thought of it before. I'm Kenyan and we're not at all demure.'

'Some of you aren't, certainly.'

She had been fourteen when he had last seen her and had conducted him and Eve on a tour of their farm, she on her pony and they on horses, she carrying a businesslike rifle across her pommel. She was only a year or so younger than Moppet, but in many ways appeared older. Except, he reminded himself, Moppet was married.

'Tell the aged ones, Uncle Harry,' she pleaded. 'I'll go mad here.'

'You won't, Susie. You'll knuckle under as everyone has to sooner or later.'

'I'd planned to run away to you and Aunt Eve when things got desperate until I found Guernsey on the map. It's a speckle in the sea. What a funny place to live.'

'Hush up, you,' Louis said. 'You are not yet too old to be sent to bed without any supper.'

'Supper. Daddy, can I have some money? We'll eat somewhere after the pictures.'

'You're not to be late back,' Louis warned.

An exaggerated sigh. 'No, Daddy.' She gave each of them a kiss and bounded out.

'Why are you insisting she be finished?' Harry asked. 'She's smashing the way she is.'

'She needs some of the corners knocking off,' Lucy said.

'Well, don't let them knock off too many. Who is she going to the pictures with?'

'A crowd of Kenyans, as she calls them. Lots of us seem to have come home at the same time, having the idea that London would be back to normal after a few months of peace.'

'It's much more normal than it was.'

'Yes, but we remember it as it used to be. We knew about the Blitz, of course, but it's hard to imagine the reality. Everyone and thing is so grey.'

'Homesick already, Lucy?' Harry said wistfully.

'A bit,' she admitted. 'And you, Harry?'

'There's nothing for me there any more.'

'You could get land,' Louis said. 'New settlers are being encouraged.'

'That is trouble with a capital T. The natives won't stand for land being taken from them for much longer, you mark my words.'

'They aren't using it.'

'That's not the point, but don't let's argue about it.'

'No. Harry, if you're ready to retire why not in Kenya? A house in Karen, say. It would be a sight more exciting than Guernsey and at least you'd be among friends.'

'Eve didn't really care for the place,' Harry muttered.

'Nairobi, you mean, or the entire country?'

'Louis!' Lucy hissed.

'Sorry, old chap, but . . .' His voice trailed off and the rest of the sentence hung in the air between them: how did you saddle yourself with another woman who refuses to live in the place you want to?

'Have you news of Mutali?' Harry asked, anxious to change the subject. 'I haven't heard from him for a while.'

357

'We thought you'd want to know and checked. He's still on the reserve being looked after by his children and grandchildren. Quite the patriarch,' Lucy said.

'I hoped he would have returned to the hotel. I'd like to think of him roaming around our old haunts.'

'There's not much call for safaris up there these days,' Louis said, 'nor any likelihood in the future, there being no sport for them.'

'Were the herds really slaughtered?' They were discussing it when Harry had been there. Seventy thousand Italian troops had surrendered in Abyssinia and had been kept in prisoner-of-war camps. They and the allied forces stationed in the country had to be fed and Kenya's teeming herds had seemed the obvious solution to the powers that were. Harry had heard that the land was empty of game but it was hard to believe. Like Louis and Lucy about the Blitz, it was impossible to match the theory to the reality.

'Yes,' Louis said gruffly. 'Perhaps it's as well you're not retiring there. Let's eat.'

Two days later Harry caught a train from Victoria Station to Portsmouth and boarded the overnight ferry to Guernsey. He had first sailed away from England in 1912 at the age of seventeen – Susie's age – when he had left for Africa on a great liner. The ferry seemed a symbol of the way his life was running downhill towards its close.

This would not do. He forced his mind to see forwards, to find a future. Part of it was with him in the shape of a three-month-old springer spaniel puppy, a several times great-granddaughter of Busy whom he had named Fly. Liver and white she was, like champion Busy. Fly, however, would never be a field trial champion, not where it counted, for she would have to undergo months of quarantine before she could compete on mainland Britain. For her this journey was one way only.

'If there are no decent husbands for you on Guernsey,' Harry said to her as he returned to her travelling basket after an early morning stroll on deck, 'we'll import one specially.'

Eve was waiting for him on the quay at St Peter Port. She kissed him, greeted the puppy, inquired about the crossing but said not a word about Olivia's wedding. She drove through the narrow streets of Guernsey's only town and into tiny, stone-banked lanes.

'We've had divine weather here,' she said. 'It's almost spring. The house is finished, nearly, and awaiting inspection by the master.'

Guernsey was making an enormous effort to please him. The sun shone from a clear blue sky and sparkled on the sea, a glimpse of which reappeared below them, and the air indeed smelled of spring, which was particularly welcome after the cold dankness of London. Inside the house the newly painted walls reflected light. Daffodils were out in the garden and were investigated by Fly when Harry took her to relieve herself and to explore her home territory.

'You have been working hard,' Harry said, back inside and having done some exploring of his own.

'Downstairs is completed, and our bedroom, but we have to wait for more paint for the rest. Everything is in short supply.'

'Your smile has performed miracles so far.'

'I don't ask where it comes from or whether it is legal. Fishing boats aren't only catching fish is my guess.'

'I'm sure you're right. The dining table fits. That's lucky, isn't it?' He was experiencing *déjà vu*. Furniture which had once belonged to Aunt Caroline and which had been in store since the house on Anglesey had been closed was now here along with rugs, ornaments, pictures and silver. The government billet in Nairobi and the flat they had lived in in London had both been furnished. This was their first real marital home.

'We can move things, Harry,' Eve said anxiously. 'I got the men to put them where they seemed best.'

'It looks wonderful,' he said.

She put her arms around his neck. 'Harry, darling, if you don't like it here we can move more than furniture.'

'I love it here and I love you.'

He bent his head to kiss her and thought: Cage? What cage?

The notion of its existence only arose when he was with people who questioned the sagacity of his second marriage, and he did not see those very often since the situation of Guernsey did not encourage any but the most determined of guests. It was easier altogether not to think about it.

Susie Fanshawe was a determined guest, but she wasn't fussed about Harry's marriage.

'I can cook, sew, iron, lay a table correctly and speak atrocious French,' she announced. 'And now I'm going home to Kenya where I shan't have to do any of it. What a ridiculous waste of time, exactly as I said it would be. Granny says I should have another season but I've refused to. I want to marry a Kenyan not an English bore, and I must hurry in case someone else snaffles him.'

'You have someone in mind, then. Is he aware of your intentions?' Eve asked, amused. She scarcely dared even consider it, but it was a pleasant change to be in young company. The friends they had made on Guernsey tended to be of Harry's generation.

'Not entirely, but I wrote to say I'd be at Race Week and would he, as it were, be my partner.'

'Susie, honestly!' Eve protested.

'I wasn't being forward, Aunt Eve, not really. I've known him for ages and he was in London last year. We – er – fumbled a bit,' she added, finally having the grace to blush. 'So I have to be there, don't I? I've booked my passage and made Granny pay. Daddy will send her a cheque.'

'Will Daddy be pleased to see you?' Harry said, relighting his pipe.

'I should jolly well hope so. I've done my stint.'

Shades of the cage. Harry escorted her back to England, for Moppet's daughter, born the previous November, was being christened, an event to which Susie was also invited. Harry had not yet met his first grandchild, had not seen Moppet since her wedding. She was living in married quarters on a naval base in Hampshire, their plans to buy a house with the help of Robert's parents having been shelved by a difficult pregnancy. He could have visited her, should have bothered, but he'd had an inexplicable queasiness about seeing Moppet pregnant.

She was the most gorgeous mother but she was only nineteen, hardly more than a child herself. She nudged her husband when Harry arrived and said, 'Daddy!' very obviously to be sure Robert Wheeler recognized his father-in-law. 'How is Eve?' she asked with a determined, too-adult politeness.

'Fit, thank you,' Harry said. 'She sends you her love and is sorry she can't be here.'

Aghast brown eyes. Do anything, *anything*, they said, but for God's sake don't lie.

Nell was there, drooling over baby Laura in a manner Harry found astonishing considering the way she had treated her own daughter. Daisy Davidson was there, she who had contrived Nell's escape from Kenya so many years ago. She was recently widowed and had returned to England for good, and was planning to live with Nell, Harry gathered. She eyed him up and down, then Susie Fanshawe standing next to him whom she knew but chose to pretend not to.

'My,' she said, 'they get younger all the time, Harry. Wherever will it end?'

Harry prayed Susie had not realized what the bitch meant and wished this was over.

Nick was there, taller than Harry, and Harry extracted

a promise from him to come to Guernsey for a week or so during the summer holidays and then poured the advantage away by suggesting Nick drank no more of the champagne which somehow Robert had managed to procure.

Nick, swaying, glared down at him. 'What do you mean by that?' he demanded belligerently.

'Only that you've had enough.'

'I hardly think,' Nick slurred, 'that you have a right to judge my behaviour.'

Harry was glad to flee from the torturer's rack into the cage.

They made a life on Guernsey. One dog was never enough for Harry and soon there was a pack of them at his heels. As before, they opened doors and there was a place for Harry on every shoot on the island, and just about every dog on each shoot had passed through Harry's hands. Eve added her bit to what she termed their cottage industry and began breeding and showing Pekineses, selling them to the neighbouring island of Jersey and to France and beyond. Harry was at first horrified by the yappy creatures and – remembering Mac – insulted by Eve's assertion that they were known as lion dogs, but he came to admire them. Eve's Pekes did not have bulging eyes or breathing problems and they were willing to go for a hell of a walk if they didn't trip over their ear fringes. He was entirely won over when Fan Tan, Best in Show three times running at the Channel Islands championships, slipped his leash at the market in St Peter Port in order to chase an Alsatian. The stall-holders swore in their Guernsey patois at their overturned fruit and vegetables, then shouted on the little 'un until Harry brought the sport to a close by a rugby tackle on Fan Tan.

While Eve inspected her boy for damage Harry went around offering compensation. No one would accept any and Harry, feeling he had to buy something, returned to

Eve with six bunches of flowers, several pounds of tomatoes, two dozen lettuces and a tortoise.

'For you,' he said.

'Harry, why a tortoise?'

'To eat the lettuces, of course.'

There were no children. Eve did not want them and Harry was relieved. He was not going to love that much again.

An unreasonable and unfair gremlin still whispered to him every so often that he should be in Africa. Susie married her Kenyan and Harry had suggested they go there for the wedding, take a holiday.

'Who would look after the dogs?' Eve said. 'No, it's impossible.'

Occasionally she went to the mainland to select new Pekineses, but never to visit her family. Their shock at the part she had played in splitting the Wittering family continued to fester, or so she believed. She communicated with her parents and sisters through Christmas cards and was indifferent when her mother wrote to say that Lulu, the dog she had used to help capture Harry, was dead.

Moppet had another daughter. It was difficult for her to travel to Guernsey, she said, with two small children, and then Robert was posted to Malta for three years.

'She hasn't forgiven me,' Harry said when he got home from saying tearful farewells, 'and I don't believe she ever will. I treated her so badly.'

'Who are you feeling sorry for? Yourself or her?'

Eve hadn't seen Olivia since the end of the war but she got on splendidly with Nick. He had remembered the promise he had made at his niece's christening but not the aftermath, or if he had he did not mention it, and visited them regularly. Having left school and done his National Service, he was working in an art gallery in London and he always brought to Guernsey a picture he said he was sure Eve would like, which she always did, said she adored it and wrote out an inflated cheque. She fussed over Nick, worried about his generally unkempt appearance – which was by design and not from necessity, for Nell made sure of that – although she did not know, let alone acknowledge, for example, the birthdays of her nephews and nieces.

She dealt with all the finances – she had all the money, her carefully nurtured legacy from her grandmother – and she manipulated the markets like a professional. That and Guernsey's liberal tax laws ensured they lived comfortably, although Eve was ever at pains to call it frugally. The top floor of their house was still unfinished. She converted it into a flat for letting out to holiday makers, but it remained sparsely furnished and no holiday-making family inhabited it. Harry wondered what the effort had been for, but Olivia did not when she arrived with Laura and Julie after a mercifully calm crossing so no one was sick.

'We're here to see my grandfather,' Laura confided to a fellow passenger as the ferry docked at St Peter Port. 'He has nine dogs.'

'How . . . interesting,' the man responded.

'Five Pekineses and four spaniels.'

'Very nice, I'm sure.'

'There's Daddy – your grandfather,' Olivia said, waving. A familiar figure in tweeds, a cap, a pipe in his mouth, waved back.

'Moppet, my Moppet,' he said when she was ashore, and hugged and hugged her. He looked at his two granddaughters. 'And have I surprises for you!'

'Have you?' Laura said. 'What?'

'Wonderful ones,' he said firmly, and she contained herself, convinced wonders would happen.

'What do we call you?' Julie asked in the car.

'What do you think you should call me?'

Julie wriggled. 'Grandfarver?' she suggested.

'That title would please me hugely,' he said.

Laura and Julie considered that where they were to stay was the height of adventure. A flat with its own door and steps to the road, its own bathroom and kitchen, the latter equipped with cornflakes and milk so they could make breakfast for themselves, was magical to them.

'It's convenient,' Eve said. 'It will stop them disturbing your father.'

Olivia gazed bleakly around. 'Convenient,' she said. 'Yes.'

But grandchildren visit their grandfathers precisely so they can disturb them. Harry introduced the girls to Alice, who helped with housework three mornings a week, and then, most solemnly, by name to each of the dogs, the Pekes in the house and the spaniels in their kennel. Then he went into the garden.

'Laura, Julie!' he shouted. 'Where are you?'

Julie cast a disturbed glance at Laura. They only knew – or only remembered knowing – one other grandfather and by that they could not judge the whole breed. Perhaps this one was forgetful. Or mad.

'We're here,' Laura said, the elder speaking for both of them.

'Yes, but the fascinating thing is you are not the only Laura and Julie around. Well, I'm blowed!' their grandfather exclaimed. 'There seems to be a bar of chocolate in a hole in this apple tree, and, look, another in that bush. You'd better grab 'em before the fairies do. Ah, Laura meet Laura.'

A shiny tortoise, greenery hanging from its mouth, was contemplating a pansy. Julie was discovered – sunbathing, Harry assured the second tortoise's namesake – a short distance away. Any relics of shyness vanished and soon the three of them were chatting away together.

He hadn't changed, Olivia reflected, sitting with a vodka and tonic (she was on holiday, after all) in the sun.

Not a bit. He still hadn't quite grown up. That night he sat in his chair, a child on a stool on each side of him, and showed them his photograph albums. The stories were word for word as Olivia remembered them from her own childhood: Mac, Mutali, man-eating lions.

'You'll never guess who this is,' he said, turning a page.

Olivia's two daughters peered and shook their heads.

'It's your mother.'

They swivelled to stare at her, then back to their grand-father, to the photograph.

'You're teasing,' Laura decided. He did, this grand-father. It was what made him so delightful.

'Scout's honour.' He twitched his moustache at them and lit his pipe. 'You tell 'em, Moppet,' he said.

'It's me,' Olivia said. 'And it's also time for bed.'

He would be sixty the next year. His hair was silver but as thick as ever and he was amazingly fit. He took them, together with an assortment of dogs, for walks on the Guernsey cliffs and had Olivia panting in his wake.

'Swing those arms and use your lungs, Moppet,' he ordered, exactly as he had on Anglesey, and the four of them, Laura and Julie taking giant strides to try to match his, swung their arms in unison and used their lungs to laugh with.

Eve took no part in any of their expeditions. She treated Olivia with the politeness due to a guest of her husband's and the children she virtually ignored – as, to be honest, they did her as there was such entertainment to be had elsewhere. Harry had them mincing the dogs' food in the kennels, a job that had once been Olivia's (she rather thought it was the same mincer) and complained that he didn't know how he was going to manage after they had left, how, in fact, he had managed before they arrived.

'We can stay here for always,' Julie offered.

'I'd like you to, but I'd get spoiled and lazy if you did.'

The children cried on their last night and Olivia promised they would be able to come back next year, a span as infinite as time itself when you are, respectively, seven and five years old.

'When Mummy was our age did she spend all her time with you?' Laura asked Harry as he sat on her bed ready to deliver their good-night story.

Olivia turned away as a curtain of anguish descended upon her father's face.

'Yes,' he said, his voice with a husk in it. 'When she was your age.'

Perhaps Eve's aloofness was due to her dislike of Olivia, or discomfort in her presence if dislike was too strong a word, but Olivia had hit upon another cause of it. Her single lunch-time vodka and tonic was every day, without exception, taken from a new bottle, and Harry only drank whisky.

'A bottle a day!' Robert said when she told him. 'That's hitting it. Lucky it's cheap there.'

'She never appears drunk. She just sort of drifts. The fact of it is that she's thirty-five and Daddy's nearly sixty.'

'She's bored of him, you mean?'

'Not of him, perhaps, but bored. She must be gazing into gloom. After thirty-five,' said Olivia, who was twenty-six, 'it's pretty much downhill, isn't it?'

'I hope not since I'll be thirty-five next birthday.'

'It would be when you are tied to a man so much older than you. You and I will go downhill together and with dignity.'

'I'll look forward to it,' Robert said.

He was leaving the Navy while he was still young enough to embark upon a second career. He'd had enough of the sea and the separations from his family.

Eve had chosen Guernsey, Olivia was sure, because it separated Harry from his family and – oh, yes – Olivia had seen the cage.

But who was in it now?

2

Eve was.

Harry was content on Guernsey, he was comfortable, he was well taken care of but, increasingly, he existed in the past, a past in which Eve had no part. It was, perhaps, unfortunate for her that Kenya hit the headlines during this period as the Mau Mau rebellion proved Harry's predictions accurate. Questions were put to him as the Guernsey expert and his answers led to reminiscences, interesting when heard the first two or three times but after that . . .

Mutali was dead, peacefully in his sleep, according to the letter from one of his mission-educated sons by his third wife. Harry was touched that the young man had bothered to write and more so by the relayed messages from his several brothers, the ones who remembered Harry, saying not all Kikuya liked what was going on and Bwana Lion-Dog should come back and give the perpetrators a good dose of his excellent swearing.

Father Patrick was dead, not peacefully. He was a victim of the Mau Mau along with three nuns at the mission he had established near Thika. The appalling news was sent by Louis and Lucy Fanshawe who had retired to a house in Karen, as they had once suggested Harry did, but had moved in with Susie, her husband and their children on their farm in the hope of helping defend them should they be attacked. It was the horrifying randomness of it, they wrote, and the way the most loyal and long-serving native servants could be forced to take the oath and conspire against their white masters. What could one do? The solution was to bar servants from the house after dark, but that offended them and made them more likely to take the oath. Yet whom could one trust? The gates of Father Patrick's mission had been unlocked by a convert of ten years' standing, and . . . no, they would not go into details about what had ensued.

'It's to do with land,' Harry said over and over again. 'The government should have been more tactful.'

'But why should the natives have the farms the settlers have sweated blood to make profitable?' asked a former colonel.

'If anyone sweated it was the natives.'

'They were paid. They were employed.'

'I had to deal with land disputes way back in the twenties. Once I –'

And on he went.

One day Eve returned from the hairdresser to find Harry slumped in his chair.

'Harry?' she said when he did not move or greet her. 'Are you all right?'

He turned his face towards her. Tears were running down his cheeks. 'Diana,' he said, groping for the newspaper on the floor beside him. 'Diana. She's dead.'

'Oh, my dear, I am so sorry.'

Eve had never met her but had heard of her, of course, for Harry often spoke of – boasted about, if the truth were told – his royal safari, and he and the Princess corresponded regularly though had not seen each other for several years.

Eve picked up the paper and read the announcement.

'What a horrible way to discover a friend has died,' she murmured. 'Poor you.'

'More than a friend,' he said. 'Much more.'

She had half suspected it but this was the first time he had come even close to an admission.

'No,' he said, already regretting it. 'I mustn't say.' He got to his feet and made for the door. 'I'm going for a walk,' he called over his shoulder.

A Guernsey fog was on the island, typical but something never mentioned in the tourist brochures. Below him, unseen, the sea crashed at the base of the cliffs.

Whom had he loved, truly loved, of the women he had known? With hindsight it was clear. There was Jilly of Dorking, but his memory of her had long since faded. There was Nell. He had needed a wife and love had been urged on by expediency – on both sides, for Nell had needed a husband – and by a wish to forget the other heartbreak. Eve. Yes, he loved her and very dearly, but that had risen from the disappointments of his marriage to Nell. Eve had tempted and he had succumbed. And there was Diana – the one woman he had fallen for spontaneously and without ulterior motive.

And there was Moppet. It was a different love entirely that he had for her and he had betrayed her shamefully; betrayed her far more than he had done Nell. Moppet had forgiven him: how? He did not deserve it.

There was a bellow, movement in the mist. For a moment he thought he was in Africa tracking a wounded buffalo, but no. He was in a field and away from the cliffs, though he did not know how he had got there, and the spaniels were among a herd of cows. They lumbered away, the wet silvering their fawn coats.

In due course Harry was informed that he had been remembered in Diana's will and some time after that a long wooden crate was delivered to the house. It took up most of the sitting room.

'I know it's a clock,' Harry said, preparing to attack the crate with a screwdriver, 'but I didn't realize it was Big Ben.'

A man came from St Peter Port to hang the pendulum and get the thing going.

'A handsome piece,' he said. He read the wording on the brass plaque on the inside of the door. 'Bagshot!' he said. 'What's the significance of the date?'

'It was her – their – wedding.'

A wedding present. A strange thing, perhaps, to leave the man who had been everything to her, but anything more personal, or that belonged in her family, would have been indiscreet. Diana had taken her discretion to the grave.

Harry, too, was discreet but the effect was the opposite to that intended. He was proud of the clock and showed it off to friends, the more so as the shock of Diana's death passed. He showed it to Olivia when she next brought the children over.

'See?' He exhibited the plaque. 'My lips are sealed,' he said. 'I'll never say a word.'

'Oh, absolutely,' Olivia said. He might as well have made a public announcement that he and the Princess had had an affair.

'The clock will be yours. I'll leave it to you in my will.'

Out came the photograph albums that night, the same stories. Laura and Julie listened, never seeming to tire of them.

'My Moppet,' he said, turning the stiff black page and forgetting who he was talking to. 'I treated her badly. Very badly. My poor Moppet.'

'I feel sorry for Eve,' Nick said. 'Life is supposed to begin at forty and she's living with an old duffer whose life is essentially over.'

'She should have thought of that before she set about wrecking our family.'

'It was a long time ago, and Mother certainly doesn't bear a grudge.'

'I bloody well do and and I refuse to give Eve a single jot of sympathy. Anyway, she prefers the sort of consolation that comes out of a bottle.'

'So would you if Robert showed everyone who visited you the clock left to him by his mistress.'

'He doesn't say she was his mistress, and anyway, she was drinking ages before that appeared on the scene ... Nick, people are dining with us tonight. If you haven't brought a tie with you Robert can lend you one.'

'I do believe,' he said, grinning, 'that's a hint.'

His careless good looks and the charm he had inherited from his father were attractive to women and he had quantities of female friends. He had never fallen in love, though, and had decided he was not the marrying kind. The art gallery, of which he was now a partner, was doing well, for he had an eye for talent and had launched some successful careers. His artists were loyal to him and most returned to him for their new exhibitions. He was probably earning healthy money but this was not reflected in his appearance, which was Bohemian and in ten years would be hippy. Olivia loved him very much and her children rated him only slightly below their Guernsey grandfather on the entertainment scale, but that was probably because he lacked the scarcity value. They rated their grandmother in London fairly highly since she took them to circuses and pantomimes, and Robert's parents, who lived quite close, were ever ready to top up piggy banks when things got tough. Laura and Julie were also honorary grandchildren to Robert's uncle and aunt, the people who had in effect raised him, and were substitutes for the children their son Douglas never had. Olivia's Aunt Celia remembered their birthdays. Laura and Julie were not spoiled, but they were rich in loving relatives and Olivia was pleased that she was able to give her daughters the kind of upbringing she had not had.

Cross fingers, touch wood. But she did not think Robert was seeing another woman and a lighted fuse was attached to her family's lives. Think? No, knew.

'Yes,' she said now to her brother, 'it is a hint.'

'I've brought a tie. Who is dining, as you so poshly put it?'

'People we were in Malta with.'

Nick pulled a face. 'Navy speak, then. Can't I eat with the kids?'

'No, you cannot.'

'Where are they?'

'At a birthday party. I'll have to fetch them soon. Laura said it's a babies' party and is nagging for an evening one for her thirteenth. Isn't it terrifying how quickly time passes?'

'I'll fetch them if you tell me where they are.'

'Nick, will you? They'd adore that.'

It was the only decent thing that had happened all day, Laura informed her mother. They'd been given balloons. Balloons! And then to be condemned to an evening of solitude when Uncle Nick was here.

'Sheer torture, isn't it, darling? Sausages and baked beans on toast in front of the television in the study.'

Nick compensated them by playing Monopoly with them for the whole of the rainy Sunday afternoon. He was very like Harry in many ways, which could have been why they had fearsome rows after a bit too much to drink. Nick went to Guernsey principally to see Eve. He had never been close to his father.

It was Nick who was rung at his gallery on a sunny May morning in 1962 by a hysterical Daisy Davidson, Nick who jumped into a taxi and ordered it to Hampstead, who confirmed what Daisy had feared but could not put into words. Nell would not wake up, she said. Would not because she had died in her sleep. Nick, shocked, distraught, still had enough presence of mind to consider his sister and while a neighbour calmed Daisy he rang Robert at work so he could go home and break the news to Olivia.

'Should I attend the funeral?' Harry asked.

'Why, for heaven's sake?' countered Eve.

'To support the children. And I was married to her.'

'It's your decision,' Eve said indifferently. She had not been to her parents' funerals when they had died within six months of each other.

Harry decided against, and fussed and fretted and tied himself in knots of guilt about whether he was right or wrong.

Something positive, however, emerged from her mother's funeral for Olivia. Nell's sister Celia and her second husband were there, naturally, and so were Sir Edward and Claire Firling. The former lived on Anglesey and the latter had a holiday house there. They begged Olivia to visit them and she made up her mind to lay the ghosts and return to the place which had such mixed memories. They went in the summer and the past was exorcised from an unexpected direction. Olivia mourned her mother, and had become close to her over the years since she had been a mother herself, and this holiday was a gentle nudge from her aunt of the period in her life when Celia and not Nell had been the closer of her female relatives. It was comforting.

They had a marvellous time driving around the island, prawning at low tide among the rocks in the bay at Rhosneigr – a skill Olivia had long since passed on to her daughters – going for picnics, having lunch or tea with the Firlings. Laura fell in love with the Firlings' twenty-year-old son and also with a Welsh boy she met fishing for dabs. For one she back-combed her hair and painted her face because, she said, he was sophisticated; for the other she went loose-haired and bare-faced for he was sure to prefer the natural look.

'I prefer the natural look,' Robert said hopefully.

'Fathers would.'

Both her loves regarded her as what she was: a school-girl. But it was another reason why Olivia saw this first of many return trips to Anglesey as special. It would be one of the last family holidays they would have, certainly the last when Laura would be more of a child than a young woman.

Nell left a tidy sum of money to be divided equally between her son and daughter. Robert and Olivia had some work done on their house and modern central heating installed.

'Do you recall me saying after thirty-five was downhill?' Olivia asked. It was her thirty-sixth birthday.

'Vaguely.'

'Rubbish, wasn't it?'

3

Harry was out shooting on his own at Petit Bôt that December among recent rain. A dog put up a woodcock, he turned, raised his gun, one foot slipped and he fell. The agony was exquisite.

'Idiot,' he grunted. 'Broken your damned leg. Now what are you going to do? Help!' he shouted, but knew there was no one there to hear. He unloaded his gun and heaved himself to one leg, using the gun as a crutch. It would make a horrible mess of the barrel, he thought, and fainted.

Not been under fire before? Don't be afraid, man. No point. Steady, sergeant, I'm coming down. It's all yours. First German bullet smack through the sergeant's head, second grazes Harry's ribs, or more than grazes. How extraordinary. His signet ring shot from his finger. Sergeant dead, soldier blubbing.

Honourable Sir Mutali, are you here bathing my brow and tending to my wounds? You got me to the field hospital, found my ring. Saved me from a lion.

Didn't save Father Patrick from the Mau Mau, though. Who saved Susie? Of course you had to shoot the buggers, Louis. Them or you, Lucy, Susie and the children. Glad you're alive.

Diana, my princess, is dead. Princess of twenty-four days.

Africa was cold and wet today, the sounds wrong. 'No, Mac, no,' he said, pushing aside a muzzle with a tongue in it.

Not Mac, not Africa. A dripping Channel Islands sky.

'All right,' he muttered. 'We won't try to walk but we're damn well getting home.'

He began to drag himself along the path. 'This is how slugs travel,' he told the dogs. 'What's good enough for them is good enough for me. If you were in a book or on television you'd fetch help. Help,' he repeated.

They gazed at him anxiously, offered another lick.

Sorry, Nell, sorry Nick. So sorry, my little Moppet.

His leg mended in time and the bronchitis developed from a chill cleared, but he had also suffered a stroke and from acting and being as fit as a man fifteen years younger than he was he became one that many years older. His grip on the present vanished entirely. He called Eve Nell. When Nick next visited he called him Louis and had a perfectly lucid discussion with him about growing coffee.

'Easy enough, eh?' he concluded. 'Could've learned, couldn't I?'

Nick warned Olivia and she booked herself and the girls into a hotel and arranged to hire a car at Guernsey airport; she did not want to disrupt Eve and, finally, agreed that her father should not be disturbed.

The changes in him were beyond what mere warnings could encompass. He looked much the same as he sat in a chair in the garden and stood up, for the stroke had not removed his old-world manners, when the mass yapping of the Pekes informed him visitors were present. He did not recognize them, though said formally he was pleased to meet them and it was nice of them to come.

'Nell will make us tea,' he said. 'The servants have disappeared. I keep telling her she can trust the natives but she won't listen.'

It was as devastating when his brain hooked on to who they were. 'My dear little Moppet, I am so very sorry,' he said. 'I shouldn't have done it. Forgive me, please.'

'Daddy, it doesn't matter any more,' she said, willing the tears away for the girls' sake.

Laura and Julie, now seventeen and fifteen, were surprisingly at ease with their grandfather in this state and seemed to know what best to do. They found their tortoises and brought them to him.

'Laura and Julie!' he said, smiling.

'Shall we mince apples for them?'

'Let's do that.'

Olivia went into the kitchen where Eve was adding half an inch of tonic to four inches of vodka.

'Tea?' she said, her voice remarkably clear. 'Help yourself.'

Olivia put on the kettle. 'Daddy's leg has healed well,' she said. 'He hardly limps.'

Eve went to the window and peered out. 'He's not there,' she said snarply. 'Where is he?'

'With the children. Don't worry, I won't let them tire him.'

'He's best when he's asleep.'

Not knowing how to respond to this, Olivia opened the fridge to get milk. It was crammed with tins. All those Olivia could see were either stew or peas. Oh, Christ! she thought, then: be positive. At least he won't starve. But if Eve believed tins belonged in a fridge what other madnesses might she commit?

Her stepmother was staring at her when she turned to put the milk on the table. 'I've always loved him,' she said, 'and I always will. You refused to recognize that, didn't you? Where would he be if not for me? Nell's dead. He'd be in a home, I expect. Would you have him to live with you?'

'Yes.'

Eve took a gulp of her drink. 'I've been happy with him,' she went on, 'but without you it would have been perfect. If only you had told him that you didn't mind and meant it.'

'I did mind. I don't now but I did then.'

'Then was the important one. Now is too late. Why couldn't you have been more like Nick?'

Olivia could have said that Nick didn't think she had been happy, and had felt sorry for her for years, but what was the point? If Olivia wanted revenge she had it: Eve being called by the name of Harry's first wife, locked in the same prison as him but in a different cell. It didn't taste sweet.

Julie chose this moment to bounce in. 'Granddad wants his albums,' she said. 'Eve, where are they?'

'By his chair. Where else?'

However awful it was for everyone else, Harry was happy. The girls were wonderful with him and, as usual, sat beside him as he went through his albums, his damaged brain spooling out Mac, Mutali, man-eating lions, word perfect.

There was a time when all the family wished with a united heart that they, too, were trapped in the untrammelled past.

A Guernsey policeman rode his bike along the road, leaned it against the wall; took out a notebook to check the address, went through the gate and rang the doorbell. Harry opened the door, Pekes fluffing, barking, round his ankles.

'Mr Wittering?' the policeman asked.

'Yes. Would you care for a cup of tea? The servants have run away but I can manage.'

'Are you the father of' – he checked his notebook again – 'Nicholas Harold Wittering?'

'Nick?' Some things he was sure of. 'Yes.'

379

'May I come in, sir? I'm afraid I have some bad news. There's been an accident. We'll need that cup of tea. I'll make it, shall I, sir? Since the servants have run away.'

Eve was out shopping and arrived home to find Harry and the policeman in the kitchen. Harry looked up at her.

'This man says Nick is dead. Deal with it, will you?' He shuffled out.

A hit-and-run driver, the policeman explained. She went to the drinks cupboard. He hated this part of the job. Who wouldn't? Someone had to do it, though. Clink of bottle and glass. Fizz. She couldn't be the deceased's mother. Wasn't old enough, for he had been thirty-seven. A tragedy.

Mr Wittering returned to the kitchen, a framed photograph in his hand. 'This was Nick,' he said. 'Poor Nick. What a dreadful thing to happen.'

The policeman glanced at the photograph. Handsome bloke. It obviously hadn't sunk in yet, the news. It was often the way, but it wasn't his business to hang around until it did. 'Is there a neighbour, a friend I can phone?' he asked.

'We'll be all right,' the woman said, half her drink already gone. 'Thank you for telling us.'

4

'He slotted it immediately into his distant past,' Laura said. 'Julie and I went over a few months later and I promise you it was as though Nick had died forty years earlier.'

'The best thing, I expect.'

'Yes. Don't ask about Nick any more. It was horrible. Horrible. After all this time I find it distressing. His money enabled your father and me to begin married life in some comfort and security, but I would a thousand times rather have had Uncle Nick and for you and Jonathan to have known him.'

'Only . . . did they –?'

'Find who did it? No. Whoever it is could be behind the wheel of a car at this moment. I hope he or she has nightmares. Emma, darling, about this guest list for the wedding. I wish you'd concentrate.'

'In a minute. Mum, did you feel sorry for Eve?'

'Good heavens, no! How could I for someone who lived with Granddad? He was great fun even when he was completely gaga. He was useless about the present but fine about Africa. We didn't think it boring – at least I didn't, although I was adult then, or thought I was, and already engaged to your father. But, yes, it must have been pretty awful being with him the whole time. I saw him for three or four days a year, and I loved him.'

'Did you like Eve?'

'I didn't the last time I saw her, not one bit. But when we were little she was – well – just there. She wasn't at ease with us, though. She wasn't used to young people, I suppose.'

'It might have been because of who you were.'

'It might. Darling, the list. Please.'

'Stephen's father said she sold a load of paintings and that's why she had so much loot, though living on Guernsey and having no children must have helped. Do you realize they hardly pay any tax there?'

'And booze is cheap. That helped.'

'Helped the cats. I went to see them and it's practically millionaires' row. Anyway, Peter says the sale of the paintings was in the papers.'

'They were the ones Nick had sold to her when he was starting out, and she sold them exactly when they were most valuable. She was shrewd. I'll give her that.'

'Nick left everything to you and Julie and it must have included paintings. Why aren't we incredibly rich?'

Laura gave a wry smile. 'Because we weren't shrewd. We thought them hideous and gave them to his assistants at the gallery. Mummy said we should offer them something to remember him by and we were relieved when they chose them. They used them to set up a Nicholas Wittering bursary for young artists.'

'Why don't I know any of this?'

'You've never asked. If you or Jonathan had been interested in art I dare say it would have surfaced.'

'A hit-and-run death,' Emma said. 'It's one away from an unresolved murder, isn't it?'

'It is an unresolved murder. It's why the wounds never completely heal. Don't ask your grandmother about him, Emma. Skip over that part. Uncle Nick died when he was thirty-seven, and that's that. Talking of your grandmother,' she continued. 'What with the guest list and the dress and all, it went out of my mind. She rang the other day and went on about a friend, a close friend, then chattered about the weather. When she heard you were coming she said you'd explain.'

'The coward!' Emma exclaimed.

'What is she up to?'

Emma laid a hand on her mother's arm. 'Could you cope with a double wedding?' she asked.

Stephen was out working when Emma arrived at the cottage, but he had lit the fire and there was a bunch of snowdrops in a glass on the kitchen table, among them a single red rose. Emma touched the soft petals. He must have bought it, which was against his principles, and neither did he approve of flowers forced into bloom out of season. The message of the rose was crystal clear, a cliché turned on its head. Emma wondered why she deserved to be so happy.

Stephen appeared an hour later, mud indistinguishable from the freckles on his face.

'Want a hug?' he invited.

'After a bath, perhaps.'

'How cruel you are.' He ran water into the kitchen sink and began to scrub his filthy hands. 'Would you like the good news or the good news?'

'Oh, the good. Definitely.'

'The house is ours, subject to the usual.'

'Stephen! Then you've decided to be sensible?'

They had found a house, 'in need of some modernization', which came with ten acres of sloping fields for which Stephen had plans. They would pay for it with the proceeds from the sale of Emma's flat to the Swiss bank which already held the lease, but the total renovation the house required was another matter and had been the source of discussion, argument almost. Emma wanted to use her golden kick in the bum, but Stephen said it was bad enough that Emma's money was buying the place and he'd feel he was a kept man. He wouldn't be properly married, he said, without a sodding great mortgage – if, that is, he could get one, for his work was spasmodic and Emma's earning power for the time being was nonexistent; not to mention the fact that the property was probably unmortgageable anyway.

'Never sensible,' he said. He dried his hands and held them out for inspection. 'Am I allowed to touch you?' A warm, homecoming kiss. 'I have missed you,' he said. 'Did you and your mum do everything you should have? Will I adore the dress?'

'Yes, and I hope so. Thank you for the rose.'

'In summer I'll show you a proper one.'

'If our getting the house is good news, what's the good news?'

'My darling old man, is what. He opened a building society account on the day I was born and has been sticking his spare pennies in it ever since against the day I shackled myself permanently.'

'And you never knew?'

'Not a dickie bird.'

'But – but why didn't he give it to you when you married Rowena?'

The smile nearly reached his left eye. 'He's awfully well acquainted with me is my old man.'

'Is it enough?'

'To assuage my raging masculine pride? Yes. Listen, my Emma, I had an idea for our honeymoon, now I can afford a splash. Shall we go to Kenya? Yes? Your face tells me I'm a genius.'

'You are.'

'I can see snow on the Equator and you can do more of your research.'

'Three birds with one stone,' Emma said. 'It's nice to know you're practical.'

'It will keep us occupied during the day.'

'Is that important?'

'Very, in my experience. How's the rest of your research going?'

'Nearly done. I've just got to kill everyone off.'

'How delightful,' Stephen said.

5

Harry George Albert Wittering slipped from his mortal coil in his seventy-third year. One could not say he departed this life, for he had done that a long time ago.

Eve refused an invitation to dine with the family on the evening after the funeral at a restaurant in St Peter Port (Restaurant! When had she last been in one of those, let alone dined out?) and sat in Harry's chair by the fire. On the table next to her – Harry's pipe rack on it – she laid out the packets of photograph tags she had bought, a bottle of white ink and an old-fashioned dip pen. She picked up the photograph albums – those bloody, lying albums which she had learned to hate – and opened the first one.

Now. Concentrate. She had to be accurate, get the animals' names right. It would not do to call an eland a gnu. Harry would not forgive her for that. A piece of paper was needed, and a pencil to mark the back of the photographs. A reference system. Yes, and a knife to scrape off the original sticky tags. Oh, and her glass was empty.

No other wife but her, no other life. Careful. She wasn't born when Harry had first gone out to Africa, was only twelve or so when Nell had forced him home. The affair with the royal princess was a suitable background. No other wife.

The irrelevant photographs burned with a pretty blue-green flame. She wondered what colour the flames were that had consumed Harry today.

Her glass was empty again.

She was shrewd, all right. Let no one doubt it. Her solicitor certainly did not.

Harry, in spite of what he had once intended, made no will but under Guernsey law a third of his estate went to his children.

'His daughter,' Eve said.

'Straightforward enough.' The solicitor glanced down at a Pekinese dog snuffling at his trousers and prayed the beastly thing wouldn't cock its leg on him.

'But my late husband had little money of his own. I took care of . . . of financial matters. How can the size of his estate be determined?'

The man tore his attention from the dog and took in the room. There was a handsome grandmother clock, and the other furniture and knicknacks were classy. He played with the spoon he was using to stir his coffee and noticed the hallmark. Solid silver and with a crest on it. There'd be more of it then. Who did that lot belong to? This was tricky, but he had to uphold the laws of Guernsey.

'Was there any property?' he suggested.

She had seen him making his appraisal. She was for ever reading how alcohol clouded the mind but it made hers sharper. She sipped her coffee. Just knowing it was in there made her feel more alert even though she could not taste it.

'Yes,' she answered, deciding not to prevaricate. She gave a small, sad smile. 'The house is mine but much of what's in it belonged to my husband. I'm sure my step-daughter would not want to take it from me, though.' She sighed and shrugged. 'What should I do? Get it valued and invite her to select a third's worth?'

'Your stepdaughter, you say, wouldn't want to take it from you?'

'Remove the things I've lived with for over twenty years? What do you think?' Prevaricate when the time was right.

'It would be awkward,' the solicitor said.

'It would be cruel.'

'Yes. She could sign a waiver, you know.'

'Could she?' Eve said eagerly, who knew very well.

'Provided there was no pressure on her to do so, of course.'

'Of course. You write to her to make certain there isn't. Explain the circumstances to her, say how distressing I would find it if she insisted on her rights.'

'I'll explain Guernsey law to her, Mrs Wittering, and ask if she would be prepared to sign the waiver.'

'You are extremely kind.'

He finished his coffee and stood, then crouched gingerly to stroke the Peke. 'Nice doggie,' he said at it.

Eve saw him out and took her cup of coffee over to Harry's chair. She could not have a proper drink as Alice was vacuuming upstairs; not everyone liked Eve's friend and hiding it had become a habit. She chased Fou-Fou from the chair – there were only two Pekes left and Harry's spaniels had been given away – and settled into it. The urn containing Harry's ashes was beside it.

'Sorry if you don't approve,' she said aloud. 'But if you'd really cared you would have made a will, wouldn't you?'

She opened the first album at the marker left in it, her reference system, and leafed backwards through the black pages. She was doing well.

Olivia opened the letter from Eve's solicitor, shuddered, and passed it across the breakfast table to Robert.

'Resist,' he said, having read it.

'How can I?'

'Because,' he said patiently, 'it's a form of blackmail. Resist.'

'I can't denude her house. What she said that time is right: she loved Daddy and what would have become of him without her?'

'Olivia, my darling, it's up to you, but she is doing you out of your father's inheritance to you as surely as she did you out of a father.'

To be ruthless and practical or believe in the essential goodness of humankind? When it boiled down to that, Olivia concluded, there was no choice. When the official waiver documents came from Guernsey she signed them.

Eve picked up Fou-Fou and hugged him. 'You don't have to be strong to win,' she told him. 'You only have to believe you are.'

This dog's ancestor Fan Tan had proved that when he'd chased an Alsatian through the market that day, the one when Laura the tortoise had come into their lives. Harry had found Julie shambling down the road, a piece of string trailing from a hole drilled through its shell. Only Harry would have stopped, made the tortoise's acquaintance, found its owner and negotiated to buy it.

Only Harry.

The photograph albums were complete, secured and put away.

She turned on the television. *Coronation Street* had already begun.

She had forgotten to wind the clock.

Her glass was empty again.

The trouble was they wouldn't leave her alone. They seemed to think she'd be interested in Laura's wedding, and later the birth of her first child. And then Julie was at it too, breeding. If Eve wasn't careful they'd be bringing their brats to Guernsey as Olivia had brought hers. She sent them odd trinkets in the hope that would keep them away, but it didn't work with Olivia. She and her husband appeared once a year. Stayed in the best hotel on the island. A special deal connected with the ferry, they claimed, or some such rot.

'Why are you here?' she demanded.

'To see if you are all right,' Robert said. 'Like it or not we feel we have a responsibility.'

Responsibility! Eve was not tricked. It had been stupid of her to allow her name to be published in connection with the sale of the paintings. She had studied the modern art market for years, first so she would have something in common with Nick and then because she had found it interesting. She hadn't realized the sale would be news, however. It wasn't that she wanted or needed the money; making it was a hobby and she should have continued doing it in private.

Robert had said she should make a will, hoping for some of it for his brats, no doubt. Except they were also Harry's grandchildren. She was only in her fifties and not ready to die yet, but consider Nick . . . And, good God!, consider who were her next of kin should she die intestate. May and Claire! One or other of them had rung not long ago. Eve hadn't sent a Christmas card, she had said, and 'they' were worried about her. Worried – ha!

She summoned her solicitor.

'I want to make a will,' she said. 'How do I proceed?'

'You give me your instructions and I translate them into the language we lawyers consider necessary for these things.'

'Is the language necessary?'

'Not entirely, but it ensures – or should ensure – that no other interpretation of your wishes can be made.'

'I see. Are you ready to receive my instructions?'

'Why, yes, Mrs Wittering,' he said, taking out his pen and notebook.

'One more thing. Are stepchildren regarded as children under Guernsey law?'

'No, Mrs Wittering, they are not.' He remembered the letter she had instructed him to write to her stepdaughter. The poor woman had signed her rights away as good as gold. He had been acting for his client and had done nothing improper, but he hoped Mrs Wittering would make reparations now.

He went away half an hour later much relieved. She had even made the stepdaughter and her husband executors.

6

Robert brought Olivia breakfast in bed on her forty-fourth birthday.

'For the most glamorous granny in Sussex,' he said.

'Granny – don't! How could Laura and Julie have done it to me?' She sorted through the cards on her breakfast tray. 'One from Canada. Do I know anyone in Canada?'

'It came the other day. I've been hiding it.'

'But it might not be a birthday card. It could be an invitation to join the *Reader's Digest*. Anything.'

'Open it and find out.'

Olivia did so. 'Well, I'll be jiggered!' she gasped. 'It's from Mo. *Mo!*'

'Who's he?'

'She. She was our maid on Anglesey. She left . . . she left suddenly. Good Lord! I must write back.'

'Have breakfast first,' Robert said, restraining her, for she was half preparing to get out of bed and go to her desk now, 'and open your other cards.'

She did so, but kept returning to the one from Mo, Mo whom she hadn't seen or heard from for thirty years.

7

Eve took the will from her shopping basket. 'Is the language in this correct?' she asked. 'It will ensure there can be no other interpretation of my wishes?'

'Yes, Mrs Wittering, once it is signed and witnessed. Are you satisfied with it? We can always make changes.'

She ignored his questions. 'Is this the only copy?'

'There is a carbon.' She had deigned to visit his office. He wondered why.

'I would like it, please.'

He hesitated. 'I assume you'll lodge the top copy here? It is usual, although of course it is your business.'

'I'll bring it to you when I've had it witnessed. In the meanwhile I'd like the carbon, please.'

He supposed there was a logic in her actions but didn't have a clue what it was. He asked his secretary to bring the carbon of Mrs Wittering's will and bade his wealthy client farewell.

Eve was not to be tricked, but she was brilliant at tricking. She had realized the lawyer could not refuse to hand over the carbon copy of her will but would be less suspicious of her motives when she had the top copy with her. If she had not he would think she had lost it and insist on making a photocopy – the things they could do these days! – and for the same reason she had not rung and asked him to send it. Also, the more he saw of composed, controlled, alcohol-sharpened Eve the more he would be able to testify as to her soundness of mind. Just in case.

She and the dogs shared a tin of stew for supper during *Coronation Street* and afterwards Eve sat at the kitchen table with the foolscap paper she had bought specially and the lawyer's version of her will.

Lawyers were supposed to be confidential, as confidential as priests in their confessionals, but Eve would not trust to that. No one would read this until after she was dead.

She picked up a new biro (she was so well prepared!) and began writing the elaborate sentences that would ensure her wishes were interpreted to the letter. It would take some time, for the friendly alcohol warned her when the pen began to slide. Her hand cramped. She should have bought lined paper. Only a third of the first page completed. Couldn't she abridge any of the repetitive rubbish?

No! The risk was too great. Anyway, it was nice to have a project.

She would be generous, but not in the ways the solicitor had thought. Not quite.

Damn you, Nicholas Harold Wittering. Damn you for dying.

Ten days on Eve handed her will to her solicitor in person, calm, controlled Eve. The long envelope, also bought specially, was sealed with wax.

'I made some changes but it's signed, witnessed and in order,' she said.

'We could have made the changes,' he said. 'They need to be initialled if they were done by hand.'

'They are initialled, believe me. Every one of them.'

'Shouldn't I check?'

'You break that sealing wax and I'll break your neck,' Eve said, smiling to show it was a joke.

Oh, Eve was brilliant. She remembered his secretary's name, that she was about to be married.

'Both my granddaughters are married,' she said. 'Or should I said step-granddaughters? So cumbersome, isn't it? They've both had babies so I'm a step-great-grand-mother. How silly, at my age!'

The girl laughed along with her. The witnesses were a couple she and Harry had known for years. Her will would be done.

They did what she had been dreading for years and brought the lot of them to Guernsey, Laura with Emma aged four and Jonathan two, Julie with Alistair aged two. She was supposed to be charmed by the children lisping 'tortoise' and produce the other Laura and Julie, but one hadn't emerged from hibernation last spring and she had given the other away. She rather thought it was Laura which had died but she really couldn't remember.

'Never mind,' Laura said, and bent to Emma. 'No, darling, no tortoise. Here's a dog instead.'

'He's very old and not used to children. I should be careful if I were you.'

Eve ignored the hurt in Laura's eyes. She hadn't in-vited them to come and disturb her. Then she noticed something on the little finger of Laura's left hand. 'Harry's signet ring!' she exclaimed. 'I've been looking for that.' She had wanted it to use on the seal of the envelope she had given to the lawyer and had been unable to find it. No wonder! 'When did you take it?' she asked.

'You sent it to me, Eve,' Laura said. 'Jules, Mummy, Daddy, I think it's time we left.'

Babies and accompanying equipment were collected amid silence.

'We only wanted to share our family with you,' Robert

said at the front door. 'They are your husband's great-grandchildren, after all.'

'I'm not altering my will.' She wasn't writing that out again.

He was going to say something else, but changed his mind and followed the others to the car.

Eve slammed the door. Good, bloody riddance. She retrieved her drink from its hiding place and made a full inspection of the house. What else had they taken? *When?*

One morning she could not get out of bed. How strange. Nothing worked. Now she thought about it, the weakness had been coming on gradually over some months. It was probably why she hadn't managed to steer the car into the garage the other day. It was surprising the damage you could do even when going slowly.

Alice had a key and would be arriving soon. If it was Wednesday. She couldn't remember. There was a phone by the bed which Eve had had installed when Harry was ill after breaking his leg, and the doctor's number was in the drawer of the bedside table. She was efficient. No one could deny that.

Dear Harry. She would lie here and think of him for a while. There was vodka and orange juice in the bedside cupboard.

8

Robert took the phone call from the hospital in St Peter Port while Olivia was out walking their dog. He called Southampton airport and booked a flight, and then rang Laura. She and Hamish had moved from London to a house the other side of Chichester and would have the dog to stay. It was a spaniel, of course.

'Is Eve dying, Daddy?' Laura asked.

'In no immediate danger, they said, but we must go.'

Not dying but asking for Olivia, whose name she had given as next of kin.

'Good God!' Olivia said.

She hoped for some kind of conciliation, or recognition that it had been neither's fault. Eve had come between a father and daughter, Olivia between a husband and wife. Things might have worked out better if Harry had been more firm, more ready to grab nettles instead of letting them sting where they willed. If he had been like that, however, he would not have been Harry, lovable most of all for his weaknesses. He would, for a start, have divorced Nell for leaving Kenya and deserting him, a thought that made Olivia reel with might-have-beens.

Eve's doctor saw them when they arrived at the hospital. It was her liver; it had been taking a terrific beating for years and it was amazing it had not given up on her before. She had a chance if – only if – she stopped drinking.

'We can treat her medical condition,' the doctor said, 'and give her time to convalesce. After that we'll warn her of the consequences of abusing herself again and let her go home.'

'That seems a bit feeble,' Robert said.

'Nothing else we can do.'

'What about Alcoholics Anonymous?'

'A splendid organization, but the major battle is won when a patient agrees to attend the first meeting.'

'A psychiatrist?' Robert persisted.

'Alcoholism is not considered a mental disorder. Any help must be sought voluntarily.'

'Then your warning,' Robert said, 'had better scare the hell out of her.'

'We will do our best,' the doctor said, and directed a nurse to take Olivia to Eve.

She was dozing but opened her eyes when she sensed a presence by her bed. The hoped-for gesture of conciliation was succinct.

'Who are you?' she said. 'Go away.'

'It's Olivia,' Olivia said, prepared to believe she had not been recognized. 'You were asking for me.'

'The moment I saw him I wanted him,' Eve muttered. 'Bad luck for you, wasn't it? Ha! Have I got surprises in store!' She sat up and reached for Olivia's hand. 'Did you bring me a drink?' she hissed.

'I'm afraid I didn't.'

'Get me one. Please . . . Moppet.'

'I don't think I ought to.' This was terrible. Worse, far worse, than Harry's reversion to the past. Olivia tried again. 'You were asking for me,' she repeated. 'What did you want to say?'

Eve sank back on the pillows. 'I've always hated cats,' she remarked. 'What a joke it's going to be. Leave me alone.'

She closed her eyes. Olivia left her and went to find Robert. 'Let's go home,' she said. 'There's nothing we can do.'

Brilliant Eve. They were trying to separate her permanently from her friend, but even without the alcohol to tune up her brain she had the measure of them. It was as though the bottle was in the next room or outside the window whispering instructions.

Yes, she said to the do-gooders, she understood. She would not drink any more. No, she did not believe she needed to join Alcoholics Anonymous; then, oh very well, she would see someone from there if they thought she should. He was quite a nice man, about her age or a bit older, and the bottle said, cooperate, be sincere, but do not join. They'll never leave us alone if you do.

'I wish you'd agree to attend our meetings,' the man said on his third visit. 'They are so useful. Do try just once.'

'I've lived the life of a recluse for a very long time,' Eve said and let off a merry laugh. 'I expect I'd need a drink to give me the courage to enter a room full of people.'

'Here's my card. Promise you'll phone if you need help?'

'I promise.'

'And may I visit you?'

'I'd be delighted if you did.'

Brilliant Eve, the bottle said.

It deceived her, though, when her convalescence was over and she was allowed to go home. Alice was there to greet her and had been looking after Fou-Fou, the only dog left. Alice fussed herself away and Eve made for the drinks cupboard. Empty. Alice must have cleared it, but on whose orders? Furious, Eve found one of her hidden bottles and poured herself, by her standards, a small one. After a few sips she felt woozy and dizzy, not blissfully adrift as she usually did. It was peculiar. She tipped the contents of the glass into the sink and made a pot of tea. In the convalescent home they had always been given tea at this time of day.

She drank the tea and was utterly bereft, bereaved. The bottle's defection to the enemy's side was a horrible blow, and there was not even *Coronation Street* to watch tonight. Alice had wound the clock and it chimed the half-hour. Half another hour and no friend to help her pass the time.

The doorbell rang and she roused herself to answer it. Her visitor was the man from AA.

'I knew the first evening would be difficult,' he said, 'so I decided to drop by.'

'How kind of you,' she said, perhaps meaning it.

He noted immediately – of course he would – what she was drinking and his approval and appreciation of the hideous liquid when she had made a fresh pot was infinitely depressing.

'You are still a relatively young woman,' the man said, slurping away, 'and, if I may say so, a good-looking one. Never forget that there's a life ahead of you.'

She stroked Fou-Fou, who was lying on her lap, and gazed into a grey, featureless future.

The man touched her arm. 'Please come to one of our meetings, Eve. It will help you, I promise. You'll get to know people of your own – of our – age.'

His smile was tender, sweetly eager. His wife had left him because of the drink, he had told her.

'I want to help you,' he said.

She sort of promised to think about it, and when he had left she leaned against the front door closed behind him and considered.

A replacement for Harry? Never!

He and the doctor at the hospital, the matron at the convalescent home, had said she would die if she drank again. Did she want to live, though?

Come to me, Eve, the bottle said, and this time it welcomed her.

The clock left to Harry by Princess Arthur of Connaught, Harry's one-time mistress, struck the hours.

Eve gazed down at Fou-Fou. He was old and arthritic and was the one thing keeping her from joining Harry. Harry had performed such a service for Mac as Eve would do for Fou-Fou now.

She staggered as she took the dog into the garden, dropped the torch, hit the door jamb. Her shoulder would be bruised, but she wouldn't be with it to feel any pain.

A stone from the rockery, smash, on Fou-Fou's skull before she had a chance to reconsider. Again and again, to be sure. Inside – such idiotic, careful fumblings to lock the door, as though it mattered – and upstairs to bed, bottle and glass safely borne.

The vodka was easy to swallow now. Just as well. There were lots of pills: those Harry had been prescribed which she had never got round to throwing away and quite a few of her own. Harry's might be worn out, but surely the cocktail would be lethal.

Dear Harry.

A thought too late: if it wasn't lethal she would probably be locked up in hospital for what she was doing. Psychiatrists trying to analyse her.

Should she have left a note? Too late for that, too.

Was this the last unconsciousness or merely tiredness? It had been, as they say, a long day.

Oh, no. Don't be sick. So undignified.

What would she tell Harry about the will she had so painstakingly written out?

Nothing. Being Harry he probably wouldn't ask.

Nick was there waiting for her. Dear Nick.

Would Nell be too, though? And, eventually, Olivia? Holding Harry back. Spoiling things.

What a very awkward place heaven was bound to be, Eve thought, as she fell into the maw of the void.

9

The solicitor ran his hand through his hair.

'This is not the will Mrs Wittering instructed me to draft,' he said. 'I'm sorry, Mrs Wheeler.'

'It's hardly your fault.'

'Yes, but I advised her about the law concerning your father's estate, about the waiver. I never dreamed –'

'Don't worry. Please.'

'Is the will legal?' Robert asked.

'Absolutely, I'm afraid. She made it some years ago.'

The coroner had decided that the balance of her mind had been disturbed when she had taken her own life, but no one could say that had been the case when she had written out this will. In fact, the way Eve had killed the dog and then herself was clinical, premeditated; and so was the way she had bamboozled the solicitor about the will. Her suicide, less than twelve hours after leaving the convalescent home, looked bad and no doubt would be the subject of inquiry and press accusation, but she had bamboozled the people there as well.

'What a business!' Olivia said. She gathered her hand-bag and coat. 'You'll tell us what our duties as executors are, no doubt, and I'd be grateful if you'd let me know when and where the sale of her . . . effects will be. I'd like a chance to bid for some things.'

They had mostly belonged to her father and reminded

her of her childhood on Anglesey. They now belonged to a cats' home.

'Yes, Mrs Wheeler, I'll do that for sure.'

He appeared so put out by the injustice he had, albeit unknowingly, helped to create that Olivia smiled reassuringly at him. 'At least the girls have a bit of money,' she said, and added, bracingly, 'and I have my father's clock and the silver. But his photograph albums, the family things worth nothing to anyone else – will I really have to buy those? And – good heavens! – the urn containing his ashes. Is that owned by the cats? We should bury it with Eve's.'

The solicitor coughed. 'I'm not really suggesting it, of course, but I believe Mrs Lapierre still has a key to the house.'

Alice, who had found Eve. In return for nearly thirty years' service Eve had left her two hundred pounds and a ten-year-old television. It had been Harry she had been devoted to, Eve only by association. Willingly she let Olivia and Robert into the house.

'You realize, don't you,' Robert told her, 'that we are intent upon theft?'

'Take what you like,' Alice said. 'I won't say anything.'

The albums, and the urn. Robert pocketed a couple of portraits of Harry's parents set into thick ivory surrounds and Olivia took silver-framed photographs of Nick, for she was not sure if these counted as 'my' family silver and she could not bear the idea of Nick owned and sold by a cats' home. There should have been pictures of her in her WRACs uniform and of hers and Robert's wedding, but they could not find them until they spotted what might have been the frames encompassing pictures of champion Pekineses.

'Robert, no!' Olivia whispered as he began dismantling the pictures. And there behind Fan Tan and Fou-Fou in their heyday were Olivia as a WRAC and she and Robert beneath an arch of naval swords on their wedding day.

Alice shifted ornaments around the table tops and mantelpiece to disguise losses. 'Anything else?' she said.

'I've got as much as my conscience will stand,' Olivia said.

'Your papa liked those china dolls. Dresden, he said they were. He'd want you to have them.'

She went to the garage to get newspapers to wrap the breakables in and returned carrying an old-fashioned suit-case, ancient luggage labels peeling off it. 'Take this,' she said. 'It's got some of his things in already.'

Game books from the 1920s, letters, some mildewed maps. They packed the photographs and albums in it and Alice produced plastic carrier bags for the rest. They stowed their booty in their hired car while Alice relocked the door, then there was a moment of exquisite embarrass-ment as Robert fumbled for his wallet, wondering if he should tip her.

She saw the movement, interpreted it and pre-empted it. 'I don't want anything,' she said. She turned to Olivia. 'I'll see you at the sale. I'll buy a little something there to remind me of him.'

Olivia hugged her. 'I'll buy it for you,' she said. 'Thank you, Alice. If there's any fuss about what we've done today blame us. We'll own up, come quietly.'

'Who's to know what's missing? It's right you should have it. In your shoes I'd have taken more.'

Robert and Olivia had dinner that night in a restaurant in St Peter Port which had become a favourite over the years, but Eve's spectre at the feast was hard to exorcise.

How could she have done it? When sound of mind – or soundish; at any rate enough to ensure that her will could not be contested – to leave to a cats' home what was by any estimate a fortune? To call Harry's family silver and Prince and Princess Arthur of Connaught's clock 'my'?

'It was guilt,' Robert said. 'Guilt for what she'd done to you.'

'A mighty odd kind of guilt.'

'She was denying it, defying it. If she'd left you everything –'

'Not the money, Robert. That was hers to do with as she wished.'

'If she'd left you everything that belonged to your father, and described it like that, she would have been admitting that he was yours and not hers.'

'He was both of ours,' Olivia said miserably. 'I hoped she would realize that eventually . . . Cats, though! And nothing for her sisters, even if she hasn't seen them for years. Nothing for her nephews and nieces who – come to think of it – she hasn't seen at all. Cats!'

'There is nothing to be done about any of it.' Robert picked up his wine glass. 'Let's just agree that when Eve wrote her will she was a very unhappy woman, whether that's right or wrong, and drink to her at peace.'

'To her and Daddy at peace,' Olivia said. 'Yes.'

The spectre of Eve retired to a corner of her mind, tucked its paws tidily under its body and dozed. Harry's soul – foolish, blameful, lovable Harry – slept soundly.

'And to you, Robert,' Olivia said, raising her glass again. 'To you for being – well – you.'

He leaned across the table and gave her a kiss. 'And finally to you, my love, for being a constant delight to me these many years.'

Part VIII

I

Olivia finished reading the last sheet of Emma's script and let it drop to the carpet beside her chair. It was caught in a draught from the fire and alighted several inches away from its fellows.

It was all fiction, of course, Olivia thought as she scooped up the pages and tidied them into·a neat swatch. But even so bits of it jerked her guts.

Would Robert mind about what she was going to do? No, never! They had talked about it and he had begged her to be happy without him, find a new life for herself. It had taken fourteen years for her to do so, fifteen if she counted marriage to Graham rather than moving to Dorset as a new life. She wondered if she would stop being a widow when she married again, or would she be both a widow and a wife? You couldn't stop being one thing because you became another, could you? – Yes! You stopped being a single woman when you got married, for example.

She went into the kitchen to check on supper, returned to the sitting room and bullied the fire into more action. She turned on the television, turned it off again (who watched this rubbish?) and was getting quite agitated by the time Graham knocked on the front door. She bolted into his arms like a lovesick teenager.

'I don't want to stop being Robert's widow,' she said.

'How are you planning to do that?'

'By marrying you.'

'Come on, 'Livia,' he said, shutting the door behind him and gently pushing her into the sitting room, 'we've both got a past and there's no use denying it. What brought this daftness on? Ah!' Seeing and recognizing the little pile of paper for what it was. 'Emma's scribblings.'

'They aren't scribblings,' Olivia said, bristling in defence of her granddaughter.

'Is it your daughters kicking up more fuss then?'

'They haven't kicked. Not much, anyway.'

'Tough on your Laura, isn't it?' he said, with his sideways look at her. 'Her daughter marrying a gardener and her mother getting spliced to a farmer.'

'We've done very well for ourselves. She should be pleased.'

'Let's hope so. Now, I've had a busy day watching the grass grow and I need a beer. What would you like?'

'A whisky, please. Just a small one. I'll get them.'

'No, you sit down and get comfortable. I'm not carping, mind, but you're always wanting to do everything. I wish you'd remember there's someone to share it.'

He ducked his head to avoid the low lintel as he went into the kitchen, leaving Olivia feeling quite weak and feminine.

He reappeared and handed her a glass. 'I do understand it,' he said, sitting on the sofa on the other side of the fire. 'Truly, I do. You'll be the third wife I've taken to Wellbeck Farm and I'm not likely to confuse you all. Robert is a part of you as the other two are a part of me – even that Cheryl who I made a right idiot of myself over.' He scratched his head in amazement at the stupid things men do before continuing, 'I reckon there's plenty of room in us for everyone, don't you?'

'Yes. Graham, I wasn't trying to –'

'I'm not much good at explaining these things, but what I'm saying is ... you keep your wedding picture, yes, and display it in your new home. And these others of your family. They are part of you like I said, and ... and I love the whole you.'

He buried his face in his tankard of beer – the tankard that had been Robert's – and drank deeply.

'Thank you, Graham,' Olivia said. 'I feel much better.'

He put the tankard down and leaned towards her. 'Something I want to know and we've never discussed, not properly.'

'What is that?'

'Why you came here to begin with. Oh, I know what you said, about the house being too big and all, but why move so far from your family?'

Olivia sipped her whisky and thought about it. 'I wanted to be independent,' she said at last. 'Have a life of my own. I hadn't, you see, since Robert died. I always seemed to be doing things for other people ... No, that sounds terrible! Just sometimes it got too much.'

2

It wasn't that she didn't love her daughters and grand-children. Far from it. It was only that . . .

Well, take one incident.

The phone began ringing as she was hefting the results of her monthly visit to the supermarket towards the front door. She hurtled forward, dropped one handful of carrier bags, fiddled with keys, opened the door, barked her shins on a protruding edge in one of the other handful of bags, ran to turn off the burglar alarm and arrived at the phone as it stopped mid-ring. She lifted the receiver and said 'Hello?', but was answered – of course she would be – by the smug purr of a dialling tone.

She slammed the receiver down and, rubbing her sore shin, swore furiously. What was the source of the desire to risk limb (if not life) to answer the phone? Whatever it was it was absurd, and she wouldn't do it again.

She retrieved the bags from the front door and took everything into the kitchen, greeted her spaniel, Rosie, fed her to shut her up, then began that peaceful counter-point to the freneticism of shopping: unpacking the bags and putting things into their right and useful places. As she always did, she marvelled at how she had come away with such a quantity of stuff. It was as though a switch operated in her head as she grabbed a trolley and marched it through the supermarket doors, programming her to believe that she was still feeding a family, or at least a hungry, healthy husband. It was the psychologists – or was it psychiatrists? – those places employed. She had read about it somewhere. They advised how the stores should be laid out and stocked and, Olivia would be prepared to bet, on other things too. Why, for example, did they only provide enormous trolleys or tiny baskets? Why not something in between so it looked as though you had a respectable load even when you didn't? Not that Olivia minded what her trolley looked like, but others might. The size, Olivia considered, beginning to be annoyed about it, was a deliberate intimidation.

Definitely psychologists. Or psychiatrists.

Thank goodness, however, for deep freezes.

She had settled down to a wonderfully self-indulgent lunch of fresh crab and an avocado pear – a whole one, and so deliciously fat and ripe that Olivia's mouth had watered when she had discovered it – and was in happy contemplation of an afternoon of Test cricket from Edgbaston and racing from Goodwood; was thinking, in fact, that there were some consolations for living alone – though after five years she should surely have found more than this really rather pathetic inventory; and was then stricken that she could weigh an avocado pear and crab salad, plus racing, plus cricket – Robert's great love – against his presence. But on the other hand she wasn't: Robert had gone and forgoing every pleasure on earth would not bring him back.

'I only said it was a consolation,' she remarked out loud.

'What?' said a voice from the kitchen door. Rosie barked and Olivia whirled round on her chair. Julie's daughter, Andrea, was there.

Olivia put down her fork. 'Hello, darling. Was I expecting you?'

Andrea shrugged her shoulders.

'I didn't think I was until tea on Sunday, but it's very nice to see you,' Olivia said, getting up.

Andrea permitted a kiss on the cheek. 'Were you talking to yourself?' she asked afterwards.

'Yes. Do you mind?'

'It's the first sign of madness.'

'That's what we used to say as children. Don't they teach you any new clichés these days? Besides, perhaps I am mad. *Is* it Sunday?'

Andrea giggled. 'It's Friday, Gran.'

'So it is. Supermarkets aren't open on Sundays, are they? No, don't answer.'

Olivia, sensing a serious threat to her peaceful afternoon, went outside. Al and Jonathan called to her from the branches of a sycamore tree in the front garden and Julie's nine-year-old Robert – who, to Olivia's consternation, was generally called Bob – was opening the back of his Aunt Laura's car. Out poured Laura's manic spaniel and Julie's brainless but sweetly obliging golden retriever. They rushed to greet Olivia and then, cowed by her fierce 'Get *down*!', went to reacquaint themselves with the rest of the garden. Rosie followed morosely. Laura emerged from the car and added another bag to the small but ominous pile on the drive. She met her mother's eyes and went on the attack.

'I've been trying to phone you all morning,' she said accusingly. 'Where have you been?'

'Out shopping. Laura, what the hell is going on?' Olivia swept her hand around to include the bags, the sycamore and the dogs.

'I'm sorry, Mummy, really, but Hamish has been invited to this business do. Very last-minute and terribly important, and wives are asked too. Honestly,' Laura said, trying to look put-upon and blasé, 'it's such a bore!'

Olivia knew her daughter far too well to be taken in. 'Where?' she asked.

'Where what?'

'Where is this important do?'

Laura mumbled something and added dogs' bedding to the pile. 'You don't mind having the children for a couple of nights, do you?'

Some believed Olivia was deaf, but she was not. Not yet, anyway. 'Did you say "Deauville"?' she inquired. 'So this business do is at the races in France. I see.'

'It's the way business is done, Mummy.'

'By mixing it with pleasure. How very nice for all concerned.'

'If I'd known it was going to come up I wouldn't have volunteered to help Julie and Jim out with the children,' Laura said virtuously.

Julie and her husband had won a cruise on the Norwegian fiords in some kind of competition. Probably, Olivia thought bitterly, one to do with the shortening of their children's names. Andrea was known to everyone but her grandmother as Andy. Al, Andy, Bob – for heaven's sake! The present grievance, however, was uppermost in Olivia's mind.

'You aren't helping out with the children,' she said. 'I am, or so it appears. Laura, this is dreadfully inconvenient. I'm dealing with the teas at the fête for the hospice tomorrow –'

'They'll lend a hand. They'd love to.'

Olivia closed her eyes at the idea of two thirteen-year-old boys loose among a multitude of crockery and old ladies, but then Andrea's hand was in hers and she looked down into such an anxious little face that the only possible thing to do was to give it another kiss to reassure it. Robert – she could not think of him as Bob! – had begun to remove the luggage from the drive, doggedly dragging each piece two-handedly into the house. Small people, even those with loving and stable backgrounds, need to make new nests when removed from their own.

'I'll have to get a baby-sitter tomorrow,' Olivia said, surrendering. 'I'm going to the theatre.'

'Emma can baby-sit.'

'She's too young. I wouldn't feel comfortable.'

'She's fifteen, Mummy. She baby-sits for all our neighbours and makes a fortune.'

'Where,' Olivia asked, for the first time noticing a lack of a full complement of grandchildren, 'is Emma?'

'At a tennis clinic.'

'Why? What's the matter with her?'

'Nothing. She's learning to improve her tennis.'

'So her tennis is at a clinic.'

'It could hardly go without her. Jackie's there and I've arranged with her mother to drop Emma here this evening.' There was an attempt at self-justification in her voice, an unspoken addition saying, 'See? I've been efficient. I've saved you the bother of collecting her.' She began to edge away. 'I must rush. Thanks, Mummy. I'm awfully grateful.'

'When will you be back?'

'Sunday – no, Monday, I think.'

'A whole weekend's worth of business. Poor Hamish. Tell him not to work too hard ... Wait, Laura, we'll have to swap cars. I can't fit five children into mine.'

Al and Jonathan hurled themselves out of the tree and followed her into the house as she went to find the keys.

'Gran, if you have Mum's car can we go home and fetch our bikes?' Jonathan asked. 'There wasn't room for them because of the luggage and the dogs, and we'll be bored stiff without them.'

'It's only for a couple of days, Jonathan.'

'Al's only here for a week, and Aunt Julie brought his all this way so we could go for rides together. Didn't she, Al?'

'Yeah.'

'Al, that's my lunch, if you don't mind.'

'Sorry, I was hungry.'

'Haven't you eaten?'

'Just a sandwich.'

'You had four,' Andrea said.

'I didn't.'

'You did!'

'I didn't.'

'Stop!' Olivia cried. 'If you are hungry I'll give you something, but please don't argue. And, Al, leave my avocado and crab alone. Here —' to Jonathan, handing him the car keys, 'take these to your mother and make sure she gives you hers. Are you hungry, too?'

'Depends what's on offer,' he replied, grinning. 'Can we get the bikes, Gran?'

'Oh, I expect so.' As he disappeared the dogs came in, tongues hanging out, tails wagging, and lapped splashily at Rosie's water bowl while she sat on her bean bag and watched in resignation. Olivia knew how she felt. 'What about them?' she asked. 'Have they been fed?'

'I think we forgot their food.' Robert went to the golden retriever and put his arms around her neck. 'Poor Truckie, she'll starve to death!'

'She's not Truckie, she's Trixie,' Andrea said.

'She's my Truckie.'

'You'll muddle her. He will, won't he, Gran?'

'I suspect she's too old to be muddled. Al, can you check for their food among the luggage? Where did you put it, Robert?'

'In the hall. And I'm not Robert, I'm Bob.'

'I'm sorry, darling, but I can't possibly call you Bob.'

'You call Al Al.'

'You call Trixie Truckie.' The sensation that she was descending to a pre-teen level was almost physical. She shook her head to clear her brain and went to the deep freeze to look over the things she had put into it such a short time ago. The click as she had entered the super-market seemed premonitory, the six-pound chicken, the three pounds of sausages and the quantity of different flavoured ice cream purely logical (though, to be fair, the latter had been intended for her grandchildren's Sunday tea). Even so she would have to find time to go shopping again. Five children and herself for three meals for a minimum of two and a half days meant feeding at least forty. Forty! And what did they want to eat now? She made her first mistake by asking, for she received four answers ranging from sausages and chips to raspberries and cream.

Later that afternoon, four hours after she had anticipated, Olivia settled in front of the television. The racing had finished but the cricket was bubbling nicely, and with Botham at the crease anything was possible. Al and Jonathan were out on their bikes and Robert and Andrea were squabbling, but quietly, over a game of Mastermind. Olivia's eyelids were beginning to close, in spite of Botham, when all three dogs started to bark and an already shattered afternoon was shattered again. Emma, wearing a Martina Navratilova headband and a short tennis dress, came into the sitting room.

'What's happened?' she demanded. 'Where have Mum and Dad gone?'

'To France,' Olivia said, struggling sleep away.

'Why?'

'Business.'

'But where are my clothes and things?'

'Upstairs. Your mother packed a bag for you.'

'How does she know what I need?' Emma said grumpily. She went upstairs and came down again a few seconds later. 'Why aren't I in my usual room? I'm not sleeping with Andy. I refuse.'

'You are in your usual room,' Olivia said wearily.

'My bag isn't.'

'I moved it,' Andrea said. 'I'm not sleeping with Bob. He snores.'

'I do not!' Robert said.

'You snuffle and snort.'

'I don't. I –'

'Can I ring Jackie, Gran?' Emma said. 'I could stay with her.' Her eyes slid away from her grandmother's. 'It will be easier since we're both going to the same party tomorrow night.'

'Your mother didn't mention that.'

'She must have forgotten.'

'Where is this party?'

'In Chichester,' Emma muttered.

'And how are you planning to get there?'

'Oh, bus,' Emma said airily. 'Or I expect Jackie's mother will take us.'

'I rather suspect Jackie's mother doesn't know a thing about it,' Olivia said, getting up and taking Emma into the kitchen away from the jug ears of Andrea and Robert. It would not do to humiliate her in front of them. 'If I ring her will she tell me she does?'

Emma flushed and did not reply.

'You weren't going to try the old one-two, were you? Pretend you were at each other's houses and be at neither? How often have you done it before?'

'Never,' Emma said, her cheeks now scarlet. 'When I heard about Mum I thought . . . I thought –'

'That I'd fall for it. Well, I haven't. Don't look so tragic, darling. You're fifteen, and very young. There's a lifetime of parties ahead of you.'

'It's only a disco, Gran.'

'Only! Where were you intending to spend the night?' Nowhere illicit, Olivia was sure. Emma, still in her tennis clothes and appearing so innocent and vulnerable, simply hadn't considered it. 'Listen, darling,' Olivia went on, 'can I bribe you and Jackie to baby-sit tomorrow night?'

She would ask Mrs Bridges to drop in, and Jackie was a sensible girl.

'How much?' Emma asked, clasping the lifebelt her grandmother had thrown her to save her face.

They negotiated a deal which included Jackie staying the night, which meant a shuffling around of other sleeping arrangements, so Andrea ended up in a room of her own and Robert on a mattress on the floor of Jonathan's and Al's room.

'We don't want the beast with us,' Al said, when he heard about it.

'And we don't need baby-sitting by two poxy girls,' Jonathan added.

Andrea chased a slice of roast chicken around her plate, eventually stabbing it with her knife. 'Al has Jonathan and Emma's having a friend to stay. Bob and me don't have anyone. It's not fair.'

'Life isn't,' Olivia said. 'It's bad luck but it's a fact. And your table matters are appalling, Andrea. When you are in my house you cut up your food and eat it properly. Don't you at home?'

'Dunno.'

'Must we have the beast with us tonight?' Al said. 'I mean, Emma's friend isn't coming until tomorrow.'

'It's all organized now,' Olivia said. 'And there's to be no more discussion.'

'But we weren't here when it was discussed. It's . . . it's undemocratic.'

'Positively dictatorial,' Olivia agreed. 'Please don't feed the dogs, Jonathan. It's bad for discipline.'

'Ours or theirs?'

'Both. And, Emma, it is rude to read the paper at table.' Her daughters were raising a tribe of monsters! Her own upbringing had been over-strict, perhaps, but this pendulum was swinging too far the other way.

'I wanted to see what's on telly,' Emma said, putting the paper down.

'What is there?' Al asked.

'I didn't get a chance to look,' Emma said, giving her grandmother a reproachful glance.

'No one is going to watch any television,' Olivia said, with the vague hope of forestalling quarrels, 'unless you all agree on what you want to watch.'

'But Gran –'

'You can have a democratic discussion about it, after supper and out of my hearing.' She smiled brightly at them. 'That's fair, isn't it?'

'And if we row,' Jonathan said, making sure of the ground rules, 'we don't get to watch anything. Is that it?'

'Absolutely.'

'If we don't watch telly we'll row anyway,' he pointed out. 'There won't be anything else to do.'

'You could have a nice, quiet game of cards.'

Four pairs of eyes informed her what they thought of that idea. The fifth belonged to Robert. He knew he was for bed and out of the calculation but he was after a quid pro quo none the less.

'Andy collected seven eggs today,' he said, 'and I only got four. Can I collect . . .' He saw his sister's face and dropped the stakes. 'Can I collect the most tomorrow?'

'Five children!' Olivia's hostess said as they were driving to the theatre.

'Six tonight. I hope I don't go home to pandemonium.'

'And your tireless work at the fête this afternoon. It's a wonder you're still alive.'

'Everything, but *everything*, has to be negotiated. The idea of questioning my elders didn't occur to me, but this lot all but threaten to take me to the European Court of Human Rights.'

'It must be exhausting.'

'I've worked out a system.'

'Tell us about it,' her host said. 'We might find it useful.'

'Bribery. Expensive, but it's only for a weekend.'

There were other costs, however. The warm darkness of the theatre was irresistible and Olivia slept throughout the entire first act.

She ended up having the children for the whole week, for Laura rang to say she and Hamish had been invited to stay in a château. Olivia couldn't refuse, but she did feel used.

She could have done with being alone on the Wednesday of their visit, when the post brought an envelope with a Canadian stamp. It was not Olivia's birthday and she knew what the news must be even before she read the black-edged card.

Mo was dead. Mo who had fought and fought against the ravages of her disease. Dear Mo: a Canadian but Welsh to the core.

'What's the matter, Gran?' Andrea said as Olivia went to her desk to write condolence letters to Max Johnstone and to Annie.

'Nothing, darling. Nothing.'

She always did what she was asked to do, and not just by her daughters. Coffee mornings, fêtes, meals on wheels, neighbourhood watch, cleaning the church (which she had begun as a temporary stand-in for someone who had broken a wrist and somehow never stopped), bring and buy sales. It was difficult to say no when you were famous for saying yes, and it was hard work. Olivia was always in the engine room since her talents – as she willingly admitted – did not include organizing. Things went wrong when Olivia was in charge, essential supplies did not materialize and her one effort at being a treasurer was best forgotten. What had started as therapy, to keep herself busy after Robert died, had developed into a manyheaded hydra.

Even so she let it carry on for several years until, ironically, she was hoist on the petard of one of the few village do-good activities she was not concerned with.

Or so-called do-good.

It was shortly before Christmas and, although Laura was doing Christmas lunch, Julie and her family would be staying with Olivia. She was checking menus and making a last-minute shopping list when the front door bell rang. She had been without Rosie for a good while now yet still expected barking when strangers attempted entry. She had been resisting it, but perhaps she should get another dog.

There were two children at the door and a car, its engine running, its exhaust sending a plume of carbon monoxide into the air, in the drive. One child – a boy, Olivia reckoned, under its winter swathings – carried a cardboard box covered inexpertly with Christmas wrapping paper, Sellotape liberally used to overcome the difficulties of corners and tears. In the box there appeared to be tins and packets of food and some limp fruit.

'For you,' the other child, a girl, said, nudging the boy.

'For me?' Olivia said. 'Why?' It was the sort of object one might swoon over had it been done by one's grandchildren when they were tiny. As it was it seemed merely shoddy.

'For you.' The boy thrust the box at her so she had to take it. 'From the children of the village for the old people,' he gabbled, obviously having learned it by rote.

'Old people!' Olivia gasped.

'Happy Christmas,' the girl added, turning the boy towards the car.

Olivia stood there holding the box, her mouth open (in speechless gratitude, they probably thought) while the car disappeared up the lane.

She took the box into the kitchen and dumped it on the table. What cheek! What interfering, infernal bloody cheek! Who had decided that she qualified for this ... this ... she poked aside the tired grapes: tins of carrots and peach slices, a packet of chocolate biscuits ... this abomination? And why?

She heard a car in the drive and hurried to look, thinking it must be the people coming back having realized their mistake, but it was Emma's sleek Porsche parking there. She got out as Olivia opened the front door.

Olivia kissed her and the air by her right ear was kissed in reply.

'Hello, Gran. Mum wants the mince pies for this evening, so I said I'd come and get them.'

'That's very kind of you, darling. You can take the puddings as well. Come in and have a cup of coffee.'

'Okay. Thanks.'

She was like her car: beautiful, expensive and soulless. Her clothes were exquisite and her make-up too heavy for the country and daytime. She jumped when the door shut and fidgeted obsessively with the strap of her handbag, folding it into a concertina and letting it out again, while Olivia put the kettle on to boil. At least, Olivia comforted herself, she is here with her family and not off with her much older and over-smooth boyfriend – or so Laura and Hamish had described him. He had been her boyfriend for nearly a year and her parents had only been allowed to meet him once. Olivia longed to take hold of her, shake the twitchiness out and some life back in. No job, no amount of money and certainly no man was worth this. Somewhere inside was a natural twenty-four-year-old girl. Or so Olivia hoped.

'What's this?' Emma's red fingernails lifted a banana from the box.

'A gift from the children of the village. To the old people,' Olivia said, her anger resurfacing. 'Indiscriminate charity is an absurd waste, and anyway how do they know how old I am? What business is it of theirs? It's great-uncle watching you. Whoever said it was quite right.'

Emma gave a brittle laugh. 'Big Brother, Gran, not great-uncle. Honestly!'

'Big Brother, then,' Olivia said, refusing to be intimidated by this painted artefact. 'The principle's the same.'

'What are you going to do about it?'

'Change my name. Move. Go underground.'

Half an hour later the beautiful shell got into the beautiful shell and drove away. Something was going to crack, Olivia thought, and a good job too provided it did no permanent damage.

There was a film of dust on the hall table. Mrs Bridges had been only yesterday but, what with her rheumatics, she couldn't keep up with the housework as she had once done and her husband who, when Robert was alive, had helped in the garden in his spare time now found mowing the lawn once a week in summer something of a strain. Olivia tried to keep the hedges trimmed and the weeds at bay, but it became more of a chore each year. The three of them, if she was to be honest with herself, charity boxes notwithstanding, were moving stealthily towards a line beyond which was . . . well, if not chaos then discomfort and worry.

In the sitting room the clock chimed away another hour that would not come again.

At this rate she would be handing out meals on wheels until she received them. Until she would be grateful for a gift from the children of the village.

There was a way to get off the treadmill without saying no. She could live rather than be lived, lie about her age if she so wished. Decide when she wanted to be considered old.

Move? Why not?

3

'I saw this advertised in *The Sunday Times*,' Olivia said to Graham, 'came to see it and that was that.'

'You decided to move at Christmas? You were in here by February.'

'The first person who viewed my house offered for it. Things can happen quickly if you force them to.'

'Laura and Julie must have been surprised.'

'They were.'

Graham tested the warmth of the bottle of wine and moved it away from the fire. He had never drunk the stuff before he had met Olivia and was getting a real taste for it. 'I'll buy you a spaniel puppy as a wedding present,' he said. 'Hey, would you like that? It's a while since there's been a dog on the farm, and what's a farm without one?'

'They've ruined spaniels, especially cockers. Ruined them! They are all ears and temperament. I can't think what my father would have said.'

'There must be the old-fashioned working kind around. We'll get one of those.'

'Maybe,' Olivia said, and in the comfortable silence that followed she contemplated the idea of her and Graham walking over his fields on summer evenings, an approximation of Busy or Rosie running before them. 'Let's,' she said.

'I'll ask around. I know blokes who are up in these things.'

He knew blokes who were 'up' in most things. He was widely liked and respected. The first impression Olivia had had of him – of a straightforward farmer who liked his pint and a game of skittles – had been misleading. Well, he was straightforward, that first and foremost, but he was also a man of the purest honesty and honour, a man who saw the world with the clearest of eyes and tried to do what was right. He made mistakes, of course, and the episode with Cheryl was an aberration, but in general his solidity was granite-like. Robert would like him, Olivia thought; he would approve.

As they sat down to supper Graham lit candles and turned out the lights. 'It's romantic,' he had said in his firm, steady way the first time he had done it, which made it more romantic than someone giving it a song and dance. Emma's Stephen, for instance: a thousand words per candle. Nice in small doses, but Olivia wouldn't want to live with it.

'Penny for 'em,' Graham said, as Olivia, having picked up the serving spoon, seemed in suspended motion.

She filled his plate and passed it to him. 'I was comparing you and Stephen,' she said.

'We do have something in common, I suppose. Both about to be shackled to women of the same family.'

'I was thinking about the way you talk – or, rather, don't. And about candles,' she added, as though that explained everything.

'I see,' he said, not pursuing it. The day he stopped enjoying her line in conversation (if there was a line) would be the day he died. 'I'm glad you're here,' he went on, 'no one more, but it is a long way from home.'

'That's what everyone kept saying, but Julie's not too far distant. I've always loved the West Country and if you're going to change your life you may as well make a proper job of it.'

'You'll even be changing your name.'

'Yes. I hadn't planned on that. It was an exaggeration.'

'At least our young folk don't give the old ones tins of carrots at Christmas time.'

'Quite right, too. Fresh ones are cheaper and much better for you. And if they did start doling things out I refuse to be old and infirm enough to get them.'

'You don't look more than forty,' he said, and in the candlelight it was true. 'You'll have help in the house,' he added, panic sneaking up on him. 'I've spoken to Elsie and she'll stay on. She's good for a few years yet.'

Olivia put down her knife and reached out her hand. He took it in his huge, rough paw.

'You told me that last week,' she said gently. 'Don't fuss.'

'I worry it won't be what you're used to.'

'Used to!' she echoed, glancing around at the room which was both a sitting room and a dining room. It was cosy but tiny, and Graham's farmhouse was many times the size of the cottage. He seemed to believe she and Robert had occupied a mansion. 'I'm used to being alone,' she said, 'so, no, it won't be that.'

'And lonely?' he asked quickly.

'Sometimes, perhaps, but that's not why I'm marrying you.'

'Why are you? Go on, say it.'

'No.'

He gripped her hand more tightly, relishing her blush. 'Go on,' he urged. 'I did earlier.'

'Because – because I love you, you fool.'

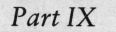

Part IX

Emma felt herself on the brink of two, possibly three deep holes. She had finished the project she had spent the past year doing; now, or when she and Stephen returned from their honeymoon in Kenya, she had to find a job – this time she had to; and she would soon be married. No, marriage to Stephen was not a hole, but she had to have something to occupy her time and, incidentally (though in reality it was far from incidental), pay her way. Stephen said if she wouldn't be a housewife she could be a garden wife. It is hard to resist the enthusiasm of the man you love and already, painlessly, she was learning Latin. She had surprised her father with it on one of his visits to Great Magister.

A garden wife. Perhaps. The long-term scheme was that Stephen would create a garden out of the land surrounding their house and open it to the public, to whom he would also sell plants from the nursery he would establish. In the meantime he would continue to do the lucrative little jobs, such as the restaurant in London, but if something bigger came along he supposed he would have to accept it though it would delay work on his own place. Things were going to be tight, even with the money Stephen's father was providing and Emma's golden kick in the bum. Every new expert who inspected their house discovered a new disaster. Not that Emma and Stephen were complaining. They would have a lot more than many other young marrieds.

The nursery could pay its way sooner rather than later – even the garden could – if Great Magister was a success and Stephen's name became well known. There was to be a grand opening in June and the PR people handling the event and the publicity in general were putting much of the focus on Stephen. Already they had moved him from the specialist magazines to the more general-interest ones. Journalists liked his personality, the way it came off the page. Every luxury hotel and conference centre had swimming pools, tennis courts, Jacuzzis, superb food, beautiful settings and access to motorways, but not an historic garden and a young, personable ('Personable!' Stephen said. 'Glory be!') gardener. Who happened to be a friend of the hottest British actor to make the Hollywood A list since . . . well, since the last one. They could be talking television if Sam –? Which he certainly would, anything for Stephen, and right now Sam could get publicity for a cockroach. None of this would necessarily help Great Magister fill its rooms, but it would do no harm to Stephen Birkenshaw. The men in suits and keffiyehs had extended his contract, realizing that, having 'finished' – Stephen's quotation marks – Great Magister's garden he had no obligation to give the PR company his time.

'I would have said I had a moral obligation,' he had told Emma, 'but they were flashing cheque books before I had the chance.'

They were extracting their pound of flesh, though: Emma and Stephen's honeymoon had been cut from five weeks to three.

'My travelling days are over,' he moaned. 'it will be a fortnight in Marbella next year.'

They were summoned to Chard St Sebastian and ordered,

mysteriously, to bring party clothes. It was two weeks before their wedding, all but a year since Emma had come here taking the first step that would so radically change her life.

'Three things, darlings,' Olivia said. 'One, your wedding present. I won't hand it over physically yet, because you can't have it until you get that *hovel* you've bought habitable. Will you ever, and where will you live until you do? Please don't tell me a mobile home, which is such a ghastly expression; or, if you must, call a spade a caravan.'

'It might be a slight hovel,' Stephen said, 'but consider the land.'

'You can't live on the land. Off it, curiously, but not on it.'

'We can stay on at the cottage,' Emma said. It was a couple of ounces back from the pound.

Olivia led them from the kitchen to the sitting room. Something about it was out of kilter, wrong, but before Emma could pinpoint what this might be Olivia stopped and indicated the clock, the wedding present to Prince and Princess Arthur of Connaught from the inhabitants of Bagshot.

'I want you two to have it,' she said.

'Gran, no!'

'Your wedding present this time round, plus a small cheque.'

Stephen bent to kiss her cheek. 'Thank you very much. We will value it always.'

'Gran, no,' Emma said again. 'You can't.'

'I damn well can,' her grandmother said composedly. 'A kiss from you, too, and a bit of gratitude, please.'

Emma complied, but then realized what was wrong. Things were gone. Gran's desk. The room was denuded, pictures, ornaments not there.

'Ah. Yes,' Olivia said, flushing faintly as Emma questioned her. 'There is that. The second thing.'

'Are you married?' Emma hazarded.

'Tomorrow. You don't need to stay for it. There's no fuss.'

'Idiot!' Emma exclaimed fondly.

'Someone's looking after here while Graham and I are on our . . . while we are away, then John's moving in. He's got a girlfriend at last. Isn't that nice? But, Emma, tell the others that there's no danger of anyone being done out of anything. No more unfair wills. Graham and I have made ones which make clear what belongs to whom. In theory John has most to lose, after all.'

'Gran, stop it.'

'Short-changed the cats, have you?' Stephen observed. 'Pity.'

'You stop it, too,' Emma told him. 'Gran, have you invited Mum and Julie?'

They had met Graham, here in Dorset on Olivia's insistence and not anywhere which could be regarded as their home ground. They were guardedly polite about their future stepfather but still astounded by their mother's plans to change her status after fifteen years of widowhood. Emma's brother and cousins were inclined to riotous comment and Emma, as senior grandchild, had had to give them serious talkings-to.

'No, I haven't,' Olivia said. 'I don't think they'd be comfortable at their mother's wedding. It's not a wedding, really. It's a thing at the register office and a do at the White Horse afterwards.'

'A bit like ours will be,' Stephen said gloomily. 'Functional.'

'Nonsense. Yours will be a ceremony in a church. I'm told a blessing is almost indistinguishable from the real thing. And, also, you have a lifetime of adventure ahead of you.'

'So have you,' Emma said. 'You're going to be a farmer's wife. That's an adventure.'

'It's a departure, certainly. Who would have thought it? Listen, darlings, you don't have to stay for tomorrow –'

'Try and keep us away,' Stephen said. 'We won't feel uncomfortable.'

'It would be lovely if you really won't, but I specially wanted you to be here tonight. It's the third thing. Emma, you won't be annoyed with me, will you?'

Emma eyed her. 'Reserve judgement,' Stephen advised.

'There's a man and his wife staying in one of the weekender's houses,' Olivia began. 'Dreadful places, they are. Empty all winter, they rip the guts out of a village. It's why I'm reluctant to sell here. It will only be bought by more weekenders unless I drop the price so a local young couple could buy it, but then surely – and who could blame them? – they'd be tempted to sell and gain the profit I should have had – or your generation will get, darlings. It's very difficult because my first duty must be to my grandchildren and not to some unknown young things, mustn't it?'

'Don't worry about us,' Stephen said. 'We've got a hovel over our heads.'

'You'll think differently when you have a brood of children to feed and clothe, I promise. No more unfair wills, I said.'

Emma let out an exasperated sigh. 'Please don't go on about your horrid will,' she said. 'It's morbid, and you're getting married tomorrow. What's so significant about the people in the weekender's place?'

'He's a literary agent, which is, I gather, a kind of broker between authors and publishers. He came into the pub one night and we got talking. Well, I said to myself, here's an opportunity. So I told him about your book and took it to him the next day.'

'You did *what*?'

'He didn't mind. I was worried that it was like accosting a doctor on holiday, convinced he'd be fascinated by the movement of one's bowels or whatever, but he was jolly decent. He liked it. Your book, I mean,' she added as Emma stared at her in horror.

'But it was never meant to be a book!'

'Rubbish. If it wasn't, why did you get that machine and type it up and everything? It's a good novel, the man says. He wants to meet you and he and his wife are coming for drinks tonight.'

'Gran,' Emma stuttered. 'How could you? It's not a novel and you know it.'

'It's as fine a piece of fiction as I've read in a long while. The man – his name is Alan something – says he'd be prepared to handle it for you, which sounds pretty sinister to me but I'm sure it's perfectly above board.'

Stephen affected shocked outrage. 'I'm not,' he protested, 'having strange men handling anything belonging to my soon-to-be missus. Not unless,' he amended, 'there's money in it.'

'There could be,' Olivia said. 'Authors get paid for writing books.'

'Then he can handle her as much as he pleases.'

'Not a modern marriage, I see,' Olivia said. 'I hope you're not promising to obey him, Emma.'

Alan Muggeridge looked more like a City whizz kid on a day off than a literary agent – or how Emma thought a literary agent should look like, although until a few hours ago she had never thought about it. His wife Georgie, he said, was his partner. He flipped through what he referred to as Emma's typescript (Good heavens! Was it really that fat?) with an intimacy and authority that made Emma feel peculiar. She fought the urge to grab it from him as he and Georgie were asked what they wanted to drink and filled glasses were brought by Stephen, who then sat in the background on a chair he had carried in from the kitchen. When he was quiet he was extraordinarily quiet. Emma glanced at him. The tawny eyes widened and the right one gave her an encouraging wink.

'Mr Muggeridge –' Emma started.

'Alan, please.'

'Alan. I never intended this, honestly I didn't. I wrote that thing for fun and . . . something else. It's not fair to interrupt your holiday.'

'He didn't mind, I told you,' Olivia said, putting bowls of nuts and cocktail biscuits on the coffee table.

Alan smiled. 'Not this time, anyway.' Again, the authoritative, intimate hand on the pile of paper. 'Emma, we've both read this and are confident we can do something with it. It needs working on, of course. Some re-writing, some twitching around –'

'Not surprising,' his wife said, 'since you didn't intend it to be a novel. Didn't you really?'

'No. No, I didn't.'

'How much fact is there, how much fiction?'

'It's mostly fiction,' Olivia said. 'Sorry, darling, but it's true. The bares bones are fact,' she explained to her guests, 'but the flesh is pure imagination.'

'I made things up to fill the gaps,' Emma admitted.

'It was mostly gaps.'

'It wasn't! There's the clock. It tells a story.'

Alan and Georgie Muggeridge twisted round and stared at it.

'And has it the plaque inside?' Alan asked.

'Yes,' Emma said, wondering whose side she was on.

Georgie had finished her inspection of the clock and was watching her. Her eyes were a bright, paraffin blue. 'Emma,' she said, 'we think we can find a publisher for what you've written, though to be a hundred per cent sure we'd like you to do some reworking, as Alan said. The point is we aren't fly-by-nights and don't want our clients to be either. Besides which, any publisher interested in you would need to know what you'll be doing next. You wrote this novel by accident. Can you write another one?'

'I – I can try, I suppose,' Emma said. This was the gaping hole: this. No longer having the company of the world in her head, no longer being under the burdensome, demanding but ultimately satisfying whip of creation. 'I will try,' she added more definitely.

An hour later Alan and Georgie Muggeridge left, reeling slightly from Stephen's generosity with Olivia's booze and from something else. They could have spent this week's holiday anywhere in Europe, for authors, friends, publishers, other agents had offered houses in the Dordogne, Provence, Lombardy, Tuscany, you name it. Somehow they had decided to accept the one in tiny Chard St Sebastian and it seemed it had produced a potential jackpot. Georgie had groaned and sworn at Alan for allowing himself to be got at in the pub and then presented with a typescript – exactly what they were on holiday from – but Emma Langton's novel was better than good.

Not Emma Langton; Emma Birkenshaw, they decided. Newly married, she'd probably want to use her married name, and if she didn't they'd have to make her see sense. Because it only turns out, doesn't it, that her fiancé is the gardener who had revived Great Magister. Had he thought of writing gardening books? they had asked. No, actually, he hadn't, but there was talk of television.

He knew Sam Sedlescombe! Sam Sedlescombe was to be his best man!

'We'd better ask them to lunch,' Georgie said.

'Before their wedding?'

'After it would mean in five or six weeks' time, and then Stephen will be in the hands of Great Magister's PR. Who knows what exposure he'll have, what contacts he'll make? It would be worth pointing out that the PR want what's best for Great Magister while we would put his interests first. He and Emma need to be orchestrated as a pair. Can't you see the young couple on the chat shows, each with a book to promote?'

'One and one making three.'

'Exactly.'

And the real jackpot, the biggie: could they get in on some of Sam Sedlescombe's action?

'They are sharks, darlings,' Olivia said. 'But very nice and I should think efficient ones. Are you sure about eating out? I could rustle up an omelette or something.'

'We'd like to take you out,' Stephen said. 'It is your hen night, after all.'

'Heavens, so it is. I'd almost forgotten. Wouldn't you, then, prefer to join the men at the Horse and leave Emma and me to let our hair down at the other place?'

He seemed downcast. 'If you insist,' he said. 'Do you?'

'No.' She smiled at him. Grandmothers weren't supposed to have favourites, but she and Emma had become the best of friends over the past year and she couldn't have dreamed up a better husband for her. And as for her own marriage tomorrow . . . well! If she wasn't so happy she would have felt ridiculous. Being in love and anticipating a honeymoon in France at her age!

Stephen put his arm around his fiancée and kissed her cheek. 'I hope you'll look as good as your gran does now on the eve of our wedding.'

'Flattery and flummery,' Olivia said. 'I won't listen to it. Darlings, I realize it's absurd, but do you mind if we drive to the Geranium? It's only that –'

'I understand,' Stephen said. He rested a freckled cheek on top of Emma's head and grinned at Olivia. 'We don't want to march back and find Graham being debagged – or worse – in the street and have no means of escape, do we?'

'For heaven's sake,' Olivia scolded, though he was near-ish the truth. Graham's friends would certainly be giving him a party and it wouldn't be fair to march into any part of it.

'And consider,' Stephen added, 'the better view we'd get with a car's headlights.'

'Oh, shut up,' said Emma and her grandmother together.

There were no scenes of debagging or debauchery on the narrow high street of Chard St Sebastian, but sounds of revelry were coming from the White Horse. Lying on the path before Olivia's front door was a bunch of narcissi, a note in an envelope attached.

'Silly man,' Olivia said when they were inside and she had read the note. She poured water into a glass jug. 'How very silly when he knows I won't be here to appreciate them.'

But she took the jug and its contents to bed with her.

'Promise you'll be like her when you are her age,' Stephen said. 'And when you think of me to look as she did just then.'

'I'll try.'

Stephen made up the fire and Emma sat on the hearth-rug, leaning against his knees when he settled himself into Olivia's usual armchair. Emma probably wouldn't be in this room again. The next time she visited Chard St Sebastian Gran would be Mrs Wellbeck and Emma Mrs Birkenshaw.

'Are you with me,' Stephen said, 'or has the fire hypnotized you?'

'With you. Shall we see what's on television?'

'In a minute. We have to be tired before we go to bed tonight, don't we? Those beds don't allow for anything but sleep.'

'Do your next favourite thing, then, and have a brandy.'

'I suppose it might help. Don't move. I'll get it.'

As he brought the two glasses over the clock chimed them a sweet half-hour.

'And hello to you, too,' Stephen said to it. 'Don't worry about the talk of hovels. We'll make the place fit for you to live in.' He handed Emma a glass and reseated himself. 'We'll have to for when people come and interview the famous novelist.'

'Or the famous gardener.' Emma swirled the liquid in the glass, enjoying the glow caused by the reflected flames. 'But it's all rather unlikely, isn't it?'

'Maybe, but who cares? The secret is to believe everything is possible and to help it happen as best one can. As it is, I already feel I've achieved the impossible.'

'How have you done that?'

'By meeting you.'

'When believing you could be a motorcycle messenger.'

'Precisely,' he said. 'Then loving you almost from that moment and, now, knowing with absolute certainty that I'll love you for the rest of my life.'

She put her glass down and turned to face him, suddenly scared. 'How can anyone be sure love lasts?'

'I know how I felt about Rowena and how I feel about you. Chalk and cheese.' Gently he kissed her brow. 'And you thought you had loved before, didn't you?'

She had to think what he meant . . . *Brian?*

Chalk and cheese, indeed!

The do at the White Horse after Olivia and Graham's wedding was a noisy, uninhibited affair, with songs, scrumpy and a speech by one of Graham's friends which included various innuendoes about skittles and darts. It seemed hilarious at the time but very probably was not. Emma enjoyed herself, though was certain of one thing: her mother and aunt would not have been comfortable.

The bridal couple left in a taxi for a hotel, to where

Graham's car had been delivered ready for the cross-Channel journey the next day, and when it was out of sight everyone trooped back inside the Horse reckoning that if you're going to get drunk you may as well do it properly. Everyone except John, who stood rooted to the pavement outside, his half-empty glass of scrumpy clutched in one hand.

Emma and John's girlfriend, Jeannie, fearful he might lurch into the street, took an arm each and tried to move him. He shrugged them off.

'I got an announcement to make,' he said. 'It's come to me like a blinding flash of light.'

'Make it inside, then,' Jeannie begged.

'No. Here and now I will. My old Uncle Gra'am is in love and I can prove it. There!' He smiled widely and took an unsuccessful aim at his drink.

'How can you prove it?' Emma said, to humour him.

''Tis obvious! He's just gone off' – scrumpy splashed as he indicated the direction – 'and he didn't tell me how to run the darned farm. 'Tis proof positive that love has addled his brains. Why –'

As they manoeuvred him in he issued a meandering recital of previous times Graham had been absent and the fuss he had made about leaving John in charge. 'Proof positive,' he concluded, and took Jeannie off to spread the news.

The noise level was now stupendous and roars emerged from the skittle alley where a game had begun. Emma was about to go in search of Stephen when he appeared beside her. He had, sensibly, decided not to compete with the Dorset men in consumption of their local brew and had stuck to beer.

'I'm one of the most sober people here,' he said, awe in his voice. 'It seems very strange.'

'Shall we go home?'

'Home. How lovely that sounds. Home with you.' He

444

took her hand as they crossed the road. Their car, a second-hand Volvo estate more practical than a Porsche for transporting plants, was in the driveway of Olivia's cottage.

'Listen,' Stephen said.

Six chimes erupted from inside the cottage into the cool spring air.

2

There was nothing functional, as it turned out, about Emma and Stephen's register office wedding. Somehow the press had got wind of Sam and Rowena's presence and had dug up the – as they saw it – juicy titbit that Rowena had once been married to Stephen. Thus the citizens of Chichester, about the Saturday shopping, got wind of it too. When Emma, her brother and parents arrived North Street was thronged with people, Sam's name buzzing among them. Police reinforcements were arriving and three members of the jazz band Sam had organized to play at the reception were getting the crowd's feet tapping.

The Langtons' way was barred by a policeman.

'This is the bride,' Hamish said, which must have been obvious by her dress: white lace over satin, three-quarter length and almost twenties in style, a white lace cap on her shining hair. It was only an hour and a half between now and the church ceremony.

The policeman summoned a colleague to help him clear a passage. 'You should have warned us,' he said. 'We would have been prepared. Got crush barriers up. We are,' he added reproachfully 'used to actors, what with the theatre. Notification is all we need.'

'It didn't occur to me,' Hamish said. 'He's only the best man, or the equivalent of it at a blessing.'

'Going on to a church, are you? Better tell us where, and the reception. Let's get you inside first, though.'

Soon they were in the register office. Stephen hurried forward, his eyes on Emma, his face suddenly pale and the freckles more noticeable than ever. He kissed her cheek and gripped her hands, for once bereft of words.

'You look . . . you look breathtaking,' he managed at last.

His parents were there, and Olivia and Graham and, of course, the cause of the chaos outside. Sam and Rowena kissed Emma too and said they were sorry about the fuss.

'They keep on apologizing,' Stephen said, his tongue back on form, 'but I think it's great. We're celebrities, even if it is borrowed.' He gave Emma the bouquet he had prepared. He did not want her carrying, he had said, flowers with wire stuck in their arses and had been nurturing these in the conservatory of Great Magister. 'It's not professional, but at least the buggers aren't being tortured,' he said.

'They are lovely. Thank you.'

'Are you nervous?'

'No. Excited, and – and –'

'That's how I feel. Full up.'

'Yes, full up.'

Another policeman arrived and Stephen joined Hamish, Laura and Sam in a discussion about crowd control. Jonathan, near to bursting but trying to be adult and cool, chatted to Rowena and to Peter and Judith Birkenshaw. Could he get Rowena and Sam's autograph? The lads in Aberdeen would never otherwise believe the famous pair had been at his sister's wedding, though it would, perhaps, be in the papers. And he had thought the whole thing certain to be a bore!

This left Emma with her grandmother and stepgrandfather. It would be an exaggeration to say she hardly recognized them, but they were undoubtedly different. A few weeks ago the prospect of a mass meeting with Olivia's relations would, Emma was sure, have reduced Graham to silence, but here he was, seeming more comfortable than Stephen in his hired tail coat and striped trousers, assured, taking the lead, kissing Emma and saying she was as pretty as a spring day.

'How was France?' Emma asked.

'Fine,' he said, a glance at Olivia. ''Cept they kept talking in a foreign language.'

'He learned some of it,' Olivia said. 'He was very good.'

Graham studied the ceiling, something that could have been the beginnings of a smile twitching the corners of his mouth. 'They have some interesting cows there,' he remarked.

'Gran,' Emma said, finally working out what was different, 'have you been dyeing your hair?'

'No, my hairdresser has. And it's not dyeing, it's streaking.'

'Ah. What is it like, then, being a farmer's wife?'

Her grandmother moved closer to her husband and put her hand in the crook of his arm. 'When you've been married to a gardener for a while,' she said, 'we'll compare notes.'

Stephen's touch on Emma's shoulder. 'We're being called,' he said. 'It's our turn.'

Twenty or so minutes later they were Mr and Mrs Birkenshaw and walked into a battery of photographers' lenses. The jazz trio, which the police had attempted to move on until cries of 'Shame!' from the crowd stopped them, began a rendition of 'The Wedding March'. Sam and Rowena hung back inside the building, but Stephen told them to come out.

'You're not stealing our thunder,' he said. 'You've created it.'

Shouts to Sam to kiss the bride, to Rowena to cuddle up to her former husband, then Sam went to talk to the press, now corralled, to their indignation, behind crush barriers. They questioned him about his next movie, when he would be returning to Hollywood, but the only thing he would talk about was the reason he was here: his friend, Stephen Birkenshaw.

Definitely not functional, but Emma felt she was really married after the service of blessing in the church during which there were hymns and prayers and things that made a wedding a wedding. And there was a congregation, a communal witness.

There were some photographers outside, but not enough to worry the constabulary – though they unnerved the local man hired by Laura and Hamish. He tried his usual patter and could sense the laughing contempt of the boys from London. A bride and groom was a bride and groom, wasn't it? You couldn't get arty and flash about that.

The congregation. Hamish watched nervously as people streamed into the marquee set up on his precious lawn, though he was comforted by the fact that it was April and the grass had the rest of spring and the summer to recover. Stephen and Emma greeted everyone individually. Elunid, old Rhys and young Rhys had come all the way from Anglesey and had brought Claire Firling. Elunid's Welsh voice bubbled above the English ones as Emma kissed her and thanked her for being here.

'Would we have missed it? Not if it had been on the other side of the world. The old ladies were game for the journey, but it would have been too much for them. Megan agreed to stay and watch over them and I promised to take them cake.' She paused for a split second. 'That's all right, isn't it?'

'Yes,' Emma said, laughing. 'I only hope Gwen approves of it.'

Elunid beamed. 'Oh, she won't, but it's the thought that counts, isn't it? Move along, you,' she scolded her husband and father-in-law. 'Emma wants to greet other guests. Don't keep her talking for ever . . . Good gracious, is that Olivia? She looks no older than when I last saw her, and that was a fair few years past.'

She swept on. Fifteen love to Elunid. Stephen had not managed a word.

'Was that a tornado or a mere hurricane?' he murmured, and turned to embrace the next guest in line: Jackie.

'Here we are, then,' Jackie said, emerging. 'I knew it would come to this after that first evening.'

'So did I,' Stephen said.

Jackie indicated Emma. 'You had her worried.'

'Part of the breaking-in process. She's not worried now. Are you?' he asked his wife.

'No, and I hope I'm not broken in, either.'

'So do I, really. She's going to be an author, have you heard?' he said to Jackie. 'She's got an agent – two agents! – and they took us out for a frightfully posh lunch. We had to concentrate like mad on which knives and forks to use, didn't we, Emma?'

Emma nodded, but she was only half listening. A grouping of people in the marquee had caught her eye: Stephen's parents, Olivia, Elunid, old Rhys, young Rhys and Claire Firling in her wheelchair were chatting and laughing, holding out their glasses as a waiter offered refills of champagne. Those people had memories, histories to exchange and had come together because of Emma's extraordinary meeting with Stephen and, without it, probably would not have encountered each other again.

Something else even more pleasing a few yards away: Emma's brother Jonathan and his cousin Alistair were in what appeared to be animated conversation with their step-grandfather. They were all waving their arms around in what was obviously a significant manner, though from this distance it was impossible to tell whether it was to demonstrate the best way of milking a cow, knocking down skittles, refining oil or doing whatever young naval officers did. Yes, the last. Semaphoring. That had to be it.

Stephen nudged her and she roused herself to receive the gardeners of Great Magister, who arrived together in a shy, embarrassed knot. Hamish, by now well acquainted with them, organized their drinks and took charge of them.

They were the last guests to arrive and Emma and Stephen were isolated for a moment, alone together for the first time on this day.

'We are enmeshed and intertwined,' Stephen said, 'and by more than Church and State.'

He had also noticed, then, the meeting bridging more than fifty years. Old Rhys had once given Olivia an apple on her birthday; Olivia had been bridesmaid at the wedding of Peter Birkenshaw's parents. Peter's aunt, Stephen's great-aunt, Claire Firling: her sister had fallen for and hunted down a married man who was Olivia's father. Old Rhys's sister had been the friend of a lonely child on Anglesey; his brother-in-law had seen Peter Birkenshaw's father killed and had shot down the German pilot responsible.

Stephen turned his wife to face him. 'Luck,' he said, 'and a huge dose of coincidence for good measure.'

'Will you always know what I'm thinking?'

'Always? I hope so. But at this moment I have to admit it's a bit obvious.'

Sam appeared, impossibly handsome in his formal clothes. Everyone was being frightfully British and pretending he and Rowena were nothing out of the ordinary, but they were the focus of furtive attention nonetheless. Their diffident attitude to their fame was no act. They had risen swiftly, they said, and could just as swiftly fall; they would enjoy it while it lasted. Today, though, Sam was taking his best man's duties seriously.

'Stop skiving, you two, and mingle,' he told them.

'Piss off,' Stephen said. 'I want a kiss and cuddle with my wife.'

'Plenty of time for that later.'

'I want one now.'

'Such a spoilt boy,' Sam sighed. 'Try not to be concerned, Emma. He might improve with age.'

'Then I'm longing for him to be seventy,' Emma said.

'That's a compliment, in case you're too dim to work it out,' Stephen said smugly. He put an arm around Emma's waist. 'The man's right, though. Let's mingle.'

The jazz band was playing and people were filling plates from a long table on which a buffet was laid out. Sam, ignoring Emma's protests that she couldn't eat a thing, collected them a plate of food to nibble at.

'You must keep up your strength,' he said.

'True,' Stephen said. 'We have a busy night ahead.'

They would be spending it at a hotel and were flying to Nairobi the following evening. Emma wondered if making love to Stephen would be different now he was her husband and thought, how absurd. How could it be different, and yet how could it be the same? She was different. Her name had changed!

'Do you know what I'm thinking now?' she teased Stephen.

'I've a hell of a good idea. Emma, my love, this is probably the best party I've ever been to, but I can't wait for it to end and for us to be on our own.'

She stared at him. 'Then you did know!'

'Is not ours a marriage of two minds?' he said, the smile climbing up his cheek.

Lovely things to savour, though, until they departed. The band, after a break for sustenance, became livelier, its beat more insistent. People began to dance. To Emma's astonishment and delight Graham led Laura on to the wooden floor where they jigged around and seemed to enjoy it. Emma would have been happier than she already was, except that was not possible.

She found her grandmother trying to persuade Robert and Andrea that Sam and Rowena would not bite them if they asked for autographs.

'Of course they won't,' Emma said, and packed her cousins off. 'Aren't you glad you married Graham before and not after this?' she asked Olivia. 'There couldn't be a better way of introducing him to the family, could there?'

'When he isn't the centre of attention and speculation? Quite.'

'You mean you'd thought of it?'

Olivia raised her eyes skyward. 'Darling, your brains have gone missing. I hope it's not permanent. Here's Rhys about to invite me to dance – or is it my grand-daughter you're after?' she asked him.

'You.' Rhys grinned. 'Remember us sneaking into the house and using the wind-up gramophone when your mam and da were out? State of the art that old thing was then.'

'I remember. And treading on your toes. Emma, Stephen's hovering so we won't be leaving you alone. Don't you think,' she added to Rhys, 'that Emma is the most gorgeous bride ever?'

'She is,' Rhys said. 'They all are on their day.'

Time, at last, after the speeches and the cake to change and leave.

'Will you still call this my bedroom?' Emma asked her mother. When she and Stephen came to stay they would be in the double spare room.

'I don't know,' Laura said. 'I expect so, for a while.' She sniffed and grabbed a tissue from the box on the dressing table.

'Mum!' Emma said.

'Sorry, but I do feel I'm losing – have lost – my daughter.'

'Okay, but consider the son you've gained.'

'Yes.' Laura blew her nose determinedly. 'And, really, I'm very happy.'

'What do you think of Graham now?'

Unreserved enthusiasm in her mother's voice. 'He's a sweetie, and Julie agrees.'

'My cup is overflowing.'

'You're a sweetie, too, to be so concerned.'

She helped Emma out of her wedding garb and into her going-away dress of printed silk. There was a linen jacket which picked up the dominant pink, and Emma wondered if Stephen would compare the colour to a plant. She recalled how she had been wearing autumnal gold the first time they had met. *Nyssa sylvatica.*

Hamish knocked and poked his head around the door. 'The car and driver are here and Stephen's pawing the ground. Shall I take your luggage?'

Laura zipped up the practical, rugged canvas bag. 'All yours,' she said.

He came in and looked at his daughter. 'Mrs Birkenshaw,' he said softly. 'A hug for your old father before you go?'

She gave him one, a private one, and her mother as well. Downstairs there were lots more and Elunid was busy with her camera and tongue, telling her husband not to forget details so there was a record for each of the two old ladies, one blind, one deaf, on Anglesey.

The car moved off, the predictable graffiti on the back windows, predictable tin cans attached.

'Now,' Stephen said, 'do I get a turn?' And a little later: 'It's a rose and I know you won't believe it but its name is "Dearest".'

'I don't think I do believe it.'

454

'Would you prefer "City of Leeds"?'

'No.'

'Dearest it is, then.'

Part X

I

Susie Dalrymple, born Fanshawe, was very large and very loud and, in spite of her claim to be Kenyan, sounded more English than Emma and Stephen. Her language was frozen somewhere in the 1940s and could have come out of an ancient black and white film starring, say, Joyce Grenfell.

She was also very – overwhelmingly – kind.

'How super to see you!' she said. 'Uncle Harry's great-granddaughter. Who would have believed it?'

There was no coincidence about this meeting, however: Susie and Olivia had been exchanging Christmas cards for the past however many years it was and after an initial letter followed by a series of crackling phone calls Susie had told Emma and Stephen they would be met at the airport and everything taken care of.

'Smashing of you to want to spend your honeymoon in Kenya,' Susie went on. 'And frightfully enterprising of you to do it on your own. Most people come on those package things.'

'If it's Wednesday it must be the Masai Mara,' Stephen said.

'Exactly!'

'Stephen is allergic to packages,' Emma said trying, unsuccessfully, to prevent her glass being removed and refilled by Tom, who was Susie's second (or was it third?)

husband. 'Only a small one;' she murmured. 'Please.' The first gin and tonic had made her pleasantly woozy. That or the sudden transportation to this foreign country; this garden in Karen – the suburb of Nairobi that had been built on Karen Blixen's farm and named after her – with the Technicolor flowers and birds, the bright blue swimming pool. Being Mrs Birkenshaw. Her husband lounging in a chair under the awning, an accustomed traveller already at home and only his winter-white skin, slathered like Emma's with sun cream, giving him away. Behind them on a bougainvillaea-swathed verandah servants were laying the table for lunch.

Stephen smiled at his hostess. 'You seem to have fixed us up better than any package could do,' he said. 'We aren't having to do anything on our own. I don't know how we can begin to thank you.'

'We love doing it, don't we, Tom? Chums of chums write and say they are coming out but are whisked off by their tours and we never have a chance to entertain them properly.' Her trio of chins compressed as she took a gulp of liquid from her glass. 'It's jolly disappointing,' she said.

She had two sons by her first husband and one of them was called Harry in honour of her godfather, her parents' friend. Harry Fielding had a farm in the Aberdares and Emma and Stephen would be visiting it during their tour of Kenya, the vehicle, equipment and guides provided or organized by the Dalrymples. After their safari they were having a few days on the coast near Malindi in a house owned by Tom's daughter. Emma had felt embarrassed by the Dalrymples' generosity until Susie's last remark. Old people could be lonely no matter how exotic their surroundings and Emma now had a twitch of guilt because she and Stephen had insisted on staying in the Norfolk Hotel for the two nights they would be in Nairobi. But they were on their honeymoon, after all, and

Emma had wanted to experience the places her great-grandfather had known. Susie and Tom had promised to take them to the Muthaiga Club later on.

'If,' Emma said, taking a deliciously cold glass from Tom, 'we told people about the service you provide you'd never have a moment's peace.' She looked at the map spread out on the table, a red dotted line marking their proposed route, solid ones indicating detours to safari lodges or the houses of friends and relations of the Dalrymples who would be delighted to provide a bed and bath should roughing it in the bush become too uncomfortable, which it was likely to do since the rains would soon begin. 'Such an enormous distance in two weeks,' Emma said. 'How long would it have taken Harry Wittering?'

'A hell of a lot longer,' Tom said. 'He had to move at the pace of his porters. Now there are four-wheel-drive Jap vehicles and the roads are better, of course. You don't need to keep to this route,' he added anxiously. 'You wanted to be independent and Joshua has designed something as rigid as the tours you were trying to avoid.'

Stephen was also studying the map. 'We'll put ourselves in Joshua's hands,' he said. 'When I've travelled before what I wanted to see was always in the same place and not, on the whole, apt to chase you.'

'The animals aren't dangerous if you're sensible, but it's as well to have chaps with you who know the ropes.'

'Joshua certainly knows those,' Susie said.

They would be meeting him in Fort Richard. He was a game warden and a descendant of H. G. A. Wittering's right-hand man, Mutali, and this was no coincidence either. Emma had asked Susie if there was a chance of meeting a living link (apart from Susie herself) with H.G.A. and Susie had arranged it. It was not as preposterous as it might appear, for some of Mutali's sons had been on the killing safaris and it was not surprising that their sons and grandsons should be involved with the modern side of the coin, the preservation of game for the tourist trade.

'He won't have heard of H.G.A.,' Emma said. 'But it's nice to know the link is there.'

Susie turned her vast bulk, encased in a flamboyant cotton print dress, to Emma. 'Olivia said you've written a book about him.'

'Well, sort of.'

'Longing to read it. He was a smashing fellow. Smashing. I loved him.'

'Most people did, it seems.'

'He was that sort. He was better at choosing friends than wives, or so my parents used to say, though I liked Eve. They – my parents – always hoped, in spite of everything, that he'd end up here next door to them.'

'Was this your parents' house?'

'It was.'

'Perhaps Harry's ghost is here.'

'Perhaps it is,' Susie said. 'Or, rather, somewhere within sight of Mount Kenya. He wouldn't recognize much of Nairobi.' She paused and sighed, and Emma wondered if she missed the good old days. Then she let out her cackling laugh and went on: 'Still, you were wrong about one thing, Emma. Joshua has heard of Uncle Harry and you'll find signs of him – material ones, I mean – up in Fort Richard.'

'Will I?' Emma said, excitement growing. 'What?'

'Joshua and the others will show you.'

'Tell me, please.'

'It would spoil it. I shouldn't have mentioned it. Come, now, it's time for lunch.'

'Am I boring you?' Emma asked Stephen. They were on the Delamere Terrace of the Norfolk Hotel and she realized that for the past half hour she had spoken of nothing

462

but what signs of H. G. A. Wittering there could be in Fort Richard. Susie and Tom had refused to divulge details.

'No, you are not,' Stephen said. 'I'm as eager as you to find out. And that's a fine thing to ask a fellow, especially a smashing one, which is what I'm sure I am, on his honeymoon. Emma, my sweet, we had a huge lunch and an enormous tea and last night was spent on a plane. Can we force down a light supper and eat it quickly? I demand,' he complained, 'my marital rights.'

'They will be given with the greatest of pleasure.'

'It's curious how they are referred to in the plural, isn't it?'

'A plural has to be better than a singular in this case, surely.'

'Mrs Birkenshaw! Another remark like that and you'll be taken to bed without any supper at all.' He stroked her left hand. 'It must be the altitude,' he said. 'Your wedding ring is doing strange things to me. How can a ring be erotic? One that size, anyway.'

She turned her hand over and gripped his. 'Have you considered room service? Or the restaurants don't close for a while yet.'

Stephen signed the chit the waiter had left on their table and hustled her to her feet. 'You brazen hussy, you,' he said. 'I am a happy man.'

They began their journey to Fort Richard at a cool seven o'clock in the morning and were there by eleven thirty. In Harry's time the journey would have taken nine hours at least, more yet during the rains, depending on the number of punctures and breakdowns. The pioneers' ox-drawn wagons, an example of which was in the grounds of the Norfolk Hotel, took days.

'Why marvel?' Stephen said. 'It's only progress.'

They had an hour to spare before they were due to

meet Joshua and Emma told Kip, sent with them by the Dalrymples to take care of the Land Cruiser (home from home, Stephen had commented), that they would like to explore Fort Richard. He, a Nairobi man, seemed astonished at the idea but was willing to help. Where would they care to start their tour? he asked.

'In the main street,' Emma said, having some mad idea that they might find the district commissioner's bungalow.

Kip shrugged his shoulders good-naturedly and shouted queries at pedestrians.

'We are in the main street,' he said then, and drove slowly along it and back. There was no building that could possibly have been a colonial bungalow and Emma realized this quest was ludicrous. She was about to tell Stephen, who was sitting between her and Kip, when he said to Kip, 'Try the Catholic church.'

Again Kip asked for directions, then turned down a side street.

'This can't be right,' Emma said. 'It should be on the main street too.'

'Not if the main street has changed,' Stephen said. 'It's nearer the river than it should have been, don't you reckon?'

The narrow road they were on was lined with dusty trees and contained a zigzag, a double dog leg. Emma gazed around eagerly. It seemed to be taking them back in time, or at least away from the showcase modernity of the street they had just left. The buildings became increasingly run-down until buildings was too good a word for the shacks made out of corrugated iron, wood, plastic bags and even bits of cars. Children crowded around the Land Cruiser as it stopped in the traffic and followed when it moved off. Kip inched right into a slightly wider road and not far further on stopped outside some gates set into a whitewashed wall topped with coils of razor wire. Inside the gates was a large courtyard enclosed by buildings, one with a cross on it. An ambulance parked outside another proved it to be a hospital.

'Father Patrick's mission,' Emma said. 'Is it possible?'

Kip waited with the Land Cruiser while Stephen and Emma, accompanied by a gaggle of children, went across the courtyard Harry Wittering had walked on often seventy years before and into the church he would not have set foot in. In here, though how often no one knew, Mutali had heard Mass said by an Irishman speaking in Latin.

Father Patrick's mission. No doubt about it. A sign on the wall near the door read: 'The Church of Our Lady, Fort Richard. A gift from the people of Cork, 1920.'

'H.G.A.'s bungalow has to be near by,' Emma whispered.

'Has to have been,' Stephen corrected. 'Redundant since independence, made of wood and no longer in the best part of town, it's unlikely to have survived.'

They went outside into sunlight. Their retinue of children had retreated to the compound gates and was exchanging taunts with an old man who was flourishing a broom at them.

'Probably arguing about who's going to fleece us,' Stephen said.

'We have so much compared to them.' Emma found the children discomfiting. They were in exuberant spirits, their smiles like half moons across their faces, they were well dressed and certainly far from starving, but they expected largesse from the white tourists who had strayed into their part of Fort Richard. To refuse them a few coins would be petty, yet to give them some would be patronizing. Emma was all for abandoning the search for H.G.A.'s bungalow – which, as Stephen had said, must have long since rotted away – and making for the hotel with its every modern convenience. Where, er – whoops! – the Africans would know their place.

'Which is to pander to the likes of us,' Stephen said when she tried to explain. 'You are an adorable, mixed-up post-colonial and you must learn to be a traveller . . . an explorer! We'll accost the ancient and discover what he has to say.'

Stephen's ability to communicate rose above minor impediments such as language and toothless gums. The old man nodded and mumbled enthusiastically and, still clutching his broom, hobbled towards the gates and the Land Cruiser. Kip, rigid with disapproval, allowed him into the vehicle and relieved his emotions by screaming at the children before driving off.

But he followed the old man's directions and they drew up on a rutted road, the buildings on each side as ramshackle as any apart from the mission and those near the river. The old man climbed out and so did Emma and Stephen. Kip, his expression possibly as supercilious as Mutali's had been when he had first encountered the inhabitants of Fort Richard, remained to guard the car and its contents from the thieves in these parts.

'We'll get nought out of ten when he reports to Susie and Tom,' Stephen said as they followed the old man down an alley. To their right goats grazed on scrubby grass among which some chickens were also attempting to scratch a living. Another swarm of children appeared and adults stopped what they were doing and stared. No one spoke. Emma grasped Stephen's arm.

'It's all right,' he said. 'When there are no gardeners about try the other international language. A smile and a wave.'

He did both and the effect was instantaneous. Emma relaxed, but was not yet sure if she liked being an explorer.

The old man came to a halt and gestured with his broom at a row of stone buildings, evidently used as storehouses. He said something, said it again louder and then tried it slower.

'Stables!' Emma said. 'That's what you mean, don't you?'

'Yes,' the old man said, relieved the idiots had understood at last. 'DC stable. Horse. Motor car.'

The stone stables the old district commissioners had needed to protect their horses from predators, adapted when motorized transport became the norm. Some DCs kept hunting dogs. Mac had lived here when lions and leopards had stalked the neighbourhood.

Emma turned and wrenched her imagination into gear. Where the goats and chickens were had been Harry's garden. The space had retained its integrity although the bungalow had gone or been cannibalized to make the shacks now occupying the area. This piece of ground Emma's great-grandmother would have called a lawn and on it she had paced and wished herself elsewhere. Emma's grandmother had played upon it with her father or her Indian *ayah*. From here Harry Wittering had ruled his district and kept the King's peace; right or wrong he had done his best and Emma was saddened to see his headquarters, and his successors', treated so shabbily. The Kenyans might not relish their colonial past but to deny it was to defy history.

Stephen rewarded the old man and they drove him back to the mission.

'Hotel now?' Kip inquired, hoping his passengers would begin to behave like proper tourists and cease this unseemly interest in Kenya's underbelly.

'Yes, please.' Stephen put his arm around his wife's shoulders. 'Don't be depressed, my love,' he said. 'Explorers don't always like what they discover. Scott ended up positively hating the Antarctic, but that's understandable, I suppose, since it was about to kill him.'

'I'm not hating this,' Emma said.

'Have you got one of those envelopes you filched from the Norfolk?'

467

She took one from her bag. 'What do you want it for?'

With his free hand he dug into the breast pocket of his shirt. 'Seeds,' he said, showing them to her before carefully putting them in the envelope. 'I'll try and grow you a canna descended from those your great-grandad knew.'

Harry would have recognized the hotel, though it had been extended and modernized since his time. He would have recognized the view, too. As the Land Cruiser came to a halt and Emma and Stephen got out, the clouds cleared from the peaks of Mount Kenya. Snow on the Equator, a ravishing sight, and Emma could understand the spell this country cast upon those who came to it. Tonight she and Stephen would be truly among it, sleeping under canvas with only a fire to keep wild Africa at bay.

'Mr and Mrs Birkenshaw?'

A tall man walked down the steps from the entrance wearing a khaki shirt and trousers of almost military neatness.

'I'm Joshua,' he said. 'Welcome.'

They all shook hands.

'Major H. G. A. Wittering's great-granddaughter,' he said to Emma. 'Mutali was my great-grandfather. They are both remembered here, you know.'

His English was perfect, the slight eccentricities of accent charming. Emma took to him immediately.

'How remembered?' she asked, the disappointments of the town forgotten.

'Did not Mr and Mrs Dalrymple tell you? No? One minute and I will show you.' He smiled at her eagerness, then leaned through the Land Cruiser window to talk to Kip. 'A quick lunch and then we leave,' he said as Kip drove the vehicle away. 'Let us go inside.'

The central part of the hotel, the old part, included the original reception area and bar, and if the town of Fort

Richard was intent upon divorcing itself from the past this place was determined to keep the marriage going. The decor was a museum to the killing days. Mounted heads of synthetically snarling leopards and cheetahs were on the walls along with lion and zebra skins, and in the bar there was a gallery of photographs which could have come out of H.G.A.'s albums: people posing by the bodies of animals.

Joshua called Emma. Called her Mrs Birkenshaw and she did not respond until Stephen attracted her attention.

'She's Emma,' he told Joshua. 'Mrs Birkenshaw her in the bush and we'll lose her. I'm Stephen.'

'Stephen, Emma,' Joshua said, indicating a middle-aged white couple who had followed them into the room. 'Mr and Mrs Fisher, the managers and part owners of the hotel.'

Mr Fisher carried a flat, leather-covered case which he put carefully, upside down, on a table before greeting them.

'This is a wonderful moment. We were so excited when Susie and Tom told us you were coming. We must take a photograph of you and Joshua,' he said to Emma. 'Would you mind?'

'No,' she stuttered, and watched in bewilderment as he went behind the bar. The attendant there, assiduously polishing a glass since there were no customers to serve, moved aside. Between horned antelope heads on the back wall were two hunting rifles and below them hung a pair of heavy, old-fashioned binoculars. Mr Fisher unlocked padlocks and lifted the lower rifle from its retaining pegs. Emma gasped and went forward to receive it.

'H.G.A.'s,' she said. 'Oh, good heavens!'

Mr Fisher handed the second rifle to Joshua and gave the binoculars to Stephen – 'So,' he said, 'you won't feel left out.'

Stephen glanced at them and raised an eyebrow. 'Glory be,' he said softly.

'Glory be indeed,' Emma echoed, gazing at the gun she held, hefting its weight.

'They are fine guns,' Joshua said, 'but we no longer use them and have had to disable them. None the less I like to make sure they are kept in good condition.'

'Read the inscriptions,' Mrs Fisher urged. 'You first, Joshua.'

Joshua raised the gun and read from the plate on the stock: ' "To Honourable Sir Mutali of the Kikuyu people who served his King and Country with honour and bravery," ' and Emma continued from the gun she carried:

' "From his friend and companion Major H. G. A. Wittering, KAR, who will never forget him." '

Mr Fisher went to the case he had left on a table and turned it over. On the top the two inscriptions were run into one.

'You next,' Mr Fisher said to Stephen.

'I'm no part of this.' He swapped the binoculars for Emma's gun. She turned them over and found the writing.

' "To Honourable Sir Mutali and Mac," ' she read, ' "with grateful thanks. Alexandra. 1923." '

'Alexandra was Princess Arthur of Connaught,' Joshua said. 'She was taken on safari by our great-grandfathers. There were photographs, but sadly they are lost.'

'I have copies,' Emma said, hysterical laughter threatening. She'd had some made from the albums thinking someone might – just might – be interested, but had never imagined a meeting like this.

'We'd love to see those,' Mrs Fisher said. 'The Princess stayed here for a night in the October of that year. It is in our records. That was when my grandfather owned the hotel.'

'Links,' Emma said. 'More than living links.' She put the binoculars down, fearful she would drop them, and leaned against Stephen. 'Mac,' she said to Joshua. 'Do you know who Mac was?'

Joshua laughed. 'Mac was a dog as big and as brave as a lion. He would face a buffalo, an elephant and not flinch. My grandfather was a little boy when he was acquainted with Mac and he exaggerated the size, I think.' He hesitated before continuing. 'It isn't fashionable to admire our former rulers,' he said, 'but I admire this H. G. A. Wittering because of the words he used of his servant. "Friend and companion" are words of respect, and he bothered to have them written down in a way that even our climate could not destroy.'

'And he never did forget him,' Emma said, remembering how her mother and aunt had been told the stories. Mac, Mutali, man-eating lions.

They did not begin their safari that afternoon, of course. There was no chance of a quick lunch after Emma had produced the photographs. Bill Fisher opened a bottle of champagne and his wife sought out the hotel's records. Emma found her great-grandmother's name in the register for 1926: she had stayed here when she went up-country with Harry Wittering and he proposed.

Emma slipped away when a bottle of brandy appeared and went into the bar. A grille was down and H. G. A.'s guns and Princess Arthur of Connaught's binoculars were back in their places behind it. The rifle case, however, was still on one of the tables and Emma ran her hand over the inscription on it. She looked at the photographs displayed on the walls. The ones she had brought, enlarged, would soon join them.

She wandered out on to the verandah and then, drawn by a seat built around the trunk of a tree in the centre of the lawn, down the steps into the garden. She sat, leaned back and closed her eyes.

How very strange that she should be here at the end of journey that had taken her from being a hard-nosed, hard-living and hard-working Yuppie to someone with no career – not a structured one, anyway – but who was at infinite peace with herself: something, surely, above the price of rubies or Porsches. Then there was the second journey, the physical one, that had led her from Anglesey here to Africa via that extraordinary encounter with a motorcycle messenger in London. Finally there was the journey, be it fictional or factual, back into time, more then seventy years of it, and across continents.

It had all begun with the will she had found which left a fortune to a cat's home. It had also, in a sense, left a bequest to Emma: herself as she was now, with a new name, a new husband and a bright new future.

A shadow fell across her and she opened her eyes. Stephen was there. He sat beside her and took her hand.

'Satisfied?' he asked after a moment.

'Yes,' she said. 'Satisfied. The circle is complete.'